Regret

LOST BOYS BOOK 2

EMILIA FINN

bee*lieve*

PUBLISHING, Pty Ltd.

info@beelievepublishing.com

ISBN: 978 1 922623 26 3 (Paperback)

Front cover photography by: James Critchley

Front cover models: Ryan Elson

Cover design: Britt @ The Hatters

Editing: Bird's Eye Editing

First printing edition 2023.

Beelieve Publishing, Pty Ltd

PO Box 407,

Woy Woy, NSW, 2256

Australia

www.emiliafinn.com

EMILIA FINN, the ROLLERS logo, the CHECKMATE SECURITY logo, STACKED DECK logo, and INAMORATA are all trade marks of Beelieve Publishing, Pty Ltd

Also by Emilia Finn

(in reading order)

The Rollin On Series

Finding Home

Finding Victory

Finding Forever

Finding Peace

Finding Redemption

Finding Hope

The Survivor Series

Because of You

Surviving You

Without You

Rewriting You

Always You

Take A Chance On Me

The Checkmate Series

Pawns In The Bishop's Game

Till The Sun Dies

Castling The Rook

Playing For Keeps

Rise Of The King

Sacrifice The Knight

Winner Takes All

Checkmate

Stacked Deck - Rollin On Next Gen

Wildcard

Reshuffle

Game of Hearts

Full House

No Limits

Bluff

Seven Card Stud

Crazy Eights

Eleusis

Dynamite

Busted

Gilded Knights (Rosa Brothers)

Redeeming The Rose

Chasing Fire

Animal Instincts

Pure Chemistry

Battle Scars

Safe Haven

Inamorata

The Fiera Princess

The Fiera Ruins

The Fiera Reign

Mayet Justice

Sinful Justice

Sinful Deed

Sinful Truth

Sinful Desire

Sinful Deceit

Sinful Chaos

Sinful Promise

Lost Boys

MISTAKE

REGRET

Crash & Burn

Rollin On Novellas

(Do not read before finishing the Rollin On Series)

Begin Again – A Short Story

Written in the Stars – A Short Story

Full Circle – A Short Story

Worth Fighting For – A Bobby & Kit Novella

Preston

LOVE IS IN THE AIR

My best friend stands just twenty feet across the room, his brand-new bride on her knees, and her lipstick messed up from contact with various appendages of his body.

That could seem dirty, depending on the level of filth one's mind possesses.

But in Cole and Maya's case, the room we share is a fairy-lit ballroom, and though her lipstick is, in fact, smudged, it's not because she's sucking off her groom in front of a rapt audience.

No. She's tying his shoelaces, because though she's a proud woman who would never debase herself for anyone, her groom—my best friend—is a pro fighter, and his penchant for training, even on the morning of his nuptials, means he's too sore to bend over and fix his own damn laces.

Or at least, that's the lie we tell ourselves as Cole lives out his lewdest fantasies on the biggest day of his life.

My best friend, my fucking brother from another mother, is a blissfully married man. And I'm... well, I'm enjoying the open tab at the bar, and the beautiful guests who walk by in formal gowns and skyscraper heels.

"You want a refill on your beer?" The bartender stops by me and sets a napkin down near my hand.

"Yeah." I slide my empty glass closer and twist to get a view of the dancefloor. Couples sway together, while a band who sings gritty soft rock jams on the stage to the left of the room.

When Maya is done tying Cole's laces, she pushes up to stand in a stunning, body-hugging, princess cut gown that, I admit, has me thinking sinful thoughts about the woman I would kill for.

I don't love her like I wanna fuck her—though, in an ideal world where such an act wouldn't betray my best friend, I sure as shit wouldn't say no. But I love her like the family she is. I love her like a sister, and though I have none of those biologically, I've brought that woman into my heart and vowed to keep her safe for the rest of time.

Because her safety is paramount to Cole's happiness. And Cole's happiness is more important to me than my own.

A result of childhood trauma, I suppose. That's what the shrinks would say. Two guys, unloved by their blood family, bond on the streets and spend their youths—their formative years—in the trenches together.

They wouldn't be wrong. Years of neglect left me without the expectation of love or loyalty from anyone else. But I sure as hell learned to care about my brother.

That thing they call childhood trauma sucks. But I'm glad for the lessons received and the friendships forged. It means I know who to keep close, and it helps me maintain protective barriers for those who *want* to be trusted, but are yet to earn the right.

"Welcome. Hey, everyone... hey! Shut up!"

The emcee—or really, the world fucking champion MMA title holder, Jack 'The Jackhammer' Reilly—holds a microphone in one hand, and a glass of soda in the other. His grin stretches his cheeks and pushes a deep dimple into one side, but his stare, because the band won't hush and guests continue to talk, makes me laugh.

He's a dangerous motherfucker, and though he bitched and whined every day leading up to today about his job as public speaker, he fulfills the task with intense vigor.

"For those of you who don't know me, my name is Jack." Then he lifts his soda and gestures toward Cole and Maya. "And they're the brand-new Mr. and Mrs. Miller. Cole asked me to stand up here today, *knowing* it would annoy me. *But...*"

While Cole chuckles, and Maya presses a blushing cheek to his chest, Jack raises his glass higher. "I'm honored to spend today with you. So just before we cut the cake and listen to boring-ass speeches from people we don't even like," he casts a look over to me, "I want to make a toast. To Maya and Cole. The sweetest teacher I ever met... besides my wife," he adds with a laugh, "and the car thief. I never asked to meet you assholes. But I'm kinda glad I did. You make life better."

"Cheers!" The guests, all sixty of them, raise their glasses and salute the new couple.

"Here." The bartender taps my shoulder and sets my beer down, then he moves along and stops in front of a blonde I don't know. "What can I getcha, miss?"

Bored with watching Jack speak, I tilt my head toward the woman, and watch her plump lips work around her request for a glass of water. I study her lean bicep as she brings a hand up to tuck stray locks of hair behind her ear, then the shimmery fabric of the baby pink dress floating around her thighs. She wears silver heels with straps that hug her calves and stop just below her knees, and because I have no shame when I stare, she turns my way and narrows her eyes when I refuse to avert my gaze.

Most would, I'm sure. When they're caught looking, most glance away and go about their business. But I was that street kid who was never taught manners. And I learned long ago that staring is the single most effective way to capture someone's attention.

While the bartender grabs a glass and half fills it with ice before adding liquid, I snag my beer and wander toward the woman whose eyes glitter almost as silver as her shoes. And above those, lashes kiss her cheeks and straddle that line where I'm not sure if they're all her, or if she's had a little salon help.

"Weddings, huh?"

Smooth line, dickhead.

But it lets her know I'm not like the slick, sweet-talking lotharios she likely encounters every other day of her life. Looking the way she does, with that body and those electrifying eyes... yeah, she gets fed bullshit lines every single day.

Guaranteed.

Setting my beer close by her hand and leaning back against the heavy wooden bar so I'm facing the dancefloor, I kick one foot over the other and grin when she can't maintain eye contact.

She's shy.

"I don't know who you are," I tell her.

A single, sharp brow raises so I see it, even with her attention focused solely on the guy pouring her water. "I don't know who you are, either." Accepting her glass, she turns to me and purses deliciously tempting lips. "That's how things usually start, right? Not knowing someone until you actually meet them."

"Well..." A soft, slow chuckle works along my throat. "You're not wrong. But I mean, I'm the groom's ride or die. So the fact I don't know you leaves me wondering..." I twist, leaving one elbow on the bar, and turn to face her front on. "Who the hell are you, and how did you get an invitation to this shindig?"

"How do you know I'm not the bride's ride or die?" She brings her water up and sips just enough to wet her lips.

Fuck, but my eyes drop to the shimmer of moisture that leaves me feeling drier than the Sahara.

"And does she realize her groom's *ride or die*," she mocks my words with a smirk, "is rude to the rest of her guests?"

"How was I rude?" I demand a little too loudly. "I asked you a question." Then I lift my chin and extend my hand. "I'm Preston. What's your name?"

She looks down, considering for a beat long enough to make my heart jump. Finally, she takes my offering and shakes. "Nicole Scott. Nicki," she amends with a beautiful smile. "And I mostly know the bride." Dropping my hand, she turns from the bar and takes a step. "I hope you enjoy your evening, Preston."

"Wait." I grab her arm—*no manners*—and watch, immediately intrigued, as goosebumps sprint along her skin and stop only when they reach the tops of her tense shoulders. Gently, I pull her back until her sumptuous hip touches the stool behind her. "Are you here with someone?"

Dangerously, her silver eyes come to mine and bore deep into my soul. "It was nice to meet you, Preston. But take your damn hand off me."

"Wh-what?"

She reaches across and pushes my hand away. "Don't touch me. Never, *ever* touch me unless I give you express permission. Which," she grips her water and takes that step again, "I did not. Now, I have to go, because I have places to be and things to do. Meanwhile, you can stay here and try your luck on the next unfortunate soul who stops by for a drink." With a flick of her hair and a disgusted shake of her head—*struck out, dickhead!*—she continues away from the bar and circles the dancefloor to stop by the three-tier wedding cake at the head of the room.

"That was brutal." With a mocking laugh, a woman with a long dancer's body and a dress tight enough to make most mouths water, stops on my other side and nods to the bartender.

That's all she has to do to ask for a drink, like he knows what she wants without words being spoken.

Satisfied and still giggling, she peers my way and shakes her head. "You shot your shot, Preston Danes. But you bungled it."

"Yeah, thanks for noticing." Taking my beer, I turn away and head toward the dancefloor.

"I'm Sophia." She snags her drink and chases after me. "I know you know already, but we haven't officially met. In fact, Cole has gone out of his way to keep us apart, but I wanted the introduction, and I rarely place value in the opinion of others when it comes to my work. So," she grabs my sleeve and yanks me around with surprising strength. "I'm done waiting for him to get off his ass and introduce us."

Sophia stands several inches shorter than my five-eleven, but she's lithe and fit; a dance teacher, according to the IRS, but something else entirely when you drill down and do a little research.

"You can call me Ace," she continues. "Those I work with usually do." She offers her hand and waits. "And you're Preston Danes. You know coding, and you come with an ability most never learn, even after a few years at college."

I take her hand, because she's pretty and I just got shot down hard enough to dent my ego. "I *could* call you Ace, but we don't work together. I *do* have an aptitude for coding, but I don't have a reason to talk to you about it." I shake her hand once. Twice. But I keep the seductive blonde in my peripherals, and puzzle over her keen interest in the multi-tiered cake. "And if Cole doesn't want us to meet, there's probably a reason for it." Finished, I drop her hand and take a step back. "You're married, no?"

Sophia scoffs. "I'm not asking to fuck you, Danes. This meet was purely professional. I like the work you did when you and Cole were a team."

I snort and turn when Nicki turns and wanders toward the kitchen doors, because, fuck, her icy stare has short-circuited my brain.

"Cole and I are *still* a team," I tell Sophia. "We'll always be a team. Last I heard, you have your own and don't need me."

"I'd like you to come down to the office on Monday and apply for a job." She circles around to stand in my line of sight, stealing my vision of Nicki and landing me instead with that of a brunette with a savage stare. "Teams are strong because they grow together. I'm intrigued by your skills, and I have enough time and interest to spend a day with you to see if you could be a good fit."

When I roll my eyes and move around her, she follows.

"I know you've moved to live closer to Cole," she presses, "which means you're looking for a full-time gig that *doesn't* come with the risk of jail time. You can't steal cars in our town, Preston. I have every single road covered, which means your cash flow is about to dry up."

"First of all, *Ace*," I stop trying to follow Nicki, and instead set my hands on my hips and my eyes on Sophia. "Word on the street is anyone who works for you risks jail time, since what your team does is rarely on the right side of the law. Second, I can take care of myself."

"You're lying," she laughs, arrogant and sure.

There are cops here as guests tonight, and when one wanders by, she literally fucking fist-bumps the dude. "No one's word, on the street or otherwise, so much as hints at jail time when associated with me," she retorts. "We're too slick for that, and the illegal things we do are to better society, so we rarely feel bad about our crimes."

"You're just a regular Robin Hood, huh? Fuck over the rich, help the poor."

"Unlike you," she counters easily, "who stole cars from the rich and lined your own pockets. At least where I come from, I help those who, in any language, sex, or location, are victims, and remove abusers from the streets. If that abuser just so happens to be fluid with cash, then I feel no remorse in redirecting those funds someplace else." She flashes a wicked smile and brings her drink up. "You know I'm good at what I do, Preston. Otherwise, you'd have already walked away from this discussion."

Fuckin' A. Yeah, I know she's good. Everyone who makes their livelihood with a computer knows of the hacker who goes by the name Ace.

Few connect Ace to Sophia Solomon, but those who do never utter the link unless they're ready to be silenced.

The fact she offers me an interview *and* the name means come Monday, if I don't impress her, I'll probably die.

Maybe. If she feels like getting her hands dirty.

"What kind of job are you looking to fill?" I grumble.

She cast the hook into the ocean, wielding bait and knowing the worm was too juicy to ignore. Now she grins, because though her reputation for savagery toward her enemies should scare me, it's her terrifying abilities with technology that have me considering a new career path.

Because she's right: I need a job, and without Cole by my side, the one I had stopped being fun a long time ago. If I have to work with someone new, it's every coder's dream to work with Ace.

"A little bit of this," she murmurs, non-committal, "a little bit of that. Come down to the Checkmate office on Monday, and we'll find something for you to do."

"Yeah," I roll my eyes again. "Because that's not shady at all."

"I'm gonna need you all to move back," Jack the emcee announces, so his voice rolls through the loudspeakers. "The bride and groom have gotta cut their cake." Then he looks to Cole and shoots him a stern glare. "Don't smush cake in her face, bro. Trust me, chicks *hate* that shit."

"Noted." Laughing, Cole leads Maya toward the extravagant cake, while on my left, Sophia melts into the small crowd, having achieved what she set out to do.

As the entire room watches the couple, I back away and leave my best friend to his happy moment. Instead, my eyes jump to Nicki, whose icy glare turns to a sweet smile that draws my attention like a sailor to a lighthouse.

She's not smiling at *me*. But hell, we're one step closer, right?

"Excuse me." I step through wedding guests, doing my best to fake manners to get by.

Considering two thirds of the people in attendance tonight are pro fighters, or married to a pro fighter, if I step on toes, I might have to defend my life. And I'm man enough to know... I can't. Not against this lot.

Finally, while everyone else pushes forward, I reach the back of the crowd and sit my ass on a barstool. I don't want to be front and center, and I sure as shit don't want to be called up for the speech I'm supposed to make at some point tonight. But as Cole and Maya pose for pictures, the captivating Nicki crosses the room and makes her way back to the bar.

I smell her before I feel the warmth of her body. Then I bathe in the sensation of her long hair brushing my arm, and her knee tapping mine as she sits on the stool to my right and crosses one leg over the other.

"Weddings, huh?" she exhales.

She cradles her half-consumed glass of water in one hand, and a cute little clutch in the other. Then she grins when I turn my head and look down at the perfect swell of her breasts in a tight dress.

Setting my beer down, I turn to her. I miss the cake-cutting, the special moment between my best friends, because I focus on the sexy blonde whose hot and cold countenance intrigues the fuck out of me. "Did you just try my pickup line?"

"Did you feel dumb saying it?" she counters with a wrinkled nose. "Because I did."

"Yeah." I twist until my knees touch her thigh and my chest almost —*almost*—brushes her shoulder. "I felt ridiculous, but experience tells me women prefer the bumbling charm over too-slick suave."

"So it's a game to you?" Glancing up and stopping with a piercing stare, she purses her lips. "All of it... a game?"

"No. I really am charming, and if you ask those closest to me, they'll tell you I have no game at all. Mostly I say what I'm thinking: good, bad, or offensive." Bravely, or perhaps stupidly, I reach out and take a lock of her hair between my fingers. Because it's right there and I fuckin' want to. "I rarely have a filter, so nine times out of ten, whatever comes out of my mouth pisses folks off. But it's always the truth."

"And the tenth?" She turns her attention back to Cole and Maya, beaming when they share cake, and gently clapping when the other guests applaud. "What comes out of your mouth on the tenth attempt?"

"Bumbling charm."

When her gaze slides my way and her eyes stop on my lips, I add, "Let's try for a general friendly conversation. That way, next time I try hitting on you, you'll be less offended and more interested."

"I'm still offended." She teases. "But listening."

Victory!

"How do you know the bride?" I ask.

She spins away from the dancefloor and around to the bar, so her hair falls from my grasp and her elbows rest on top. Now, I get a view of the perfect arch of her back and the muscles in her triceps that imply thrice-a-week gym classes. Setting her clutch on the bar, she answers, "Business. How do you know the groom?"

"We basically grew up together. Are you here with someone?"

"I'm not," she admits, wrapping her hand around her water glass.

Whether intentional or not, she shows off an *un*adorned ring finger. *Not married.*

"Me either. I asked the bride if she'd be my date." I remain in place so my legs hug her chair and, when she looks my way, she has no choice but to be a mere half a foot away. "Maya said no."

"I mean, that's fair." Smirking, Nicki brings her water up and sips through the straw. "Have you known the bride long?"

"As long as Cole has known her. But she's a sweetheart, and I'm eighty percent devastated I didn't meet her first."

"Sounds serious." Tilting her head my way, her eyes dance as she asks, "And the other twenty percent?"

"Is happy I came alone. If I hadn't, I wouldn't be sitting here with you."

"Oh geez." She looks to the mirrored wall at the back of the bar and sits up taller. She's humored by me, but her cheeks warm and her shoulders bounce at my expense. "That was smooth, Preston. Holy moly," she lifts a hand and shakes it the way someone might if they burned their fingers. "Smooth as butter."

"I wasn't trying to be smooth," I chuckle. "It wasn't a line. If I had come with someone else, I wouldn't be sitting here with you. That's a fact."

"Even if she was just someone you'd met recently? A casual date?"

"Even then. I'm offensive, but I'm not an asshole."

She snickers under her breath and glances down at her water, while behind us, Jack Reilly talks more shit about the friend he claims is *his*, when we all know Cole is *mine*.

"Even if she was casual," Nicki murmurs to herself. Then glancing my way, she raises a brow. "So you would describe yourself as loyal?"

"I'm the most loyal person I know," I tell her seriously. "That's not even a flex. It's just who I am in my soul. If I consider someone my friend, family, or responsibility, then they remain that way no matter what. If I'd brought a date tonight, even if I later decided I wasn't feeling *it* and wanted out, I would remain loyal until our date was complete. I'd get her home, make sure she was safe. And then I'd walk away knowing I was the best person I could be."

When the bartender wanders back this way, I lift my hand to get his attention, and try the Sophia-nod to order my drink.

Either he thinks my legs are as nice as the dancer's, or he's simply good at his job, because he grabs a glass and starts pouring.

I assume it's the latter.

"Cole saved my ass a thousand times over the years," I continue contemplatively. "Literally and figuratively. That means he can trust me forever."

"Even though eighty percent of you wants to bang his wife?"

I choke out a laugh and accept my drink when the bartender sets it down. "I don't wanna bang her. I wanna marry her and live a disgustingly content life with someone sweet and selfless and kind. If she bakes cupcakes, then even better. Hell, she can keep dating Cole if she wants, since our marriage is one of the arranged kinds. I would know she still loves him."

"Noble of you." Nicki's long, blonde hair falls across her shoulder, so the loose curls touch the top of the bar. "I can bake. Like, really well."

"Yeah? Now who's flexing?" I inch just a little closer until her perfume is in my lungs. "Was that a pickup line?"

"No, it's fact." She sits taller again, snickering, and leans to her left to take back some of the space I took from her. "I got an Easy Bake Oven for my fifth birthday, and I haven't stopped since."

I got a kick in the gut and a broken arm for mine.

But those aren't the details one likes to hear when flirting with a stranger at a wedding. So instead, I ask, "Favorite thing to bake?"

"Brownies," she answers instantly. She doesn't even have to think about it. "They were the first thing I truly struggled with. I kept messing up the recipes, or overcooking them. Sometimes undercooking. I know they're nothing special to most bakers, but they were a genuine challenge for me, back when I was trying to do better." Turning my way, she allows her smile to curl up seductively. "Now that I've got it under control, I take a lot of pleasure in baking them. Then I enjoy eating them."

I look down at her flat stomach, doubting she's eaten anything but lettuce in her life, only to bark out a laugh when she releases her core muscles and creates a roll beneath her dress.

"Hot," I snigger. "Your muscle control is commendable."

"Yes, well... Some could say eating baked goods six days a week is bad for me. Others might consider it an opportunity to practice sucking my stomach in. Do you have siblings? Older, younger?"

"None." I accept her change of subject and bring my gaze up to stop on her icy eyes. Not icy like unfriendly, but the silver sure as shit cuts through a man when she's not wearing a smile. "I'm an only child biologically," I explain. "Cole is my brother because of love. Though, like Cole, I probably have a dozen half-siblings floating around. But none I know of. You?"

"I have a younger brother. He's grown now, but in my mind, he'll always be the baby." At a thought that passes through her mind, she flashes a wicked smile. "I bake for him a lot, too. And his boss and work friends."

"*And* his boss?" I whistle under my breath. "Jesus, Nicki. You're spreading the love and ruining men. Now you'll never know if your brother is actually good at his job, or if his boss just keeps him around for the brownies and hot sister scenery."

"Hot sister scenery," she scoffs. Dismissive, she goes back to her water and drags the tip of her finger around the lip.

Note to self: she can't accept compliments.

"I'm sure he carries his own career. It's dangerous," she adds thoughtfully. "They have to trust each other with their lives. So I'd like to think that if Axel was bad at his job, they'd set him aside to keep everyone safe— even at the cost of a batch of brownies."

Axel. Dangerous. Trust. I catch the tidbits she offers, and probe for more. "Is he a cop?"

Like a switch, her eyes burn dark, and an impenetrable wall comes up. "No. He's not a cop. In fact, he possesses a healthy dislike for cops."

"So..." I bring my beer up to buy time. For her unexpected temper to subside, and for her glare to notch back down to a flirty stare. "What does he do for a living?"

"He's a firefighter." Lifting her water, she tips it back until she empties the glass, then she sets it down again and looks to me with a forced smile. "Do you live here?"

Willing to play, I glance around the ballroom. "In this hotel?"

"In this city." She rolls her eyes. "I know the bride and groom live a town over. I wasn't sure if you—"

"I'm sort of in between," I cut in. "Cole and I grew up here, but he moved, and he's never coming back, so I signed a lease last week for a place just outside his town. Ya know, to be closer to my family, try to woo Maya over to divorce court, that sorta stuff."

Instead of laughing, Nicki moves off her stool and slides a manicured finger beneath her bottom lip, somehow perfecting her already perfect lipstick without the use of a mirror. "Are you driving to your new place tonight, or staying in the hotel like everyone else?"

"Staying here for the night." Narrowing my eyes, I study her up and down and turn, since she's intent on leaving. "You?"

"Staying." She nods over my shoulder, nerves in her gaze, and shaking hands for reasons I can't pinpoint. "Preston—"

Then my name echoing somewhere far away penetrates my senses.

"Preston Danes," Jack's voice comes louder now. Louder. "Hey, douchebag! It's time for the best man speech, so get your ass up here and speak, or I'm passing over you and getting on with the show."

"What?" I twist on my stool and come face to face with Cole, Maya, Jack, and sixty of their closest friends and family. "Huh?"

"Speech," Nicole snickers. With a look that errs toward *'you're an adorable idiot'*—which is not the same face one might make to express *'you're suave and sexy and impossible not to fuck the first night we meet'*— she grabs her clutch and walks away, leaving me to the spotlight, and pushes through the kitchen doors on the far side of the room.

"You have ten seconds," Jack growls. "You're wasting my time and messing with our schedule. And since I don't like your thieving ass anyway, I'm not inclined to wait for you to sort out your shit."

It's like spending hours in the dark, and then having a spotlight shoved in my face. Or like floating in a warm bath, only for the water to empty out and leave me flopping in the cold.

That's how it feels to have a discussion with Nicole—just the two of us while we talk and explore and, *fuck yes*, flirt—but now she's gone, and I'm left to navigate real life with her absence.

"Fuck." I cover my eyes when an actual spotlight beams my way, then I slide off my stool and pick up my beer before cutting a line through the crowd and slowing beside the cake and a blushing bride whose husband kneads her ass in his hands.

Finally, I snatch the mic from Jack and turn my back on him, because I have no desire to fake manners. He's a dick, and I don't care for his approval.

"Um..." I glance out at my audience, then to my right, to the only two in this room I love. "Well... Maya and Cole," I start. "I wr-wrote something before tonight. I swear, I prepared a speech. But now that we're here, and I'm looking into your eyes..." My throat burns dry. Because I don't do public speaking. Or speaking about my feelings—like... ever. "That shit I wrote now feels dumb."

Pressure builds throughout the room the longer I take to say the things I'm supposed to say. Guests fidget, and the kitchen doors swing open to reveal servers moving through with heaped trays.

On the return swing, I catch sight of Nicki perched on a stainless-steel counter, a pastry in her hand, a devious smile playing across her lips, and her eyes burning into mine.

She's... a million things, I guess. She's a contradiction. She's shy, but she's not. She's softly spoken, but not really. She's not interested in wedding hookups with strangers, but she came back to me when she didn't have to. She tried my line, and stuck around long enough to let me know she's interested too. She walked away just seconds after a burning glare when I mentioned cops. But now she smiles and watches me stammer my way through the world's worst best man speech.

She's hot and she's cold. And right now, she's enjoying my public humiliation.

"Uh..." When the door swings shut once more, cutting off my view and leaving me a loner in front of all these people, I bring my attention back to Cole and Maya. Then to *The Jackhammer,* who quickly tires of waiting for me. "I, uh—"

"And you're done." Jack comes around and reaches out with a lightning-fast sweep of his arm to steal my microphone. But I'm quicker, so I spin toward the bride and groom and focus.

On love.

On them.

On the fact that, if Cole, a lowly street thief whose childhood was no better than mine, can have a day like today and spend the rest of his life with a woman like Maya, then maybe, just maybe, there's a chance for me yet.

Unlikely, I admit. *But possible.*

"Maya and Cole," I start again, setting my beer on the cake table and slapping away Jack's grabbing hands. I step away to find my own space, then I extend my free hand and wait for Maya to take it, since holding Cole's would just be weird.

"I grew up with the groom," I tell everyone. "Back in the day, we were just a couple of kids whose stomachs were too empty, and our brains too big. As was typical with kids with nothing to do and no one to answer to, who often find trouble to occupy their time, that's..." I laugh. "That's what we did."

I pull Maya closer so she slips under my arm. She's not mine. She's nothing if not completely and totally his. So though she hugs my side, she watches her husband like he hung the moon and all the stars. She watches him now the way I probably did, back when I was a kid and getting my ass kicked by an older dude.

Big, bad Cole Miller didn't then, and doesn't now, tolerate bullies. So he laid that asshole out and kept me safe when he had no reason to feel loyal. He just did it, because he's the best guy in the world.

"I know some of you hold a grudge," I continue. "Because Cole's introduction to your family came with a little petty theft."

"Petty?" Jack barks out. "It's called grand theft, stupid. It was cold and calculated, and it was targeting *me*. None of that is petty."

"Well, even so," I chuckle. "Some of you still obsess over the time the Jackhammer almost lost his ride. But that's not who I see when I look at this man."

I meet Cole's eyes and feel my heart kick, because I don't love anyone on this planet. Not my mom. Not my dad. Not even myself most of the time. But I love Cole. And I love his wife.

"This is the best man I know. And I don't mean that the way some folks throw words around for the sake of hearing themselves speak. I mean it with every part of my soul. And Maya," I look down at her beautiful eyes, only to chuckle when she glances up and shows off glistening tears.

Because if I don't, I might find myself getting emotional too. "She's the very best woman I've ever met. She's strong and brave and smart and sweet. She's sassy, and she tries so very hard to be as badass as me and Cole."

"Hey!" She tries for offended, but ruins it when she reaches up and swipes tears from her cheek. "I'm a badass."

"If you say so, doll." I press a kiss to the top of her hair and squeeze extra tight. "When the best man on the planet met the best woman, it was inevitable we'd end up here today. Maya, in a pretty dress, and Cole, wearing a tux he hates. Good food." Then I peek across at Jack and smirk. "Mediocre company. I don't do speeches well," I bring my gaze to Cole, "I don't have the fancy words you deserve. But I want you to know I love you, bro. All the way till the zombie apocalypse. And when those fuckers are trying to peel your skin back for dinner, I promise to do everything I can to stop them."

"Weird sentiment," Jack grumbles. "Freaks."

"I'm so fuckin' proud of what you've achieved this past year," I push on. "I'm thrilled you met Maya, and I consider myself fortunate that I get to watch you guys grow old together. We both know our lives have been lacking in positive examples of healthy love. So the fact you did what you always do, taking shit into your own hands and creating that foundation for us both, means more to me than you can ever know. Now *you* get to live it, and *I* get to watch, learn, and enjoy." I carefully release Maya and step closer to Cole. "Thank you, brother. Till the zombies."

"Aw, shit." He sets his drink down beside mine and closes the space between us, pulling me in for a tight hug. "I love you, Pres. That was beautiful."

"It was crap." I pat him on the back as we pull apart. "But it was meant with love. Every single word. I'm so ridiculously happy for you guys." Reaching out, I bring Maya in again and sandwich her between us until she grunts. "Please never stop inviting me to Thanksgiving dinner."

"Never." Blubbering, Maya opens her arms wide and engulfs me in the biggest cuddle her small body is capable of. "All three of us know what it's like to be let down by the family we were born into. So when we have a chance to create one with our hearts instead—"

"We don't let it go." Cole sets his meaty palm on the back of my head and drags me in closer. "Every birthday, Pres. Every Christmas, Easter, and Thanksgiving. Every single holiday. You have my word."

"And every Friday night dinner," Maya adds, "Purely because we love you and want you around."

Nicki

YES. NO. MAYBE. I DON'T KNOW. CAN YOU REPEAT THE QUESTION?

"Go out there, girl." Megan—the wedding planner—is a woman I met only in the last couple of weeks. She's beautiful, she's boisterous, she shoves mini quiches in her mouth, and when the kitchen doors swing open and we glimpse Preston Danes hugging the bride and groom in the middle of the dancefloor, she smacks my shoulder so her palm meets bare skin and her slap makes me scowl.

Growling, I bring my angry gaze to her. "Don't hit me!"

"Don't be a pussy," she shoots back easily. "You look at that man the way I look at these platters of food. So go," she brushes me off the counter until I touch down on painful silver stilettos. "He already showed you his cards. You know he's interested. But you're the one who keeps walking away, so if you want something to happen, you're gonna have to be the big girl and initiate it."

"No, I can't—"

"You can!" Tossing a mini rice ball between perfectly glossy lips, she comes around the counter and pushes me toward the door. "Men are simple creatures, Nicki. They wanna see boobs, they wanna see ass. Hell, after the speech that dude just gave, I'd say all he needs to see right now are your come-hither eyes, and he's gonna trip on his feet to get to you."

"I don't even know him." I skid to a stop and hold the doorframe so she can't shove me out. "I've literally never met him before tonight."

"All the better," she teases. "You deserve a night of naughty sex, Nic.

One-night stands are supremely underrated. Exploring your sexuality with someone you don't know is..." she purrs. "Amazing. *And* he's a brute." She shoves the door open so it swings on the hinges and draws attention from anyone who might think to look this way. "He's got a sexy smile, his eyes like to eat you up, and I feel he'd consider it his duty to help you find your G-spot."

"*You're* a brute." I twist in place, almost rolling my ankles, and meet Meg's glittering eyes. "I can't just approach a guy I don't know and expect to have sex with him."

"Sure you can."

Just as the words leave her mouth, a man with dark hair and beautiful green eyes wanders by with a beer in his hand. She grabs his tie and yanks him close. Then she smacks a kiss to his lips that leaves me breathless and wondering.

She holds me, and she holds him, which means I become the third wheel in a public exchange of saliva. When she's got her fill, she breaks the kiss and reaches up to wipe a smudge of lipstick from his top lip. "I'm in room four-oh-three tonight, handsome."

"Yeah?" He steps closer, grinning like he's won the lottery without ever buying a ticket. "What time you heading up there?"

"Gimme an hour." Placing a hand on his muscular chest, she pats once, twice, three times, though on the third, she gives a little shove and sends him on his way. Glancing back to me, she winks. "And that's how it's done."

"You're not seriously going to sleep with him, are you?"

She grits her teeth and takes a step further into the room, nudging me from safety and tiptoeing me into the ballroom. The band plays again, now that the speeches are over and the guy Meg just kissed is freed to pick up his guitar. "I most definitely will sleep with him tonight. He's sexy, he kisses well, and he has those eyes like Preston. Ya know, the kind that promise to eat a woman up if she asks nicely."

"You want me to *ask* him to eat me up?"

Too loud! Too much.

Soft chuckles roll from a group of wedding guests who stand close enough to hear every word we speak. Turning back to Meg with fire flaming in my cheeks, I change my tack and plead instead of fight.

"I'm not like you, Meg. I can't do that."

"I suggest you try." She nudges me toward the couples on the dance-floor and smacks my ass so I gasp in surprise. "It's all about attitude. If you act shy and weird, it's gonna be shy and weird. But if you act like the queen you are and take charge?" She sighs. "I promise you're gonna have an amazing night."

"I'm working." And yet, I tuck my clutch beneath my arm and snatch a glass of wine from a passing server. "I can't hit on the wedding guests."

"I'm working too," she counters. "Doesn't mean I won't let that guy with the tongue rock my world in an hour."

Placing her fingers beneath the base of my wine glass, she pushes up until I drink, drink, drink a little more. And when the glass is empty and my heart pounds, she takes the crystal away and replaces it with another.

"This'll help," she explains. "Chug it, then go say hey. I bet if you let him, he'll take charge and lead the night. You just have to sit back and see where he takes you."

"You're not worried he'll kill me and wear my skin?"

She barks out a laugh loud enough to draw that particular guy's gaze. "He's best friends with the groom. I think that's called a personal recommendation. If he's a dick, you get to smack the groom for it."

"Nicki?"

I squeak at his voice—*super uncool of me*—and spin to find Preston Danes standing just two feet away.

Preston got a fresh haircut for tonight, evidenced not by the inch-long mop on top, but the sharp lines that make way for a fade along the sides and back. His lips, thick and smiling, are surrounded by week-old stubble that, at the very sight of it, makes my thighs quiver.

Oh god. My heart thuds in my chest, but Meg's words ring in my mind. *Act shy and weird, and it'll be shy and weird. But act like a queen...*

"Uh... hi." I bring my second glass of wine up and drink, hoping and praying he can't see the tremble in my hands. "I liked your speech," I mumble around the lip of my glass. "I didn't hear all of it. But the bits I did, I li—"

"Do you wanna dance?" He thrusts a hand forward so the tips of his fingers brush my stomach. His eyes are a blinding, bright blue as they pierce mine; the kind of blue you catch only once or twice a summer, when there are no clouds and no smog, and you're brave enough to look up at the sky in the filthy heat.

He swallows, so I notice his Adam's apple bobbing in his throat. Then with a gentle hand on the sharp line of my hipbone, he drags me forward until I stumble against his chest.

"Uh…"

"Great." His lips curl into a devious smile, while his hands make quick work of relieving me of my wineglass and setting it someplace else. Wrapping one arm around my body to snatch my clutch and stuff it into his back pocket for safekeeping, he sets his palm on my back, while the other takes my hand and twines our fingers together.

"Tell me something about you." Just like Meg promised, Preston takes the lead and presses my cheek to his muscular chest. "Something I can't possibly know."

"I mean…" Exhaling, I allow myself to have this moment. To rest in a stranger's arms and not think about how I'll feel tomorrow. Or about the troubles I'll have to face when we're done. I ignore my responsibilities and silence the voice in my head that screams I'll regret this when the sun rises next. "You can't possibly know anything about me. You don't know me at all."

"I know you have a brother," he counters with a smile. "And that you like to bake. I know you know the bride, and that you were recently fighting with that other blonde chick about something. Oh," he pulls back and grins, "I also know you take life really seriously."

"How could you know that last one?"

"Because you're dancing with a stranger," he comes in closer again, so his stubbled chin brushes along my cheek and his words float into my ear. Secret enough they're only for me. "But you keep looking around to see who's watching you. You're self-conscious and nervous." He turns his face in so I swear, *I swear*, I feel his lips on my temple. "Tells me you're not used to frivolities or spontaneity."

"Which kind of implies you are." I shake his hand off, but only so I can wrap my arms around his neck and lean closer. *If I close my eyes, if I can't see anyone else, then maybe they can't see me.* "Are you spontaneous, Preston?"

"I am." And to prove it, his hands slip along my torso. Lower. Lower. So I feel my pulse somewhere I haven't felt it in a while. "I'm the king of midnight adventures, long drives to nowhere, and sneaky drive-thru visits whenever my stomach says to go that way."

"And I..." A soft chuckle rolls along my throat. We couldn't be more different if he rode elephants to work and lived in Australia. "I'm the queen of an eight o'clock bedtime, routines that keep my day moving, and carrying a planner in my handbag that would devastate me if I lost it."

He considers my answer for a long beat, holding me close as we sway to a slow song that reverberates somewhere deep in my chest. Finally, he pulls back just far enough to catch my eyes. "It's after eight o'clock now."

"I know!" Laughing, I step in again. *Be a queen. Be confident.* "Special circumstances and all that. What do you do for work?"

He snorts. "Okay, I see. We're up to the formal interview questions. I work with computers." Turning us, he weaves us further into the crowd. Like he thrives on attention, and knows for every person who sees us, my heart will thunder harder. "I work with software and stuff all day. Who is your best friend?"

"What?" Startled, I meet his eyes. "How the hell did you jump topics so fast?"

He only shrugs and places a hand on the back of my head to bring me closer. "Spontaneity. When you need to vent, or celebrate, or scream about the world, who do you call?"

"You mean, like, a girlfriend?" I ask. "You're asking who my squad is?"

"Right." Wrapping me up tight and dropping his hands, he draws patterns against my back. "Who is on your speed dial for those moments?"

"I don't have a female best friend," I admit. Closing my eyes, I draw a deep breath to fill my lungs, then I exhale again and smile. "But whenever anything happens to me, good or bad or something in between, I call Axel."

"Your brother?"

One point for Preston: he listens. "Yes, my brother. We know everything about each other."

"So when he bangs a chick at a wedding and he wants to tell someone about it?"

I snort. "I wish I could tell you he calls someone else. But yeah. Those exact, specific circumstances haven't occurred, but sure, when he's at a bar or whatever, and he's spending time with a woman, or on a random Sunday morning when I'm feeling fresh and caffeinated after a peaceful Saturday night sleep, and he's waking up groggy, hungover, and with a chick whose name he possibly doesn't recall, he calls me."

"To tell you he got laid?" Preston's disbelieving curiosity makes me grin. "Like, *hey sis, I just made this chick squirt allllll over. It was tasty and fun.*"

"No!" I smack his chest and pull away, only to laugh when his hands are faster and he yanks me back in. "He doesn't tell me *that* stuff. Jesus. He tells me he *hung out* with someone. Or he says he *slept over*. On the rare occasion when he's not feeling great, he tells me she was crazy or whatever."

"Crazy?"

"Yeah. Like, she tore him up with her nails, or she asked for some really wild, freaky stuff. Axel is kinda goofy and outgoing—"

"So, your opposite," Preston cuts in.

I shoot him a playful scowl, but he's not wrong. "I'm just saying that Axel's been known to attract women who are also weird and outgoing. And though I doubt he judges most of what they want in private, sometimes there are limits. And when those limits are being tested, he tends to peace out and call me to whine about it."

"And just so we're clear," he pushes me away from his body, only to hold my hand and twirl me. It's surprisingly romantic. Heated. And then he pulls me in again so we clash and his cologne snakes deep into my lungs. "This is your brother, your *full-blood* brother, who tells you of his freaky conquests?"

"You're making it sound worse than it is." I cinch my arms over his shoulders and exhale. "Now stop talking about my brother. It's ruining my mood."

"Yeah?" Preston's hands are large, enveloping, as his fingers track from one side of my back to the other. "And what kind of mood are you aiming for?"

Be shy and weird, and it's going to be shy and weird. But be a queen...

Leaning back to catch his eyes, I can't help but feel that just looking at this man is like standing on the edge of the world and preparing to jump.

"Spontaneity," I murmur, simultaneously hoping he does and doesn't hear. "I guess I'm looking to stay up past my bedtime. Maybe aim for a midnight adventure."

"Fuckin A."

He's more confident than me. More outgoing. While I'm dancing with a stranger and worrying about the possibility of a stress-induced stroke, he merely grins and slides a hand up to weave through my hair. Closer. Closer, he brings us together, so his breath feathers along my tongue.

"Will you stab me if I take you on an adventure?" His murmuring lips brush over my cheek. It's almost a kiss. Almost the most action I've had in... too long. "Nicki?"

"Umm." I push up to my toes—my take on confidence, when really, we both know he won't reject me at this point. "I mean," I amend just a moment before our lips touch, "I won't stab you. *Yes please* to the adventure."

"Alright. To midnight adventures." He closes the space between our lips and slides his tongue inside until an involuntary sigh escapes from somewhere deep in my chest.

His hands grow tighter, his palms hotter, so I feel the burn through the thin fabric of my dress. He tilts his head to the side, his tongue dueling with mine, and when a soft whimper rolls along my throat and leaves me breathless, he changes our pace from a gentle examination to something a hell of a lot more demanding.

"Come with me?" He breaks our kiss but drives his lips along the sensitive column of my neck. He bites so sensations sprint through my blood, then he soothes with a long stroke of his tongue, so those sensations all head toward the same point inside my body.

"Nicki?" he repeats when I say nothing. "Will you come somewhere with me?"

"Sure." I squeeze my eyes shut and try so very hard to get out of my head. To not obsess over the thoughts racing through my mind, and instead concentrate only on what's happening right now. On this man and how it feels when he touches me, and not on what the rest of the world is doing. "I trust you."

"Well, hell." He chokes out a laugh and pulls back, but he takes my hand and starts walking. Too fast. Too conspicuous as we pass the bride and groom. "At no point did I say you should trust me." He leads me past the cake and through the ballroom, then yanking a heavy door open, he tugs me into a brightly lit hall and straight toward a trio of elevators. "In fact, it probably wouldn't be good for you to trust me." He slaps the call button and pushes me up against the wall until I crash with a gasp, and his teeth latch on to my neck.

His hands explore my hips. My waist. His thumbs tease the swells of my breasts, and his cock, hard beneath his pants, presses to my stomach and steals my breath.

"Preston, I..." I tip my head back and study the adorned ceiling while he makes a feast of my neck. My heart thunders, and the pulse between my legs makes it almost impossible to think of anything but him.

"Jesus," I hiss when he bites. "Preston."

"In." He drags me away from the wall and into an empty elevator, then he crushes me against the back wall and searches his pockets for a frantic second before finding his room card and waving it across the sensor. Slamming the side of his fist to the button for the eleventh floor, he comes back to me, ravenous, and devours. "You taste like sugar and sin, Nicki. I had no clue that was my favorite flavor."

"Smooth." I snicker, but that turns to a guttural groan when he slips his hand between my legs and cups me.

My dress remains between us. My panties, too. But the fact he would be so brazen so quickly leaves me floundering for stability and sense.

"Jesus."

"Out." As soon as the doors slide open and we're presented with an empty hall, he pulls away, holding my hand in one of his, and slipping the second into his pants to rearrange whatever is uncomfortable. "I'm in eleven-seventy-three." His steps are fast, too fast, so they almost turn to a run that I have to jog to keep up with. "What don't you like?"

Don't fall down. Don't be shy and weird. Don't trip in your shoes.

Oh god, did you shave?

"Nicki?"

"Huh?"

He brings us to a stop in front of his door and slides his card in front of the sensor. Shoving it wide and tugging me in, he tosses the card to the floor and slams me against the wall so I hit with a thud and my breath catches in my throat.

Bending just a fraction, Preston grabs my thighs and lifts me so I cry out in surprise. Then he swallows down every sound I make and fights my tongue with his own. "What don't you like?"

"Um..." Can't breathe. Can't think. Can't focus on anything except his steel-like length crushing against my core, and the purse he tosses to his hotel room floor. "Tuna. And tomatoes. And liars."

"No." Chuckling, he swings me away from the wall and crosses a messy room until his shins touch the end of a massive four-poster bed. Then he drops me so covers puff up around me, and my legs simply... fall open. "I meant sexually, weirdo."

He stands over me, panting, cataloging, and tugging at his tie. He loosens it just far enough, then pulls it over his head and drops it down beside my thigh. "You need slow? Fast? Gentle? How do you feel about oral sex?"

"Uh..." I'm having sex with a stranger. I'm having sex, period! Oh god. *I'm in my head. I'm in my head!* "I'd rather you just... *do*, ya know? And if I don't like it, I'll tell you."

"And if you *do* like it?" He tears his shirt open to reveal a chest covered with a smattering of dark hair. My fingers itch to touch, and my lips tremble to taste. Leaning closer, he sets his fingertips beneath my chin and draws my eyes back to his. "Will you tell me that too?"

"You want positive reinforcement?"

Slowly, a sly grin works along his lips. "First and foremost, I wanna know that you're enjoying yourself. But second..." He stands again and goes to work on his belt, yanking the leather from each loop, and sets it on the bed beside his tie. "I guess positive reinforcement is my love language. If you tell me I'm rocking your world, I'm gonna keep on doing it. But if you're silent and I don't know, then maybe I'll change things up right when you needed me to stay there."

"Ruining my orgasm." I smile and look down at the long trail of hair that leads into his pants. "That would be a tragedy."

"So tell me when it's working." He shoves his zipper down and pushes his pants next. "Tell me when it's not."

Extending his hand and taking mine, he yanks so fast that I squeal, then he flips me so I land on my knees, with my face pressed to the covers. "It's not that I don't think your dress is amazing," he grabs the fabric and bunches it around my hips, "but I was really curious what you have going on underneath."

"Oh god." I close my eyes—it's my defense, I swear. It's my escape when everything feels too intense. "Preston."

"I like these." Sliding his fingers just beneath the lace fabric of my panties, he strokes my butt cheek so the simple touch of his flesh on mine feels like a thousand bolts of lightning. It's not a painful sensation, it's just... a lot.

"I was never the dude who liked thongs. They just seem so... I dunno." He pushes the fabric aside and reveals one whole side of my ass. "Impractical and uncomfortable. But these..."

Slowly, he moves away from my ass and reaches up to the zipper of my dress. Torturously, tauntingly, he brings the zipper down so pink fabric falls from my torso and drapes to the bed. "These are cheeky and sexy. They let a man wonder and hope."

Bending, he presses a kiss to the center of my back, then bites until I cry out in surprise. "This is like unwrapping a gift, Nicki. And gifts might be my second love language."

"You've done a great deal of soul-searching." I pant. And writhe. But still, I try for witty comebacks. "You have an entire list of things you want from a woman."

"A self-aware man has to be a good thing, right?" Gliding his fingertips along my spine, his touch sends goosebumps sprinting all the way to the top of my head and down to the soles of my feet. "Typically, I know what I want, so I communicate that with whoever needs to know." Setting his fiery palm on my bare ribs, he pushes me to the side so I fall back to the bed and look up at his intense stare. "It means I know what I don't want, too. And I figure, miscommunication is a waste of everyone's time." Setting his knee between my legs and resting all his weight on one elbow, he lowers down to take my bra-covered nipple between his lips.

My spine arches in response. I squirm beneath his body, and the pulse between my legs grows headier and headier until I can't focus on anything else. "Preston..."

"So, since I intend to be straight with you—" Pulling away, he chews on his bottom lip and waits for my eyes to roll back to his. Then he gently tugs my bra down to reveal all of me. "I kinda hope you'll do the same in return. I can't read your mind, but I can listen. So tell me what you want, Nicki. Tell me now and save us both the torture of wasted time."

I can't say it. I can't say what I want!

But there is something I desperately need. So I set my hands on his shoulders and push down.

My heart is in my throat, nerves making it impossible for me to breathe. This man has not once given me reason to think he's not interested, and yet, my intrusive thoughts come charging in.

What if he's disgusted? What if he doesn't want to?

"Mm..." But of course, he makes good on my every filthy desire. "You wanna come on my face, Nicki?" Moving to his knees on the floor, he rests his elbows on each side of my thighs and studies me.

I feel my pleasure soak my panties. I feel it dribble free and bring a burning blush to my cheeks.

But Preston takes his time, palming my thighs and opening me wide. "I want you to use your words." He stares along my body, smirking when our eyes meet and my breath stops in my throat. "Tell me what you want so there's no confusion. I'd hate to assume, only to do something you don't want, and have you running out of here regretting ever meeting me."

"I don't..." My face burns crimson. My heart sprints in my chest. And the more I have to *think*, the less I get to be in the moment and simply *feel*. "Preston, I can't..."

"Do you want me to lick your pussy, Nicole?"

Oh god. My stomach twists. A gush of pleasure soaks my panties, and when I try to lift my legs, to close them and lock him out, Preston's firm grip holds me in place so I whimper.

"Nicki?"

"Yes." I cover my eyes and pull in a deep breath. "Yes, I want you to do that."

"Good."

He buries his face between my legs and bites my clit through the fabric of my underwear, sending spears of ecstasy rolling through my blood and a cry escaping from deep in my chest. He plays with me through my panties, groaning, as though this brings him genuine pleasure too.

Finally, he reaches up and takes the waistband of my underwear with his fingers, then bringing them down, horrifyingly slow, he stops for just a beat before exposing all of me to his hungry eyes.

I let my hands fall away from my face and look down at his intense stare. Then I swallow, because he grins... like this is all a fun game for him.

"Preston, I..."

"You look good up there, Nicole." He drags my panties down and sets them on the floor somewhere I may never find them again. Then he slides the tip of his tongue along the inside of my thigh.

The stroke of his tongue is like lava on my skin, then the coarse scratch of his stubble sparks that lava to a wildfire.

"I don't know if you know this," he pulls my clit between his lips and sets a hand on my belly when I almost spring off the bed, "and I don't know if this applies to all men, but for me..." He suckles on my clit, groaning when a wash of pleasure floods between my legs and makes a mess of his bedspread. "This view," he grunts, "seeing your sweet pussy, and your tits, and your beautiful face, all at the same time?" Impatient, he slips two thick fingers through my folds and holds me down when I cry out. "It's enough to make me come without you even touching me."

"Oh god!" Tears make my eyes itch. "Preston."

"Say Preston *first.*" He pumps his hand and draws me closer to an explosive peak. "Then God. This is my hard work, not his."

"Oh geez." I don't mean to laugh. Or cry. Or make whatever the hell sound comes from my soul. But I cover my eyes again and shake my head. "You're so egotistical."

"It's who I am." Pushing up to his feet, he comes to rest over my chest, but he continues playing with my pussy with one hand. Pumping, punishing. Using the other, he reaches up and pushes my own hands away from my eyes. "Dirty talk gets my engine revving, beautiful. Tell me I'm your god, and I'm not sure either of us will survive the night."

Slamming his lips to mine and his tongue inside, he transfers to me the flavor of... me. And though my brain insists that should be gross, my heart and soul and libido say the opposite.

"Fuck, you feel good beneath my body, Nicki."

"Do you have a condom?"

I can hardly catch my breath. I don't want to think tonight. I don't want to obsess, or worry, or dissect a simple act. I just want to do.

And I want him to do it to me.

"Preston?"

"I do." He slows his fingers and circles my clit with his thumb. "But it's not time for that yet. I still have so much—"

"Now." I sit up, pushing him back, and work to shrug out of what remains of my dress. I grab Preston's boxers and push them down to reveal a deliciously thick, enticingly ready cock, then I encircle it with my hand and have him calling out with just one glide.

"You only get one chance." I quicken my pace and force myself not to slide his length into my mouth.

I mean, I probably should. Tit for tat and all that. But I can't bring myself to do it. I can't break down that barrier of intimacy with a man I just met.

But I squeeze my fingers tighter and glance up to watch this powerful man lose control of his body.

He wraps a hand in my hair and holds on tight enough he *could* hurt me. Just one yank to the side, and he could send me spiraling into a dark place I never want to revisit. But he doesn't tug. He doesn't abuse.

Jesus, he's the king of living in the moment and enjoying whatever pleasures are handed to him.

"One time," I continue when my throbbing pussy makes me desperate. "One chance. Then I'm never gonna see you again."

"All the more reason for us to savor." Glancing down, his burning eyes lock onto mine. "One night means I'm gonna explore everything you've got. I don't want a quickie."

"But I do."

I release his cock and grin when he cries out at the loss, but then I bend to his trousers on the floor. I grab his wallet from the back pocket and flip it open—since everyone knows we can find a condom there— then I take it out and toss the rest away.

I study the silver package. I turn it over to make sure there are no imperfections, then I look up to Preston and swallow. "It wasn't left in the sun or anything, right?"

"Promise." He snatches the foil packet and tears it open with a savage growl reverberating through his chest. "You about to run out on me, Nicki?"

"Not if you don't give me time to think." I take the slimy rubber from between his fingers and set it on the end of his cock. Slowly, carefully, I roll it along his shaft and grow more breathless the longer it takes to reach the base.

So much. So thick.

And for tonight, it's all for me.

"I don't want the awkward chit-chat and getting-to-know-you phase of sex." I set my hand on his back and pull him forward a step so I can press a biting kiss to his abdomen. "I don't want that. I just want the act. The sex."

"Wow." The single word comes out a little short, but when I look up, his smiling lips smooth out the fraying of my nerves. "If I said that to a chick, she'd slap me for being a one-track-minded jerkoff."

"I'll be that person." Reclining back onto my elbows, then flat on the bed, I reach up and sigh when he follows me down. "We both know what this is," I pant. "And it took a hell of a lot of trust for me to get this far. To be in this room with you. So now, I just want—"

"The sex." He wraps his arm beneath my back and picks me up effort-lessly to carry me along the bed. He crawls on his knees, holding all of my weight with one arm, while he uses the other to hold himself up. Then he settles my head on a silky pillow and buries his lips against my pounding throat. "If you change your mind."

Pushing my thighs wide, then picking one leg up and resting it on his shoulder, his eyes burn with hunger and panic in one. Desire, and *this can't be real*. Reaching down and circling his sheathed cock in his hand, he comes closer and sets the fiery head at my opening. "Fuck, Nicki. If you change your mind and want slower, you just tell me, and I'll stop."

"Okay."

I move my hands along his back and reach down to cup his muscular ass. Then I pull him up, surprising him with my move, and whimper when his cock spears deep inside my pussy and my walls flutter tight to hold him in place.

"Shit!" I squeeze my eyes shut when my release threatens. I'm so close. So ready. "Fuck, Preston."

"So tight." Slowly, he rolls his hips forward and starts a rocking pace that has his dick teasing every nerve inside my core. When I cry from how good it feels, he turns his face and bites the side of my knee. "So fucking perfect, Nicki."

My lungs clamor for air, and my pulse scrambles too quickly. Too erratic. But I switch off my brain and feel. Experience. Absorb.

I'm having my first ever one-night stand, and hell, but it doesn't feel as cheap as I thought it would.

"Preston..."

"Tell me what's working." He quickens his pace and squeezes his eyes shut when he finds what turns him on. "Tell me what's not, babe." Blindly, he brings his hand away from my leg, but swings in again and spanks my ass until I cry out. "Fuck."

"That works," I tell him breathlessly.

If I was using my brain right now, I might acknowledge how surprised I am that being spanked is a turn on. I might even obsess over how I assumed that would be the world's shittiest turn *off*. But I'm not thinking. I refuse. I absolutely say no to using my brain. So I reach up and cup the back of Preston's head instead.

His eyes snap open at my contact, then they burn when I pull him down and slam my lips to his until his tongue comes out to play.

"I guess I like it rough," I tell him between biting kisses. "I like it when you're being bossy."

"Fuckin A." He glides his hand along my thigh and up to stroke my ribs. His hips slam against the backs of my legs, and when my pussy clenches tight with my pending orgasm, he sends his hand on a frenzied exploration of my body.

My breasts, then my chest. He strokes my jaw, and breaks his mouth away from mine, only to latch on to my neck and bite hard enough to make me cry out.

"I'm going to come." My hips move now, too. They piston and search for release. "Preston."

"If you come," he pulls away, but keeps pounding. Keeps moving. "You're gonna take me with you. I'm not ready for this night to be over."

"I'm not willing to risk my orgasm." I twist and try to turn us over.

I'm not nearly strong enough to make him go anywhere he doesn't want to go. But he understands my request, so he drops to his side, then rolls to his back and drags me with him so we don't disconnect for even a second.

The momentum helps propel me up onto his lap, then I keep our pace going. I roll my hips and grind down so my clit gets a little attention. Then I grab Preston's hand and bring it up to cup my breast. "I like it a little rough," I whisper. "Remember?"

Invitation received, he surges up and takes my nipple between his teeth, biting down till I scream. "I like that you like it rough," he pants. Cupping my ass, he pulls my cheeks apart and bruises my flesh with his fingers. "I like that you're scared to ask, but brave enough to get the

31

message across." He wraps his arm around my hips and holds my weight, then he thrusts upwards to fill me to bursting. "I like that you wanna cry when you come."

"Oh god." I drop my face to his shoulder and hold on for the ride. Because he refuses to play second fiddle. He refuses to let me be in charge. "Preston."

"Fuck!" he barks out when my clamping walls squeeze him tight. "Nicole."

"Now." My release comes out on a sob. My orgasm seizing my body and holding me captive, while beneath, Preston keeps working. Pistoning his hips and dragging me across the fire.

I come with a violent burst that empties my lungs and leaves me holding on or risk falling to the floor. Then Preston explodes too, a vicious detonation that fills his condom and ignites a second release from deep inside my soul.

My hips twitch and my heart thunders. My nails bite into his shoulders, and our lips come back together so our tongues duel.

If the hotel were to burn down around us, I wouldn't know.

If my phone wants my attention, I don't hear it.

There could be an earthquake outside, and I wouldn't be able to differentiate it from the way my body and mind shake in this room.

"Shit." Panting, Preston breaks the silence and presses a gentle kiss to the corner of my lips. His breath bathes my skin, his teeth, nipping my jaw. He drops a second kiss to soothe where he bites, while deep in my pussy, his dick twitches with the aftershocks of something I'm not sure either of us are ready to explore.

"Fuck, Nicki." He keeps me wrapped up close. One arm around my hips, and the other, across my back like a reverse seatbelt. "Took my breath away," he accuses, though his words come with a pleased smile. "Not often people can manage that."

A surprising snicker rolls along my throat, and though I don't mean to, I bring my hand up and slide my fingers through the longer locks atop his head. "I, uh..." I draw a deep breath and try, so very hard, to keep my brain away. To stay out of my head and not overthink this predicament I've found myself in. "Well..."

"Stop it." Easily able to read my inner turmoil, Preston stands from the bed, carrying me with him so I'm still pinioned on his cock, but then he sets me on my feet and slowly slides out until my breath comes out on an exhaled gasp. "Stop thinking about running away."

He leaves me standing by the bed and strolls toward the bathroom. I don't see him once he crosses the threshold, but I still know, somehow, that he peels the condom off and drops it in the trash. Then the faucet flips on.

"Stop overthinking everything," he calls out as the tap turns off and a squeak of the towel rail makes me jump.

Finally, when my eyes go to the floor in search of my clothes, he heads back into the room and sweeps me up into his arms so I scream louder now than I ever did while we were having sex.

My arms instinctively wrap around his neck and my body curls into his for fear of being dropped. But then he walks us around to the side of his bed and yanks the covers back to make space for me. "Do you like TV?"

"Wh—" I look around in a panic as he sets me in the middle of the mattress. "What?"

He snags a television remote from the bedside table, then climbs into bed beside me and pulls the covers up. Pointing the remote at a flat screen mounted to the wall, he switches it on, then he slaps the light switch until we're bathed in darkness. "Funny or heart-jerking?" he asks as the TV flickers to life, roughly folding me closer so my cheek presses to his chest and my leg comes up over his thighs.

Hair covers his chest and tickles my cheek, and without my express permission, my hand comes up and my fingers move through the dusting of dark coverage.

"Let's go with funny," he answers himself, since I don't seem to intend to. "*Schitt's Creek*?" he rumbles. "Or *Brooklyn 99*?"

He selects the cop show and tosses the remote somewhere toward the end of the bed, then he pulls me in close and pretends like all is good in the world.

Like we're an old couple lazing about after a long day.

"Stop thinking, Nicki." Sighing, he places his fingers beneath my chin and drags my face up till our eyes meet. Then when I think my brain might explode, he flashes a devilish grin. "You're doing this to yourself. But it doesn't have to be nearly as scary as you're making it."

"I should go home."

Self-fulfilling prophecy, maybe.

Self-sabotage, probably.

I attempt to push up to my elbow, but Preston cuts me off and pulls me back down again.

"I'm not gonna hold you here against your wishes," he speaks quickly when my eyes flash with fear. Challenge. Contempt. "This isn't one of those situations. But I'm gonna try to get you to turn off your over-analyzing brain for a minute. Because if you do, I think you'll realize this isn't so bad."

Releasing my face, he wraps me up tight and presses the world's sweet-est, softest, most panic-inducing kiss to the center of my forehead. "Give resting a try," he murmurs when I close my eyes.

Tears burn the backs, and my hands shake from nerves. But his calm countenance somehow chips away at the armor my psyche so tirelessly attempts to build.

"Give yourself an hour where you don't have to worry about anything outside this room." He sets one last kiss on my temple before turning back to the television. "Two episodes. Then who knows, maybe you'll have fallen asleep because you're so fucking comfortable."

"You think you know me?"

Fight it, Nicki.

Stay the night, Nicki.

The way I wage war within myself is more chatter than I'll ever need. Having a man on the outside making demands too only adds to the noise. But then his hand drops to my naked hip, and his fingers stroke soft patterns against my skin.

He draws pictures, I think. Maybe shapes. Or letters. He spells things out, or solves math equations. I don't know what he's doing, but it soothes the frantic sprinting of my mind. It gives the synapses in my brain something else to focus on.

Jesus, whatever he draws, it tugs my consciousness that way, and away from my racing thoughts.

"Feels nice?" he murmurs, while on the television, Detective Jake Peralta tries his damnedest to woo Amy Santiago into a night of frivolity. "Rest, Nicki. Slow things down."

"Can we watch the other show?" My throat burns dry, but Preston's stroking fingers help slow my thundering heart. "Please."

"Of course." He pushes up quickly and snatches the remote, then flopping back, he drags me close again and hitches my leg back across his. "You don't like the nine-nine?"

"I just don't want to watch it," I mumble. Closing my eyes, I work to pace my breathing and not think about the phone I hear vibrating somewhere in this room.

It's my phone, I know it is. But it's not an important call, so I remain in this bed and snuggle closer to a complete stranger.

When I exhale a deep breath and Preston feels me relax, his hand goes back to my hip and resumes its constant patterns.

"Good girl," he rumbles. "Now sleep."

Nicki

MIDNIGHT ADVENTURES... OUTTA HERE.

My eyes stay closed for hours... so many hours. But the television drones, and eventually, Preston sleeps. His hand falls limp, and when the sound of his soft breathing penetrates my ears, that elixir he created with his fingertips washes away so my intruding thoughts come sprinting back.

Get up, Nicki.

Crawl out of this bed and run the hell away.

It smells like sex in here.

But he smells so good.

What if he wakes when I move, and then we have to face that awkward chit-chat all over again?

Why can't I just go to sleep like a normal person?

I could, I admit to myself. *If I was in my bed. Alone.*

Go to sleep, Nicole! Or get up and leave.

Pick a fucking lane and use it.

"Dammit," I groan under my breath.

Gently, so ridiculously carefully, I turn away and cautiously push the blankets off. Dragging just one leg out, painstakingly slowly, I twist my hips and turn until my foot touches the floor. Then I follow with the second until I'm sitting on the edge of the bed, and the light from the television is all I have to light my way.

Setting my hands on either side of my thighs, I slowly push up to stand, and when the springs inside the mattress moan from my movement, I grit my teeth and pray with all my heart and soul that Preston stays asleep.

He's a nice guy. In fact, he's really friggin' cool. But I'm not sure I was built for this life of spontaneity and casual sex. I wasn't made for adult dating—not that this was a *date*—and I'm sure as hell not equipped for sharing a bed with a man, or awkward mornings-after.

So... I have to leave.

When Preston remains asleep at my back and completely still despite my disturbance, I push the rest of the way off the mattress and grab the first piece of fabric my hands touch.

His shirt, with the musky scent of aftershave and a soft side of... I sniff the collar as I shrug it on. *Whiskey, maybe.* I slide my arms through the sleeves and reach to the front to fix the buttons, then I sigh when my phone buzzes again.

Always demanding my attention.

Always screaming at me to devote my time there.

Tiptoeing across the room and stopping by the pile that is my dress and shoes and tossed purse, I snatch my phone from the clutch and sigh, not only at the seven percent phone battery I have left, but the twelve missed calls and seventeen texts.

"Jesus Christ." Ignoring every notification and instead navigating to a different text screen, I pull up my brother's name. Because he's my best friend. He's my person.

If I wanted to use Preston's words, I would describe Axel as my *ride or die.*

So although I'm all but naked, and reeling from an evening of things brothers shouldn't know about, I click on his name and start typing.

Hey. You awake?

While I wait for his reply, I slowly back up to the luxurious wing-back chair in the corner of Preston's room, and sitting down with the world's slowest movements, I release an anxious breath and open my texts from another man.

Where are you?

Are you working tonight?

I have a quick question about June. Call me back.

Nicki? I tried to call you.

Hello? Nicki?

Nick. I'm on shift all night, so call me back.

June said you're in the city tonight. So call me when you're finished working.

Nicki? Why aren't you answering my calls?

Nicki?

Annoyed, I reach up and play with my earring. It's a nervous tic, a way to expel the energy pulsing through my veins. But my fidgeting hand grows more intent when my phone vibrates all over again.

It's like Noah *knows* I'm holding it. Or maybe he's simply that persistent. But the device *buzz, buzz, buzz*es and sets my temper alight.

Angry at his constant intrusions, I cast my eyes to the clock on the bedside table, and beside that, to Preston's muscular body draped across my side of the mattress. Then I scowl and end the incoming call.

Jumping back to my texts, I type, *It's two in the morning, Noah. I've been asleep. I'll call you tomorrow.* Then because I know he'll keep trying, I place his number on a restricted list that I know enrages him to the point of obsession. It means his calls and texts go straight into a queue, and don't bother me until I enable them again.

It'll mean hours of badgering tomorrow, and a lengthy discussion about why I shouldn't do that to him, and why this proves he can't '*trust me to do the right thing.*'

"Ugh." Moving back to my text screen with Axel, I bring my fingers up and nibble on my thumbnail as the three little bubbles move, letting me know he's awake and texting me back.

It's two in the morning, Feeney. Why are you awake?

I choke out an almost silent laugh and write back, *It's two where you are too. Why are YOU awake?*

My body clock is all messed up, he types back immediately. *I'm used to 24s, so I can't sleep yet. You okay?*

I cast a look back to Preston. To his broad back, etched with muscle, but smooth, unlike his chest. I study the thick column of his neck, where I'm quite certain I bit him at some point in the last couple hours—though the thought doesn't leave me terrified like I thought it might.

While he sleeps, I can finally relax and simply... look. And appreciate. And relive.

But then I remember the phone in my hand and the question my little brother has asked.

Typing, I tell him, *I did something bad. Something outrageous. And I don't want to tell you about it. But I'm freaking out a little bit and don't know who else to talk to.*

Axel: *Okay... are you safe?*

Me: *Yes.*

Axel: *But you had sex?*

Me: *I didn't say that!*

Axel: *It's two in the morning! I'm reading between the lines. So I'm gonna ask again: are you safe? Are you okay?*

Me: *Yes, I'm safe. I'm okay. I'm not afraid. But shittttttt, I'm freaking out.*

Instead of receiving a reply text, my screen changes to an incoming call, while my little brother's goofy grin fills the photo box and *usually* makes me smile. Because he's set to have calls alert me immediately—unlike Noah, who is always set to vibrate—my ringtone bleats loud enough to make me jump.

Preston stirs in his sleep, exhaling a noisy breath, then drags my pillow down to become his little cuddle friend.

Panicked, I accept the call and shove up from my chair, then I dash into the bathroom in the dark. My feet are sensitive to the coarse carpet, and a moment after that, the cold tile, while the hem of Preston's shirt brushes my thighs and sends shivers racing along my spine just as easily as his fingertips elicit the same response.

Ducking through the doorway and closing it at my back, I walk to the toilet and close the lid. Then I sit down in the darkness and bring the phone to my ear. "Axel," I whisper. "Now's not a good time."

He chokes out a laugh so loud, it's obvious he's not afraid of waking a one-night conquest. "You got laid, Feeney. What the fuck?"

"Shut up," I hiss. "Why'd you call me? You knew I was somewhere not conducive to private discussions."

"And now you're echoing," he giggles. "Tells me you snuck into the bathroom. My big sister's a fuckin' hussy! How's it feel?"

"Like I'm gonna strangle you the second I see you. What do you want?"

40

"To know that you're safe." Lowering his voice, he turns a little more serious. "Why are you freaking out? Is he an asshole?"

"No, he's..." I rest my elbows on my knees and my face in my hand. Then taking a deep breath, I let it out again until my chest empties. "He's really nice, actually. Like, he's confident and arrogant and a little crude. But he seems like a good person beneath that."

"Did you feel unsafe while spending time with him?" He cuts through my over-analysis and so easily arrows to what's important. "Did he push boundaries or take something you weren't willing to give?"

"Well..." I frown. "No, but—"

"So why the fuck are you freaking out? It's two o'clock in the morning, Nicole. You should be in a sex coma, not hiding in a bathroom and calling your brother."

"You make it sound worse than it actually is." Grumbling, I sit taller and glance toward the closed door, fully expecting Preston to barge through. That would be my luck, of course. "I don't like how it feels to sleep in a bed with someone else."

"So kick his ass out and catch some shuteye."

"This is his room!" I bite back. "I can't kick him out, Axe."

"Wanna bet? You go back into that room, Feeney, and tap him on the shoulder. Wake him the fuck up. Then you hand him his shoes and tell him he's sleeping in the lobby downstairs. Any decent dude would take his shit and leave you with the room."

"But it's *his* room. I can't just kick him out."

"Sure you can. Women have done it to me. And guess how I responded? I left," he answers before I can ask. "Like a fuckin' gentleman. Any dude who wants to get snippy for being told to skedaddle won't have to worry for too long. I'll come introduce him to my fucking fists until he relearns how to speak with a lisp."

"You're an animal." Dropping my head back and resting it on the cold tile wall, I rub the heel of my palm over my eyes. "I can't believe I... ya know."

"Had sex?" he sniggers. "I know. I'm processing too."

"I let a man bring me to his room," I clarify. "And then I did that thing—"

"Had sex."

"And then I stayed in the bed long enough to let him fall asleep."

"It's weird, right?" I know he's my brother. And I know this is a conversation verging on crazy. But beneath all that, I know he's smiling. "He must be a smooth talker to get your guard down like that."

"Smooth talker," I ponder sadly. "Or I'm just an idiot who hasn't learned her lesson. What if he's just like every other guy out there, huh? What if he's a dick, and I've just instigated a nightmare of bullshit I'm gonna spend years trying to undo?"

"See, I hear you, Feeney, and I sympathize with your hardships, but what if... and hear me out..." he teases. "You just had no strings attached, no repercussions, no drama sex with a decent guy?"

"Axel—"

"Did you use protection?"

"What?" My heart skips in my chest. "Wildly inappropriate."

"So you didn't?"

"Yes! We did. But you don't need to—"

"Then you're gonna be fine," he cuts in, interrupting what we both know will turn into a tirade. "No STDs, no babies, no drama. Go back to bed, Nick. Let the man hug you, then tomorrow, come home and I'll spray you with Lysol."

"You're an asshole." But my smile notches up when he cackles. "Go to sleep, or you're gonna be wrecked when you're on shift tomorrow."

"Nah." He grunts as he moves, so in my mind, I see him readjusting in his recliner and finding a new comfortable position. "I start shift tomorrow night at six, so it's best if I stay awake tonight, then sleep tomorrow after you get home. That way, I stay on the right sleep schedule. In the meantime, I'm gonna watch me some more *Brooklyn 99*."

"Ugh." I roll my eyes and push up to stand from the icy cold toilet seat. "I'm so sick of that show, I swear."

"Because Jake is funnier than you?" he taunts. "Or because you project your trauma onto everyone else and expect the rest of the world to fit into the same tiny box?"

"Shut up." I make my way to the mirror and catch just the outline of my face from the moonlight fighting to penetrate the small square window above the shower. "I'm gonna hang up, grab my things, and sneak out."

"Man-eater," he tosses at me. "You just use 'em, then dump 'em. Never thought I'd see the day sweet little Nicole Feeney would chew a man up and spit him out."

"Nicole Scott," I return through pursed lips. Setting my free hand on the lip of the basin and drawing a deep breath into my lungs, I exhale again and close my eyes. "I'm Nicole Scott, and I have been for a long time. It is what it is."

"Maybe that's what your license says. But I know what I know. Now go back to bed. Get some sleep, and maybe some morning fuckery. Tomorrow, you come back to real life and bullshit. But tonight, and for as long as it's dark, you get to be Cinderella. Don't waste the opportunity."

"Yeah..." I see stars behind my eyelids. Constellations. I have a million thoughts chasing each other. And a man in the next room, hugging a pillow that smells of me. "I'll talk to you tomorrow, Axel. Save me a seat at the breakfast table."

He scoffs. "It's your table, sis. Don't be home too early, okay? Pretend you're on vacation. Go to the buffet and get yourself a breakfast you would never have back here. Sip your coffee slowly. Have a looooong shower and pretend you have nothing else to worry about in the world."

"Unlikely." Opening my eyes, I blink through the stars and study my silhouette in the mirror. "Before you go?"

"Mm? What's up?"

"Have women seriously kicked you out of your own hotel room?"

He barks out a playful laugh. "Once or twice. Believe it or not, I tend to bag the good girls who have existential crises because they've banged a stranger. So they hide in the bathroom and have a panic attack, then they tiptoe back into the room when they think I'm asleep, and they do the weird *yes-no* negotiation in their head about whether they should wake me up."

Relatable. So ridiculously relatable.

"So you do the gentlemanly thing and go?"

"I do. Because good girls need gentle hands. And there are way too many *nice guys* out here who make us all look like sociopathic assholes. The dude you selected out of *allllll* the guys at that wedding must be pretty cool, considering you gave him even a second of your time. Trust your instincts, Feeney. You've got them. You've just spent way too many years questioning them."

"It's hard to know what's instinct," I whisper past the lump in my throat, "and what's overthinking."

"Well…" He considers for a moment. "You gotta feel it in your stomach. When I'm walking into a structure fire in the middle of a shift, when my eyes are burning, and maybe I'm tired from a long day. When I'm walking toward a wall of fucking flames, Nick, I could stand there and overthink it all, or I could trust my gut and go where I've gotta go."

"I don't know h—" Frustrated, I bite off my words and shake my head. "I don't know how to tell the difference between what's real and what's projection."

"Your gut." I hear him move, and then the squeak and click of the footrest locking into place on the recliner in my living room. He grunts, then stands, though I don't know where he's going at this hour.

"You've gotta try to quiet your brain and listen to your stomach. It takes practice, but eventually, the right message gets through." Feet shuffle against hardwood floors, then he stops at my fridge and opens the door so I hear glass bottles rattle together. "It's worked for me so far, anyway. Haven't died in a fire yet."

"Ugh!" I slap the porcelain sink and growl. "Axel! Don't say things like that and tempt the universe to screw everything up. Jesus!"

"And now you're worrying about me," he chuckles. "Means you're not overthinking the dude in your bed. While your brain is on fire, search your gut and figure out what it's saying about him. Then go to sleep and get some rest. You need it. You're only twenty-five, Feeney, but you hold stress like you're forty-five."

"Charming." I pull the phone away from my ear to check the time. It's now closer to two-thirty than it is to two, so I bring the device back to my ear. "I'm hanging up. I'll see you in the morning. And stop calling me Feeney."

He completely ignores my request and asks instead, "Did I help stop your panic attack?"

"Sure. But you replaced it with a new freakout about your work. Good job, douchebag."

Unbothered, he chuckles. "All part of the little brother package. I'll see you when you get home, then we'll high-five over your newest filthy conquest."

"You're disturbed, disgusting, and lack appropriate boundaries."

Hanging up, I stare down at my black screen and smile. Because I love him anyway. I love him more than almost anyone else on the planet.

But what are you gonna do now, Nicole?

Glancing up at the mirror, grateful that I can't clearly see my face, I draw a deep breath and work to psych myself up.

Go back to bed? Snuggle in? Plan for a morning orgasm?

Not likely.

I push away from the sink and approach the closed door in silence, then opening it up and slipping back into Preston's room, I stop by the side of the bed and look down at the man who now starfishes across the entire mattress.

Sheets barely cover his ass, while muscle flexes in his shoulders so my eyes are drawn to the hard lines. He's taken over the bed, which means for me to get back in, I would have to move him. I would need to disturb his peace and risk waking him up—and it's already been established I don't intend to face the awkward chit-chat that inevitably comes after casual sex.

Breathing out a somewhat disappointed sigh, I begin collecting my things, using the television to illuminate my way. I grab my dress and shoes. Panties. I don't swap out and leave Preston's shirt behind. Instead, I take it with me. Because I'm a thief, I suppose. And I like the idea of keeping it as a token of that one night I got a little wild and did something purely for me.

Making certain my buttons are secure, and stepping into my panties, I cast one last look around the room and snag my clutch from the floor near the closet. Finally, I turn the television off so Preston can rest in proper darkness. Then approaching the door in a now-pitch black room, I follow the strip of light underneath until my hand touches the cold steel handle.

Pulling it open and feeling a stab of guilt for the harsh light glaring into the room, I look back for half a beat and study the man who took and gave tonight. No strings attached. No pouting. No weird manipulations or games.

Just... sex. A mutual exchange where neither of us had to feel used or abused, and yet, we both got to find completion.

How utterly refreshing.

Stepping across the threshold and into the stark hall, I twist back and let the door slowly swing closed. I guide it so the lock snicks, but without the loud *click* that'll wake every person on this floor. Then I turn away and do my first ever walk of shame.

My makeup is no doubt clownish by this point. My hair, surely pointing a thousand different directions. I'm barefooted, holding my heels like a common... well, *spontaneous* woman. Preston's shirt is all I have to maintain modesty, and beneath it, my thighs burn in the very best way.

Jesus, why do I insist on walking away, when I know that tomorrow, next week, hell, next *year*, I'm going to wish I'd bathed in this moment for as long as I possibly could?

Because I'm a toxic jerk whose therapist makes a fortune in inconsistent one-hour increments.

I head to the elevator and step inside, then out again on the ninth floor. When I find my door, I take my room key from my clutch and press it to the sensor until the little light turns green. Then I slip through the door and pray no one is in the security office right now, witnessing my half-naked stroll through the halls.

Instead of going to bed and falling flat on my face to rest, I pack up my things and call this trip to an end. I have a fast shower, and fold Preston's shirt with the utmost care. I slip into a pair of sneakers, and a slouchy shirt that shows off one shoulder and most of my collarbone. I brush my teeth and push wet hair off my shoulder. I set my planner into my oversized purse—not at all like the clutch I've carted around all day—and my laptop after that.

Then casting one last glance over my room and making certain I haven't forgotten anything, I look regretfully toward the untouched bed and sigh.

I didn't even pull the covers back. I didn't get to sit on it.

Last night was supposed to be a mini vacation away from home, paid for by a crew of really sweet professional fighters, and complete with a three-course meal and exorbitant hours of Netflix binging. Instead, it turned into an existential crisis, fantastic sex, and an orgasm that ended a years long dry spell.

"Could've been worse," I grumble as I let myself back into the hall.

I hiss when the corner of my bag scrapes my thigh, then clomp-step my way to the elevator and out to freedom.

Into my car. Headlights on to battle the middle of the night darkness, and stereo up to hide the *clunk-clunk-clunk* of my old and dying engine.

I pull into a drive-thru on the way out of the city and I buy a coffee to get me through the drive home. Then I settle in for the one-hour trip, dissociating from everything that's happened in the last twelve hours, and operate on muscle memory until I cross over the train tracks leading into the town I was born and raised in.

The bride and groom live here too, but I guess they wanted the fancy venue in the city for their party. They wanted elegant and grand and colorful and amazing. So I loaded up my car and went where they asked me to go.

Pulling onto my street and turning down my music, I slow out front of my Victorian-esque, two-story home, and smile at the beautiful garden I tend whenever I have time. I park on the street, since Axel's truck is in my driveway, then slide out of my car, carefully closing the door so I don't wake my neighbors. I leave my luggage in the trunk, but I scoop up my purse and lug it along the footpath that cuts down the middle of my yard.

The television illuminates my living room window, but I don't hear any sound.

Finally, I trudge up the porch steps and allow my smile to stretch across my face. Because maybe I'm in the middle of a crisis, but I'm home. And home is where my heart is. Always and forever.

That's why it's easy for me to let go of people like Preston Danes and the experiences he may offer me—inside of a bed or out. It's easy to push all that aside and point myself back toward home, because the rewards far outweigh the miniscule risk of missing out on something good.

A risk I happily take every single day of my life.

Slipping my key into the front door and twisting it in silence, I push the door open... and startle when I find my little—but much bigger than me—brother standing at the bottom of the stairs.

Axel Feeney is twenty-one years old, one of the youngest firefighters on his crew. He's six feet tall, and a slightly too-trim hundred and eighty pounds. His shoulders are broad, and his hips are slim. And though we both know he still has more growing to do, he steps forward now and pulls me into a crushing hug that empties my lungs and makes my eyes burn with tears I have no reasonable explanation for.

"I knew you'd come straight home, Feeney." He grunts and squeezes me extra tight. "You're your own worst enemy."

"I couldn't sleep there." I press my ear to his chest and feel the first trickle of relief inside my heart. "I couldn't sleep in that bed with a man, Axe. I didn't want to do it."

"And that's your choice." Pulling back, he presses a noisy kiss to my cheek, then holds my arms so we remain connected, but a foot apart. "I'm proud of you for knowing your boundaries and enforcing them. I know that took a lot."

"It took so much," I choke out something that is half laugh, half sob. "I was all over the place with indecision."

"And now you're home." He takes my purse without asking and sets it on the floor by the living room entrance. Then he slings his arm over my shoulders and starts us up the stairs.

Because he knows where I need to be. He knows where I need to go.

It's not that I can't share a bed at all.

It's just that I can't share a bed with a man.

"She went to bed around eight," he whispers. "Asleep by eight-thirty. She had Pop Tarts for dinner, and enough lemon soda to soak her mattress."

"You're an ass," I snicker. But I hurry my steps and head toward the bedroom door, third on the left, after we reach the stair landing. "What did she really have for dinner?"

"Cheese pizza with extra cheese. She did have lemon soda, but we shared a can, and she finished it around seven, so she had plenty of time to pee. Noah tried to call the house a dozen times, but I told him to fuck off and get a life." Then he stops at the door and beams while a moving night-light casts stars all over my daughter's bedroom ceiling. "She hasn't stirred since I put her down. But she was hoping you'd be here when she woke."

My heart melts as I study my daughter's soft brown locks. Her thick bottom lip pushed out in a pout, and her long, black lashes kissing her cheeks. She sleeps on her back, with her arms above her head and her legs bent at the knee.

I have a picture just like this, but from when she was in my stomach.

"Go to sleep, Mama Feeney." Axel presses a kiss to my temple and gently shoves me into the room. "You know you're dying for some shuteye."

"You need to stop calling me Feeney." I pause in the middle of my baby's bedroom and push my sneakers off. "*Her* last name is Scott." I glance back and meet Axel's eyes. "I'm not changing mine back and leaving her out here all alone—and Noah will never allow me to change her name. This is the life we have now, so stop picking at it."

"Yeah, well, it's a pretty decent life," he says with a soft grin.

I come up on the other side of the bed and pull the blankets down, then I slide in beside my daughter and sigh at her amazingly soft skin. Fixing my pillow and dragging her small body closer, I close my eyes and exhale.

"Yeah," I whisper. For me. For her. For Axel. "It's a pretty good life."

"Goodnight, Nick. Sleep well." Grabbing the doorhandle and pulling it closed most of the way, Axel's footsteps echo all the way along the hall until he's on the stairs.

Then, as though she senses me near, June smacks her lips and turns toward me. "Mommy?"

"Shhh..." I brush her hair back and set my lips on the center of her brow. "It's still nighttime. Go back to sleep."

"Kay..." She wriggles close and stops only when her face rests in the crook of my neck. Then she sighs and floats back to sleep. "Love you."

"I love you too, June Bug. With my whole entire heart."

Preston

REALITY STINKS, MAN.

Sunlight shines through my windows, burning my eyes, but it's the absence of a warm body beside mine that brings me out of my slumber.

I lie on my side, a sheet covering my bottom half, and my thigh straddling a fucking pillow. As I peel just one eye open, I squint and frown at the harsh morning light that makes it feel like my retinas are bleeding.

She's gone.

She ran, just like I knew she would.

Flopping to my back and exhaling a heavy sigh, I spread my arms and legs wide and take stock of what the fuck happened since Cole got hitched yesterday.

Vows. Food. Speeches. Cake. Dancing.

Nicki Scott.

Blonde. Beautiful. Witty... but scared.

Outspoken... but vulnerable.

Sheltered... but secretive.

Slitting my other eye open and waiting for them both to adjust to the fact it's a new day, I glance around my room and groan at the early hour.

Whatever hour it is, it's too early.

Could she still be here, I wonder, *and I'm just too stupid to notice?*

With a guttural grunt, I push up to sit and peer to the wing-back chair in the corner of the room: empty. To the bathroom: door open. I peek back at the television: off. And then to the exit, and know she left through it long ago.

Wiping my eyes and stifling a deep yawn, I crawl along my bed in search of my pants. Taking my phone out of the pocket when I find them, I check for missed calls.

I have a few. Same with emails and text. But none need to be dealt with now.

Instead, I jump over to an app I've been working on for the past year, and open it up to find a zillion notifications from the last twelve hours. Most were from the wedding, when people were everywhere, and bodies surrounded me. So I follow the timeline until there are just two: me and Nicole.

And then at two-eighteen this morning, when a couple became just one.

She snuck out while I slept, and now I can't know where she is, because I never got her number. We never discussed a *tomorrow*, and though my app can alert me to bodies in my vicinity, it can't differentiate whose is whose, and it sure as shit can't lead me to Nicole.

"Fuck." Tossing the phone to my covers and pressing the heels of my hands over my eyes, I yawn again and roll my head side to side.

I tried to get her to stay. I tried to provide her with a safe space and somewhere to rest for a night.

But she was a flight risk from the moment we met.

I knew that. *She* knew that.

Now... it's over.

Tilting my head to the side and peering at the clock on my bedside table, I moan when the time reads nine-twenty-three. Early for a guy whose life tends to happen in the hours between ten and three, but well after a respectable hour for everyone else.

Setting my feet over the edge of the bed and pushing up to stand, I snag my phone and head into the bathroom. Flipping a little music on so I'm not in here *all* alone, I switch the shower on, step into a steaming stream of hot water, and make quick work of cleaning up.

I wash my hair and run a handful of soap over my face. Then I lean out of the shower cubicle and grab my toothbrush, smearing paste on the bristles and shrugging at the puddle of water I've left on the floor that'll become a slipping hazard when I'm not paying attention.

Brushing my teeth and making a concerted effort *not* to touch my cock each time a flash of Nicki Scott passes through my mind, I finish up within minutes and shut the shower off again.

Dry off. Drop my towel on the floor.

I head back into my room and pull on a fresh pair of jeans and an ACDC concert t-shirt. I push my hair back and glance into the mirror to make sure I'm presentable, then I drop into the wing-back chair and pull on a pair of socks.

Jeans and boots today, when I was relegated to a suit last night, and black leather shoes that made me feel like a dickhead.

If I never have to wear that shit again, it'll be too soon.

Finishing one boot, then working on the second, I scowl when something sharp stabs the back of my thigh. But it's not until I push up to stand that the soft thud of metal hitting the thin carpet makes me stop.

Glancing down with curiosity, I inspect the shiny silver earring that glints in the rays of sunlight spilling through the hotel windows.

Bending, I scoop up the bauble and bring it closer, studying the baby pink stone held to the center with a claw. Then the hook at the top that stabs through a wearer's earlobe, and the shiny diamonds surrounding the gem that give it a glittery finish.

It can't be a ridiculously expensive earring; it doesn't feel like it is. But it makes me smile as I twist my hand, and spears of sunlight make it sparkle in every direction.

Like Cinderella left a shoe, Nicki has left behind a trinket of her own.

Not that I'll travel the city and make women try it on for size. That would just be creepy. But I close my hand around the shiny silver, and drop my fist into my pocket. Then heading back to the bathroom to grab my phone, I skid on the wet floor and chuckle to myself when I risk total paralysis because of the mess I left.

But do I clean it up?

No.

I turn the music off and slip my phone into my pocket, then I head out. Out of my room, and into the hall. I step into the elevator, and though I know the chances of me seeing her are slim to none, I keep my eyes peeled for any sight of blonde hair and silver eyes.

"Preston! There you are." The moment the elevator opens on the restaurant level, Maya's magnetic smile brings mine up in response.

She wears a sundress today of yellow and white, and wedge heels to help her tiny frame stand just a little taller. And though she's married to the man she fucking adores, she drops his hand now like he's last week's trash, and rushes forward to wrap me in a hug that steals my breath away. "I was hoping we'd see you at breakfast."

She smells of flowers and summer days by the water. Not at all like icy-Nicole's scent of sugar and sex. But pulling back, clueless to the thoughts that pass through my mind, she scoops my arm with hers and leads us toward Cole, who stands at the check-in stand of the restaurant.

"You left early last night," she chatters happily. "I swear, I saw you one minute, then the next, you were gone."

Morose, I shake my head and pat her hand. "You shouldn't be this obsessed with me, Maya. Your husband is gonna get mad as hell if he finds out about us."

"You ass." With a roll of her eyes, she swings her free hand out and smacks my stomach so I bark out a fast laugh. "You wish I was half as obsessed with you as you are with him."

Releasing her with a chuckle, I stop in front of Cole and pull him in for a fast side hug. "Hey, bitch. Sleep well?"

"I haven't slept yet." With a smug grin, he takes his wife against his side and starts into the restaurant when a server grabs menus and leads us in.

She walks all the way to a table in the far corner that overlooks the city through massive floor-to-ceiling windows, and when Cole comes around to pull out a chair for Maya, the server watches them with hearts in her eyes and a bottom lip that drops from desire.

She's blonde. She's beautiful. Her body is deliciously curvy, even in a bland work uniform of navy slacks and a branded apron. But though I try desperately to stir a little want in my mind, I can't find it. Not a spark to be found. Not even a flicker.

"Dammit."

"What?" Concerned, despite Cole's gentle kiss to the side of her neck, Maya's eyes shoot across to me. "What happened?"

"Fuck." Unhearing, or perhaps uncaring, Cole pulls a chair out on Maya's left, then drops in with an exhalation of exhaustion, and flips his empty coffee mug like it'll fill by magic. "I'm so fucking tired, man."

"What time did you leave last night?" I flip my own mug when the server stops by our table with a coffeepot. Then I brush Maya's concern off with a reassuring smile and a deep inhalation of caffeine.

"Thank you," I murmur for the server. Then to Cole, "Did you stay till the end, or duck out early?"

"Stayed till about midnight," he answers on a yawn. He doesn't cover his mouth, because just like me, he was a kid raised on the streets where theft was encouraged if you wanted to eat, and manners were only for the upper crust of society. "About half of our guests were still partying when we were done."

"But they were all friends," Maya adds around the lip of her coffee mug. "It's not like they needed us to stay and entertain them." Her eyes are too pink, and the bags beneath them are large enough to carry a weekend of luggage. But she smiles anyway, resting against Cole's shoulder when he pulls her in. "Where'd you go?"

"Out." I smirk when she doesn't look away, and sip when her lips flatten. "I had better places to be than my ex-best friend's shitty wedding."

"Ex-best friend?" Cole sneers. "I'd ask what I did wrong, but I know you're only looking for attention. I refuse to reward your petulance and give it to you."

"*Petulance.*" I grumble around these big words he uses, now that he married a rich girl. "Well, from where I sit, it looks like you're pretty fucking cozy with the Jackhammer. You have a new bestie now? Trying to think of a way to let me down easy?"

"Like I said," he moves from sipping his coffee to straight out chugging it. "Looking for attention. My loyalties remain solid, so if you're feeling insecure, I suggest you check your hormones and change your tampon."

"Which is such lovely dinner table discussion." Maya, the daughter of rich, snobbish geezers, complains, but smiles when a server comes back with a notepad. "Mmm. I'm starving."

"Are you ready to order?"

"Yes please."

While Maya leans to the side to give the server all of her attention, Cole comes my way and bites out a hissed, "Where'd you go?"

"Out." I flash a grin and relive memories from last night—Nicole's taunting smile, her electric eyes, and her round tits that tasted of powdered sugar and every man's filthy fantasy. I think of how tight she was wrapped around my cock, and better yet, how much trust it took for her to even exist in the same room as me.

It doesn't take a genius for one kid of trauma to recognize another. Maybe she's not a *kid* of trauma, but I guarantee she has a metric ton of baggage sitting heavily atop her shoulders that weighs down every thought and decision she ever makes.

But since Cole's pointed stare remains squarely on me, demanding more than a brush-off answer, I shrug and bring my coffee back up to sip. "I was with someone. She was really fucking cool."

His brows jump high on his forehead. "You fucked one of my wedding guests?"

"What we did," I cut in, searching to protect Nicole's modesty, since mine was long ago tossed in the trash, "isn't up for discussion. But sure, I spent time with one of your wedding guests."

"What?" Maya inserts her face in the gap between me and her groom. "Who?"

"None of your—"

"Everyone who came last night came with a date," she charges on with wild eyes. She leans closer and basically wedges Cole out of our conversation. "Like, *everyone*. Whose marriage did you break up, Preston Danes?"

"You're so fucking dramatic." I roll my eyes, and because I'd rather not consider her words fact—that everyone in attendance was already paired up—I bring my coffee back to my lips and work to ignore the earring in my pocket.

It burns like a dirty secret and weighs like an anvil, while in my mind, Nicole's pointed *no* when I asked if she'd come with someone plays on repeat. Soothing. Comforting.

"Not everyone, obviously. I got to talking to someone at the bar, I specifically asked if she was single—*"Didn't I?"*—and then we hung out. That's all you need to know."

"No, seriously." Maya reaches across and grabs my jaw, yanking me around so coffee sloshes over the rim of my mug and her nails dig into my skin. "Every. Single. Person. At our wedding, besides you, came with a date."

"False." *But she was so nervous. Fidgety. Flighty. Cheating?* "No. Nicki wouldn't—"

"Nicki?" Dropping her hand and frowning, Maya settles back against Cole's side to think. "I don't know any Nickis."

My heart thuds once, painfully in my chest. "What?"

"I didn't invite any Nickis to my wedding, Pres." Relieved, Maya exhales a heavy breath and settles back with her coffee. "Geez, here I was thinking you were about to break up a fighter's family, and Cole would need to protect you. But I didn't invite any Nickis, which means you hooked up with a chick who crashed our party for the free booze." Then she sniggers. "Classy choice."

"Uh... no." I reach into my pocket and take out her earring. Because it's a connection I crave. An assurance she was real. "She spoke of you. She *specifically* said she knew the bride."

Cole snorts. "Did you tell her you knew the groom before that?" He slides the pad of his thumb along the column of Maya's neck and sends her into a puddle of goo. He doesn't even know it, since his attention is on me. But I see her orgasmic eyes. Her devilish smirk. "If you mention knowing the groom, of course the party crasher's gonna claim the bride. C'mon, man." He reaches across and slaps the center of my forehead. "We've done this before. You know the drill."

Scandalized and a little pissed, Maya twists to face Cole. "You've crashed weddings?"

"Free food." He drops a kiss to the tip of her nose. "Free booze." Another kiss. "Dancing and drinking and fucking around?" Then he laughs. "Yeah, Maya Elizabeth, we've crashed weddings. I'm embarrassed Pres was swindled by a regular hustler, though. That's just humiliating."

"She wasn't hustling!" I glance down when a server sets a packed plate of bacon and eggs by my elbow, then I look to Maya's knowing grin and glower. "She wasn't hustling! She spoke of you by name. She was an actual guest."

"She was lying to you." Maya snags her silverware and unwraps them from the fabric napkin. "Plain and simple. Either she lied about being invited and snuck in for a free night of drinking and dinner, or she lied about her name. Because I wrote every single place card yesterday morning, and I promise you, there were no Nickis on my guest list."

"You're wrong." I fist the delicate earring in my hand and scowl down at my breakfast. Then I pick up a thick slice of toast and take a bite. "She was there. She was invited. And Nicki was absolutely her name."

57

"Maybe you snorted cocaine," Cole jokes. "And you got so high, you didn't realize you were just tugging your own dick."

"Crude!" Maya smacks his chest and shoves him off when he tries to pull her close again. "You speak unnecessarily. And you," she turns to me with a grin. "Got swindled." She picks up a rasher of bacon and bites off the end. "How does it feel?"

"Shut up."

"Must be a dent to the ego," she giggles. "The car-thieving, computer-hacking '*street thug*,'" she does the finger quotes around the last two words to taunt me. "You got hustled, Pres." She takes another smiling bite of bacon. "I hope it was worth it."

"She didn't hustle me!" Anger courses through my blood and surprises me with its heat.

I push up from the table and slide the chair back in. Leaning over Maya, I get close enough that her pupils grow larger. "Your brain isn't working right. You have a friend named Nicki. She's blonde and pretty and has a smart mouth, and I'm *never* hustled." Then I press a noisy kiss to the center of her forehead.

It's violent and impatient and surprises the shit out of her.

"I'm heading home in the next hour," I tell them.

"*Home* home?" Cole asks. "Your apartment?"

"Home, as in my new place." I turn back and grab my uneaten break-fast—because I'm still hungry, even if my friends are dicks. "I have a job interview tomorrow, and absolutely no fucking clue of the mess I'm walking into at this new house."

Then I point a finger in Maya's face so her eyes focus on the tip and cross. "If I need fresh sheets, I'm taking them from your place. Same with food. Because *I'm* a fuckin' hustler." I snatch up my coffee and stride out of the hotel restaurant.

I'm the idiot who draws eyes in the elevator for carrying a plate, but I long ago stopped giving a fuck about what people thought about me. I was the dirty kid with tattered clothes and too many visible ribs. Torn shoes, and shaggy hair. Black eyes, and semi-regular broken bones.

From the moment I was old enough to notice, I became desensitized to folks staring at me, and holding a plate is *low* on the ladder of shit people have double-checked me for.

"What?" I challenge a smirking woman, only to glare when her smile grows in response. "It's rude to stare at people."

"And it's dangerous to bark at my wife," the dude on her left sneers. "Watch yourself, bruh."

As soon as the elevator stops on my floor and the doors slide open, I charge out again with a huff. "Whatever, man."

"You're pretty grumpy for a guy who got lucky last night." The blonde, whose handbag is almost as big as her body, grins when I spin back.

Winking, she taps the close-door button and finger-waves as the solid silver doors slide closed again. "See ya."

My new home is a house. Not an apartment, not a trailer, and not an old, abandoned warehouse on the industrial side of the city, with smashed windows and enough bags of chips to choke a teen. It's an actual cottage on the outskirts of a small town, with broken rafters hanging from the roof, and overgrown gardens spilling with wildflowers and prickly weeds.

The plot of land that comes with my cheap-ass rental boasts enough space and surrounding trees to make it difficult to see the neighbors, and when I stand on the rickety porch out front—praying not to fall through and break my shin—I get a nice view of rolling hills that turn to dense forest.

This place is private, and though it's drafty and lacks heating and cooling, it's the exact right amount of *'no one is nearby'* that I crave.

"You're welcome to repair anything you want." The owner kicks rocks in what was probably once a circular driveway. The foundations remain of what *was* there, if you dig beneath the surface of trash and neglect. "Inside could do with a lick of paint," he continues, "and the toilet wobbles, so take care with that. But otherwise..." Dropping his hands into his pockets, he pulls one out again and offers me a keyring.

One key. One furry ball keychain with which it hangs on.

"Rent is due on the first of every month. But if you think you're running late, you can just let me know, and it'll be—"

"I won't be late." I accept the key and slide the keyring into my pocket. Nicki's earring remains, a talisman that she was real. A promise I wasn't hustled. "Where's the closest neighbor?"

"Couple minutes that way," he nods to the south. "It's a quiet road, though, and doesn't get a lot of traffic. The only time you might hear anything is when the cop who lives a mile or so up is called on duty in the middle of the night. But even that is rare around here."

"There's a cop on this road?" I glance in the direction my landlord nods, then contemplating, I drag my bottom lip between my teeth. "Okay."

"Your internet will be spotty out here," he adds. "It's just the way it is. But if you drive into town, there's a library that has free—"

"That won't be an issue."

Moving down the steps of the porch and heading to my truck, I grab a box from the back seat and slam the door shut again until rusted flecks of paint chip off and float to the ground.

Some could say I'm an animal for not having a nicer car. For not having something I can race across the city and outsmart the cops with. But that's Cole's lot in life; *he* wants the sexy Mustang with the smooth ride and rumbling engine. I just want... a ride. And I don't much care if she's sexy.

Hefting my box and passing my landlord, I head back up the porch steps and swing the rickety wire door open so it squeaks on its hinges. "I think I've got it from here," I mumble. I don't even bother taking my new key out, since everyone knows this cottage has neither been used nor locked since nineteen-seventy-something. "I'll send you a text if I need anything else."

"Alright." The old man bends to grab a smooth, round rock from the ground, then bouncing it in his hand, he turns on his heels and heads back to his car. "You know where to find me if you need anything. I'll see you around, Mr. Danes."

"It's Preston." I shove the creaking wooden door open and make an '*oops*' sound in the back of my throat when it bounces off the wall and vibrates back my way. Stepping through the doorway and wrinkling my nose at the tang of moisture in the air, I catch sight of a round table in the middle of the small kitchen, so I set the box down with careful hands, then turn back and prop the door open to invite a little fresh air in.

Crossing the room and opening a weighted window, I start a cross-breeze that helps transport the scent of mold out, but as I head into the living room to open more, my phone vibrates in my pocket with a ringtone I always answer.

Taking the device out, I bring it to my ear. "Hey, Cole." I pass a lumpy couch and vow to never sit on it unless I suddenly like the idea of bugs crawling into my skin. "Are you guys home?"

"Yeah. We just pulled up at the apartment. Maya wanted to stop in and visit her folks before we left the city, so..."

I open the living room window and scowl, not because of mold or bugs or rotting walls, but because of Maya's parents. "Why the fuck would she go there? They're assholes."

Cole chuckles. "Because we didn't get all her diaries yet, so we're pilfering them one at a time. Her parents are too fucking arrogant to notice, and too self-absorbed to check. They noticed the missing salt and pepper shakers, though."

I choke out a laugh and push musty old curtains aside to let daylight into my new living room. "Cutest little kleptomaniac I ever met. How's married life, man? Suffocating?"

He snorts. "It's been one day." But then he sobers. "And no. Not even a little bit suffocating. I'm just saying, she's lucky she loves her job and isn't ready to take a break yet, because I'm sitting over here ready to make babies and keep her at home forever."

"Jesus." I step away from the window and cross over to the dark hallway. "How times have changed, huh? Cole Miller, the dude who was never gonna settle down. Now you're domesticated and giddy about it."

"Yeah, well... Shit just clicks, Pres." I don't know what he's doing on his end of the line. Maybe moving through the apartment he shares with Maya. Or flopping onto his couch. Or making a protein smoothie in the kitchen that's far more updated than my own. "It just... when she's the right one, those plans you make for yourself shift to the left. The plans that still work with her in them stay, but those that don't, get tossed."

"And you're not mad that your plans have been hijacked?"

He chuckles, soft and almost pitying. "Not even a little. I get mad now if whatever I'm supposed to be doing doesn't fit her."

"Like training at the gym?"

"Like training at the gym," he laughs. "It's my job, so it's not like I hate it. But man, when I have a fight coming up and my hours get heavier… when that shit eats into my Maya time?" I don't see him, but I know he shakes his head. "Makes me cranky. Anyway…" He exhales. "What are you doing?"

"Walking through my new place."

I come back into my kitchen and begin unpacking the box I brought inside. I don't have pots or pans or silverware to fill my drawers. But I have laptops, routers, and a fucking satellite that makes my landlord's *'you might have crappy internet'* a non-issue.

"I'm pretty sure rats will eat my corpse overnight," I tell my best friend. Lowering my hand and changing our call to loudspeaker, I set the device on the table and go about assembling my things. "And if they chew through my cords, I'm going on a fucking rampage."

Pulling out my laptop, I barely stop short of giving it a hug.

I'm a sentimental man when things matter.

"Place is cute," I murmur after a moment. "In a *'probably gonna get murdered by the weird cornfield people when I close my eyes'* kinda way. I should update my will and make sure Maya gets all my stuff."

"You're so fucking dramatic. There's an apartment available in my building, dipshit. You could've been our neighbor."

"So take a hint," I taunt in response. Flipping my laptop open and hitting the power button, I watch as the screen lights up. "I don't wanna be your neighbor, bitch. The only reason I'd live that close is to bang your wife, but since she likes me too, and chances are she won't say no, it's best I stay here and not risk our friendship."

"You're an asshole," he grumbles. "My wife will *never* stray, so don't flatter yourself. And good," he huffs, "I didn't want you as a neighbor anyway. I was just being polite."

I bark out a laugh and pull out a chair when I realize I'm not leaving this table for the foreseeable future. "Having a full-time girlfriend has really fucked with you. You never bothered with being polite in the past."

"I've evolved," he counters.

Ignoring him, I study the screen in front of me, frowning at the reports I set to auto-run during the hour-long drive from the city to here.

That chick Sophia Solomon who wants to offer me a job is as slick as they come. She's a monster when it comes to hacking any device. Whether it's a random mom-and-pop setup, or the fucking intelligence sector for the U.S. government, I'm not sure she's ever been denied access.

So, me being me, I thought I'd try my hand at accessing her system.

If I can be better than her, then I don't need her. And if I can't, then taking a job at her company and learning from her is the next best option.

"Did you figure out who you banged last night?" Cole asks after a minute of silence. "Is the reason you can't remember her name because she rattled your brains and rocked your world?"

"Her name is Nicole." I stare at the security walls Sophia has surrounding her corporation, and start chipping away with fast strokes of my fingers across the keyboard. "And I'm not here to discuss what we did and didn't do. Did you find her on your guest list yet?"

"Dude!" he laughs. "I'm telling you, there's no one. You're either delirious, or she lied to you."

"She didn't fuckin' lie to me."

I come up against a trap Sophia has laid for anyone ballsy enough to consider knocking on her door, but I skirt around the virus that would chew up my computer and spit it out, and then I keep scaling Mount Solomon.

"Her name is Nicole," I repeat. "She's got blonde hair that goes to her shoulder blades, and icy silver eyes that set a man on fire if he says the wrong thing. She's only an inch or so taller than Maya, and probably about fifteen pounds heavier. She wore a pink dress, silver shoes," *and black underwear.* Though the last is for me to know. Not for him. "She has perfectly straight teeth, but for one on the bottom that is a smidge out of alignment. But it's cute," I add quickly. "She wears her nails short, but painted them to match her dress. And she sure as shit doesn't like a guy grabbing her arm or stopping her when she intends to walk away."

"Pres—"

"She has a brother named Axel. He's a firefighter. I don't know about her parents, I didn't ask. She doesn't wear a wedding ring—or any jewelry, actually, except for a pair of silver earrings."

"Jesus, man." Cole's voice turns softer. "Are you okay over there?"

I tear my hands from my keyboard and watch in horror as a second trap laid down with Griffin Technology jumps up to attack me.

"What?" I keep my hands away. Wait it out as their bots search for their intruder.

Already, I've penetrated their first line of defense. But if the first line could be described as a hundred soldiers, then what comes after that is equivalent to a thousand.

"You're obsessing over a chick no one knows," Cole presses, clueless to the war I wage on my laptop. "You noticed the fucking color of her nails and got a bio on her family, but you don't know her name or who the hell she is."

"I do know her name!" Taking a breath as Sophia's security passes me by, I sit forward again and continue my trek. "It's Nicole. Fuck, don't you listen to me at all?"

"There. Was. No. Nicole. At my wedding." He enunciates each word, then ends them with a sigh. "You don't obsess about women, Pres. So what the fuck?"

"I'm not obsessing," I growl. "I casually asked about a woman I met. That's it. It's you and Maya who're making this into something it's not. Shit."

I gain access to Checkmate Security's financials with a click of a button. Something to celebrate, I'm sure, except it was way too fucking easy.

"What do you know about Checkmate?" Carefully, I take a look around their servers and make mental notes of each fact I find.

Checkmate enjoys a casual five million dollars in turnover a year, but spend four and a half on salaries, kickbacks, and expenses. They have a fund set up for pro bono work that is always being exercised, and another, separate file with *my* name on it.

Narrowing my eyes, I click on the link and follow it down the line.

"Cole?"

"Um... Checkmate?" He audibly rubs a hand across his jaw. "I dunno, man. Run by a couple brothers and their military cohort. Bishop, there's two of 'em... that's the name and the faces that go with the personal security."

"Three of them."

"They..." He pauses. Then, "What?"

"Three Bishops," I correct him. "The third is known by Griffin, but they all share a father. Theo Griffin is a fucking magnate, you know that? Multibillionaire with enough tech to make Steve Jobs look like an amateur. What's up with Solomon?"

"Hm?"

"Sophia Solomon," I clarify. "You said Bishops run the joint, but it's Sophia who has everyone's balls in her purse."

"Does she?" I hear his non-committal shrug. "Dunno. She was at the wedding last night."

"I know she was at the wedding," I laugh. "She solicited me."

"Wait..." Silence beats for a minute. "For sex?"

"For a job, stupid. She wants me to come into the office in the morning and interview to become one of her team. Fuck knows why."

I follow the thread of files with my name on them and grin when I find background checks she's obviously already run.

She knows how much money I have in the bank: not a lot. What I drive: a piece of shit. Where I live: my apartment, *and* this cottage. She knows my social security number, my private health status, my medical records, and how much I owe the IRS.

"Jesus, Cole. She's thorough. She's got my records all the way back to birth."

I check the medical records and scour the list of hospital visits I endured as a child. For the first time in my life, I see the notes the doctors and nurses made, the reports they sent over to child services, though I know nothing ever came of them.

"She doesn't much care for HIPAA either. No way she should have access to what she does."

"Not surprising..." Cole makes a casual sound in the back of his throat. "The guys down at the gym consider her family, so who am I to argue with them? How do you know what files she has on you?"

I click over to another folder labeled *PRESTON DANES: PRIVATE*. Frowning, I open it up and squint closer at the million files that populate with dizzying speed. "Because I'm in her system."

"What the fuck do you mean you're in her system?" he demands. "Pres! You can't be in Sophia's system. She'll kill you!"

"She's not as slick as she thinks she—"

My words cut off with a snap when a skull and bones populate my screen, and a moment after that, a message that reads '*Wannabes try, losers burn, students learn. See you at the office tomorrow.*'

Then my computer shuts down.

"Wait." I shake my laptop, like that'll somehow fix whatever the fuck has happened. "Hey!" I hit the power button, then I jam my thumb over top and hold it down. "Hey!"

"What?" Cole asks. "What's wrong?"

"She shut me the fuck down!"

I shove up from my chair so the old wooden legs scrape along linoleum tiles, then I drag my moving box closer and take out another laptop.

I have a dozen, though the fastest, most up-to-date machine gets the most use.

I switch it on and breathe a little easier when the lights illuminate my keyboard. Then I wait, wait, wait as the main screen loads, and finally type in my password.

I switch the wi-fi on and wait for my satellite to connect. From no bars, to five bars of internet. But before I can do anything, a familiar screen pops up.

'Step away from the computer, Jackass. It's the weekend. Your IP address has been flagged, your VPNs are useless, now your system has been shut down. Fuck off, and go outside like a normal person. Next time, you'll know not to try to mess with my security. Lukewarm regards, Ace.'

"Dammit, Cole!" I slap the machine closed and grab out a third from my box—but I don't open it. I don't dare connect it to the internet and risk another casualty. "Fuck!"

"She got you, huh?" Chuckling like this is all a joke to him, Cole sips at something on his end of the line, and then grunts, so in my mind, I see him kicking his feet up and getting comfortable. "Tell me you pissed off Checkmate without telling me you pissed off Checkmate."

"Fuck you, Miller. She's lucky I don't go down there and rain hellfire on her fucking company."

"Uh huh," he sniggers. "Folks who *do* don't speak about it. Those who speak about it aren't gonna do shit."

"Fuck you!" I pick up my phone and push away from the table, then charging through my kitchen and onto the rotting porch outside, I stop at the top of the steps and sneer when a couple of deer wander by my truck. "Tell Maya I said hey."

"Okay," he snickers. "Will do. Tell Nicole we said hey. Oh wait..." he adds with a cackle. "She doesn't exist."

Snarling, I kill our call and shove my phone into my back pocket, then

I drop my hand into the front and take out her earring. The tiny, glittering silver. The baby pink rock, and the hook at the top that loops through her ear.

"She exists."

My stomach feels off, because I don't have a computer to work with—and that, to me, is the equivalent of being naked in public. My heart thuds, because I was with a woman last night. A beautiful, single, but ridiculously unavailable woman. And my head aches, because I've tried all day to remember her every feature, and the more time that passes between then and now, the fuzzier she becomes.

Because according to Maya, she never invited a Nicole to her wedding. And fuck if that knowledge isn't screwing with me.

With an exhale that leaves my chest empty, and a shake of my head that attempts to rid my mind of an impossible conundrum, I take out my phone again and unlock the screen.

Hitting dial on my second most called number, I refill my lungs and wait as the line trills. Once. Twice. On the third, the call connects, and her smile, even without hearing her voice, penetrates the line. "Hi, Preston."

"Maya." I walk to the edge of my porch and bend my legs to sit. "No screwing around, okay? No jokes, no mind-fucks, no bullshit."

"Uh... Okay." She evens her voice. "What's up?"

"Did you invite a Nicki to your wedding?"

"No." Deadly serious, she continues, "I swear I didn't. I'm aware that's not the answer you want, and I know I was messing with you earlier. But no, Pres. There were no Nicki's at my wedding."

"Fuck." I bring a hand up and rub it across my face. I scratch my nails through the short stubble on my chin, and when that doesn't ease the tension that makes my jaw ache, I reach up and run my fingers through the hair on top of my head. "Alright. I'll talk to you later, okay?"

"What are you gonna do for the rest of the day?"

I glance up at the shingles hanging from my roof, then down at the pile on the dirt that've already fallen. I peek to the massive fir tree that lays across the driveway: a casualty of a past storm, probably. Then I look to my truck, and in the back, my suitcases.

"I'll hang out here and settle in," I mumble. "I have to unpack."

"Do you have linens there?" she asks softly. "Pillows and sheets and blankets and stuff?"

"I dunno." Dropping to my feet and swiping my hand across my ass to pat away dirt, I hold the phone close to my ear and head toward my truck. "I'll drive into town later if I need it."

"Come *here*," she counters. "You won't find a store open late on a Sunday afternoon that sells linen anyway. Besides, you can come for dinner. I wanna see you."

"But it's Sunday." I set our call on loudspeaker, then I drop the phone in a box, and heft the box from my truck. "Your vows promised Fridays and holidays."

She scoffs. "My vows didn't mention you at all, Preston Danes. But my offer for dinner stands every single night. Forever. That doesn't mean I'll cook every time," she adds with a laugh. "But there will never come a time I won't wanna share a meal with you."

"Wanna play cards?" An odd sadness sits low in my stomach, leeching into my heart so it feels impossibly heavy buried deep in my chest.

I went to sleep with a beautiful, complicated, complex woman in my arms last night. But now, it's as though she doesn't exist. I have her name, I know what she looks like, and I even know who her brother is. But I can't look her up, since my computer was shut down by a hacking ballerina.

"I feel like playing cards." I continue up my porch steps and inside my little cottage. Setting the box on the table beside the first, I grab my phone again and head outside to keep unloading. "Do you think it's too late to annul your wedding and marry me instead?"

"We already consummated." She snickers before adding, "Multiple times."

"Ugh." I toss the phone into a third box and heft it out of my truck. "There you go, Maya Blake, breaking my heart without a care in the world."

"So let me feed you tonight. I'll see you around six, okay?"

"Yep." I move back into the house and set the box on the floor. "I'll see you at six."

Nicki

THIS IS ME

Mondays are my most dreaded day of the week. Work is hectic as I catch up after a Sunday off, my brain is often fried from a busy Saturday, Noah typically has Mondays off work—giving him more time to harass me—and June is in school.

Which means everyone except the one I want talks *at* me and demands my attention.

"We have the Warrander wedding at the end of the month." Hannah, my colleague, barrels into the back with my planner in one hand, and a pen in the other. She's tall, olive tanned, and has no curves to speak of, despite working inside a store that peddles butter frosting and full fat whipped cream on the daily. "They want four tiers, Nick. Have they signed off on the final design?"

"Yep." I work on cupcakes for the store, piping icing onto the top now that I'm done baking them. Rainbow isn't my favorite, but they sell well. And for a single mom who has a mouth to feed and no choice but to succeed no matter what, I choose what sells over what fulfills my artistic side. "It's all written up over," I lift my chin toward the wall I consider my game plan for the month.

My planner is where I keep the minute details, like costs, dates, and delivery times. But my wall is like a vision board, with flavors and tiers, designs and goals.

"These are almost done, too." I move on to the next row, the seventh of ten rows of ten. "You can start moving them out now. That'll make room for what I've gotta do next."

Scowling, Hannah sets my planner down, but picks up a heavy tray of cupcakes and wanders to the front of the store. "Your life would be easier if you moved into the apartment upstairs," she calls back. "You wake up at three o'clock every damn morning, then you spend hours baking at home and transporting everything here. But if you lived upstairs," she adds, allowing her voice to grow louder, "you could leave June sleeping while you use the ovens down here. Save yourself a step."

"I'm not leaving my home, Hannah." I move on to the next row as the radio plays somewhere far away, and my hands work by muscle memory. I don't have to think about what I do anymore. Especially not toward the end of my workday. I just *do*. And when I find that rhythm, that's when my heart sings with happiness. "I'm not leaving my daughter in bed upstairs, in an apartment smaller than my kitchen in my home, all so I can come down here and get lost in my work."

"It would save you a lot of trouble," she returns. "That's all I'm saying. Plus, smaller place means less cleaning."

"Bigger place means my daughter gets her own room. It means I have a home office, and a kitchen large enough that baking at three o'clock is a pleasure. It means," I speak louder and continue onto the final row, "June wakes to the scent of cupcakes, but she doesn't have to stay in her room all alone and wait for me." Lifting my hands when the beautiful Hannah comes back my way, I meet her gaze and smile. "It means a garden for my baby to play in. And a backyard. And a swingset in that yard. And a garage. And—"

"Alright! Fine." She snatches the next tray of cupcakes and heads away again. "I was only trying to help, sheesh."

"Finding shortcuts in my personal life isn't helping, Hannah. But finding me a shortcut in work is. I know you mean well." I grab my bag and set it on the stainless-steel counter, then I wipe my hands on my apron and follow her into the front of my store. "But if you want to help, find an easier way for me to transport stock from home to the shop. That'll save me time."

The bell hanging above the front door jingles, drawing my attention up and a smile to my lips when a man I know by face, though we're not friends, wanders in with a twin girl on each side. One of them has dark hair, dark features, and olive skin much like Hannah's, while the other is blonde and blue, her sister's opposite.

"Go look at the cupcakes." Kane releases their hands so they dash across the tile and plaster their noses to the glass displays.

Like they do every time they come in here, they arrow for the cabinet filled with rainbows.

"Hi there, Mr. Bishop." I set my elbows on the counter and study the tattooed... well, *thug*, who watches his daughters like they're everything he loves and needs. Then I look to the twins and wave. "Hi, girls. I *just* finished icing those. You came at the perfect time."

"Cupcakes," the blonde one hums. She scrunches her little fists and vibrates with excitement. "I *love* cupcakes."

"I know you do." *I see you in here at least every other day.* "Do you want me to start making other colors?" I peek at the darker twin. "Pinks? Purples? Polka dots, maybe?"

"Rainbows!" she shouts, though it's a giddy explosion, not a spoiled demand. "Rainbows are so yummy."

"We'll take two rainbow cupcakes, please." Kane, the dad, wanders closer and sets enough cash down for ten cupcakes.

His cologne fills my lungs, and the bulges under his jacket are enough for me to know this man is dangerous. But his smile when our eyes meet is a reminder he's on our side—whatever side that is. He's here to protect our town, not hurt anyone in it.

"Keep the change, Ms. Scott. That cake on Saturday night was delicious, by the way. I didn't hear a single complaint."

"Heh." I snatch up his money and walk to the register to ring up the sale, while Hannah takes out the cakes and passes one to each twin. "Thanks. I owe you for recommending my little bakery to the bride and groom."

"It wasn't me." Grinning, he glances down at his rainbow-mouthed twins and purses his lips. "Cole said cake, my babies said they know just the place." Reaching back, he slips his wallet into his pocket and fixes his jacket again to cover his gun.

Or guns. Who knows how many he has.

He's not a cop, though. He's not even mall security. He's something else entirely, and though that *something else* could look a little on the...

unsanctioned militia side, he's friendly with the police. And the police force in this town is one of the best I've ever known.

Ironically, I've known a lot of officers. I've had up close and personal interactions with many, and more often than I'm comfortable admitting, they've left a bad taste in my mouth and not an ounce of trust in the people who're supposed to protect us.

"Well..." Shaking off that thought, I clear my throat and fix my smile. "All the same, I appreciate the recommendation. And the night out," I add as an afterthought. "I got to wear a pretty dress and eat a nice dinner. I got a hotel room," *though I never slept in it,* "then I was home to see my baby when she woke."

"Sounds like the perfect night to me."

He glances over his shoulder a mere second before the door opens again and the bell rings to let everyone know we have a visitor. But Kane's friendliness noticeably dials down when a plain-clothed police detective wanders in.

He wears a gun on his hip, too, and a badge right beside it.

Noah Scott is six feet tall, though he wears shoes with a one-inch sole, like he feels that extra height somehow makes him a better man. He works out at least once a day, shaves in the morning and at night, keeps a comb in his car— since that's not as pretentious as carrying it in his pocket—and though his and Kane's eyes meet, his keep on moving as he makes a beeline to where I stand.

Luckily for me, the counter forces the distance Noah wishes he could remove.

"Nicki." He leans across without invitation, so his badge and gun clank against the glass, and cupping my face with unrelenting fingers, he presses a kiss to my cheek.

It's all very European, I suppose. The kiss hello. But I don't like it. I don't want it.

I've *never* wanted it.

Unfortunately, Noah has never much worried himself over what I do and do not want.

"You look great, Nick." Pulling away, my ex-husband's snake-like stare is, to the rest of the world's population, pretty. He's handsome and charismatic. Charming, and has the perfect eyes to ears to nose and lips ratio, according to... some teen magazine, when selecting the *world's sexiest man.*

He was born with the perfect mask to dupe women into falling in love.

After all, he got me, hook, line, and sinker. As quickly as we met, we married and had a baby. Then, before the ink had dried on June's birth certificate, he allowed that mask to slip away.

His kindness was a farce. His charm, a show. Everything he did was to benefit him, and every interaction he ever took part in was to bolster his ego.

He had everyone conned, and me, trapped with a newborn baby and no way out. But he never managed to get along with my brother, which meant the mask was never good enough to get past Axel.

I was a woman living inside a domestically abusive marriage—a role I had to accept my own heaping serving of responsibility in—but although it took me entirely too long to voice my truths, the moment I did, my baby brother came to my rescue and pulled us out.

Noah slept with countless other women throughout our marriage, he controlled our finances, sabotaging my work prospects so I couldn't gain independence, and because cops watch each other's backs, even when their comrades are assholes, I had nowhere to escape that didn't come with a patrolman's eyes.

Thankfully, as time often manages, proof of Noah's behavior became obvious to everyone. Not just one-off offenses, but repeated patterns. Not just singular lies, but falsities built atop falsities, until it came to a point that he had to obey the judge's orders, or risk everything: his career, his reputation, and his finances.

The last, of course, was a language he spoke.

Noah Scott is motivated purely by control and money. The second, he can no longer hold over me, thanks to my thriving shop. But the first... he retains through my daughter.

Co-parenting with this man is the bane of my existence.

"Hey, Noah." I school my features and back away from the counter so he can't reach out for me again. Then I move to the rack of fresh bread and rearrange loaves, though they were perfect already. "What are you doing here?"

"I came by to see you." He follows me around the store, like we must remain in the same close distance at all times.

He sets his hands on his hips and adopts a swagger in his walk, so when I glance back, I see the wink he shoots toward the little girls.

They scowl in response.

Children and animals, I swear, aren't fooled by the mask.

"I finished up night-shift and figured a drive would be good for me." He passes a watchful Kane Bishop and props his elbows on the display cabinet. "Where's Junie?"

At school, you asshole. But I lean to my left and direct a pointed stare toward the clock on the wall. "School's not out till three."

"Which is..." He brings his hand up to check the watch on his wrist. "A little over an hour away."

That's generally how time works, jerkoff.

When I say nothing out loud, Noah only exhales an amused chuckle. "You're nearly done for the day, right?"

"Hm?" I grab the empty trays Hannah has yet to put away and start toward the prep area out back. "I still have a bunch of stuff to do. Sorry I can't stick around and chat."

"Hey! You can't—"

Hannah's protest brings me around to find Noah stopping at the entryway that separates the front of the bakery from the back, which is clearly staff-only.

When our eyes meet and mine narrow, his only dance with humor.

It's like he thinks he has a right to be here. Like we're still married, and he somehow has a claim to my hard work.

"It's an hour." His lips crinkle with an arrogant smirk. "Let's get coffee, then we can pick June up from school together."

I set the trays on the counter with a *clang* and ignore Hannah's panicked stare behind my ex. Shaking my head, I pick up a used icing bag instead and wield it as though I intend to use it. He has no clue what it is, or that it's useless now that it's empty.

"I have to work, Noah. And June has soccer practice this afternoon, which means we can't get coffee. But I'll have her call you when we're eating dinner. You can talk to her th—"

"Well, why don't I hang around till dinnertime?" Moving closer, he grabs my arm and squeezes tight enough to let me know he can become a bigger annoyance if I don't stop brushing him off. "I'll sit out there," he pokes his thumb over his shoulder, "have a coffee and something to eat. I'll come to soccer practice, too, since June's my daughter and I have as much right as you do to be there. Then we can have dinner together. Ya know." He grins so his toothy smile will burn against the backs of my eyelids when I close my eyes tonight. "Like a family."

But we're not a family, you self-centered, entitled asshole! "I'm sorry." I gently pry my arm from his hand, and grunt when he makes me work to get free. "We're busy."

"Nick—"

"You must be exhausted after night-shift." I wander toward the industrial dishwasher and tug the door open so a waft of steam escapes and warms my face. Immediately, I set my piping bag aside and take out pots instead, walking them to their shelf for storage until tomorrow. "June's soccer practice is boring. It's where I work on order numbers for next week, so I won't even get to talk. Then dinner is just plain old spaghetti bolognese, and I know you hate that."

"We can order in."

"The beef has already been defrosted." I go back to the dishwasher for the next pot. "And I can't afford to waste like that." *Pay your child support, you deadbeat piece of shit.* "But I'll tell June you were here. She'll be excited."

"Fine." Hard-faced, with anger boiling in his eyes, he turns on his heels and takes off like a shot. "I'll pick her up myself. She can blow off soccer and be with me instead. Maybe then, you'll deign to spare me a little of your time."

My heart thunders as I dash in his wake—only to stop on a skid when Noah turns back.

"June has to go to practice," I rush out. "She risks her spot on the team if she doesn't go. I build my entire schedule around her extracurriculars so we can make it work. You just randomly showing up and changing things hurts her."

"So now you're trying to tell me how to raise my daughter?" He grabs my arm again—a fucking instinct he has, probably borne of the way he handles the criminals he arrests—and squeezes.

It's how Preston grabbed me the other night when I tried to walk away, but not the same.

Not nearly the same.

"You don't get to sign her up for every sport on the planet to prevent her spending time with me, Nicki!"

"We have orders." I again pry my arm from his hold, and swallow when I find Kane Bishop standing just three feet away, his eyes burning and black, like there's no heart or soul behind them.

But it's not me he glares at.

"Noah..." Clearing my throat, I bring my gaze back to my ex and search for de-escalation. "She's busy today, okay? That's not meant to hurt your feelings. It's just her life; she needs practice to stay on the team, and the fitness is good for her sleep. But we'll call you tonight when we settle in with dinner, and you can take her out after school tomorrow, okay?"

He says nothing. He only stares. Deep, deep into my soul.

"Okay?" I repeat. Leaning in and steeling myself for the revulsion I feel in every pore of my body, I wrap my arms around his torso and give him the physical touch he craves. "I'm not trying to upset you," I tell him softly. "I'm just trying to provide a stable routine for our daughter." Pulling back, I leave his hand when it lowers to my hip. I don't like it, but it's better he touches me than punish our daughter. "That's what we both want, right? For June to be happy?"

"Sure..." Lying, like he does every other time he opens his mouth, Noah nods and takes a step back. "You're absolutely right. June is my main priority."

Lie.

"She always has been," he continues. "Her happiness is all I care about."

Lie. Lie.

"I'm so glad I got to see you, Nick." Leaning closer, he presses a friendly kiss to my cheek, so it lands dangerously near the corner of my lips. "You look beautiful today, even though you've been up half the night."

"Ha." I force a shallow laugh and reach up to wipe my cheek. It's an instinctual move, but thankfully, Noah perceives it as insecurity, rather than what it actually is: my disgust at his lips touching my skin. "I'll text you in a little while, okay? And then you can let me know your plans for tomorrow, so June knows what's happening."

"Yep."

He turns toward our audience and snags a cupcake from the rack without asking. Without using tongs. Without washing his fucking hands or paying for the item he never earned. He takes a hefty bite and waves for the twin girls, then he's gone.

Through the heavy glass door, and past the ringing bell. He heads to his car, parked on the street outside, and when our eyes meet through the window, his smug grin lifts before he slips on a pair of aviator sunglasses that notches up the revulsion in my blood so I almost vomit in my mouth.

"Well, he seems like a fuckin' peach." Kane sweeps his blonde twin up in one arm and presses a noisy kiss to her cheek. Then he nods to summon Hannah's attention. "Can I get a dozen more cupcakes boxed up? If I don't take any back to the office, Aunty Soph is gonna kill us, isn't she, Luna?" He tickles the girl's ribs, and smiles when she cackles. But just beneath the surface of his humor is a raging inferno, a result of unofficially meeting the self-proclaimed *amazing* Noah Scott. "Aunt Sophie can become homicidal when she's hungry, can't she, pretty girl? She'll smell the icing on your breath and know we cheated her."

"Aunt Sophie likes cake." The other twin presses her nose to the glass as Hannah boxes up the treats. Her hands are sticky, and her lips leave behind a smudge that I'll come around and clean once they're gone. But for right now, she watches Hannah's hands as though in a sugar-induced trance. "She likes cake a *lot*."

"Well," I smile. "I'm glad."

When Kane reaches back to grab his wallet, I shake my head and extend my hand to say stop. "Free of charge."

"Oh please." He chokes out a scoffing laugh and takes out enough cash to pay for thirty. "Consider it the only child support you'll receive this month." He winks, then, "Give me a receipt, then they become a tax write-off anyway." He sets his money on the glass display and bends to set his daughter on her feet. "I'm taking these to work, I'm gonna become the most popular guy around, and then I get to offset my expense with the taxman. It's win-win-win for me. My beautiful Rose! Can you get the door for Daddy?"

"Oh, let me help." My nerves batter and send my pulse skittering, but I dash around the counter and help the toddler pull open the heavy glass.

The breeze outside today is fresh and perfect, and the second the door is out of the way, gusts rush into my store and stir up the scent of sugar in all its forms.

"I'm sorry about..." I tilt my head back toward the counter. "Ya know. What you saw. I didn't mean—"

"To be impregnated by a douchebag?" he asks with a sly grin. He shifts the box of cakes in his muscular arm and takes the door, holding it wide enough for his babies to pass through. "It's gotta be tough having to fake being nice to that asshole, Ms. Scott. I don't envy your situation."

"You can call me Nicki," I reply in a tone friendlier than my nerves want.

My survival instincts shout at me to retreat. To find a quiet space and simply... *be*. There. Alone. But my therapist encourages me to be open to the good people.

To learn to differentiate between sharks and dolphins.

Sharks, in this analogy, are easy enough to translate. They're the assholes. The predators. The selfish ones who hurt everyone they come in contact with. Which makes the dolphins the friendly type.

Sharks, dolphins. Red flags, and green flags.

Jesus, this tattooed mountain of muscle with a potty mouth and enough weaponry on his body is, somehow, today, my dolphin.

"Thank you for sticking around," I tell him. "He would have stayed longer if you hadn't."

"Cowards usually shut their mouths when they have an unwelcoming audience." He casts a glance to the sidewalk outside to make sure his girls are safe, then he brings his eyes back to me. "The school won't release your daughter to him on a non-court-ordered day. You have my word."

"No, I..." I bring a hand up to wipe my cheek. It's a natural response, I swear. "He's a cop in the city, not here. And my relationship with June's school is pretty solid. One of the teachers there is sister to the chief here, so for the most part, we're insulated pretty well."

"I know that teacher," Kane smirks. "And the cop. But though I bring my babies here almost every single day, I've never stopped to introduce myself to you."

"You're Kane Bishop." My eyes drop to his hand when he places it between us.

He wants to shake mine. To formalize our introduction. But he reads my body language quickly, and when I take a step back, he nods and slides his hand under the box to support his cupcakes.

"I-I'm sorry," I stammer.

"No need." He lowers his chin in a kind of farewell. Then he takes a step back as well. "You can call me Kane," he adds, his foot in the door's way, the only reason it doesn't close. "You know where to find me if you need a hand, okay? No strings."

I know he works in security and acts as a bodyguard, of the highly paid variety. So since I have no money to toss around, I snicker and take another step away. "Thanks, Kane. Enjoy your cupcakes. Next time you come back with the girls, they eat for free."

"And take from your daughter's mouth? Nah." He releases the door and turns on his heels. "Let's ride, Chicken and Nugget! Aunty Soph probably already knows we have these."

"We're gonna go visit Aunty Soph!" cheers Luna, the blonde one. I don't know if she's Chicken or Nugget, but she grabs her sister and gallops like a cute little pony. "Dance this afternoon, Daddy?"

"Dance *every day*," he chuckles, the sound fading away as the door shuts and locks them and the wind out.

Finally, with hands shaking from adrenaline, and a pesky blush filling my cheeks and letting the world know I'm embarrassed, I turn away from the door and head back around to the other side of the counter.

"I'm going to the school early," I tell Hannah. Without stopping, I move into the back of the store and resume unloading the dishwasher. "I wanna make sure Noah isn't there causing a scene."

"They won't hand her to him, right?" Hannah follows me to the dishwasher, but when I snarl at her close proximity, she lifts a massive pot and holds it between us as a shield. "You said they won't—"

"It's a legally gray area." I set cake molds on the counter to my right and focus on drying them off, instead of obsessing on everything else wrong in my life. "We have court orders, so they probably won't. But he's her parent too, Hannah. And he comes with a badge. So if he wants to get noisy, do you think a first-grade teacher is going to stand up under that and refuse him?"

"Well, they should." As soon as the dishwasher is empty, she grabs dirty dishes and begins the re-fill. It's a never-ending cycle inside this bakery; one I only tire of when Noah comes around and zaps me of energy. "June has a right to safety and security, Nick."

"But the courts place priority on a man's right to see his child, even when that right infringes on the child's well-being. So until June's an adult, we're slaves to his moods." I stack one cupcake mold on top of another, so they crash together and echo through the store. "Things are just easier if I work *with* him and smooth out the difference for my daughter. Hopefully, she never has to feel the jagged edges."

"But you put yourself out for slaughter," she argues, "and, what? Hope you don't bleed on your baby?"

I scoff and dry the next mold with vicious swipes of my hand. "It is what it is."

At another jingle of the bell above the front door, I stare into Hannah's eyes and communicate, wordlessly, to stop talking about my private life. "Go serve that customer. I'm finishing up here, then I'm heading out for the day. You'll close up at five?"

"I always do," she singsongs.

Closing the now-full dishwasher and selecting the wash and rinse cycle, she blows me an air-kiss and sashays her ass toward the front of the store.

"Oh, well hey there, handsome. I love it when firefighters visit me in the afternoons."

"Hey, Han." Axel's voice is besotted and bothered at the same time. "Nicki in?"

"She's rage-cleaning in the back."

I roll my eyes and take more care when I set the next mold down.

"Her bastard ex dropped by," Hannah continues, "and he was as charming as always. Want a cupcake?"

"Sure."

Axel's heavy boots clomp along the tile flooring as he moves in my direction. He pauses for a moment—to accept his dessert, no doubt—then he continues on and stops in the doorway exactly where Noah did just ten minutes ago. "What happened?"

"Nothing." Finished with my pile of molds, I pick up the lot and take them to the shelf to be stored until next time. "He wanted to hang out this afternoon and get dinner together. I said no." I head to the storeroom in the corner and reach in blindly to grab my car keys, then I move back to my table and collect my bag. "That was the end of it. And," I loop my finger through my keyring and reach back to undo my food-smattered apron. "I'm done talking about it. I'm going to pick June up from school."

He glances to the clock and narrows his eyes. "It's two o'clock."

"So I'll sit in my car and work until the bell rings. Geez." I lift the halter strap of my apron and tilt my head to free my ponytail of the fabric, then I ball everything up and drop it into one of the old buckets I use to transport things home that need to be washed. "Aren't you on shift?"

"Sure am." He brings his cupcake up and takes a noisy bite. "But the crew wanted cake, and I happen to know a chick in town who makes those."

"So you drove over here to get them? While on shift?"

He takes another bite and smiles a rainbow icing grin. "No. The crew and I just got done washing the rig. They're outside now, waiting for me to bring them food."

"Jesus." I look to Hannah behind him. "Box up a dozen, please. Get them moving so his truck doesn't block traffic any longer."

"Yeah," he teases, "because all two cars out there will create bedlam. You're cranky, Nick, and everyone knows that's how you get after Detective Douchebag drops by. Now you're going to the school early, which means he threatened you."

"He didn't threaten me!" I pick up my bucket of laundry, and snag my planner as I pass it. "He expressed an interest in wanting to see us today. I said no, so he said he would take June instead. Which sounds great, by the way," I come to a stop in front of my much taller younger brother, "except it was in retaliation for my rejection, not a genuine desire to spend time with his daughter. So again, I said no. He'll make me pay for that disrespect, but not today." I turn away and continue deeper into the back of my store, heading toward the rear exit.

"Today, I'm picking her up. I'm getting there early, I'm taking her to soccer practice, because that's what she's expecting to do, and while I'm there, I'll gently mention that her daddy wants to spend tomorrow afternoon with her. It's not part of our usual plan," I call back. Kicking the door open, I squint into the sunlight outside and groan, because exhaustion is kicking my ass. "She'll be sad, because she doesn't *want* to see him. But it's my job to juggle what's best for her, while also bending over for the courts and fostering the relationship between an abuser and an innocent child."

Stepping outside and setting my bucket down by my clunky old car, I unlock the door and toss my purse into the passenger seat. "I swear to god,

Axel," I don't speak too loud now, because I know he's followed me to the back door, "if I hear '*You're alienating him*' one more time, I'm going to strangle a judge."

"He's a piece of shit, Nick. We both know it."

"Alienation isn't even the appropriate word to use!" I grab my bucket again and take it to the trunk, only to growl when I find yesterday's still sitting there. "That's just a bullshit word abuser's sling around when they're losing control."

I slam the trunk shut and come around to the driver's-side door. Putting one foot inside the car, and one arm on the frame of the open door, I meet my brother's gaze and try to fix the forlorn expression on my face. "Ya know what? It's whatever. We've been juggling. Everything is fine, and I'll make damn sure everything *stays* fine. Go get your cupcakes, and tell Nix they're my gift to your crew." Bringing my hand to my lips, I kiss my fingers and blow it back to my brother. "See you when I see you."

"Yeah," he sighs. "I'll see you when I see you." Frowning, he leans against the doorframe in most of his turnout gear. The pants and boots, but with a muscle t-shirt wrapped around his chest, and suspenders circling his shoulders. His hair is smooshed down, making me wonder if he's been wearing his helmet all day or a hat. Or both, off and on.

"You'll feel better once you have June," he adds when I don't move. "Cuddle my niece and tell her Uncle Axe loves her. I might even stop by after shift to give her a hug."

It's funny how when my brother mentions a spontaneous visit, my heart softens and my smile notches up. But when Noah uses the exact same sentence, it's nothing but a threat.

"She'll like that." Dropping into my seat and closing the car door, I switch the engine on and wind my window down. "We both would," I admit. "You make life better, Axel. Just by existing."

"Aw man." He pushes away from the building and stomps his way to my side of the car. Leaning down, he presses a kiss to my forehead and lingers a minute longer. "Life shouldn't feel this hard, Feeney. It's supposed to be a fun adventure."

I pull away, not because his touch repulses me, but because he's right: I'll feel better once I have my baby in my arms. "I had my adventure. I fell in love and got married. Then I got a divorce. Now it's time for June to have her adventure."

"You're the best mom I know," he rumbles. Taking a step back and rapping his knuckles on the roof of my quietly sputtering car, he winks when our eyes meet. "The. Best," he repeats. "Tell June I'll see her soon."

"Yeah."

Fixing my seatbelt and holding my breath when the constant vibration of my engine misses a beat and everything seems to stutter for a moment, I breathe again when the rhythm evens out. Then I put my car into reverse and back away from Juniper's Bakery.

It's the one dream I held onto through years of bad marriage and raising a baby who needed me. When Noah was wearing me down and siphoning our funds anywhere but into our joint accounts. When I was asked by a friend to bake a birthday cake and I thought, *wow, something just for me*, though of course, that was stomped on too. Juniper's was what I thought about while my baby slept. It's what I planned while she needed to be burped. It's what I hoped for while she screamed from colic, and while I walked the halls of our home just so we could get a little quiet and Noah could sleep.

Because although I was exhausted and would've given anything for a little sleep myself, his moods always came first.

So while he slept and June napped, and the world was quiet and my brain swirled from exhaustion, Juniper's is what I imagined. And the moment our divorce papers were signed and the ink had dried, I opened a new bank account, baked the very best cake I could with the few dollars I had, then I swallowed my pride and asked my brother for a little help.

It wasn't my finest moment, asking him for money. But it led to what I have now, and to free pastries and cakes for Axel for the rest of his life.

Pulling the car into the old alleyway that runs behind most businesses in this town, I straighten out and push the shift into drive, then I make my way toward June's school just a few blocks away with an engine that splutters, and a stereo that is either always too loud, or too quiet.

An hour later, the bell rings, and with my anxiety rocketing into the next stratosphere, I fidget with my keyring and wait on pins and needles as children spill out of the school and parents rush forward to collect their babies.

I could be one of those parents. Sprint through the doors and make a huge, noisy scene. There could be loud hugs and whoops of delight.

Shouted '*How was your day?*' and '*Did you miss me?*' But June abhors that kind of attention.

She's only six, but she's been abused for every one of her six years by a man whose only pleasure in life is to steal the light from a female's eyes. Wife or daughter, it doesn't matter to him. Adult or child. Noah Scott can't feel good about himself unless he's knocking someone else down. And though it's my fault June is stuck with him for a father, though that's my mistake to bear for the rest of our lives, I refuse to add to her trauma by being a mom who draws attention to her when she doesn't want it.

So I stay inside my car, and enjoy the knock of my heart when she comes out the double front doors of the school and stops on the concrete steps.

Through my windshield, our eyes meet, hers knowing where to go, since I park in the same spot every single day. And when she starts down the steps and heads in my direction, I finally have the go-ahead to open my door and push out of the car.

While a couple hundred other children run and barge through clusters of people, and holler with glee for the end of another school day, June, with her shoulder-length hair tied into two pigtails that bounce as she walks, silently makes her way to me, and then wraps her arms around my hips the moment we're close enough.

She presses her face to my stomach and exhales so hard, I could almost wonder if she's held her breath all day long.

"Hi, Mommy." She squeezes extra tight and links her fingers at my back so I can't escape.

I wish I could bend down and hug her back. I want to be a more active participant in this hold. But my job, as her mother, is to support her every want. And that first hug at the end of every long school day is all about her. She wants to wrap me up tight and grunt in the back of her little throat. She wants to be in control, when so much of the rest of her life is controlled by everyone else. So I let her hold on, and I run my fingers through her hair while she gets what she needs and fills her emotional cup.

"I missed you today, Mommy." Pulling away, but keeping her hands on my hips, she folds her neck back and looks up until her silver-gray eyes lock onto mine. "I got all my spelling words correct."

"You did?" I lower into a crouch, now that I can, and stop on her level, marveling at her lashes, which are so long, they tap her sun-kissed cheeks. "I'm so proud of you, baby. What else happened?"

"Charlie climbed the biggest tree." Twisting, she points at a massive linden on the far side of the playground. "He got all the way to the top."

"He did?" I peer at the tree in question, knowing it's damn near eighty feet tall, and Charlie, six years old. "Why did he do that?"

"Because the Devil Twins bet that he couldn't." Wanting to giggle, but not quite ready to, she firms her quivering lips and steps in again to wrap her arms around my neck. "He got in big trouble from the teacher on duty."

"Well, I would hope so. Climbing that high is very dangerous." Closing my eyes and setting aside the thought of a first-grader almost killing himself today, I breathe in the scent of my baby girl instead, covered in dust and wafting with the smell of craft glue and god knows what else. "I missed the heck out of you today." Pulling back, I meet her sweet gaze. "Did you have fun?"

"Uh huh." She releases me and climbs through the driver's side door. She knows she shouldn't, and her backpack makes it all the more difficult, but we both know our car is a piece of shit. At this point, who even cares about muddy footprints on the middle console? "Are we going back to the store so you can work before soccer?"

"Nope." I slide in after her, and watch in my rearview mirror as she tosses her bag down and climbs into her booster seat.

She fixes her own seatbelt and smiles triumphantly when the *click* indicates she's safe. Then she meets my gaze in the mirror, so I add, "We're going home to get changed. Mommy would like a quick shower, too, just to clean work off my skin. Then we're going to practice. And after that, Uncle Axel said he's gonna drop by around dinnertime."

"Oh!" Her little eyes light up with glee. "What's for dinner?"

"Anything you want, baby." Starting the car and checking to make sure I don't mow someone else's child down, I pull out of my parking space and head toward the exit. "I haven't taken anything out of the freezer yet. Plus, you got all your spelling words correct. Sounds to me like you get to choose."

"Not spaghetti," she grumbles. Like her father, she hates the stuff. And because I'm not an asshole, I never cook it for her. Though of course, Noah needn't know that. "Can we have creamy pasta?"

"With the chicken?" I pull onto the quiet street and turn the car toward home. "Of course."

"That's Uncle Axe's favorite too," she chirps, happy now that she's in her safe space. Me. This car. Routine. That's what makes my daughter's soul sing. "He loooooves the boscaiola, Mommy. He always slurps it up till sauce gets on his chin."

"Uncle Axel is a child." I huff, though she knows it's all in good fun. "He's excited to see you tonight, babe. He dropped by the bakery just an hour ago and bought a zillion rainbow cupcakes for him and his friends."

"He likes those," she sniggers. "I wonder if he has another baseball game soon." She brings a finger up to stroke her chin, like an old-school murder mystery screen actor. "I like the baseball games, because Uncle Axe is the fastest runner there."

"Maybe. Those games are for charity, and there are always charities that need help. So I guess there could be a game coming up. You can ask him tonight, if you want."

"Okay." Relaxed, she looks out the window as we move through residential streets and head home.

She trusts me to make the world a better place. But though I do everything in my power to smooth out the jagged edges, there will always be those that cut her.

"Uh... June?" I pull onto our street and slow down as we approach our driveway.

When she meets my gaze in the mirror, I swallow down my dread and do what needs to be done. "Daddy dropped by the shop today."

Immediately, her shoulders come up in defense.

"He's going to call you later tonight, okay? He wants to chat and hang out. And tomorrow, I think he's going to pick you up from school."

"What?" Her voice shakes. "No, I don't want—"

"I bet if you ask nicely, he might take you out for ice cream."

"But, Mom—"

"And it's only for an hour or two. Then you'll come home to Mommy again, and we can get ready for bed."

"I don't wanna go!" Tears fill her eyes already. Heartbreaking, soul-shattering tears that make my throat tighten. "Mommy, it's not the weekend, and—"

"I know, baby." Pulling into our driveway and cutting the engine, I grab my purse and sling it over my shoulder, then I lean into the backseat and unsnap June's seatbelt. Finally, I meet her glistening gaze and lie. Like I always have to when it comes to Noah. "It'll be fun, okay? Daddy wants to see you."

"Will I have to spend the weekend with him, too?" She's only six, but she long ago learned how to measure time. And better—*worse?*—how to negotiate with it. "If I go tomorrow, can I stay home on the weekend?"

"No, baby." A heavy sigh rolls along my throat so my exhale makes her hair flutter. "No, it's Daddy's time this weekend, so if he wants you to go, you have to go."

"But it's your time tomorrow!" She shoves her seatbelt off and charges forward in her booster until we're almost nose to nose. "It's *your* turn tomorrow, so I should get to stay with you."

"But Daddy would like to spend time with you. And since you spend *most* of your time with me, it's only fair—"

"But it's your time!" she bursts out. "Mommy, I want to spend time with you and Uncle Axe. Daddy is mean when I'm with him, and the drive to his house makes me sick in my tummy."

"I don't think you'll go to his house tomorrow." I have to swallow the tears in my throat, or risk my daughter hearing them. "It's just an afternoon playdate. But I'll pack your special medicine for the weekend, okay? You can take it before you leave, so your tummy doesn't hurt for the drive."

"But, Mommy—"

"Baby," I cut her off with my stern voice. Not because I'm mad, and definitely not because I think she's wrong. But because if she refuses to go tomorrow, he'll punish us both, and though I've always taken the abuse he doles out to me if it means saving her, it's the psychological bullshit he thrusts upon our daughter that causes the most damage. "I need you to spend time with Daddy tomorrow afternoon, okay? You can ask him for ice cream, show him the park, and then come home. It'll be an hour."

"Do you want me to go?" Her jaw wobbles with pain, and her eyes dance with devastation. But she reaches across and holds my face, like she knows I have to look away to lie to her. "Do you *want* me to go?"

No. No. Never ever do I want you to go. But I need you to, to save us both worse when the weekend rolls around.

"Yes." I turn my face and press a kiss to the middle of her dirt-covered palm. "Yes, babe. I would like you to spend time with Daddy tomorrow. But it only has to be quick, then I'll be so excited for you to come home."

"I'm gonna tell him I have a tummy ache." Secure in her plan, she releases me and grabs her backpack. "After we get ice cream, I'm gonna tell him I have to poop. Then he'll bring me home early. And if Uncle Axe is at the house when I come home, Daddy won't hang out long."

She's too smart for her age. Too understanding for a child.

She shoves her car door open and climbs out onto the concrete driveway. Slamming the metal shut behind her and waiting for me to follow, she flashes a devious grin as soon as our eyes meet over the hood. "Can you invite Uncle Axe over for dinner tomorrow night too, Mommy?"

"Sure, baby." I flatten my lips when they want to smile, and make sure to grab my buckets of washing from the trunk. Then I follow my clever girl inside. "I'll ask Uncle Axe when he drops by tonight. Or you can ask. Now go upstairs and get changed for soccer."

I set my buckets inside the front door and take her bag when she spins, unsure where to put it, then I pat her butt and send her dashing toward the staircase. "Don't forget your socks before coming down."

Turning, I close the front door and flip every one of the three locks I long ago had installed. Finally, I spin on my heels and follow her up. "Mommy's going for a shower, June. But I'll be out in five, then we're leaving."

"Okay!" She slams her bedroom door in her haste, then shouts, "Sorrrrry!"

Shaking my head, I move into my bedroom at the end of the hall, then into the attached bathroom that constantly vacillates between smelling like a sugar factory, and resembling one that bottles perfume. Stripping off my clothes and switching on the shower, I step into the boiling spray and wash my cheek first.

Wherever Noah Scott touched, I scrub. Because I chose to leave my marriage three years ago. I made that choice for me and my daughter. And though he remains in our lives and manipulates his way into more time with us, I still have the freedom to wash him off again.

Someday, when June is grown and I no longer have to abide by a court order, he'll have had his last opportunity to touch. To kiss. To be in my space and dirty the world I'm creating for our daughter.

But until then... boiling showers will do.

Preston

IN THE WILD

"Slide on in, Danes."

Sophia Solomon, the dominatrix ballerina, the computer destroying, soul sucking, sex on legs seductress, walks a lap of the Checkmate Security office, pacing behind me as I sit at her desk. She wields a Twizzler stick the way others might wield a cat o' nine tails, and when I only stare at the fucking firewalls leading into Griffin Technology's servers, my hands off the keyboard, and my heart thundering in my throat, she stops with a quiet snarl and rests her hand on my shoulder.

"I said," she murmurs savagely. "Slide on in."

"You want me to compromise Griffin Tech's system?" I glance around the large office, the half a dozen desks spread out across the room, and the gazes that pulse back at me from those who came to watch the show.

A guy with one real leg, and the other, a fucking machine part.

Another guy—he has to be seven feet tall—with enough firepower strapped to his thigh, my asshole puckers each time our eyes meet.

And Jay Bishop, *married* to the ballerina... His lips peel back further every second her hand remains on my shoulder.

"I don't..." I turn in my chair, knocking her hand free as I move. But then I'm left to look up at the beautiful woman as she unapologetically towers over me. "Griffin is your family."

"Griffin is a competitor in the tech world," she counters smoothly. "He might be my husband's brother, but he's a threat to my income."

Circling around and perching her ass on the corner of my desk, she folds her arms and pushes up what little breast she has. "He's a sweetheart," she snickers. "And he's coming to family dinner tonight. But I asked you to do something for me, Danes. So either you'll do it, or you'll go back to the streets and find a different job."

"You want me to destroy your brother-in-law's security?" I repeat slowly. "How the fuck do you know someone else won't jump in while his system is down and cause more damage?"

She brings her candy stick up and takes a fast, smiling bite. "I guess that's a risk we have to take."

"But it's not!" I shove up from my chair and walk away from the desk. "You think you can try out this tough girl act and have me fuck with the dude, but I know what Griffin is, okay? I know what he's capable of, and I know if I compromise his system, not only will he break my fucking hands, but chances are, they won't find my body again."

Smug, her chest bounces with soft laughter. "You afraid, Danes?"

"Afraid? No! But realistic?" I spin back and meet her calculating eyes. "Hell fucking yes. If I compromise his security, even for a minute, he loses multi-fucking-billions of dollars. Men have killed for less, Ace. So how about you give me a different test and stop setting us both up to be murdered?"

"You can't do it?" she asks instead. "It's a straightforward task. I'm already in. So unless you prove to me you can do the same, what the hell use do I even have for you?"

"Give me something else! Or I can just *tell* you what I'd do. Would that suffice?"

She scoffs and pulls out her chair, flopping down so the base squeaks from her minimal weight. "You're a pussy. And you can go." Dismissive, she flicks her wrist toward the door. "We don't need you."

"You get off on playing with fire." Angry. Hell, peer pressured, as men stare me down and mock me with their eyes, I come back around to the right side of the desk and shove Sophia's wheely chair to the side, then I kiss my life goodbye as I slowly, maliciously dig beneath the security walls Griffin has in place to protect his oodles of money.

"He's going to kill me," I bite out.

But I scale a wall using Checkmate's lightning-fast technology, and take solace in knowing that *when* he finds his intruder, it'll have Sophia's name all over it. Her computer. Her office. Her command.

That might give me just enough time to slip out of town and change my name to Max Power.

"He's working on a new operating system for his phones." I cruise on past the schematics he leaves out for anyone to pilfer, then I slam up against a firewall that promises the destruction of every hard drive within a thousand-mile radius.

Well. Not literally. But still, the threat is clear.

"He's got something hidden behind this wall, which kinda makes me wonder if the OS he left out is only for show. A distraction," I ponder. Reaching out as my back rejects the angle I'm bent at, I drag Sophia's chair over and pointedly wait for her to take a hint and stand again. Then I bring it beneath my ass and drop to straighten my aching back. "He has nearly twelve thousand people on staff. Do you understand that?"

I spare a fast glance for Sophia, then peer to the doorway when Kane Bishop wanders in with a box in his hands and his twin daughters dancing their way into the room.

"So what?" Distracted, Sophia charges forward and snatches the box of cakes from Kane's lithe grip. Opening it up so I glimpse *JUNIPER'S* on the top, she takes a rainbow cupcake and sets the rest down in front of the one-legged man. Turning back to me and peeling away the cupcake's paper cup, she takes a bite and somehow still scowls atop rainbows and sprinkles. "What about them?"

"Twelve thousand families who could be out of a job if I fuck this up."

"Nah." She takes another bite and steals a second cupcake before everyone else dives in. Then she wanders my way and sets the cake by my right hand. "Once you do the job, you get a reward. But until then…"

I push the cupcake away and continue delving into Griffin's servers. "He has fail-safes here for the casual… *adventurer* with a laptop. But it's pretty basic stuff."

"Uh huh. It comes in layers, so he can collect data on who's trying to sneak in. The hobbyists drop out in level one. Those who've done a year at community college fall away in level two." She perches her ass on the corner of the desk and grins. "Those who did a four-year degree and have a modicum of skill tend to slide on through till about level six."

"This isn't a fucking game, ya know?"

"Hey!" Kane picks up his dark-haired twin and covers her ear with his hand. "Watch your fuckin' language, kid."

I pause in my work and press my lips together. Because his words carry genuine threat, but his daughter flashes a goofy grin and bats her dad's hand away.

Shaking my head, I drop my gaze again and go back to work. The sweet scent of sugar makes my mouth water, but I focus on what I'm supposed to do, and not on the ballerina with icing on her chin.

"Those four-year graduates who do okay usually get their asses handed to them and their machines destroyed," she continues, scrunching her cupcake paper and dropping her eyes to the one she gave me. "And then there are the folks with God-given talent and a tendency to access any damn thing."

She watches my cake the way some would watch a lover they so desperately want. She traps her bottom lip between her teeth, her eyes hooded and hungry. "Those are the folks we offer a job."

When I reach out and take my cupcake to set it on the other side of the desk, she snaps out of her reverie and brings her gaze back up to me. "Then Griff and I fight over who gets to keep the new talent. Right now," she leans onto the desk and peers at my computer, "you don't have a job offer."

"Fuck off." I grumble it under my breath, because Kane continues to glower. But I go back to my exploration of Griffin Technology's system. "What makes you think I'm asking for a job, anyway? It's me wondering if you're worth my time."

She only snorts and grabs her blonde-haired niece when the girl moseys closer. Hitching the toddler up onto her hip and stealing my cupcake to give to the girl, she smiles for me. "If you say so. Are you in yet?"

"No." I bite out the word and double down on my focus. "I find it concerning you run this supposed *legitimate* business," I lift my hands and do the finger quotes, then I bring them back down and continue working. "But what you really are is a thief, a hack, and a glutton." The last, I'm referring to her candy and cake consumption in the last ten minutes. "You bring children in here like it's a daycare, but you're probably on every Most Wanted List the FBI has ever published."

"I'm on no such list." Unworried, she tickles her niece's stomach, and laughs when the little girl giggles. "Only those four-year graduates who *think* they're smart end up on lists. They're good enough to pass levels one and two, but aren't nearly skilled enough not to get caught."

She peeks toward the clock and purses her lips. "I should warn you, Griffin has failsafe timers. You've been in for, what, two minutes now?" Considering, she presses a kiss to the kid's temple. "You have a minute before he destroys you."

"What?" With my heart in my throat and my hands shaking with adrenaline, I refocus on the screen in front of me. "Didn't think to tell me that two minutes ago?"

"Why should I? When you work for me, the shit we're paid to do doesn't come with a cheat list and hand-holding. Always assume you're on the clock. Don't dilly-dally like this is a Sunday stroll. Rosalee?" She meets the hungry stare of the dark-haired twin. "How was your walk with Daddy?"

"We got cake," she answers happily. "And Daddy got cranky."

"What?" Intrigued, Soph turns her back on me and faces her brother-in-law. "It's a bakery, Bish. How the hell can you get cranky in there?"

"I don't like cops." He casts a look toward the one-legged guy. Then he flashes a grin. "Most of 'em think they're big because they've got the badge." Then he brings his attention back to Soph. Behind her, sweat trickles along my spine as I work through the layers of protection that Griffin has set up around his servers. "I especially don't like dudes who treat women like shit and hide behind a badge to do it."

"What happened?" Soph pushes off the desk and crosses over to the box of cake. "Who is he?"

"Dude she used to be married to. Still has to share a kid. He wants her back, and he'll use the kid to do it."

"Then he's an asshole." Soph snatches up the bakery box and whirls to come my way. "Ten," she counts, and takes a step. "Nine. The clock's ticking, Danes. Did you climb those walls yet? Eight."

"Shush!" My thoughts sprint as quickly as my fingers type. Like Cole sidesteps a jab inside the octagon, I evade a malicious trojan whose job it is to decimate me. "Stop talking, jesus."

"Five," she teases. "Four."

"Ace!"

"If the clock beats you, you've screwed us all. Three."

"Fuck!" I shove back from the desk and throw my hands off the keyboard. "Done! I'm in." I push up from my chair so it continues whirling once I'm gone, then I wipe the sweat from my brow and pass the little girls who watch me like I'm strange.

Considering the family they're raised in, that's quite the statement about how I look right now.

"I'm in," I repeat. "He's exposed. I never agreed to this!" I turn back and point my finger at Sophia. "I create little fucking apps that follow people, Ace. I steal cars, not by breaking the steering lock, but by tricking the computer inside. I'm not even a four-year graduate, so this shit you asked for is ridiculous."

Phones ring throughout the office. Not just one or two, but all six... or eight. However many there are.

Across the room, the dude with one and a half legs answers the phone on his desk and sets the call on speaker. "Checkmate Security. How may I direct your call?"

"What the fuck are you doing, Ace?"

Oh god. Oh fuck. Is that Theo Griffin?

"Get the hell out, asshole!"

"We've just identified vulnerabilities in your security, Griff." Giggling, Sophia drops into my deserted chair and taps at her keyboard. "Time to tighten up or lose your bank balance."

"Sophia!"

"Stop swearing in front of my babies," Kane grumbles. "I'm not playing, Gunner."

"Gunner?" I search the bionic man's eyes, then desperately, I look to Jay. "What the hell is happening?"

"You just got yourself a job," Soph answers instead.

Then picking up the phone on her desk, she selects Griffin's line and brings the call to her ear. "He's fresh, Griff, and he slid under your wall in less than three minutes. But we'll catch up after work and fix this shit before someone else screws you over." She stops and flashes a giddy grin. "Now say thank you."

She's insane. And arrogant. And fucking ballsier than anyone else I've ever met.

I don't think Griffin thanks her, because she makes a soft scoffing sound in the back of her throat, then sets the phone back in the cradle and makes her fingers dance on the keyboard to prop up the damage I did and put in place temporary measures to keep others out.

"I'm working on something," she murmurs for me. "There's this family in New York I want dissolved—but first, we have to follow the line back and find out who they have on their payroll, what they're selling, and how to penetrate their walls."

Hitting enter, she sits back and folds her fingers in her lap. "Your official position here will be IT support for the residential security systems we peddle to regular joes. You'll take their calls and talk them through whatever they fucked up. *That*," she emphasizes, "is what you tell the IRS and anyone who asks. But what you're actually doing is searching for liabilities in the Mancino family mafia. You'll use your skillset to navigate their property on a physical level—"

"You want me to go there?"

"No." Pushing up to stand, she circles the desk and opens the box of diminishing cupcakes for her perusal. "You'll work remotely, but I want eyes on the property, and eventually, some kind of vehicle that will deliver explosives."

"Wait." I shoot a shocked glance to Kane, and then to his brother. "Explosives?" I raise my hands in surrender and shake my head. "Been there, done that, don't intend to repeat the experience."

Impressed, she selects a cupcake and wanders toward me with eyes that glitter like the devil's. "Ethan 'Box' Bannin." She takes my hand and turns it so its palm side up, then she sets the cupcake in the middle. "You think I wasn't watching him after he hurt Maya?"

"I don't—"

"I knew you'd come for him. And when you proved me right, I knew you had the guts for what we need here at Checkmate."

Quieting my voice, I lean closer and grit my teeth. "I won't kill on your orders, Ace. I'm not a gun for hire."

"I'm not asking you to kill anyone. I just want a little noise and light—when the time is right," she adds with a smile.

Placing her hand beneath mine and pushing my cupcake up till I smell the sugar, she winks. "First, you get our tech inside that mansion. The rest will come later."

"I'll find a way in," I negotiate. "Remotely. I'll set you up. But I won't arm a damn thing, and I won't hit the trigger."

"But... Box," she whispers, smug. "You've got the stomach for it."

"I did that for Maya." I peel the paper from my cupcake as adrenaline drains from my system and my blood sugar dips low. "And for Cole. They're the only people on this planet I would kill for."

"Well," she smirks when I take a bite of fluffy, delicious heaven. "Lucky for everyone else, I'll do it for a tidy sum, or a righteous reason. You build the arc, Noah. I'll drive it."

"Ugh." Kane comes across the room so I catch him in my peripherals. "*Noah*. That was that asshole's name." He hooks his daughters around their hips and hefts them up to carry one on each side, then he starts toward the back exit. "I'm taking the chicken nuggets to their mom, then I'm heading out to make sure Nicki isn't bothered by that fuckwit."

"Nicki?" I spin fast enough to almost clip Sophia's jaw with my elbow, then I dash across the office and yank Kane around with enough force, I know damn well he'd pull a piece if he wasn't wielding his children. "Nicki who?"

He looks me up and down with a scorching stare and shrugs my hand off. "Scott," he answers slowly. Measured. "You need to stay the hell away. She's already got man troubles, and surely has no time for you."

Turning away, he continues through the door and heads into the garage out back. Then he's gone, and I'm left holding half of a cupcake while the remaining Checkmate staff watch my back.

"I could've told you that," Sophia sniggers. "Nicki was at the wedding on Saturday night. I sure found it curious that she disappeared about the same time you did. Then she rolled back into town in the dead of night while you slept."

"She ditched." I toss the last of my cupcake in my mouth and groan at how delicious it is. "But since you're so smart, you can tell me where to find her."

Laughing, she picks up the now-empty cupcake box and walks it to the trash. "I don't think I will. It'll be more fun to watch you search."

"Ace—"

"Besides," she brushes her hands together and runs the tip of her tongue along her bottom lip, "Bish said to stay away. She's got troubles, and you're a guy who pulled the trigger that one time for your friends. Jay?" She wanders toward her tatted husband and waits for him to stand. "Wanna buy me more cake? That last batch was delicious."

"Always." He pushes the chair back under his desk and comes around to sling his arm over Sophia's shoulder, then he tugs her in tight and presses a kiss to her temple. "Then it's time for dance. Though I kinda feel like watching soccer today."

She chokes out a giggle at whatever their inside joke may be, and lets him lead her away. "I'll send you my offer letter," she calls back to me. "See you here again tomorrow. You get paid monthly, but the first check comes in advance so you can feed yourself."

Stopping at the door, she turns back and leans against the frame while waiting for my eyes. When she speaks again, the teasing is gone from her voice. "I'll provide you with a computer, and Griff will get you anything else you need. You won't always have to work in the office. Honestly, once I'm confident you're doing the job, I won't care where you do it, so long as it's getting done. But just so you know," she taps her knuckles to the wall. "I'm proud of you. Well done."

"For breaking through Griffin's security?"

She shakes her head and slowly pushes away from the wall. "For pulling the trigger and doing what was right for Maya, even if what was right wasn't lawful."

Stunned, I take a step back and drop my hands into my pockets.

She's congratulating me for killing a man.

I wasn't in the same building as him. I wasn't even in the same city or zip code. But I ended a life and felt no remorse for my actions.

"Sometimes, you just gotta do what needs to be done," she continues. "Especially when the cops won't do it for you." Turning on her heels and lacing her fingers around Jay's once more, they head out the back door and leave me standing speechless in the middle of Checkmate Security.

My new workplace.

My new... family?

"Shit." Taking stock of my new reality, I feel the scrunched up cupcake wrapper in my fist and taste the sweet dessert still on my tongue. Then I meet the hard gaze of the guy with one leg. "I'm going home." Striding away, I push through the building and head into the sunlight outside.

I have groceries to buy and a fridge to stock before I risk another morning without caffeine. So I head to my truck and slide in so the cab squeaks on its chassis. Starting the engine and pulling away from the curb, I drive toward Main Street with a shopping list playing through my mind.

I'm a simple man who likes simple food. Bread. Milk. Maybe a little ham or turkey to make a sandwich. Coffee for the mornings, and Coke for the afternoons. I never got the chance to enjoy fancy dinners or expand my palate as a child—what, with all the starvation and neglect competing for my attention—which means the elaborate, expensive restaurant meals others prefer are lost on me.

Instead, as I pull onto Main Street and pass Franky's Diner, I remember the fried chicken they make, and the delicious lasagna that makes my mouth water, and know I'll become a regular.

When Maya isn't cooking for me, the guys down at Franky's will.

Reluctantly, I bring my attention back to the road. Traffic is a little heavier now, with the after-school crowd puttering through—though, 'heavy' traffic here is a slow day compared to in the city. Still, most parking spaces are being used, and bodies stroll the sidewalk in search of afternoon treats. Kids race around, while moms race after them.

Amid all that, I catch sight of long, blonde hair tied up in a high pony-tail, and the sharp cheekbones of a woman I swear, *I fucking swear*, I know.

"Nicole?" My pulse thunders as I fight to keep my eyes on the car in front of me, but also on her as she continues in the opposite direction.

After a brief battle with my window, I wind the fucker down with my left hand, then abruptly slam my foot to the brake and come to a jolting stop when the car in front of me pauses to let another into the constant stream of traffic.

"Nicole! Hey!" I shout loud enough to draw dozens of sets of eyes.

Mercifully, Nicole's, silver and daring, become one of them.

Loaded silence hangs between us. Secrets and late nights and stomach-cramping sex. Early morning sneak outs, and mid-morning wakeups... alone.

Children whoop in the street, oblivious to the war that wages between two intimate strangers, and vehicles putter along, but I care about none of it, so long as her eyes are on me.

But just as I open my mouth to call her name a third time, to urge her closer, she darts away. Panicked and quick-footed, she drops her head and charges on.

"Hey!" Frenzied, I unsnap my seatbelt and shove my door open to chase. Fuck my truck, and screw whoever gets mad about where I leave it.

But the little hatchback riding my tail honks their horn loud enough to draw everyone around.

Everyone but the one I want.

"*Nicole!*" I drop my foot out the door until it touches the road. "Hey! Fuck."

"Dude!" The occupant of the car behind mine sticks her head out the window. "Move!"

Growling, I whip my head back around.

But Nicki is gone. Disappeared. Hiding somewhere I can't know unless I scour every shop, and demand to be let into every single back room. And fuck, but I think she commands more loyalty in this town than the new guy who may or may not have a job working for the crazy Sophia Solomon.

"Move!"

Hooooooooonk!

"Dammit." Pushing back into my truck and slamming the door shut, I fix my seatbelt and roll my vehicle forward the twelve feet available before I have to stop again.

Gripping the steering wheel in my hands, I search the street, both for somewhere to park and for the seductive blonde who took my breath away when no one else ever has.

The siren whose mind keeps mine spinning, and whose troubled undertones speak to something deep in my soul.

I catch sight of long legs and bouncing hair in my rearview mirror, but she cuts around a corner half a second later, once again disappearing from my life and leaving behind a wash of disappointment that sits heavy in my chest.

Why can't I let her go?

And why does she insist on not being found?

"Move!" The car behind mine honks again, setting my teeth on edge and making it so I barely keep my temper on lock. "You have space, asshole! Let's go."

Nicole

NEAR MISSES AND HEART PALPITATIONS

My phone vibrates constantly with Noah's name flashing across the screen and demanding my attention while I work, and June's desperation *not* to spend time with her father this afternoon grows headier with every minute that passes.

But Hannah bops around the store with a dance in her step and a metric ton of energy pulsing from her veins as she busily restocks the bread rack.

"How is she?" Axel sits on the steel counter ten feet from me and eats a croissant the way a cow eats grass. Messy, unsophisticated, and noisy. "Does she know Dickhead is picking her up from school?"

"His name is Noah." I spin an eight-inch, double layer birthday cake and work frosting onto the sides. I don't know whose birthday it is, but I *do* know they like chocolate marble sponge and have an eye for pretty flowers. "We may think he's a dickhead," I continue through tight lips. "But he has a name, and June better not hear any except the correct one."

"Right, but Dickhead isn't here right now," he counters with a toothy grin. He pats his hands together to rid them of pastry, and when Hannah bounces by and places a glazed donut beside his thigh, his smirk grows that much larger.

While my eyes roll.

"Stop feeding him," I grumble. "One a day is good. More than that and he'll need bypass surgery."

"Stop raining on my parade, Feeney." He picks up his donut and swings his legs the way he did as a child. "Nix has us running around so fuckin' much, I can never have enough carbs."

"Perhaps." I set my spatula down and walk to the mini fridge I keep out here for the sake of convenience. Taking out one of those protein breakfast replacement shakes, I walk it to my brother and set it down with a firm *thud*. "But sugar doesn't fuel muscle. It rots it away, so you end up weak and dumb."

"Sugar doesn't impact my intellectual abilities," he sniggers. But he grabs his protein anyway and shoves the rest of his donut into his mouth. "You didn't answer my question. Does June know he's coming to get her?"

"Yes." I head back to my counter and continue frosting the cake. "She knows. I packed a card game in her school bag, in case Noah has no freakin' clue what to do that doesn't include driving around town and making her carsick, then I told her we'll do something special for dinner as a reward for tolerating his shit."

He snorts. "You didn't say it like that, did you?"

"No." I spin my cake and fix the spots where coverage is thin. "I said we'd do something special to celebrate a big day being over. Are you coming to dinner?"

"Sure."

He glances across when my phone vibrates again and Noah's name flashes for my attention, then he rolls his eyes and sits tall. "He's obsessed."

"He struggles with relinquishing control." I mean, that's what those '*healing after abuse*' books say, right? "He's a single child who has never been told no. He holds a powerful position within the police force, his uncle is friendly with the mayor—which only adds another level of '*can't touch me*'—and for several years before I left, I never said no to him." Looking across at my brother, I reach up and wipe a single, pesky hair off my cheek. "He's only doing what he's always done. *I'm* the one who changed things up."

"Right. And God forbid you advocate for yourself and your daughter." Defiant, he leans across and kills Noah's call with a fast swipe of his finger. "Never taking no for an answer because his mommy taught him to be that way doesn't make him someone to pity or pander to, Nick. He's a grown-ass man who chooses the prick life."

When the phone vibrates again, surprising Axel and bringing a nasty scowl to his face, he snatches it up and answers before I can tell him to stop. "What?"

"Axel!" I toss my spatula and sprint around the counter. "Axel!"

"She's working, Dickhead. She's busy earning money to raise her daughter, because your deadbeat ass doesn't pay a cent to help out."

"Axel!" My heart thunders at the repercussions his behavior will invoke. "Stop it!"

"I said she's working," he pushes on anyway. Raising his free hand and pressing it to the center of my forehead, he keeps me away and unloads his bad mood on my ex-husband. "You know what time it is, Scott. And you know she works for a living. So instead of blowing up her phone every three fucking minutes, why don't you go pick up another shift and send that money this way? Ya know, since *apparently* your current income doesn't cover your fair share of raising a little girl."

"Axel!" I smash my fist into his ribs and find temporary satisfaction when he grunts in pain, then I grab my phone and check the clock on the wall.

Juggling the device and bringing it to my ear, I turn away from my brother and loathe the ball of dread sitting deep in my stomach. "Noah? Hey. Wh—"

"Who the fuck does he think he is?"

Noah, predictably, loses his shit and launches into a rant from hell.

Funny. He never bites back when he and Axel are in the same physical space.

"Nicole!" he continues savagely. "What the fuck?"

"I'm sorry." It's too deeply ingrained. Too beaten into my psyche. Even when I haven't done anything wrong, I apologize to this man and hope his bad mood doesn't last long. "What's up?" Then I remember the time. "Are you on your way to get June?"

"I'm in the fuckin' car," he sneers. "I was on my way there, but now I'm wondering if I should keep her for a few days. Ya know, to let the men you invite into our daughter's life cool off and not be a danger to her."

I spin and shoot a filthy glare at Axel.

"He's my brother," I grit between tight teeth. "You know he's not a danger to her. And no, you will not keep her for a few days."

"What are you gonna do to stop me? You've given me written permission to pick her up today. Maybe I'll keep her through the weekend and give you both space to learn your place in my daughter's life."

"*Our* daughter's life," I cut in. "And we have court orders for this very reason, Noah. Because the judge felt it was important for June to have stability. And you taking her when it pleases you, and returning her when you get bored is not stability."

"I've booked you in for a five o'clock reservation." Hannah's angelic tone brings my hackles up and the hair on my arms standing on end. Turning in a panic, I meet her playful eyes. "Table for you and Eric, right?"

"What?" From fire to ice, Noah's voice turns to a chilling dagger. "You have a date tonight?"

"I know you don't have long," Hannah presses, digging my hole deeper and causing me more grief than I need today. "You're outta here at four. But since Noah's getting June Bug from school, that gives you just enough time to shower and change. Eric confirmed dinner at five is fine for him."

"Who is Eric?" Noah's words slow, but I know damn well his thoughts speed. "Nicole?"

"No one. I..." I glance toward a wildly grinning Axel, and snarl when he slides off the counter and toe-taps a weird jitterbug dance with my employee. Frustrated, I shake my head and ignore my idiots. "Are you on your way to get June?"

"No, I have to work." *Lies. Lies. Lies.* I know, because his mouth is open. "I was calling to tell you I got busy and can't—"

"But a minute ago, you said you might pick her up and keep her till the end of the weekend. Noah, are you—"

"I'm busy. Which means you have to collect her from school."

"But school is getting out in ten minutes!" I bark out. "I planned my day expecting you would collect her."

"Our court orders state she's with you today," he counters so fucking smugly. "If you can't take care of your responsibilities, then maybe you're not cut out to be June's primary caregiver."

Rage bubbles in my blood and threatens to spew all over anyone who dares to come near me. But I've had practice dealing with his bullshit over the last couple of years. So I slow my breathing and calm the words I *want* to say, then reach back and steadily tug on the string that secures my apron closed.

"It's fine. I'll pick her up." I hold my phone between my shoulder and ear, and pull the dirty apron away from my body. "Can we expect you to collect her on Friday?"

"Wait, you're picking her up?" Hannah presses a silent high-five against Axel's palm. "What do you want me to do with your reservations?"

"Of course I'll be there Friday." So fucking casual. So serene. It's like Noah hands me his anger to hold, so he can go back to being charming and sweet. "I always fulfill my obligations, Nicole. You should look within yourself and try to understand why you can't do the same."

"Of course." I measure each and every word as I cross my kitchen. Class ends in just ten minutes, but I slow my movements. I refuse to rush. Because the school is only two minutes away, and I won't be baited by this man. "Thanks for calling to let me know you can't pick her up." I drop my apron in a fresh bucket and reach into the storage closet to grab my bag and keys. "We'll talk to you in a couple of days."

"Have her call me tonight," he tosses in before I can end our call. "I'll want to know how her afternoon was. Especially since she'll be disappointed Daddy had to work."

"Mmhmm." Through tight lips, I wander back to stop in front of Axel and Hannah. "I better run now so I can get to school in time. Chat later."

Gripping my phone in a steel hold and pulling it away from my ear, I mash my thumb against the screen and kill our call. Then I glare at Hannah with enough venom to make her take a step back. "What the hell? *Who* is Eric?"

"Your fictional date." Her breath escapes on a nervous laugh. "Noah was coming to take June because he knew it would hurt you. Then he got wind you had something better to do, so he changed things up. *Everyone* knows he wants to control you more than anything else. In his mind, he's just ruined your date."

"I don't have a date!" I spin on my heels and pass the cake I've only halfway finished. "Put that in the fridge till I get back. Then call the client and tell them I'll be an hour late on delivery."

"Wait." Chuckling, Axel strides half a dozen long steps and catches up to me before I escape out the back door. He grabs my wrist and yanks me around, then sighs when I turn with tears burning the backs of my eyes.

"Aww, Feeney." He pulls me in for a hug that knocks the air from my lungs. "Don't cry. He's not worth it."

"He keeps trying to mess with me." I tighten my fist around my keys and focus on that pain, instead of the slick anxiety roiling in my stomach. "He wants to take her because it annoys me. Then he dumps her when he thinks *that'll* annoy me more. He can't stand the thought of me dating, so he would literally forfeit his time with June just to stop me from doing it."

"He's an asshole, Feeney. We already knew that."

"He's going to jerk us around forever." Pulling back and sniffling up the dread I feel, I bring a hand up to wipe beneath my eyes. "Most days, it's fine, Axe. I can take it. Because maybe I had the exact right number of coffees that day, and a reasonable amount of sleep, and June is worth it. But sometimes, his shots get me between the ribs and hit their target."

I drop my hand to the place on my side that almost feels like a stitch. That odd ache people sometimes get when they've run a race. But it's a pain only Noah can inflict. "He'll *always* have energy for this, because he has no responsibilities besides the job he does poorly. Whereas *I'm* always under-slept, under-fed, stressed out, and living on eggshells. It's not a fair fight," I whimper. "And now I have to piss off a client, because I committed to a four o'clock cake delivery I can't make."

"I'll go get June." He peels my car keys and purse from my hands, but bundles them together and wraps his free arm over my shoulders. Walking me back toward my cake, he squeezes me extra tight like he knows I need his strength. "She'll be thrilled. I'll bring her here to hang out, but I won't leave till you're done with that cake. Then we're gonna go find Eric and get you a date."

"Shut up," I laugh. And cry. And smack his chest when he snickers in response. "I don't have space in my life to date, Axel. We both know the mess that'll turn in to."

"Just another filthy one-night stand, then." He presses a kiss to my brow and taps my nose when I groan. "Get back to work, I'll go get June Bug, then we'll have dinner together." Releasing me when we're at my table, he turns to Hannah and gives her a real high-five. "It was nice working with you, kid. Good thinking on your feet."

"No problem, Probey." She flashes a wicked grin and follows him out to the front of the store. "Just doing my civic duty."

"Probey," he scoffs. I don't need to watch his progress to know where he is. I can tell from the echo of his boots on my tile floors, then from the ring of the bell above the door. "I know you know I'm cooler than that." Stopping in the doorway, he calls back, "Wipe your tears, Feeney. June's coming home with us. Once you catch your breath, you'll realize it's actually a good day. Oh hey, man."

Feet shuffle, and guys mutter between themselves. Then Axel is gone, and I'm left standing where I began when Hurricane Noah blew through and attempted, again, to mess with my life.

I pick up my spatula and sniffle back the mess trying to leak from my nose, then I look down at my shirt and know, if I don't find an apron, I'm going to regret it.

"Hey, Hannah?" I set my spatula back down and hurry toward the front of the store. "I need a—"

"Welcome to Juniper's," she cheerfully greets our new customer. "What can I get for you?"

I skid to a stop in the section between the front and back of the store, desperately gulping for air and breaking out in a ridiculous sweat at the sight of Preston freakin' Danes studying the cakes in our glass display.

His attention is on the baked treats, his eyes down, and not on me.

Turn around, Nicole. Run away!

But I was never that good at saving my own life, so all I manage is a shocked intake of air that grabs not only Hannah's attention, but Preston's too.

He stands straight, like someone plugged his spine into an electrical outlet and shocked him. Then his summer-blue eyes scan me from the top of my head to the toes of my icing-smattered boots.

"P-P—"

"Nicole," he breathes out.

He wears black jeans today, and a shirt that clings to his chest. The very same stubble that left my thighs trembling a few nights ago now moves as his lips curl into a grin, and the hair atop his head, the long strands I ran my fingers through on Saturday night, now lay limp and sexy enough to make my fingertips tingle.

"You're..." He looks to Hannah, then to the massive backlit sign on the wall that says *Juniper's*. Then he brings his gaze back to me and shakes his head. "You baked the fucking cake."

"Wh-what?"

He digs his hands into his pockets and lets his stare burn dangerously hot against my skin. "I asked about you. I asked Maya and Cole who you were, and they *swore* they never invited a Nicki to their wedding."

"I—"

"You baked the fucking cake!" he repeats. Taking his left hand out again, he opens his palm and shows off the paper wrapping I use for our cupcakes, scrunched into a tight ball. "You weren't a guest," he declares. "You baked the cake, which is why I couldn't find you."

"Couldn't fi..." I'm lost. Confused. Devastated. Reeling. "Why are you here?"

"Because I ate one of those rainbow cupcakes yesterday and damn near came in my shorts."

Scandalized, Hannah claps a hand to her mouth and turns a bright shade of red.

"I knew it was a Juniper's cake," he continues, "I saw the box. So I came down after work today to find what else is available." Slowly, dangerously, a sly smile crosses his lips and damn near leaves me breathless. "Your baking tastes as good as your body, Nicole."

Hannah squeaks.

"I should've known I was eating something you made."

"Oh god." Hannah squirms. And shakes. And sizzles with a blush. Her eyes swing between me and Preston. But when I say nothing, she approaches the counter and offers her free hand. "You must be Eric."

Thoughtfully, he shakes her hand and narrows his eyes. "Preston." Then he drops it again and peers my way. "Eric?"

"A metaphor," I volunteer on a shaking breath. Because I guess I still do what men want, even when I really shouldn't. "Uh... Preston, I don't—"

"Know how not to run out in the middle of the night?" Stalking closer, he stops again when he stands almost exactly where Noah did when he came in yesterday.

But he's not Noah. His hair is wilder, and his stubble... unheard of for my ex-husband. He's broad across the shoulders, and powerful in his stance. But it's his stare. It's the way he just looks, and looks, and looks, when most others grow self-conscious and look away.

Finally, he peeks toward the sign on the wall and raises a questioning brow. "Juniper's. Family name?"

"It's actually—"

"No." I take a step forward and silence Hannah with a single look. Then I paste on my best customer-service smile and grab a paper bag from the shelf beneath the counter. *Serve him, get him out, move on with my life.* "What would you like to eat? Cupcake?" I offer, fake-cheerful. "Pastry?"

"Well..." His ocean-blue gaze studies me. It's slow and concentrated. Intense and unwavering. "I wouldn't mind eating you again. I didn't get enough on Saturday night."

"Lawd have mercy." Hannah grabs an oven mitt and uses it as a fan. "I feel like I missed out on a *whooole* lot of backstory from the weekend, Feeney."

I look in her direction and narrow my eyes.

"Why does she call you Feeney?" Preston steps to the right and takes up my field of vision. Demanding my attention and saving my staff member from burning to death. "What's Feeney mean?"

"It means I need you to decide what item you'd like to purchase." Shaking the paper bag so it makes a snapping sound in the air, I find my customer-service smile again. "I have work to do, and I'm sure you have somewhere else to be."

"Not really." He rests his hip against the glass case and folds his arms. Then, as arrogant as he was on the night of the Miller wedding, he smirks and undresses me with his eyes. "I'm done for the day, and you..." He peers back toward the small sign that hangs in the front door. "Are open for two more hours."

"Hannah's rostered on till five." I open the display fridge and snatch out a cupcake, since we know he enjoyed the first. Shoving it into the paper bag and destroying the frosting, I spin the bag in my hands and twist the top closed. Then I set it on the counter with a sugary sweet smile. "I have *different* work to do," I continue my original train of thought. "I have a birthday cake to complete, and I'm absolutely done letting men interrupt my day. So..." I push the cake a little closer to him. "On the house, in payment for your graceful and silent exit. It was nice to see you again, Preston." I turn away to leave. "Have a nice li—"

Lightning-fast, he wraps his broad hand around my wrist and pulls me up short so my feet slip on the tile and my hip raps against the counter when I sling back his way. Then our eyes meet, and his nose damn near touches mine.

"It was my pleasure seeing you again, Nicole. Seriously," he purrs, extra deep in his throat. "My *pleasure*. I know you don't like me grabbing you," he glances at his hand, "so I'm sorry for doing it."

"Then let me go." I even my voice. Soften my tone. But the craziest part of all is the fact my stomach doesn't rebel at the thought of being touched. My heart races, sure. But not for the same reasons it does when Noah grabs me. "Let me go *now*," I repeat. *But why is my voice breathy?* "I have things to do."

"See…" He leans a little closer. And then leans in a little more, so the things he says are just for me—even with Hannah close by and desperately attempting to listen in. "I would leave, but your pupils got bigger the second you saw me. Your breath started racing." He grins when I lick my dry lips. "And your nipples hardened beneath your shirt."

Oh god.

"So, although your words say one thing, your body is telling me something else."

"Preston—"

"I can be gentle," he whispers. "And I can be respectful. But fuck, I'm kinda hoping your body and your mind can get on the same page sometime soon."

"L-let me go." I open my fingers and stretch them wide, though I know he's not hurting me. "My words are all that matter right now. They're all that matter *anytime*."

"Your words are a front you're putting on. To save your dignity. But your body…" He chews his bottom lip and draws my eyes down to the movement. "Your body says you like what I can do for you."

"Pres—"

"Incoming!" Hannah zooms across the store and shoves our hands apart, startling me from my thoughts of Preston and a hotel room. Of his stubble on my thighs, and his tongue on my pussy. My brain tosses out the images of him holding me on his lap, and the face he made when we were close to completion.

It's a lot like the face he was making just a moment ago.

But now, Hannah yanks us from our memories and lobs the cupcake bag at Preston's chest so he's forced to catch it.

Almost immediately, the bell rings above the front door, and my eyes move, too slowly, to my brother walking in with my six-year-old on his hip.

"Axel!" Hannah chokes out a nervous giggle that sets my brother on edge.

His eyes shoot to me, then to the back of Preston's head. But June is her usual self—happier, really, because her uncle picked her up instead of her dad.

"Hey there, June Bug." Hannah steps away from me, drawing my daughter's attention. "Do you want a cupcake? How was school?"

"Hey, Feeney." Suspicious, Axel's movements are measured and slow as he sets an oblivious June on her feet and pats her butt to get her moving. Then he crosses my store and narrows his eyes when an involuntary groan rolls along my throat.

"What's... uh..." He stops on Preston's right. "What's going on?"

"Hey." Fixing his expression and turning, Preston meets Axel's apprehensive stare and offers his hand. "Cakes here are good, huh?"

"They sure as shit are." Axel pumps once. Twice. A third time before releasing his hand and setting June's backpack on the floor by his feet. "Tension is feeling kinda thick, though." He brings his gaze back to mine. "What's wrong?"

"Nothing, I—"

"She was a little startled when I came in here," Preston pushes on with a wicked smirk. Then he nods toward Axel. "You guys are related, huh? Same eyes."

"Axel Feeney," he responds. "Brother. And you are?"

"Preston Danes." He drags the corner of his lip between his teeth and chuckles. "A friend of Nicole's."

"Oh god." I lay my arms flat on the glass case and press my face down. *I don't want to see this. I don't want to hear it.*

"We met at the wedding," he adds nonchalantly. "We, uh... had a good time."

"Oh shit." My brother isn't the kind that'll try to intimidate a suitor, or have that *'will you treat my sister right?'* talk. No. What Axel is, is the high-fiving, *my sister got laid* kind. "You're him."

I crack one eye open and whimper at my brother's lopsided grin. "You're the dude."

Pleased, I suppose, Preston smirks. "I'm the dude."

"Man." Exasperated, Axel rolls his eyes. "Why didn't you go to the lobby and let her get some sleep? Then she might've stayed the night."

"Axel!" I shove up straight and flatten my lips when June peeks across. Bless Hannah's sweet heart, she works her ass off to hold my daughter's attention. "Stop."

"In the lobby?" Preston folds his arms and tilts his head to the side, as though the action helps him process his thoughts. "What do you mean?"

"She was having a mini-seizure on Saturday night because she wanted to sleep."

"Axel Feeney!" I reach across and smack his shoulder. "Stop it!"

"But you were there," he continues, sniggering and rubbing his arm. "She was so tired, man. But having someone in the same room was..." Instead of finishing his sentence, he brings his hand up and makes a cutting motion across his throat.

"Wildly overdramatic gesture," I grunt. "You're leaving now, right?"

Hurt, Axel's eyes whip back my way. "Me?"

"No." I look to Preston and reuse that customer service smile I've practiced over the years. "*You*. You have your cake, and I have work to do, so that means—"

"You wanna hang out?" Arrogant, Preston turns to Axel. "There are chairs outside, and I have the rest of the afternoon off. I'm kinda new to town, and my best friend is busy over at the Rollin On Gym. You're a firefighter, right?" He casts a sly side glance my way. "I'd love to buy a first responder a coffee."

"Oh, well, shucks." Axel flashes a wicked smile. "That's generous of you."

"Don't." I grit my teeth and lean closer to the pair. "Don't you dare, Axel."

"Sure!" He claps Preston's shoulder and takes a step toward the door. "A friend of my sister's is a friend of mine. And I'm off shift for the rest of the day."

"Sweet." Preston winks for me, then turns away with his cake. "I'll see you around, Nicole."

"June Bug." Axel claps his hands and waits for her to spin. "Wanna come to the park? It's a nice day, and you have the entire afternoon free."

"Okay!" She waves to Hannah and skips toward Axel. Snatching his hand and looking up at Preston, she breaks and melts my heart in the same second when she offers him the other hand. "Are you coming to the park, too?"

"I am." He lowers to a crouch and shakes her little hand. "My name is Preston." Then he peeks up at Axel. "You look kinda like your daddy, did you know that? Same eyes."

My soul shrivels. My heart stings. My whole entire fucking being ceases to function.

And June shakes her head. "That's not my dad! My dad is a grumpy butt. This is my Uncle Axe."

"Oh?" I see it in Preston's eyes. The way he tries to understand. The way his brain works over the possibilities. It takes him an eternity—and yet, a millisecond—but when it happens, his eyes shoot wide. "Oh!"

"Juniper Scott." She flashes a megawatt grin and stands tall, proud of her name, knowing this entire business is dedicated to her.

Everything I do, everything I am, is for her.

"I like your eyes," she adds sweetly. "They're really bright."

"Well..." His voice crackles as he peeks my way. But he's quick on his feet. His brain, fast, as he pushes up to stand. "Thanks. I really like yours, too. They're very pretty, kinda like..."

"My mom's!" she fills in, like everyone inside this bakery needs to hear her say it out loud. She grabs Preston's hand, so she walks between the two men, but gazes back my way as she leads them to the door. "Bye, Mom! I'm so happy Uncle Axe picked me up from school today."

"Yeah." I drop my face against my arms, and groan as the bells above the door jingle. "Me too, baby. I'll see you in a little bit," I add, since I really do have to finish that cake.

"Uncle Axe," I call out, my voice breaking from an overwhelming surge of anxiety rolling through my stomach.

When he turns back, I shake my head.

That's all I've got.

It's all I can communicate, as Preston's sly grin remains notched high.

"I've got her." Axel winks, like that somehow fixes all my problems. Then he swings June onto his hip so her hand drops away from Preston's, and her body ends up on his other side. "Go do your work. Ignore your phone. Life is fine."

And then he steps through the glass door and walks away. With my baby. And my one-night stand.

"Oh my god." I want to cry. And scream. And curl up into a ball, and smash something just so I can hear it shatter.

"What in the fresh hell is going on?" Hannah charges around the counter and stops an inch to my left so her perfume fills my lungs. Then she exclaims, louder this time, "What the hell, Feeney!?"

Preston

WELL, THAT EXPLAINS IT

S he's a mom.

And carries a different last name than her brother.

Which means...

"She's married?" The instant *Juniper Scott* dashes away from her uncle and makes a beeline for the swings in the middle of the park along Main Street, I drop my ass to a bench and set aside my destroyed cupcake. Then I rest my elbows on my knees, my face in my hands, and tilt my head to see the brother she spoke of on Saturday night.

The one she adores.

The firefighter.

The one who has her back, no matter what.

"Nicole is married?"

"Divorced." Axel Feeney was cheerful inside Juniper's. Playful. But maybe that was a show for Nicole, because he sure as hell isn't my friend anymore. He looks me up and down with eyes that speak of murder—he would clearly commit it for her—and a jaw that lets me know he's holding on to his temper by a weak thread. "You're the dude she hung out with at the wedding?"

"I mean..." I nod, aware we both know '*hung out with*' is code for something else. "Yeah."

"She called me at two o'clock that morning, mid-meltdown, because you were in that room and she wanted you to leave."

"She wanted—? I didn't..." I exhale a noisy breath and glance back to the little girl on the swings. Her sweet ponytail, and her tiny body working tirelessly to get the swing moving. "I didn't know she was melting down. I was asleep, man."

But I forced her to stay, I have to admit to myself.

She wanted to leave earlier, but I picked her up and dragged her into my bed.

"She's twitchy, huh?"

"With good fuckin' reason," he grits out. "I'm not gonna be the guy who tells you her life story and gives you a cheat sheet to fuck with her. But I'll tell you this: she has a hell of a radar on her now, and she knows when a dude is full of shit. She has low tolerance for guys in general, she still has to see her ex damn near daily. Her daughter is her *main* priority, her business comes second, and I assure you, she'll die protecting both. I'm sure you had a good time banging a single chick on the weekend, Preston, but you need to know she's not that person in real life. She's busy, she's boundaried up, she has no time, and less patience than anyone else you'll ever meet. And if you think you get to step in and cause her grief..."

"You'll fuck me up." Nodding, I look down at my hands and think. Wonder. Ponder. Plan. "Is her ex abusive? Is that why she's the way she is?"

"She's perfect the way she is," he cuts in. "And I'm not gonna tell you anything she hasn't already. Ask her your damn self. If she doesn't answer, it's because she doesn't want you to know."

Fair.

Rolling my bottom lip between my teeth, I go back to watching Juniper. "She kept her married name?"

"She won't go back to Feeney for as long as June Bug stays a Scott."

Twenty feet away, *June Bug* throws her head back and squeals when a black Labrador lopes into the park and sniffs at her feet.

"Does she wanna fix her marriage?"

"Nope. June!" Axel's eagle eyes watch the dog closely. "You okay?"

"I'm okay!" She squirms and rolls and risks falling straight to the ground if she slips. But her hands grip the chains of the swing. "S'okay, Uncle Axe! She's gentle." Then she cranes her neck and pins him with a look. "We should get a dog!"

He chokes out a laugh and shakes his head. "Not happenin', cutie. Mommy is busy, and Uncle Axe spends too much time at the firehouse to commit to a pet."

Settling back in his seat while the owner of the dog wanders across the park—a woman I recognize, and a little boy I've heard rumors about through Cole—Axel glances my way. "She doesn't want her marriage back. Fuck," he snorts, "I'm pretty sure she didn't want it in the first place. But she has a daughter with that man, and he's not showing any signs of fucking off and leaving them alone. So she's co-parenting the best she can, and you couldn't pry that married name from her cold, dead hands for as long as June has it." Shrugging, he exhales a deep sigh. "It is what it is."

"Is he local?" These are things I should ask Nicole. *But why am I asking them at all? I don't know her. I don't know him or the kid.* But my mind spins anyway, desperately searching for the puzzle pieces that make up Nicole Scott.

"The ex," I clarify when Axel's lips remain tight.

"He lives in the city, but he pops up whenever the fuck he wants. He calls the rest of the time."

"Things amicable between them?" *Why? Why do I care?* "Juniper called him grumpy."

"He's an asshole," Axel grunts. "And you don't get to speak of her so casually. You just met her."

Confused, I ask, "Nicole?"

"June." He swings a fiery stare back to me. "You can meet a woman at a wedding and have a good time. Fuck, man, I'm here to encourage it, because Nick needs to think about herself a little more often. But it's not like June has a constant stream of men coming through her life. I won't allow it, and Nicole sure as fuck won't even consider it. So that means June gets me. *I'm* the stable, decent, safe male role model in her life. Her father is the one who walks in and out and leaves behind a trail of devastation every time he does. And you..." he looks me up and down. "You're nobody."

"Does he hurt her?"

Confused, his brows pull tight in thought. "Nicole?"

"June." I bring my gaze around to the little girl who chatters with a boy much larger than her, while fifteen feet across the playground, his mother watches on. "She said he's grumpy. But she's a kid, so that might actually translate to *he's a piece of shit who belts me for fun.*"

I've only just met her. Literally minutes ago. But I was a kid whose dad liked to belt him, too. I was a child in a shitty situation with no voice and nowhere to go.

"So," I repeat for *Uncle Axe*. "Does he hurt her?"

He shakes his head, releasing my heart from the vise I wasn't aware was there. "Physically? He wouldn't dare. He knows I'd kill him—and that's if I even get there before Feeney. But—"

"Why do you call her Feeney?" Curious, I grab my cupcake bag and slowly tear it open to reveal its crushed contents. The prettiness has been ruined, but the taste, I'm certain, remains the same. "That chick at the bakery called her Feeney, too."

"Because sometimes she's gotta be reminded who the fuck she is." He snatches the cupcake from me with a noisy snap of the bag, and before I can demand it back, he takes a heaping bite.

"She was born a Feeney," he speaks around his mouthful. "Beneath the new name and the divorce and the court orders and her attempts to co-parent with a fuckwit, she's *my* family. Not his. And maybe she'll keep the other name until June Bug is grown, but she's not a Scott. Not in her heart or soul. Also," he glances my way with rainbow frosting on his lips, "it's the psychological bullshit he does to June."

Perplexed, my brow lifts high on one side. "Huh?"

"You asked if he hurts her. I'm saying he doesn't hit. He wouldn't dare. But he fucks with her head and works his ass off to destroy the sparkle in her eyes." He looks back to his niece and watches as the boy pushes her swing higher. "She's the purest, smartest, sweetest little girl you'll ever meet. She's wise beyond her years, but we all know that's code for *'she's lived in a toxic environment and had to survive it'*. She knows what her father is, Preston. She doesn't know the words for it, but she sure as fuck feels it in her stomach every time he's around."

He brings his shoulders high in a shrug. "But the courts say she has to go to him every second weekend. So that's what happens. Mostly, she puts up with it. She takes her teddy and a few extra snacks in her backpack, and she gets through the weekend with that asshole. But she's always happy to come home. And for the first couple of days after she's back, she's feeling big feelings, and those are the days Nick is the least available to the rest of us."

"Because she's sad for her kid?"

"Because her kid needs a fuckin' hug and a reminder that she's special and amazing and worthy of love that doesn't hurt."

Sitting back and bringing one leg up so he rests his ankle on the opposite knee, he adds, "Love that is healthy doesn't hurt. And love that hurts isn't healthy." He slides the last of my cake through his lips. "Now tell me, who the fuck are you?"

I frown. "What?"

"You're Preston Danes. You're the dude my sister met at a wedding, and according to her midnight meltdown, you hug a fuck of a lot and have no trouble sleeping with a strange woman in the room." His eyes flicker between mine. "But who are you? Where did you come from? Who are your people, and what's your job?"

"Uh..." It's the *'what are your intentions'* talk, but a little more subtle. "Preston Danes, like you said. Only child to a couple of assholes. Cole Miller is my best friend, and Maya Blake might be the best woman I've ever met in my life. I work in IT," *sort of,* "but I used to steal cars for a living."

His brow quirks at that, but it's best I tell him now before he figures it out on his own.

Offense over defense, right?

"I moved to town over the weekend, though I've been spending most of my time here for a while. I'm renting this old cottage just past the train tracks, I had a job interview at Checkmate, and—"

"Checkmate?" His eyes narrow, exactly how I expected they would. "You work in security?"

"I work in IT," I reiterate. "Computers. Tech support, mostly." *Ha! Sort of.*

"Ever been married before, Danes?"

I snort. "Never."

"Kids?"

"None."

"That you know about," he retorts. "How many running around because the baby mama didn't wanna tell you?"

His question gives me a moment of pause before I shake my head again. "None. Those I've known intimately have remained in my life to a certain degree—"

"Friends with the exes?"

"Friend*ly*," I correct. "We don't chat or hang out, but there isn't a single one I couldn't expect a glowing character reference from. I'm a decent person, Axel. Not always good..." I chuckle.

When Juniper throws her head back and laughs, I peek her way to watch. The Feeney family genes are strong, so my heart skips, because she looks a hell of a lot like her mom, but with brown hair instead of blonde.

"I do the right thing by the people who deserve it," I murmur. "And I won't tolerate those who don't. I enjoyed spending time with Nicole on Saturday night. I sure as fuck had no clue she's a mom or has an ex-husband. Honestly?" I look back to Axel, "It doesn't look promising that she's gonna give me a minute of her time in the future. But if I see her ex around, and he's stealing that little girl's sparkle..." I think of Ethan 'Box' Bannin, then I think of sweet Maya in the hospital after that asshole fucked her up. Broken ribs, black eye, blood in her vomit.

Smiling now, I look back to Juniper and know without a doubt in my soul that she has an ally in me. "I'll take care of what needs taking care of."

"I'm gonna jump!" She squeals and kicks her feet, while the dog sits on its haunches, and the boy slows the swing.

He's only six; I know that, because Maya was his teacher last year. But he's sensible, so if June is saying she's going to jump, he's clever enough to slow the swing.

"Uncle Axe!" she hollers amid silly laughter. "Are you watching? I'm gonna jump."

"Don't break your leg, June Bug." He scrunches my cupcake bag and brushes crumbs off his shirt, then he pushes up to stand and wanders closer to the boy. "Your mother will destroy me if I bring you back all busted up."

"I won't break my leg." She vibrates where she sits. And loosens her grip on the chains.

The little boy frantically works to slow the swing, but without simply grabbing it and slamming her to a jolting stop. And the dog... well, the way she walks around to June's front almost makes it seem like she's going to catch her.

Or get crushed in the process.

"Ready?" June wiggles her legs. "Uncle Axe! You ready?"

"I'm ready, Bug." He strides to the left side of the swing set. "Maybe slow it down first. You're still going too high."

"Not too high!" She peels one finger off the chains, settling a heavy blob of dread in my throat. Because she's going way too fast for a kid her size to jump off. "Ready?"

"Yo!" I shove up to stand and prepare to run. "She's gonna fly, like, ten feet, man."

"Setty!" June shouts.

Axel's eyeballs seem to sweat, and his hands come up in preparation.

"Go!" She releases her hold at the very apex of the swing's arc and flings through the air. Ten feet high. Twelve.

The dog jumps, and the mom grits her teeth.

I dash forward a step. Then two.

But Axel sprints toward the front of the swings, scaring the dog back, and catches his niece so she flops into his arms with a grunt of exhaled air. Then he laughs when she wrinkles her nose and frowns at his interference.

"Uncle Axe! You messed me up."

He presses a noisy kiss to her forehead and carries her back my way. "You were gonna mess yourself up, Little Feen. Uncle Axe saved you a trip to the ER." He stops five feet in front of me and tips his chin. "Buy me a coffee some other day. Say goodbye to Preston, Bug."

"Goodbye, Preston!" Her eyes dance with happiness, and her smile is something... other. Beautiful and delirious and distracting and lovely. "It was nice to meet you."

"It was nice to meet you too, Juniper."

It baffles me that instead of smiling, I frown. That instead of enjoying the little girl's innocent spirit and the way she keeps her uncle on his toes, I turn instead, my body instructing me to follow them.

I don't, of course.

I can't.

But fuck, I kind of want to.

Leaving me in their dust, Axel carries her away. And when they're twenty or so feet from me, he changes his grip and monkeys her around to his back.

Still, I watch them. And I think of Nicole. Of the woman from the wedding, the one who presented herself as single and somewhat interested in a brief romance. Then I think of the Nicole I met today. Still stand-offish and shy, but with a sharp tongue and firmly held boundaries.

She's a mom. A divorcee. She runs a business, and provides a healthy male role model in her daughter's life in the form of her brother.

"Shit." With an unhappy scowl as the Feeneys step off the sidewalk at the end of the block and continue toward Juniper's Bakery, I sit on the bench where I started, and again drop my face into my hands.

But then I push up again, too much pent-up energy bubbling in my veins, and start toward Main Street. Not to follow Axel, but to get to my truck.

Unreasonably angry, though I can't explain exactly why, I snatch the phone from my pocket and hit dial on Cole's name.

He's probably at the gym, training for his next big fight—a suspicion that's confirmed when the call rings out and his voicemail picks up. So I hit the red icon on my screen and dial Maya instead.

Since school is out and the children have left, she'll be more inclined to answer.

"Hello?"

I exhale an explosive breath and push my hand up through my hair. "I found her."

"Who?" She's still at the school, I can hear the sound of chatter and a soft radio bleating somewhere in her vicinity. "Preston?"

"Nicki." I put my head down and continue along the sidewalk toward the bakery. And hell, but I kind of hope Nicole isn't near the window to see me pass again. Not now. Not today. "She was your fucking cake chick, Maya. She owns Juniper's Bakery."

"Oh." Then, "Oh!" Her voice comes out on a squeak. "You kept saying Nicki, so I didn't... Nicole Scott," she murmurs. "Oh my gosh."

"You know her kid too, don't you, Maya?" I lower my tone and breathe a little easier when I catch sight of my truck. "She knows Charlie Reilly, that massive fighter kid. And he was your student last year. So that means—"

"Yes," she whispers. "Holy cow, yes. June was in my class last year, too."

"Dammit, Maya!" I unlock my truck and slide into the driver's side. Juniper's Bakery is just a few stores down, but I close my door and set my call on speaker, then I start the engine and back away before Nicole thinks

I'm a total fucking creep. "I was blindsided! When you knew who I was talking about all along."

"I didn't know she..." She hesitates for a moment. "Pres, I didn't know it was *her*."

"No?" Straightening the truck in the street and pushing the stick into gear, I putter away and turn toward my cottage.

I could go to the gym. Or to Checkmate. Hell, I could go to the school. But the last might land me a date with the cops if Nicole gets a wild hair and thinks I'm checking up on her life.

"Well, I found her," I continue. "By accident, that is. Because I went looking for an afternoon snack at this bakery I'd heard of. And *whatdoya-know*?" I growl. "There she was, still fucking beautiful. Standoffish as always. But then, *but then*!" I'm on a roll. And angry. And bewildered. And fuck knows what else. "A little girl walked in and introduced herself."

"Oh god," Maya exhales. "Shit, Pres."

"I thought she was Nicole's brother's kid. They have the same fucking eyes. But noooo," I snarl. "Juniper, as in Juniper's fucking Bakery. And Nicole is her *mommy*. Because the woman I banged at a wedding is a mom! Apparently."

"Are you..." She considers her words for a moment. "Are you mad she's a mom, Preston? Like, is that the issue?"

"No! I'm mad that I know exactly where she is now, but I can't go there. I'm mad that I can't stop obsessing over seeing her again, but she doesn't want me back. I'm mad because her kid is the cutest little thing I ever saw in my life, and she's outgoing," then I think of the swing, "and so fucking brave! Little kids with abusive dads aren't outgoing or brave unless their moms have busted their asses to protect them. And you know what else I'm mad about?"

I hit the indicator and turn at the end of the block.

"Maya? Do you know what I'm mad about?"

She sighs. "What?"

"I'm mad, because I mentioned Juniper having an abusive daddy just now, and you neither denied it, nor acted surprised. Which tells me I'm on the fucking money. So now I'm even *more* mad, because how can someone abuse a little girl?"

A pained groan works along my throat. Because she's so cute and innocent. So sweet and deserving.

"Do you know the dude?" I ask her. "He gets Juniper every other weekend, which means he probably picks her up from school. That means—"

"Yeah," she sighs, interjecting as I pull the truck across the railway lines heading out of town, "I've met him. As her teacher, who spent every school day for a year with her, I know about her life. Kids tell on their parents, Pres. The good and the bad. So I know her dad makes her feel crap about herself, and I know he's on her mom's case every day looking to chat. I know he doesn't pack her enough food for lunch, but she never complains. She only has two school days a month where he's in charge of dressing her, brushing her hair, and packing her food. So she deals with it in silence, because she knows she'll go home to her mom at the end of that day, and Nicole will be able to fill her tummy again."

"Fucccck." I have only a few triggers in my life; one of them is a parent who abuses their child. The other, a child with an empty stomach. "She goes hungry?"

"Yeah," she admits softly. "Sometimes. Not because he's broke or wants her to be hungry. He's just..." I wait with bated breath for her to think up the right words. "He doesn't bother himself with her needs. He's one of those guys who considers himself really important. He's so busy focusing on that and thinking about his ex-wife, that the kid is just a blip on his radar. Someone he's forced to spend time with so he can keep Nicole tethered close."

My brows come close together so I feel the severe line they create down the center. "He doesn't *want* to spend time with his daughter?"

I'm pretty sure she shrugs, but because I can't see her, I can't know for sure. "I don't think he's interested in her at all. His end game has always been to control his wife, so—"

"*Ex-wife,*" I cut in angrily. "She's his ex-wife."

"Jesus," Maya exhales. "You're seriously wound up about this. Yes, his *ex-wife,*" she repeats with a verbal eyeroll. "I doubt he loves her. But guys like him... it's a bit like my mom, ya know? They enjoy the control. They enjoy making others miserable. And since June is the bridge to Nicole..."

"How do you deal with people like that?" Slowly, I turn off the main road and head onto my bumpy driveway. The massive tree still lies across one side, and potholes take up most of the rest of the space. "How do you deal with your mom?"

"Non-contact," she murmurs. "Mostly. I speak to her when I must, and ignore her the rest of the time."

"And Nicole?" I ask. "What are the chances she can do that?"

My best friend's wife scoffs, though there isn't a lot of humor in the sound. "She's gotta parent with him. For as long as June is a minor, she never gets to escape him."

"And that," I bite out and cut my engine, "is why she's the way she is. Boundaries up, zero tolerance, and with no time for anyone else."

Snatching the key from my ignition and pushing my door open so it squeaks on the hinges, I push out and slam the door shut when my boots touch the driveway. "She's been burned, Maya. She's not risking the fire again."

"Are you *this* interested?" she asks, disbelieving. "You sound really freakin' emotionally invested in someone you met one time, Preston."

"I'm interested enough to want her to be happy. And for her not to have her abuser sitting on her back every day for the next, what..." I do the math in my head, "twelve years. I was invested enough to want to find that woman I met and fool around some more. Because apart from you and Cole," I slip a different key into my front door lock, then shove the door open to reveal my messy kitchen, "I don't sleep with other people around, Maya. I never, ever, *ever* sleep unless I'm alone. So the fact I could, and so fucking heavily that she was able to slip out, means something to me. But now she's a momma bear who would rather set me on fire than risk my touch burning her."

"She just..." Maya pauses for a long beat. "I don't know, Pres. She's a total sweetheart. Maybe you don't know that person yet, but I swear, she's so kind and selfless. She supplements classroom craft supplies, even though she doesn't have to. She brought some to me every term last year, and I know June's first-grade classroom gets them too. She goes out of her way to communicate with her teachers, letting us know her co-parenting relationship is... tough. But she never disparages him. Ever. She just says that things are tense and he's not always receptive to feedback or communication, but if there's anything anyone needs, she's ready and willing to bridge that gap in case he drops the ball."

She lets out a deep breath. "I watched that little girl for an entire year and saw how she was each day. Nine school days in a row, she was her usual bubbly, perfect self, but on that tenth day, after spending the weekend with her dad, she would come back to me so friggin' sad. She was dirty, her hair was knotted, her teeth were furry, and her belly was grumbling. Bags under her eyes said she wasn't sleeping, and the emotion in them said she was feeling big things, but waiting to get home to mom before letting them out."

"Things are so messy and fresh there." Pulling out my dining room chair, I lower with a huff and press a palm to one eye. "That little girl is so sweet, Maya. I saw outgoing and brave, but you mention her abuse, and I'm seeing two entirely different kids in my mind."

"She can be brave and outspoken on her mom's days," she explains, "because she's safe and supported. That doesn't mean she's not neglected on her dad's days. It just means she's resilient."

"I'm so fucking sick of people calling abused kids *resilient* and thinking it's a compliment. Jesus, Maya." I drop my hand and sit back to look up at my ceiling. "What the hell do I do with this?"

"With what, exactly?" I hear her chair squeak, then the soft slide of a desk drawer. "What do you need to deal with? Maybe I can help."

"Nicole." I focus on the stretch I feel in my neck from the way I sit. The tug of my throat. The tickle of hair on my forehead. I anchor myself in the now, so I don't get lost in the little boy who wandered the streets with an empty stomach and no mom to make him feel safe. "I really liked spending time with her."

"So... ask her out. Gently," she adds with a soft laugh. "*Very* gently. And be prepared for her to say no. Because, like you said, she's inclined to set you on fire first. It's how she survives, after what she's been through."

"So I'm already on the back foot," I argue. "Because of some other asshole's actions."

"If she's worth it, then you won't mind. And if you do mind, then I suggest you don't approach her at all. She deserves better than a bitter guy who considers her to be hard work... and I think you agree."

"What about Juniper?"

My question catches her by surprise. "Huh?"

"What do I do with Juniper?"

"You sure as hell don't tie her to a tree out back so you can spend time with her mom!" Giggling, she sobers quickly when I don't join in.

"Uh..." Serious now, she still coughs out the odd residual chuckle. "Well... okay. So they're a package deal. Forever. Whoever you *think* you met at the wedding doesn't matter. Because *this* is who she is—a mom, a business owner, and insanely busy. I assure you, she'll never be sorry for having a daughter, and she won't apologize for working hard to support that little girl. She won't choose anyone or anything over her child, and should you ever think you deserve to come first, well..." she whistles under her breath, "we circle back around to you not approaching her in the first place.

"Chances are, she won't be able to go out at night," she warns me. "Not for a long time, anyway. But *if* she agrees to hang out with you some more, she'll want to do it when June isn't around. Since having random men around her kid isn't something she would do, it means you get the dregs of what time she has left. And since she has June most of the time, and work always, it means that your *getting to know you* dates will be few and far between. Sound too hard yet?"

Straightening my back and sitting tall, I frown. "No. I—I'm thinking. I'm cataloging everything you're saying."

"Start slow," she continues. "We all know you're the million-miles-a-minute Preston, but that won't do you any favors here. If you push, she'll push back."

Yeah, I think to myself. *I noticed already.*

"And once she's done pushing back, she'll turn her ass around and walk away. *And* she'll feel relief doing so, because you're an additional stressor in her life, and she could do with offloading a few of those."

"Why the hell am I a stressor?" I bite out. "I don't intend to fuck her around."

"Because you're a man," she throws down coldly. "Because you're not a part of the routine they already have. Because you're a risk. And because, to people like her, time is a commodity she doesn't have a lot of. So to spend some of it on you is an investment she may not be willing to make. And if she does," she adds with a smile in her tone, "be thankful. Because instead of wearing an uncomfortable dress and painful shoes and hanging out with a source of stress, she *could* be sitting at home with guac on her face and a glass of wine in her hand.

"She already has good options for her limited time, Pres. So to give that up and invest in you will take trust. And consistency. She's gonna make you work for it. Oh," she adds as a final thought. "And her ex-husband is a cop."

She drops that news like she's merely mentioning the color of his hair.

"A detective, to be specific. So not only do you have to worry about him finding your rap sheet and jamming it up your ass, but even if you were a perfect choir boy with nothing but praises all over, he's still gonna make things hard on her if he finds out she's dating. He wants her back, Preston. And you're sitting here telling me you might be the guy who stands in his way."

"Shit, Maya—"

"*If* you're still interested," she brings her speech to a climax, "if you're still willing to put in the work, then get ready. Because it's gonna be slow, and it's gonna take patience. But..." Dreamily, she sighs. "I like her. And I like June. A lot. Anyone who gets to be in their lives, in my opinion, is very lucky."

Nicole

TRUTH BOMBS

"What happened?" I shove through the front door of my home, knowing my brother purposely brought June back here instead of to the bakery.

He didn't want to come back to the shop and explain himself, and he knew I'd be tied up for another couple of hours and unable to rush out.

But now I'm free, and my heart has yet to slow since my brother, my daughter, and my one-night stand walked out at three o'clock.

"Axel!" I slam my bag to the floor in my living room and stomp from hardwood to carpet. With my eyes zinging from one corner of the room to another, I search for the duo I know are here.

"Axel Feeney!" I charge back out of my living room and head into my kitchen. "If you don't come out here, I swear to god, I'm gonna tear the skin from your—"

"Yo, psycho!" He pushes up to stand and reveals himself on my back porch through the kitchen window. With a cupcake in his left hand and a half-consumed beer in his right, he flashes a mischievous grin and turns again, so my gaze jumps to June on the ten-foot trampoline in the middle of our backyard.

Springs rhythmically squeak, telegraphing exactly where she is. If my temper could have subsided just a little, I would have heard her and known precisely where they were. But no, because anger and nerves and anxiety swirl in my blood.

"June Bug baked, so grab a cupcake and take a breath," he calls back. "Then come out here, but leave your bad mood in there."

"Leave my bad mood," I grumble, unable to tamp down the feelings surging through my body.

I take a sharp left and catch sight of ten cupcakes on a cooling rack, and beside them, a piping bag filled with icing that's an almost fluorescent purple I have no clue how they achieved. My face is wrinkled in unhappiness and my breath puffs out like an angry bull's, but I grab a cake and violently tear the paper off, feeling no remorse for the crumbs that flitter to my floor.

I'll mop them up later, and make my sour mood worse when I have to scrub because they've been trampled onto the tile.

Heading to the back door and slinging it too wide too quickly, I growl when it smacks the wall and bounces back to slap my thigh. Axel's eyes swing my way, and his expression turns arrogant, like he's happy the door is doling out the punishment I deserve.

"Hi, Mommy!" Bounce. *Squeak.* Bounce. *Squeak.* Bounce. *Squeak.* "Did you get a cake, Mommy?"

"Hi, baby." I lift my half-destroyed treat and hold it the way one might a glass of champagne. At a wedding. When a certain handsome stranger is making his best man speech.

Damn that charming asshole!

I come to a stop beside my lounging brother so my hip touches his shoulder and his smile rolls outward like a *vibe*. But I don't look his way. I don't take my eyes off my cake. "What the hell happened after you left the shop?"

"Got to know your special friend." Smug, he watches my daughter like she's the start and end of everything in his life.

It shouldn't be like this. He should think about his own relationships, and maybe making a daughter of his own. But he can't, because I'm too dependent and in need of him in our lives.

"I kinda like him," he continues. "Has a brain in his head and a solid grasp on being a reasonably decent human being."

"'Reasonably'?" *Don't look down. Don't peer his way.* "Why reasonably?"

He shrugs, then smirks when June waves from the middle of the yard. Thankfully, she's too far away to hear us when we're not shouting at each other. "Do a flip, Bug! Show Mommy what you were working on."

Oh god. Sure. Let's add a broken neck to our long list of crap to handle this week. "Be careful, baby."

"I like him, because he's not a people pleaser," Axel finally says, setting my pulse racing just a little faster. "He's real. He's not sorry for who he is, and he's sure as shit not sorry for liking you."

"He..." I wrench my head to the side and meet his gaze. "He said that?"

"You're fishing for compliments," he teases, "and you're not very subtle about it." Relaxed, he tosses the second half of his cupcake into his mouth and talks around the intrusion. "He didn't say it, Feeney. But his eyes do. His body language. Every fucking word that comes out of his mouth, even when they're not your name, says he's interested."

"Axel, I can't—"

"He got the surprise of his life today. Finding out the woman he wants to see more of is a mom." He lifts a questioning brow. "I don't know the right procedure for all that, since smart women don't tell strangers they have kids. But fuck, Nick, she stunned him good."

"Well, he—"

"And still," he cuts in before I can go on. "He handled it. He didn't stumble, and not once while we were at the park did he give me the feeling he resented you or her for it."

"Of course not! If he thought he could, even for a single second, I would—"

"Yeah, yeah." He rolls his eyes. "You'd make him rue the day and *blah blah blah.*" He goes back to watching June. "We know, Rocky."

"Why the hell are you mocking me, Axel? Why are you mad at me for protecting my baby?"

"I'm not." He brings his beer up for a sip. "You're the one who came out here with a bad attitude. I'm only matching your energy. You wanna be pissy, I'll be pissy too. You wanna cheer the fuck up, then I'm here for it. She nearly broke both her legs at the park today, by the way."

Shock makes my eyes jump wide. "What?"

"And he was gonna mow every fucker over to help her." Grinning, he sips again and hides his smile behind the bottle. "He was discreet about it.

131

EMILIA FINN

He wasn't gonna impose—he was just the backup if I messed up. But fuck if he wasn't ready to throw down and protect this kid he just met."

"He's…" Frowning, confused, I snatch Axel's beer and bring it to my lips to chug most of what's left. "He's not, like, weirdly obsessed with her, right? Do I need a restraining order?"

He snorts. "No, I think he's just a protector in general. Of kids. Of people who matter. I think you mean something to him, and she obviously means something to you. So though he'd just met her, and it would be wildly inappropriate and weird for him to feel *anything* about her right now, he was ready to protect her simply because she's yours."

Contemplative, I hold the beer bottle to my lips and inhale the scent of alcohol, weak as it may be. "And remind me again how my daughter was in a situation where she needed to be protected?"

He chokes out a laugh, then finally growing weary of me standing while he sits, he grabs the hem of my shirt and roughly yanks me around until my ass slams to the Adirondack chair set beside his. He built these in woodwork class in his senior year of high school. They're more solid than anything I'll ever get from a store, and come with the bonus of his name burned into the armrests.

"She was on the swings at the park and wanted to jump." Relaxing again, while I fuss with my shirt and push hair off my neck, he turns just his head and meets my gaze. "Ya know how we used to do it as kids? Swing as high as we can go, then jump off and try not to kill ourselves?"

"Mmm." I tip the last of his beer back and swallow it down, while twenty feet away, June does a flip on the trampoline and lands on her back with a grunt. "You told her no, right?"

"No," he chuckles. "I told her to have the time of her life. It's what kids do. But when she was getting a little too much air and ran the risk of shattering both of her ankles when she landed, I caught her instead. But your boy—"

"I don't have a boy." A nasty scowl slides across my brow. "Or a man, or anything in between."

"Whatever you say. But he was there, sneering at that Reilly kid, who came along to push her on the swings. He was ready to throw down for a little girl he'd only just met, and when I asked about him and his people, he answered—no bullshit, no excuses, and no glamorizing unglamorous shit. He's just…" he shrugs. "I dunno. Decent."

132

"A glowing recommendation." With a roll of my eyes, I look back to June and take a calmer bite of my cupcake. "What did he say about me?"

Axel sniggers. *Fishing. For. Compliments.* "He thinks you're beautiful, smart, savvy, and he'd like to take you out to dinner."

Stunned, I bring my gaze back around to my brother. "Really?"

He shakes his head, firming his quivering lips instead of smirking. "No. But he was thinking those things, and it's obvious you'd be receptive to a request."

"You're an asshole." I reach out, holding the neck of the beer bottle, and tap his kneecap so his reflex kicks in and a yelp escapes his throat. "I'm not receptive," I tell him. "I'm unavailable."

"Then why are you so interested in what we said and did?"

"Because you took my daughter to hang out with him! And he's..."

"The guy you banged?" he teases. "It's okay. We all know."

"The man I spent time with," I grit out. "It's horribly inappropriate to introduce my daughter to random men."

"Lucky I didn't tell her Mommy did the dirty with him, then, huh?" Rubbing his knee and stealing the bottle before I swing a second time, he sets it on the opposite side of his chair and drags his bottom lip through his teeth. "He was just a guy I was chatting with. That's all it is for her, and that's all it ever has to be. Just like she meets the guys down at the fire-house. But now lemme ask *you* something..." Expectant, he turns my way and lifts a brow. "What do you want from all this?"

"Nothing. I—"

"Am afraid of commitment," he nods. "I know. But what do you *want*, Feeney? You want a fuck buddy? You want a date once a month? Do you want him to walk into the lake and never come out again?"

I glower and study the net surrounding the trampoline. Hard. "You're my brother. This discussion isn't—"

"I'm also the only guy in your life that genuinely cares about your happiness. And let's not forget *you* called *me* from your lover's hotel room."

"Ugh!" I slap his leg and feel my bad mood slip away when my brother squeals. "Stop saying lover. And fuck buddy. And *commitment*." The last makes me shiver, but not for any reason that's good. "He's just a guy whose—"

"Very presence makes you look twice. Three times." His lips curl higher. "Four."

"Axel—"

"He's decent. He cares about people other than himself. He's forward," Axel chuckles. "Forward enough to drag you out of the shell you're so obsessed with staying inside. He's not pussyfooting around and taking care not to ruffle feathers. But he left you in a daze and smiling after that wedding, which has to mean something."

"Sure." I shrug. "It means he was the best sex I've had in..." *Too long. Perhaps ever.* I shake my head. "Doesn't make him a good person. He's just... ya know, that first meal a starving person gets after famine. To them, anything is good."

Immaturity is my brother's most prominent personality trait. So he giggles like a child and chokes out, "You said *sex*." Then peering across the yard, his attention moves to June as she clings to the trampoline net and watches us. "What other tricks you got, Bug? Show Uncle Axe before he has to go home."

"Home?" Her eyes widen in panic. Then, like bouncing is currency and that currency keeps him here, she flings herself to the center of the mat and sends the springs squeaking again. "You're staying for dinner, right?"

"Mm..." His cheeks warm and his eyes slide my way. "She wants a daddy figure, Feeney."

"Don't even." I press the heels of my palms to my face and groan. "She has a daddy. We don't like him very much, and she often comes home with new traumas I wish she never had to know. But I'm not shopping for a man to step in and complicate the bullshit we're already living."

"You have such a way with words." Sniggering, he reaches out and circles my wrist with his palm, then he tugs my hand down so I can no longer hide. "But you still didn't answer my question. What do you want?"

"I want peace," I whine. "I want sleep. I want a week where I get complete and utter cooperation from the man I'm legally obligated to raise a daughter with. I screwed up when choosing who I would procreate with, Axel, and now, she," I glance over to an oblivious June and sigh. "*She* pays the price for my screwup. I want to hit pause on my life and have more sex with Preston. But I can't, because pausing life isn't a thing, and having sex with him has proven to not be without stress and strings."

"What stress?" He readjusts in his seat and sets his left ankle on the opposite knee. "What's he doing that is stressing you out?"

"Axel, I—"

"Is he harassing you?" His jaw tightens at the thought. "Stalking you? Blowing up your phone? Demanding your attention? Driving past the house? What, Nick?" His glare grows more dangerous with every question he asks. "What's he doing that's making you hurt? Because maybe I thought he was decent, but if he's not—"

"He exists," I whisper. Because I'm embarrassed. Ashamed. "He literally exists, and that's it. That's all he's done. He doesn't have my phone number, so he can't blow it up. He doesn't know where I live, so... same. Before this afternoon, I literally hadn't seen or spoken to him since the weekend, so harassment and stalking are out too. But it's just—"

"Noah drives by the house," he rumbles softly. "He stalks, and calls it checking in. He's the reason your phone battery is always dying, and it's because of him you're terrified of inviting someone new into your life. Because fuck, what if you end up with more of the same?"

"You're mocking me." Pushing up from my seat, I turn toward the back door and head into my kitchen to pour a glass of wine. Because I need alcohol to cloud my senses. Because I owe Axel a beer, and myself, time alone. "I'm already drowning," I tell him through the window, low enough only he can hear. "Every single day is a shit fight where I live in fear of what's next. Every single day, Noah's coming at me with new drama, and even when that drama doesn't exist, *especially* then, he creates it for us both."

I take out a bottle of sweet white wine from my fridge, then snag a glass from the rack on top. "I can't date someone else, Axel. Even if I wanted to, even if I tossed caution to the wind and risked finding myself another man just like Noah, I can't date, because I don't have time. And I definitely don't have the energy to deal with the blowback if Noah finds out."

"So you'll let him control you forever?" He doesn't get up from his chair. Doesn't even turn to speak. "Your fear of more drama means he maintains that control, and you... die alone?"

"Good lord." I pour until the liquid touches the very brim of my glass.

Short of an emergent ER visit tonight, I have nowhere to be, but a hell of a lot of nerves to dull. "I'm twenty-five years old, Axe." Re-capping the bottle and placing it back in the fridge, I take out a beer and hip-bump the door closed. "Twelve years from now, I'll still be young enough to find someone to spend my time with."

"Perhaps." When I come out the back door and step onto the porch, he peers across and waits for me to wander closer. "But considering the current pickle you've found yourself in, it's apparent that your body and mind want you to meet someone *now*."

"It was a one-night stand." I set his beer on his armrest, and my wine on mine. Then lowering with a heavy exhale, I sit deep in the chair so it's almost a hug. "He's just a guy I never intended to see again. Grownups do it all the time, right? Casual sex. Mutual orgasms. Each party walks away, and life goes on as it should."

"Sure. That's how it's supposed to be." Still, I said *orgasms* and *sex*, so he sniggers. "But it's not how it went for you. You were in a different city, at a wedding where you knew no one but your client. You went to a guest's room and had sex, and now..." He grabs his beer and grins, "dude has a job just three blocks from your shop, and a home just a few minutes from yours. That, darling sister, sounds like the universe is fucking with you."

"Right." I bring my wine to my lips and take a mouthful. "Because it hasn't already picked on me enough. I don't know what I did to deserve this kind of wrath, Axel, but I swear, it's uncalled for. I'm a good person."

"So maybe consider a change in perspective."

When June stops bouncing and reaches up to unzip the net, Axel bounds up from his chair with more energy than I ever remember possessing, and starts across the lawn to save her.

"Maybe this isn't supposed to be punishment." He grabs my daughter and monkeys her around to his back before starting in my direction. "Maybe it's a reward. Because life has already shit on you, and now it's time for you to experience something good."

My eyes meet an interested June's. My brain acutely attuned to knowing what I can and cannot say in front of her—despite the fact my brother freely cusses in front of her. "That would imply smooth and easy," I tell him. "Rewards aren't supposed to be so stressful."

Curious, June tilts her head to the side the way Axel and I are both known to do when we're thinking. "What does stressful mean, Mommy?"

"Uh..." I sip again and try to empty my glass before she asks what's in it. Noah's a master manipulator and interrogates criminals for a living. My six-year-old can't stand up to the pressure, no matter how much she wishes she could protect me. "Stressful is like when something feels really hard," I try to clarify. "Like, when your brain and your tummy feel weird. I was saying to Uncle Axe that something good, like a reward, shouldn't feel stressful. And if it's stressful, maybe it's not a reward."

"I got an award at school today."

"What?" Surprised, I sit taller in my chair. "You got an award? Did you bring it home? I didn't see it yet, baby."

"Yeah." When Axel comes to stop in front of the porch, June shimmies off his back and comes around to wrap me in a sweaty side-hug. "It was a reward because I read for fifty nights in a row. But Mommy..." She pulls away and stares deep into my eyes. "I had to get up at assembly in front of *everyone* to get it. It was a reward," she explains. "But it made my brain and my tummy feel gross. That was stressful for me."

"Ha!" Axel snags his niece around the hips and drops a noisy kiss on the top of her head. "Such a smart girl. Sometimes, even good things are hard work, huh, Bug? Doesn't make it a bad thing. It just means, if you really want it enough, you gotta work for it."

"Hush." Setting my wine glass on the porch beneath my chair so it won't be kicked over, I push up and take my daughter's hand in mine. "Show me your award, baby. Is that why you made cupcakes? To celebrate? I tasted one. It was delicious."

"It was?" Thrilled, she skips toward the back door now that our day is done. School is finished, and the shop is closed.

I'll have to wake in the early, delirious hours of tomorrow morning and start again, and before that, I'll need to facilitate a call between June and her father, all so he can check in and make sure I'm not on a date— with the fictional Eric, or anyone else. But I long ago learned the importance of compartmentalizing that crap for the sake of living right now.

"Uncle Axe and I worked really hard on them, Mommy." She swings the door wide so the handle bounces off the wall. "They were still a bit hot when I was doing the icing, so it messed up a little."

"But they were still so yummy." Smiling, I set Noah aside, and

Preston, and hell, even Axel, and instead, I take a seat at my kitchen counter and wait while June races to her school bag and dashes back to show off an award made on cardstock. "Fifty nights of reading, honey. I'm so proud of you."

She uses the handles on the drawers to climb onto the counter and sit in front of me. Then she turns the certificate my way to show it off. "Do you 'member when I couldn't even read at all? I didn't even know *and* or *if*."

"Of course." I lift my hands and wait patiently for her to pass the card to me. "This is so amazing, Juniper. Mommy is so freakin' proud of how much you've been practicing since last year." I peek across the kitchen and stop on the corkboard already filled to the brim with awards just like it. "Do you think we should pin it up? Or would you like to hold onto it for a little while longer?"

"You can pin it." She shoves to her feet when I stand and cross the room, then vibrates entirely too near the edge as I hurriedly pin. "On the side, Mommy. Don't cover up my kindness award!"

"Sit down, June." I watch her, even while I watch the placement of her certificate. "I don't want you to fall."

"Above that one," she ignores me. "On *top of*, Mommy. Not—"

"Sit down, honey." I pull her certificate away from the wall and hold it up as ransom. "Sit down, or get down. *Then* I'll pin this up."

Huffing the same way Axel does when he's cranky, she drops to her butt and exhales.

"Thank you."

While Axel wanders back through the door and pauses on the threshold, I follow June's instructions and find the exact right place to display her newest achievement.

"I'm so happy for you, baby." Turning back, I move quickly to the counter and sweep her up into my arms to press a kiss to her temple. "What do you want for dinner? Then Daddy would like to call you."

"*Uggggggggh*." She rolls her eyes into the back of her head. "Daddy makes me call too much."

Yes, honey. He does. Because that's how he controls us.

But if I say no, he makes life so much more difficult.

"It'll be fun," I tell her instead. "Besides, you got to go to the park with Uncle Axe today, huh? You even said yesterday that's what you wanted."

"I know." Starry-eyed, she gazes across at him. "It's like my wish came true." Then she grabs my face and smooshes my cheeks. "I liked Uncle Axe's friend, too. He was nice."

"Uncle Axe's f—"*Preston. Dammit.* "Okay." Too stupid to come up with something better, I lower her to her feet and tap her butt to get her moving across the kitchen. "I mean... Cool."

Axel is too pleased. Too self-righteous, as he swings her up into his arms.

"Shut it," I snap.

"What?" Laughing, he toe-tap dances his way deeper into my kitchen. "I didn't say anything."

"Don't use your face like that either." I make my way to the messy cupcake station and start scooping crumbs into my hand to be tossed into the trash. "I'm making dinner for everyone. Then Uncle Axe is going home, June Bug is calling Daddy, and Mommy is having a really long, really hot soak in the tub."

"Guys dig that," Axel taunts. "Want me to find out your reward's phone number?"

"No!" I snatch up a tea towel and whip it so fast, the end cracks in the air. "Jesus, Axel. Boundaries, man!"

"Mommy!" June throws her head back and cackles. "You're so silly."

"Mommy got super cranky at Uncle Axe today." At the counter, while she eats her dinner and talks into the screen of her tablet, June gives her father everything he doesn't need to know about my life.

What Axel and I argue about is never that serious, and it's not like I can expect a six-year-old to censor herself, but I sit on the couch in my living room and close my eyes.

"She whipped him with a towel, Daddy."

"She did?" He's too intrigued. Too interested. "She must've been really mad, huh? What was she so angry about?"

None of your business, asshole.

"It was joke angry," June recovers for us both. "She laughed, and he laughed even more." Silence hangs for a beat as she fills her mouth. "I got to go to the park today after school, 'cos you didn't pick me up when you said you would."

"When I..." His tone changes, the way I've heard it a million times during our relationship. "It's not my day, Junie. Daddy didn't say he would pick you up."

"Yes you did." She's young enough to still call people out without realizing the undertones to a conversation. "You told Mommy you wanted to hang out with me this afternoon, so she told me. And that's why you were supposed to pick me up from school."

"No." He's so calm. So measured. *Gag me.* "It's Wednesday, which means it's Mom's day. Did you get confused again?" He makes that good-natured chortle sound people do, except his is an act. He's gaslighting our daughter, and by extension, me, instead of taking responsibility for his bullshit behavior. "Mommy can be so forgetful sometimes, huh? She works so much, it's not surprising she sometimes messes these things up."

I work so much because raising a little girl doesn't come free, you lying sack of abusive shit.

"Don't you get mad that Mommy works so much, Junie? Does she ever even play with you?"

"Prick," I grumble into my glass of water. Water, because if I drink more wine, I'll wake up miserable when my alarm chirps tomorrow morning. "Prick," I repeat. "*Prick, prick, prick.*"

"*You* had to work today," June responds easily. "That's why you couldn't pick me up."

"Wha—"

"But Mommy plays with me all the time. We play cards almost every single day. And we practice flipping on the trampoline."

That's a lie—or at the very best, an extreme stretch of the truth. But she knows who he is, and what he does to her.

She doesn't have a label for it yet. But she has the feelings in her gut.

Gaslighting equals sick in her stomach.

"And Uncle Axe plays with me *heeeeaps*," she adds, almost too cheerfully. "He's like a kid, Daddy. He's so silly."

"Mm." The one topic Noah won't touch with a ten-foot pole. "Who took you to the park, Junie? Mommy had to work, right?"

*You know I did, you slimy shit. You canceled **knowing** I was in the middle of a job.*

"Uncle Axe took me to the park," she answers. "And his friend."

His friend.

Preston.

My heart stops in my throat and threatens to make me sick.

"And I saw *my* friend there too," She pushes on, oblivious to the heavy reality her words carry, if only Noah knew. "Charlie was a boy in my class last year, and he came to the park with his mom. So we played for a bit."

"Is his mom dating Uncle Axel?"

Inappropriate! I shove up and set my glass on the coffee table, but before I can charge in and end their call, June's laughter peals loud.

"What? No! Charlie's mom is married to the fighter, Daddy. The one who can never be beat."

Yeah, jerkoff. Talk shit about his wife so he can come beat your stupid ass for being disrespectful.

"Plus," June continues, whispering now. "I think there's a baby in her tummy. Charlie said at school that he thinks he's getting a new brother or sister. Isn't that exciting?"

"Sure." He's bored now. Talking of people who don't serve his needs holds no interest for my ex-husband.

"Wouldn't it be exciting if Mommy had a new baby in her tummy?"

"What?!" Noah's voice rises about seven thousand octaves, while on the couch, I sink into the cushions and cover my eyes. *Escape. Run away.* "Is Mommy thinking of having a baby in her tummy, June?"

Inappropriate.

"No." She giggles and fills her mouth with more of her dinner. "Mommy needs a husband to make a baby. And you and Mommy got a divorce, so..."

I have never, ever, in my entire life, mentioned the *D* word to my daughter. *Ever.* So the fact she knows it says a lot about Noah's inability to spare our daughter the burden of grownup issues.

"Well, you never know, June," he counters with a smile in his tone. "Mommy and Daddy are talking about dating again."

"*What?*" I throw my hands off my face and push up to stand. "Hey!" I charge out of the living room and into the kitchen. "Noah. Hi." I paste on a smile and snatch the tablet from the counter in front of our daughter.

Just seeing his face makes my stomach dip. Just looking into his eyes reminds me of the years I spent cowering under his wants and needs. Honestly, my first instinct is *still* to please this douchebag, but my brain is getting faster at remembering my self-imposed boundaries.

I walk the tablet out of the kitchen with just a single glance to June to let her know I'll be back in a second, then I charge up the stairs and lock myself in my bedroom.

Finally, I let it rip.

"Inappropriate! Wildly, horribly, *ridiculously* inappropriate to tell our six-year-old child such a blatant, emotionally manipulative lie."

"What?" He's never been one to take responsibility. For anything. Ever. And he doesn't bother himself with anyone else's mood when they think he's done something wrong. Case in point: the way he sits back in his recliner now, cool as a cucumber and brimming with satisfaction that he got me on the phone. "You seem wound up, Nicki. Is everything okay?"

"You told our daughter we were thinking of dating! She's six, Noah. To a child, that basically means we're getting back together."

"So?" He reaches somewhere off-camera, then comes back with a handful of cheese puffs to shove into his mouth. "How am I a bad guy for giving our daughter hope?"

"Because it's a lie!"

This entire conversation, my energy, my anger, every single word I speak, is a reward to the man who manipulates every situation to secure my attention. He got exactly what he was aiming for.

"We aren't getting together, Noah. We're divorced for a reason, and you telling June we might reconcile is horrible and cruel."

"It's only cruel if it's something she wants. And if it is, then have you considered that *your* refusal to reunify is the problem? We're here because of you, Nicki. Because of *your* selfishness and inability to cooperate or communicate."

I hate you. I hate you. I hate you!

I firm my lips and my voice. "I'm hanging up. I will not entertain this conversation, and every time you bring it up to our daughter, I will end your call and protect her from your poisonous words."

Pushing away from my bedroom wall and opening the door, I move into the hall and head downstairs. "And I'll have you know I've documented your lies."

"My lies?" he barks out. "What lies?"

"The fact you claim to have never asked to pick her up today. That Mommy must be forgetful and silly. That's a lie, Noah. It's manipulation. It's gaslighting. And it's denigration. All of which are against our court orders. These things have been documented and will be shared with my legal team."

I reach the bottom of the stairs and look deep into his eyes. Usually, I stare at his nose. Or the center of his forehead. It sends him insane, and it saves me the added trauma of seeing them when I'm trying to sleep at night. But for this, I make sure he's paying attention.

"Don't call me, Noah. I'll communicate with you about June if I need to, and I'll have her ready for her weekend with you. You'll collect her from school on Friday, and drop her off Monday, which means *we* do not need to talk about it."

"Nicki—"

"Enjoy the rest of your evening. If you need anything else, email."

"Nicki!"

I hit the big red button at the bottom of my screen, then I close the cover and press my back to the wall. Closing my eyes, I breathe in... something. Serenity? Patience? Forgiveness, maybe.

The device chirps again, demanding my attention. Raging against being set aside. But I shake my head and silence the call.

When it starts vibrating a second time, I switch it off and lift my shoulders in search of strength. And bravery. And hope that Noah won't win this battle of wills.

Finally, I move into the kitchen and fake a smile for my inquisitively watchful daughter.

"Did Daddy hang up?"

"Yep." I walk to my junk drawer and toss the tablet in so it bounces against birthday candles and random cookie cutters. Scissors. Chopsticks. With a fast sweep of my hand, I slam the drawer closed, then I turn back to my baby and fake a serene smile. "Daddy said goodnight, and that he loves you. He said he can't wait to see you this weekend."

Preston

AND AGAIN

Thursday passes in a blur of Juniper's sweet treats—purchased and collected by someone *not* me—and eye-bleeding hours as I sit at my new desk and spitball ways to infiltrate a mafia family's tech system.

Because that's my life, I guess. I used to steal cars, and now... well, I guess I'm stealing from the mafia.

Way better.

Thursday night, I eat dinner at Cole and Maya's, and spend hours playing cards in their living room, which keeps me out until close to nine in the evening—though that used to be the time I *started* my revelry. *Oh, how times have changed*—then I end up at my rickety kitchen table, where I have a fancy new Griffin laptop, and enough software to make a man like me jizz in his pants.

I was once a poor boy who couldn't afford to eat, and whatever tech I had came from salvaging parts and building my own. Now, I have Griffin logos everywhere in my home, and access to anything else I could ever think of needing.

In exchange for those pretty, new devices, my job is to infiltrate a well-protected, wealthy, and extremely cautious family's servers. Not just to fuck with their money, but to have the ability to control anything. *Everything*. And not let them know we're doing it.

Friday is spent inside the Checkmate office. Bishop brothers come and go, and every time they pass through, they make me wonder what they do to benefit the company.

I understand they're the name and finances behind the security firm. But what do they *do*? Because I'm so fucking sure it's the ballerina who holds everyone's balls in her cute little dance bag.

Theo Griffin himself drops by and carries with him a grudge I'm not sure we'll ever recover from. And soon after that, Jessica, Kane's wife, brings in those twin girls, and flitters around the office like a ditsy socialite intent on twirling her way through life; an image I could believe on appearances alone, if not for the fact I *know* she's a shark lawyer who wipes courtroom floors with her adversaries, and leads her thug husband around by the hairs in his nostrils.

Maybe that's her schtick... to have people think she's simple. So when she destroys a man and tears shreds from his face for daring to go toe to toe against her, it comes as that much more of a surprise.

A lot like Sophia, I suppose. A *type* the Bishop brothers are drawn to.

"I think you're making this too complicated." Sitting back at the boardroom table, surrounded by half a dozen mercenaries I probably could've gone my entire life not knowing, I meet Sophia's eyes only. *She's* my boss. She's the one I answer to on this. "You're asking for me to slide in remotely, when it would be so much easier to just... let their soldiers do the work for us."

"How?" Sophia is a fidgety soul, unable to sit still, unable to not chew on something every minute of every day. So she flicks the end of a pencil against the wooden tabletop with one hand, and with the other, reaches across to steal a sour gummy worm from the pile Jay stacks tall. "They're Mancino's soldiers for a reason, Danes. They're not stupid. So how do you suggest we use them?"

"Drop a USB stick on Mancino's property."

I bring my gaze around as Theo Griffin scoffs at the simplicity of my plan.

"Wherever he or his men go, we drop a stick," I press. "Load them up with malware, let the idiots pick one up and plug it in. Then we have control."

Unimpressed, Sophia purses her lips and glares around at every man at the table. "Any of you *ever* pick up a USB stick and plug it into a computer I gave you, I'll kill you with my bare fucking hands." Then she brings her gaze back to me. "That's basically guerilla warfare and lacks the subtlety I asked for, Danes. Do better."

"A party invitation?" I smile, because she's a tech goddesses who gets off on being sneaky and vicious, and I'm just a street kid who doesn't mind crashing through walls to gain access to somewhere I shouldn't be.

Maybe she's *asking* for quiet and subtle, but she brought me in knowing who I am and how I operate. So fuck it, I present her with *Preston Danes*.

"We find out who Mancino associates with: business or personal. We clone an email that would typically come for him, so it looks completely normal. A supply drop, or a party invitation. Hell, we copy his gas bill and send that over, intercepting the real one so he's none the wiser. He or his people click a link, and we slip in, easy as that. Then we have control."

"We don't need control," she counters savagely. "We need eyes."

"Having control doesn't mean we slap a fucking page on his screen that says he's a dead shit and we've compromised his server. Once we're in, we can see whatever he sees. We can create or delete his contacts. We can intercept anything incoming or outgoing. And we can collect whatever data you need for the cops and take him down. Having control also means you can clone his system and switch him over to the dupe. We'll have the real thing to hand to whoever you're looking to give it to." I lounge back in my seat and wait. "Tell me I'm wrong."

"You didn't..." She looks at Griffin. Then Jay. She casts an eye to a man I now know as Troy 'Romeo' Rosa, then she comes back and narrows them on me. "You didn't drop a USB stick or interact with Griffin on Monday. Yet you slid through his system."

"With sweat in my asscrack and a hell of a risk when I found out about the timer. *And*," I look to him, "he knew the moment I was in. I'd scaled his walls, Ace, but it was like jumping the fence at a major league baseball game. It can be done, but everyone sees you doing it, and a minute later, you got security laying you out and smashing your face into the grass. You want us to be in, but for him not to know? I suggest you try my way."

"USB drop or a party invitation?" Her nostrils flare with impatience. "That's the *best* you've got for me?"

"They're practical solutions. Just because they're not pretty or come with an obnoxious *fuck you* doesn't make them useless."

My back is to the glass wall that oversees the rest of the office, but when Romeo's eyes flicker over my shoulder, I follow his gaze and find Axel Feeney in the middle of the office, smiling and chatting with the boisterous secretary I learned on my first day is named Dolly.

Dolly lacks filters and social boundaries, and she doesn't much care about consent when touching another man's body. Though, as long as your last name isn't Bishop or Griffin, she tends to leave you be.

Mostly.

But she's got Axel blushing like a pre-pubescent twelve-year-old, and me, curious as fuck why the hell he's here.

Rotating back to Sophia, I push up from my chair and grab my laptop from the table. It's like a security blanket for me, going everywhere I go. "I'll be back." Turning away and pushing my chair in, I stroll to the boardroom door and swing it open fast enough that I draw Axel's eager attention.

Dolly strokes the man's chest, and murmurs something filthy that makes his ears red. But when our eyes meet, sending thoughts of Nicole passing through my mind, he seems to straighten a little.

"Axel?" I switch my laptop from one hand to the other as I approach the pair. "You good?"

"I wanna talk." He looks back to Dolly and pats her hand away before taking a step in my direction. "Alone."

My heart squeezes in my chest for reasons I can't entirely pinpoint. But after a glance to the boardroom, where half a dozen Checkmate staff watch us through the glass, I set my laptop on my desk and tilt my head toward the front end of the building. "We can walk."

At his nod, I head through the hall and into front reception, past Dolly's desk, then through the front door and into the afternoon warmth outside.

The sun is harsh, painful against my eyes after eight hours indoors, but I continue onto the sidewalk and slow my steps when Axel falls into pace on my right.

I dig my hands into my pockets to play with the earring I haven't set aside since I found it, and peering across at Axel, I lift a brow in question. "Are Nicole and Juniper okay?"

His jaw clenches so the muscles stand out in stark contrast when shadows from the trees fall across his face. "You haven't been around since Wednesday."

Curious, I puzzle at his words. "She doesn't want me around, Axel. Trying to force my company on them would be shitty."

"Did you ditch because she's a mom?" he demands. "Or busy? Or—"

"Someone's ex-wife?" I finish, because I know that's where he was going. "No. She's a mom, that's cool. That's her journey. She's busy, because she's got a kid to feed. She's someone's ex-wife; sounds to me like it's his loss."

I peer across and wait for his eyes. "I'm led to believe Scott was the issue in that marriage. And Nicole is..." I consider for a moment. "Insanely closed off to risking her time or attention again. What do you want me to do? Harass her until she calls the cops and has me escorted off her property?"

"No." Scowling, his brows pinch with dissatisfaction. "But there's a difference between harassment and showing interest."

"Dude," I shake my head, "she *knows* I'm interested. Pretty sure she knows where to find me, too."

"She's never gonna come looking," he bites out. "*Never*. Because she's busy and stressed and anxious and hella gun-shy when it comes to men. So that means you gotta—"

"Gotta what?" I hurry around to step in front of him. "Cut the shit and lay it out straight, Axe. You *want* me to pursue her? Are you in charge of her romantic life now?"

"She likes you." His words come out on an exhale that makes my throat tighten. "She's not gonna say it, and she's not gonna come searching for you. But she fuckin' likes you, Danes. And seeing as how I don't get the urge to smash your head against a brick wall every time I see you, I'd say we have a solid foundation for *something*."

"Something?" I question. "You want her to date?"

"I want her to breathe! I want her to think about her own happiness for a minute before she kills herself with stress. And I want to *not* see the worry that was in her eyes last night every time June mentioned going to her deadbeat dad's for the weekend."

This weekend? "She—"

"I've brought you up a few times since Wednesday, Danes, *always* when she was busy doing something else, and I swear to fuck, she brightened every time. She tried to pretend it was nothing, and she sure as shit acted cool about it all. But when I mentioned your name, she was just a little freer. It didn't last long, but for that second—"

"I'm just a guy." I shove my fingers through my hair and groan. "I like her too, Axel, but I'm just a man she met one time. How do you know I won't hurt her? How can I step up and tell this woman I won't fuck her around, when, honestly, I can't know if that's true?"

"So you intend to screw with her?"

"I don't know what I intend! I don't *date* women. I just... ya know."

At the words I don't say, his eyes turn a dangerously darker shade of gray.

"Maybe I could try," I concede. "But fuck, I'd feel like a dick if I accidentally hurt her. And she's got June, so it's not like we have a lot of room to—"

"I'm not shopping for a husband for my sister, Danes. And I'm not looking to adopt a stepdaddy for June."

"You're..." I narrow my eyes. "You're not?"

"No! I'm saying Nicole is home for the next three nights. Alone. June Bug is with her dad, Nick only has one cake to deliver tomorrow for a wedding, and I'm on shift the entire weekend. That's... it. That's three whole nights where she could, *maybe*, be receptive to a friend hanging out."

"You realize you're pimping your sister out right now, right?" I turn on my heels and head back toward Checkmate, lest the nerves swirling in my stomach get the better of me. "You're telling a guy you don't know that she'll be home alone."

"A guy I'll smear against the fucking concrete if I find out he's hurt her."

He slams his hand onto my shoulder and swings me back around until we're eye to eye. My blue, to his silver. "Call me crazy," he continues, "but I don't think you're gonna harm her. Not on purpose, anyway."

"No? And what makes you so sure?"

"Because you came out of your meeting as soon as you saw me inside Checkmate. Because you asked about Nick *and* Bug, not because you wanted to slide into my good books, but because you give a shit. And because you like her, but you've stayed away from the shop since Wednesday, though I know for a damn fact your ass has eaten a metric ton of Juniper's cakes in the last two days. You're respecting her space. Though, it's funny... you weren't doing that before you realized she was damaged goods."

"Hey!" I snap. "Who the fuck said she's damaged goods? Because I know I didn't."

His lips peel into a sly grin. "See? You give a shit, Danes. So I'm gonna give you her number. You're gonna maybe get a hunger for something glazed in the next hour or so, and then you're gonna head over to the shop and save my sister from working herself to death."

"So... I just do as I'm told?" My stomach jumps at the thought of being used. But hell, I'm not all that mad about it. "And you're telling me to go bang your sister?"

His eyes narrow to dangerous slits. "I'm telling you to drop by Juniper's in the next hour," he grits out. "And force Nicki out of her spiraling cycle of lonely independence while she counts down the seconds until her daughter comes home again. She knows June Bug is abused in that home, and she knows there's nothing she can do about it. So do you think she should spend the next seventy-two hours obsessing over something she can't change? Or smiling because the new dumbass in town asked her out?"

"Sounds like the perfect aphrodisiac," I roll my eyes. "*I know you're thinking about your child being with your former abuser right now. But how about we fuck the weekend away and mess up the sheets as many times as we possibly can? Come on, it'll be fun.*"

He starts past me, slamming his shoulder against mine and knocking the air from my lungs. "If you can't take her mind off her troubles, then you're not nearly as slick as you think you are." Then he spins and walks backwards. "And since you're that much of a soft cock, don't worry about it. There're a hundred other single dudes in this town who'll happily take her out."

"Wait..." Panic bubbles in my blood as I dash to keep up. "Who else is asking her out?"

He laughs. But he turns and starts toward his truck parked out front of my office. "Every unmarried man in a hundred-mile radius." He searches his pockets for car keys, then pulls them out to beep the locks open. "I don't know if you've noticed, Danes, but she's beautiful, smart, and hardworking. She's everything a lot of men are looking for, so forget it." He stops by his car door and opens it wide.

It doesn't squeak the way mine does.

"She likes you, and you like her. That's the fuckin' truth, and the only reason I came down here today. But you're a pussy, and I'm not here to hold your hand through a situation I'm already uncomfortable with."

"And by *situation*," I stop in front of his truck and press my fists to his hood, "you mean organizing your sister's sex life?"

"*Date*," he growls. "Not sex. She felt safe with you, Preston." His eyes soften on those words—surprising us both, I think. "I specifically asked her if she felt unsafe."

My heart races faster in my chest. Faster. "Wh-what did she say?"

"That she was never afraid. And maybe that doesn't mean much to you, since you don't really know her. But for someone like her, who literally fucking twitches whenever *anyone* who isn't me or June touches her..." he shakes his head. "It means a lot. It means there's something there."

His words are like physical blows. One, then another. And another.

"I've played a bigger role in co-parenting June than Noah ever did, which means I'm in their lives every single day, Danes. I see my sister *every, single, day*. She's been asked out a million times since her divorce, and she's had a million more opportunities for a one-night stand after a wedding."

"Jesus, Axel." Strangely, I bring a hand to my chest, and frown when his words sting. "That doesn't make me feel good to know."

"It hurts because you care." Cruelly, he digs his blade in. "Whatever becomes of all this, whatever she says or does, and whatever role you may someday, a *loooooong* time from now, play in June's life, you care. And Nick cares. But if you're waiting for her to come to you in lingerie and profess her fucking crush, it's never gonna happen."

Sliding into his truck and slamming the door shut, he starts the engine and winds the window down so I can still hear him. "She twitches when men touch her, Danes. That physical contact terrifies her."

Did she show me that fear? I think to myself. *That night at the wedding, or during our time in my room... No. Her desire and her receptiveness to everything I did to her body...*

"She doesn't do that for me."

He flashes a wide smile and pushes his truck into reverse. "Exactly, stupid."

Backing away from the curb and coming to idle in the street, he rests his elbow on the frame of his door and reaches the other way to snag a ballcap from the passenger seat. Settling it on his head and shadowing his eyes, he tips his chin. "I'm heading on-shift now, and June Bug is readying for a miserable three days with her sperm donor. What are you gonna do about Nick's weekend?"

He doesn't wait for my answer; though, even if he did, I'm not sure a lot of traffic would collect behind him.

When his truck roars away from Checkmate, leaving me standing alone in the warm afternoon sun, I come to a decision faster than it takes me to choose what I'll eat for dinner.

Which is scary, considering what's at stake.

Spinning on my heels and charging back into my office, I head to my desk and grab my Griffin laptop.

"Preston?" Soph steps out of the boardroom and leans against the wall, watching me with folded arms. "Your workday doesn't end till five."

"Correction: it ends right now."

I snatch the power cord from the wall, and smirk when my carelessness makes Sophia snarl. "My contract is to infiltrate Mancino's systems. It doesn't matter where I do the work, and I know for a fact you're not ready to push in yet, anyway. So I'd say I can take off an hour early today, and make up for it at home over the weekend." I look to Jay, who comes through the doorway next. "I'm going home."

"No, you're going to Juniper's Bakery." He fists a handful of gummies and tosses them into his mouth. "Don't act like Soph doesn't have ears on every block of this town." He lowers his head and grins. "I don't know if I'm disgusted by Feeney's *cojones*, or proud. But since I don't have a sister, I'm leaning toward the second. He's on a mission to get that woman laid."

I tuck my laptop under one arm, and ball the cord in my fist on the same side. Then I extend my free hand and point it straight between his eyes. "Don't talk about her sex life. Ever." Then I look to Sophia and raise a brow. "It's illegal to listen to private conversations without consent or a court order."

"What are you gonna do?" she laughs. "Tell the cops? Oh, I know." She accepts a silently offered gummy worm and tosses it into her mouth. "Maybe you can call Detective Noah Scott and report it to him. You would have to tell him the content of your conversation, though, so..."

"Fuck that asshole."

I don't even know him. Never met him before in my life. But I see him in my mind, and I want to rearrange his face until Nicole could never again pick him out of a crowd.

But I shove my chair back under my desk instead and take keys from the top drawer. "What else do you know about him?"

Smug now that she's caught my interest, she shrugs. "I know his pertinents. His date of birth and which hospital he was born in. I know his medical and criminal history, and I have a copy of both his marriage certificate, and the one that has *divorced* stamped on top. I know where he lives, and how long he's lived there. That he fucks women most nights of the week, and that he did so even while he was still married to Nicole. I know he's got two on the hook right now, each clueless to the other and oblivious to the ex-wife's existence at all." She reaches around and takes her cell from her back pocket. "You think I don't know everything about everyone in this town, Danes?"

"But he doesn't live in this town." Though I'll be damned if I'm not impressed. "And if he's a cop, he could have your ass if he finds out."

"He *is* a cop," she presses, like she doesn't appreciate being doubted. "Fact. But even if he finds out, he's gotta prove it. And I'm saying right now—" She wanders away from the wall and winks when the one-legged bionic guy steps into the room. "I can't say cops bother me all that much. The good ones are already my pals, and the shitty ones deserve a cattle prod up their assholes."

She makes her way to an unmanned desk, but flicks her wrist in my direction. "Enjoy your weekend of fornication. Don't break her heart. Come back to work Monday with something better than '*let's drop a USB stick in Mancino's yard and hope he picks it up*'."

I roll my eyes and take another step toward the exit. "Don't act like it's a bad plan just because you didn't think of it first. You like the flash and glamor wherever you go, Ace, but in reality, we just have to get the job done."

"Kinda like that time you danced on a thug's lap in a glittery thong," Jay grumbles. "Then climbed his back and slit his throat open." He glances to me and forces a tense smile. "Coulda dealt with that *whole* issue with less glitter, I reckon."

I peer to Sophia and purse my lips. "My point exactly. I'm out." I move away from my desk and carry my shit toward the hall. "Don't call me unless it's important."

"I'll call you whenever the fuck I wanna call you," she shouts at my back. "I own you now, Danes. It's a universally known fact."

"Uh-huh." I head toward reception but lift my hand in a wave that vibes more like flipping my boss the bird. "See ya."

I catch Dolly's playful grin as I pass through, though I keep going. "Have a good weekend."

"Mmhm. You keep pissing that puny ballerina off, Mr. Danes, and you and I will get along just fine."

I don't know her beef with Soph, and I have no clue how deep it runs or why the busty receptionist still lives, but it brings a smile to my face as I head outside and make a beeline for my truck.

I have three nights—seventy-two hours—to whisk Nicole away and keep her mind off where her baby will spend her time. And if I can manage it, I'll keep her from working herself to death too.

Sliding into my truck and setting my things on the passenger side of the old bench seat, I close my door and take satisfaction in the deep groan of the hinges. Then starting the engine and checking the street behind me, I back out and roll to a stop as I move the gear into drive.

I'm gonna head home first. Take a shower, and eat something that contains a modicum of protein. Because maybe Juniper's cakes are deliciously sinful, but they're made specifically to leave a man weak.

I have an hour before Nicole clocks out and leaves her store. Which means I have fifty-nine minutes to get myself organized and stroll through her door to stop her escape.

Game on.

Nicole

GAME OFF!

I shove through the glass front door of Juniper's and hear the tinkle of the bells above, but they don't bring me nearly as much pleasure as they do most other days of the week.

School is out, and June is with her dad. I know this because I just watched him pick her up.

Noah's weekends are literally the only hours I ever get to myself, but knowing where my baby girl is, and with whom, makes it damn near impossible to switch off and appreciate the time I have.

Instead, I obsess over the damage Noah callously inflicts on a little girl in retribution for her mother's actions. I fear for the despair I'll need to mend on Monday afternoon when I see her again. I worry over my sweet baby's innocence, and her simple, day-to-day well-being: is she hungry? Is she sad? Is she huddled in the corner of her part-time bedroom, counting down the seconds until she can come home again?

Every time she's gone, I desperately try to convince myself to rest. Stressing about things won't change the outcome, and worrying over whatever is happening in that home helps no one. But saying and doing are two entirely different things, and up to this point in my life, I've yet to master the art of *not* anxiously overanalyzing the uncontrollable.

"Hey, Feen." Hannah rhythmically sweeps behind the counter and sways her ass to the soft melody of Taylor Swift's newest single. "You got that cake to the Densons?"

"Yup. All delivered, signed, and paid for."

I take out my planner and flip it open to today's date to make sure I've done everything I need to do leading into the weekend. "I'll bake three dozen more fairy cakes for tomorrow morning," I recite for us both, "I've finished the wedding cake for the Truemans. Also, I had a last-minute birthday cake order come in."

"And god forbid you take a little time off." She dances and sweeps, her gentle movements a stark contrast to her biting remark. "Did you see June Bug before she left?"

I shrug my shoulders and hunch over my book to tick each item off my list. "From afar. If I got too close and Noah saw, he'd have insisted I join them."

She sticks a finger in her mouth. "Gag."

"And when I inevitably told him no," I continue, "he'd accuse me of interfering with his time by being anywhere near the school."

"His mood swings and manipulations are just so..." She hugs the broom the way a woman might hug a bouquet of flowers. "Wholesome, dontcha think?"

"Yup."

She's being facetious. As am I. Neither of us need to point it out.

"So she's gone, and I won't hear from them again until Monday. Oh, also," looking up, I wait for her eyes, "I was considering this new line of pastries for the shop. We could start out slow and get a consensus from customers to see if they like them, then we can decide whether to make them permanent or dismiss the idea."

"Sure." She sets her broom aside and switches it out for a dustpan. "Because you have so much free time on your hands." Lowering into a crouch, she scoops the mess off the floor and sniggers. "This is your toxic trait, by the way."

Scowling, I drop my gaze to my planner and focus there. Where I can be productive and distracted. "You're out of line and exceptionally disrespectful."

"Which are *my* toxic traits," she giggles. "Except, I quite like them. Chill, Feeney. We have enough stock to get us through the weekend, since you enjoy working yourself to the bone on Noah's Fridays. Why don't you save the fairy cakes till Monday, and if you're extra good and I think you've deserved it, we'll discuss the new pastry next week once Bug is home and you're feeling less self-destructive?"

Giving up on my act of working, I set my pen aside with a *clank* on the counter and glance across to meet Hannah's playful expression. "You seem to forget which of us is the boss, and which is the spoiled brat who chose to work in a bakery instead of finish high school because," I lift my hands and do the finger quotes, "*No one tells me what to do.*"

"First of all," pushing up straight, she dumps the contents of the pan into the trash, then she sets her hands on her hips. "You're digging up ancient history, and I don't appreciate it. That's petty and embarrassing, and you're better than that. Second, that cutie is here."

"What?"

The front door jingles open, and the sound of the bell sends my heart surging into my throat. But it's not until Preston's icy blue stare beats relentlessly against mine that my stomach threatens to revolt.

"Oh, hey there, Preston!" Hannah quick-steps to the sink nestled in the corner and washes her hands with soap and warm water. Drying them off and slipping on a pair of gloves, she makes her way to the display cabinet and peruses her options for a moment. "I know you enjoyed the rainbow cake the other day, but..." Deciding, she snatches out a cupcake that comes with a caramel glaze and melted pieces of chocolate in the center.

Grabbing a paper bag and setting it inside, she flips the parcel to close the ends, then she places it on the counter and smirks. "On the house," she adds too cheerfully. "Because it's Friday, my boss is in an unusually happy mood, and she just allocated me a free cake fund I get to spend weekly."

Curiously, reluctantly, he peels his eyes away from mine and peers toward Hannah. "Huh?"

"Feeney was just saying how she's thrilled to have the weekend to herself," she continues easily, "and how she bought a couple of steaks from the store to grill up. Axel was supposed to eat the other one, but now he's working."

Resting her arms on the display cabinet, she pauses for a beat and sighs dreamily for her one true love. "He works almost as much as she does. But anyway," she shakes off the thought of my little brother and forges on with her devious plan. "Two steaks, one grill, one lonely woman."

"Hannah!"

"Nicole doesn't *need* company, of course. But she was just saying it's been a hot minute since she last saw you. So if she happened to run into you this afternoon, she might invite you over for steak."

Preston's intense eyes whip back my way.

Nerves swirl in my stomach. I don't have steak, and even if I did, I have no clue how to cook the damn things without turning them to leather. "Hannah, you need to sto—"

"So what do you think, handsome?" She charges around the L-shaped counter and stops beside me. "You wanna hang out for dinner?"

"With you?" His eyes flicker to her. Then back to me. "With—"

"With the boss lady," she laughs. "I have a date with my television tonight, and who knows, maybe I'll text Axe and tempt him into talking to me."

"Talking?" Coming to his senses, albeit slowly, Preston meets my assistant's eyes with a playfulness weaving into his expression. "He doesn't even talk to you?"

"Not privately." She wrinkles her nose. "And definitely not in the middle of the night, even though we *both* know he's on shift and wide awake." She rolls her eyes and mimics my quoting fingers. "It would be disrespectful to Nicki, and to myself, because he's my boss' brother and much too old for me." She drops her hands. "Which is not true, by the way. He's, like, two years older. At best."

Preston's smiling stare jumps back to me. "She's crushing on your bro?"

I snap my diary closed and slide it back into my purse. "Everyone has a crush on my brother. He's handsome, charming, and by all of society's standards, his career choice makes him a hero."

Dragging my bag off the counter and looping my arms through the straps, I force myself to smile for Preston. "Enjoy your cake. And your weekend. Hannah," I give her a half-hearted wave. She deserves far less after her *two-steaks-one-woman* bullshit. "You can lock up. I'll be here when you arrive in the morning."

"Bah humbug, Nicole Scott!" she shouts as I walk, so her voice echoes all the way to the other end of the building. "I said, bah. Hum. Bug! Go," she hisses, not for me. "And tighten your shirt, man. If you screw this up, she's gonna close up faster than that chain pizza place that tried to open shop in town last year."

"Oh god." I close my eyes and groan at the state of... well, my life.

My assistant is insane, my brother lacks boundaries, and my vagina... is tempted by a second round with Preston Danes.

If only I could cook steak.

Opening my eyes again, I charge toward the back door, knowing my car is out front, but having no desire to turn around and walk past Preston. "I'm going home, Hannah. Stop sexually harassing my customers."

"So *you* sexually harass them!" She stops in the doorway between the front of the store and the back, and when I peer her way, I breathe a little easier to find Preston *not* following me.

Tight shirt or otherwise.

"Stop being such a prude, Feeney! It's unattractive."

"Stop being so dramatic, Hannah!" I shove the back door open and squint at the harsh afternoon sun blaring in. "It's a fireable offense."

Stepping through the doorway and double-checking I have my car keys, I slam it shut again and listen as the lock clicks home and secures the shop from anyone who thinks they can wander in freely.

Funny, it was a lock installed only *after* Noah began behaving like it was his God-given right to come and go whenever he pleased.

Moving into the alleyway out back, and then circling around the block, I allow my heart to slow with each step I take.

Thanks to my late afternoon cake delivery, I couldn't park directly in front of the store when I got back. That means I won't have to step in front of the glass wall and see Preston again. It means I won't be harassed by Hannah, or badgered by my very own brain, because there's a very real part of me that wishes I could be... well, less of a prude.

Juggling my keys and selecting the one I need, I approach my car with both eyes discreetly on Juniper's front door. *Don't come out here*, I silently plead. *Don't come out here.*

I slip the key into my driver's side door, frowning when I don't hear the telltale snick of locks. But I grab the handle and pull it wide anyway.

Maybe I didn't lock up when I got out earlier.

After reaching through and tossing my bag into the back, I lower into my seat with an undignified huff and twist to grab my seatbelt. But I let out a loud, ear-splitting scream when I find a man where there should be empty space.

"Fffff!" I swing out with a wild hand—and smack Preston's arm.

My brain clicks over quickly, promising that I probably won't die from my intruder. But while fear washes away, my temper holds on for the ride.

"Dammit, Preston!" I slap his chest again, only to let out a dangerous growl when he catches my hand and chuckles. "What the hell is wrong with you?"

"You were gonna shout *fuck*." Entirely amused, he holds my wrist when I try for a third whack. "Good-girl Nicole Feeney has big-girl words hidden in her temper."

"My name is Nicole *Scott*." I yank my arm free of his hold and consider stabbing him with the sharp ends of my keys. "How the hell did you get in my car?"

Sliding a slow, gentle hand across his arm as though to soothe the ache I created, he continues to grin when my eyes naturally drop to the movement. "I opened the door, of course."

"And you're gonna tell me I left my car unlocked," I snarl. "Right?"

"No." He turns in his seat so one leg comes up to rest against the center console. "I helped myself."

"Helped yourself..." My eyes narrow to dangerous slits. "To my locked car?"

"Yes." He flashes a wicked smirk and drags his bottom lip between his teeth. "Your car is old as fuck, Feeney. I'm surprised no one has stolen it yet."

I bark out a ridiculous laugh and stab the correct key into the ignition barrel. "Safest car in this state and the next. No one wants my bucket of crap. Now, if you could," I wave my hand toward the door, "get the hell out."

"Mmm, I'd rather not." His eyes are too bright. Too playful, considering the midlife crisis I experience every time we're within touching distance. "I seem to recall a dinner invitation."

"Yeah." I tilt my chin toward the store. "From Hannah. She's being loyal, because I saw you first. But go ahead, you have my blessing. Tell her she can pursue you now."

Unbothered, he snickers under his breath. "She's more interested in fucking your brother. Which is a fun coincidence, since I have similar feelings about a different Fee—"

"My name is Nicole *Scott*!" I grab my seatbelt and swing it across my torso until steel meets the catch down by my hip. "I don't know what you think you heard, Preston. But you have no right to—"

"I heard you married someone with the name Scott," he cuts in casually. "But you're divorced now. I also heard you're dynamite in bed. Oh wait." He postures when I look his way. "I got that from firsthand experience."

"And now you know. So leave." I lean across—*Big mistake. Massive mistake!*—and shove his door open.

Damn him and the aftershave that fills my lungs. Damn his damp hair, and his soulful eyes that peer down into mine. Damn Preston Danes to hell and back, because I want him almost as much as I want to punch him in the face.

"Please go away." Quieting my temper, I sit tall again and press my hands to my lap. They shake, and I hate that they show my weaknesses so obviously. "I have somewhere to be, and you're in my car uninvited, being inappropriate, and verging on violent."

"Oh please," he scoffs. "You know I'm not gonna hurt you—unless you count smacking your ass or biting your clit, right when you're about to come on my face."

My breath comes out on a staccato that almost leaves me dizzy.

"I understand you have a history, Feeney."

"Don't call me Fee—"

"I get that you've had a shit time with men. But I'm not your ex, so I shouldn't be tarred with the same brush you bought to flog him with."

"Sure. So I just... blindly trust you?" I swallow down the nerves in my throat before they back up and choke me. "Men are perfectly trustworthy, so I should just... write the last one off as an anomaly?"

"No," he counters seriously. "There are a lot of really fucking shitty guys out here. I'll be the first to tell you that. Which means I'm glad you've got your shields up. But you gotta open the door sometimes. Just a little. Give me room to get my foot in there, so I have a chance to at least teach you that not all dudes fucking suck."

"Oh!" I turn back to stare at the shopfronts in front of my car. "The *not all men* speech. I haven't heard this one before. Go on." I twist back and meet his eyes. "I'm riveted."

"You're bitter and mean," he teases. "But you were the same way on the night of Cole's wedding. And still…" He looks down at his lap to show off what I'm pretty frickin' certain is a banana in his boxer shorts. *You know that's his cock, Nicole.* "I enjoyed our time together."

"You're despicable! And unwelcome."

"I'm interested," he argues easily. "And so are you."

"I'm not."

"You're a liar." Bravely… or perhaps stupidly, he closes the space between us and presses his lips to the warm skin behind my ear.

His teeth weave magic with my senses, and his tongue follows to send tingles sprinting along my spine.

"Your breath is choppy, Nicole. Your nipples are peaked. Your tongue won't leave your lips alone, and your pussy…" He pauses, like he somehow knows it'll slowly send me insane. "Is wet."

"You're rude and presumptuous." So why, *why* are my thighs slick with want? "I can't do this, Preston. I won't."

"Because you're busy?" He nibbles on the shell of my ear, and chips away at the armor I cling to so desperately. "Or because you're scared to admit you want me too?"

"I—"

"And remember," he cups my jaw, forcing me around until our lips feather close. "We already fucked once, which means I already know you want me. The worst is over. You already let your guard down… and guess what?" He slides his tongue out to seduce my bottom lip. "I didn't hurt you. In fact, I'm pretty sure I gave you the best orgasm you've ever had. Then *you're* the one who ran out and left me feeling rejected."

"You didn't…" I can't catch my breath. Or collect my thoughts. "You didn't feel rejected."

"Because I'm a guy, and guys aren't allowed to have feelings or insecurities?" He drags my lip between his teeth and lowers his hand so the tips of his fingers trail along my collarbone. "I was pretty fuckin' bummed when I woke on Sunday."

"Super bummed." *Stay strong. Stay firm.* "So bummed, you haven't come back to my store since you found out I'm a mom."

He brushes his knuckles across my peaked nipples, and chuckles at my frantic inhalation of air. "I was being respectful. There's a kid involved now, and I'm not here to freak you out or make you think I'm a threat. Had I kept coming into your store, you might've thought I was a fucking creep."

"But breaking into my car is acceptable?" *Who the hell am I kidding? He's about three seconds from getting exactly what he wants.* "Preston, I—"

"Dinner?" He bites my jaw, and groans when an involuntary sound rolls along my throat. "Steak?"

"I don't actually have any," I whimper. "Hannah was playing with you."

"So we'll go buy some." He sets his hand in my lap, which only draws my attention down to the pulse throbbing wildly between my legs. "I can cook it," he continues with a deliciously grizzled voice. "When was the last time someone else cooked you a meal?"

"Tuesday." I close my eyes and simply... feel. "When I ordered pizza."

He coughs out a fast laugh and slides his palm closer to my core. "Let me cook you steak tonight. Then I wanna fuck you till you're sore."

He bites my neck and presses his knuckles to my clit, so I jump from the electricity pulsing through my veins.

"My place or yours," he grits out, holding onto his hunger with a tight grip. "If you choose yours and you don't want me to sleep in your bed, that's fine. I can leave."

"You want a booty call," I breathe. Barely. "Sex, then you're done."

"No." He pushes my hair off my shoulder and slides seductive fingertips along my collarbone. "I want you to be comfortable. I want you to not regret the time you spend with me. So if you just wanna fuck and then have me leave, that's what we'll do. But don't forget, I'm offering dinner first."

He turns his hand between my legs and grinds the heel of his palm across my pulsing center. "Home-cooked. I'm offering all night. I'm offering whatever the fuck you want, because I swear to god," he groans, latching onto my neck with a violence that makes the blood in my veins turn to lava. "I haven't gotten you out of my head since the wedding. Do you have any clue how much it sucked to not wake up to you? Or to find out you're a fucking ghost, since, according to Maya, there were no guests named Nicki? Or to find out on Wednesday where you work, but be forced to stay away so I don't scare you or Juniper?"

"Don't say her name." I shake my head and pull away to give myself space to align my thoughts. "Don't—" *You don't get a claim to her. You don't get to be another man who could hurt her.* "Don't."

"Okay." He pulls his hand from between my legs and instead, slides it up my thigh and beneath my shirt to caress my stomach.

I work in a bakery. I'm a mom. I'm not a washboard-abbed, flat-stomached supermodel like those women at last weekend's wedding.

"Dinner?" he asks softly. "Just one night. I'm begging you."

"One night, and you'll leave me alone?" I'm folding. Folding. Flopping to the floor like a stack of wet playing cards.

"If you want me to." He wraps his large palm around my ribs and makes me feel small. Delicate. Sexy. "I won't have had enough," he peppers a kiss to my neck. Then my shoulder. My chest. "I could have you every single night for a year, and I'm not sure I'd be done. But if you want just one night and then me out of your life..."

"You'll go?"

He chokes out a strained laugh. "I'll go... but I'll get fat buying cakes from your shop, in the world's least threatening way. And maybe in a month or two, you'll accept another *one night*. Then another a month after that. Eventually," he bites down on my shoulder and draws a desperate whimper from deep in my chest. "You might think enough of me to ask me for a weekend."

Pulling back, he shows me bright blue eyes, darkened with want. "Guys wanna be asked out sometimes too, Feeney. We have feelings."

I roll my eyes and pull away from him, then setting my head against the rest, I take a moment to breathe. To think through my options and pray I don't choose wrong.

I can luxuriate in a night of good sex with a guy who has already proven he's... *reasonably* string-free.

Or I can go home and have time to myself.

I could hide away and try to call June, knowing Noah won't accept the c—

"You're overthinking." Preston's strong fingers pinch my chin and drag me around until our eyes meet and I find myself swimming in ocean-blue perfection. "You overthink every situation," he murmurs. "Isn't it exhausting?"

"I have to." Turning away again, I force his hand to drop away and give me space. "I have so much to consider, and if I mess things up—"

"You're off work." He rolls his bottom lip between his fingers; a thinking pose, I guess. And his next choice, after I refuse to let him hold me. "Your daughter is away for the weekend. Your brother is working. Your life is..." He stops and grins. "Free and clear. You have a window to play with, Nicole. So play with the fuckin' thing and quit overanalyzing."

"You oversimplify things," I growl. "I still need to bake for the shop tomorrow. I have a daughter who might try to call. I have a uterus, but I refuse to have more babies. And dammit, Preston, sex leads to those, even if you don't mean for it to."

For the first time, perhaps ever, I've shocked the man who has a comeback for everything.

"Holy shit, Feeney." He rubs a hand across his face and laughs. "You go deep, huh? It's casual sex and a steak dinner, not a marriage proposal. I have rubbers in my wallet, and your hypersensitivity about this risk implies you're on the pill."

"Well...yes."

"That's double protection. But if we get slammed with world-changing news after that, there are other options available."

"Sure," I bite out. "At the expense of my body and my hormones. Not to mention my mental well-being."

He drops his hands and turns in his seat. "So you're never gonna have sex again?" His voice is too loud. "Your pussy is far too sweet for you to stop, Feeney. You're still young. Don't quit on me yet."

"You're crude." I fold my arms and look out my side window. "Always so forward and rude."

"And yet," he leans into my space and brushes the tips of his fingers across my still-peaked nipples. "You want me. My place or yours?"

I'm a glutton for punishment. Or maybe I'm finally giving myself a moment to be a twenty-something-year-old woman with needs that haven't been met in years... except for last weekend.

"Mine. It's safe," I explain. "I know where everything is, and you know to take your ass home after we're done."

"Fine." He drops a noisy kiss on my cheek and turns to his door. Pushing it open so the hinges complain, he steps out of my car, but rests his hand on the roof and leans back in to catch my eyes. "I know where you live. I'll buy steak, you go home. You get a ten-minute head start before I arrive. If the front door is still unlocked when I get there, we both agree you want this night as much as I do."

"Yep."

A million thoughts sprint through my mind, but I straighten my torso in front of my steering wheel and ignore Hannah's face pressed to the shop window a few doors up.

Twisting the key in my ignition barrel, I have every intention to race home, speed-shower, and contemplate running away. But my engine only rolls... and rolls... and tries so very hard to start.

Frowning, I turn the key back toward me and take it from the barrel, then I insert it again and try a second time.

My poor piece of shit car only makes the *rrr-rrr* sound.

"Uh oh." Not at all upset like I am, Preston's goofy grin is enough to set my temper alight. "Sounds to me like you've got car troubles, Ms. Feeney."

"*Scott*," I snarl. Then I yank the key from the ignition, shove out of my car, stalk onto the sidewalk, and steam toward my store. "Hannah!"

"Yup?" She pops away from the window with flaming cheeks and eyes dilated, like she was watching something she kind of likes, and stops in the doorway, trembling with giddy happiness. "You okay?"

"My car's not starting." I throw my keys and watch them hit the floor and skid to a stop a foot from her shoes. "Keep these here, I'll ask Axel to help me tomorrow."

Then I spin away and let the door close at my back.

"Drive me home." Demanding, unkind, I charge toward Preston's truck and wait by the passenger door for him to unlock it.

I have to be mean. I *have* to be bossy. Because if I stop and allow myself to think, I might start obsessing about my unreliable car and how close I am to a mental breakdown.

"Please," I add, when he only stands by his hood and watches me. "I'll take care of my car tomorrow."

"Well..." Considering for a moment, he shrugs and makes his way to the driver's side door. "Alrighty. Guess we're going grocery shopping together."

"Absolutely not."

When his locks disengage and he opens his door, I remember my purse in my car, and dash that way to save it. Though the chances of someone stealing in this town—unless your name is Cole Miller or Preston Danes —is slim to not at all.

Slamming my door shut again and jogging back to Preston's truck, I ignore his hungry stare. I ignore the lust in his eyes, and the way he flexes his hands around his steering wheel, like that somehow relieves the tension bubbling in his blood.

Climbing into the passenger side, I twist and toss my purse onto the backseat. Then I turn the other way and grab my seatbelt.

Anything so I don't have to meet his eyes.

"We're not going grocery shopping." I snap the belt into the catch and cross my legs, because I guess I'm feeling closed off and irritable. "That's unnecessary. I have food at my home."

"Plus, grocery shopping with your one-night stand is just too... domesticated, right?"

"Way too domesticated. Let's go."

A pair of sunglasses hang from the visor, and when I catch sight of Hannah's delighted face pressed once more to my shop window, I snatch them down and push them onto my face. Then I hope for that feeling I was experiencing in my car to return.

The one where my pulse was throbbing, and my blood was too warm for comfort. The one where Preston's hands and lips were on my skin, and my brain stopped working for just a damn minute.

"Please." Vulnerable when the truck remains in place and the engine, off, I turn to Preston and show him my nerves. "Please, let's go before I chicken out."

"Okay." Serious now, he slips his key into the ignition and starts the engine so it purrs in a way mine never has, then pushing the stick into reverse and resting his arm across the back of my seat, he pulls away from the curb and into the street.

"But if you change your mind," idling for a moment as he straightens the wheel and slides the gear into first, he looks across and gently tugs the glasses from my face to reveal my terrified eyes. "If you don't want to do something, you just say so, okay? This is no pressure. No guilt. No bull-shit manipulation. I don't ever want to have sex with someone who isn't as keen as I am."

Dropping the sunglasses back in place and winking, he turns straight in his seat and releases the clutch. "'No' is a whole sentence, Feeney. And I have two ears to listen with." Slowly, he starts the truck forward so we're rolling along the street and heading toward my home. "You want takeout or something while we're out?"

"No." I drag my lip between my teeth and bite to pull my focus away from what the hell I'm doing. "I'm not hungry yet. Plus, I already said I have food at home. We'll make something."

"So dinner still stands." Chuckling, he turns at the end of the block and continues on. "You're doing great, Nicole. I feel super welcome."

"How do you know where I live, anyway?" I study each street sign we pass, and scowl as Preston confidently navigates neighborhoods in a town he's lived in for a week. "Stalking?"

He snorts. "I work for Checkmate, babe. I know where everyone lives."

Preston

EASY DOES IT

S he's gonna make herself sick one of these days. Nervous and scared. Overthinking and obsessively analyzing. I feel her nerves in the air, her tension and worry making my own heart race faster.

But the fact she still wants me to come with her, that she's still here and saying yes, means so much more than a casual *'sure, we can fuck'* spoken by any other woman.

She's terrified. But trusting. And hell, she's taking me to her home. Her safe space.

Even if she's chewing her thumbnail and radiating waves of anxious energy through the cab of my truck.

Pulling into her driveway, I slow to a stop and take the shift out of gear, then yanking on the brake and cutting the engine, I look to her as the music cuts away and silence beats down on us like a physical wave.

She doesn't look at me. Doesn't smile. Doesn't make small talk. She just mutilates her fingernail and bounces her knee.

"Hey?" When her face edges toward pale and her thumb threatens to bleed, I reach across and wrap my palm around her wrist. Pulling her hand away and waiting for her eyes to come to me, I test a gentle smile. "You need to stop freaking the fuck out. This is feeling a hell of a lot like non-consent."

"No, it's..." She shakes her head and carefully tugs her arm free of my grip. Then reaching back and grabbing her monstrous purse, she pushes out of her side and wanders to my side of the truck.

She doesn't open my door, but she waits, nervously looking anywhere but at me.

Putting her out of her misery, I snag my keys and open my door.

After swinging my legs out and dropping to my boots on squishy grass, I slam the truck shut, and swallow when she grabs my sleeve and starts toward her porch.

"I want this," she mumbles, her face turned toward the house so I can barely hear. "I swear I do. I'm just..." She stomps up the porch steps and, releasing me, reaches into her purse to take out her house keys, separate from the set she tossed at Hannah.

Maybe her car breaking down is a common occurrence, so she long ago separated the set that would need to stay with the mechanic.

Unlocking her door and pushing it wide to reveal a front foyer dominated by a beautiful hardwood staircase, she turns back to me and glances up from beneath her lashes. "I'm still new to the casual sex scene. So I don't..." she shrugs. "Ya know, nerves are allowed."

"Well, sure." I set my hand on her hip and lead her inside. "But if paralyzing nerves are *all* you feel when I'm around, then maybe I'm not the right one for—"

She kicks the door shut and spins so fast, half of me thinks she's gonna sock me in the face. But instead, she tosses her handbag to the floor and wraps her arms around my neck, then she plasters her lips to mine and...

Jesus. Is she racing toward the finish line? Trying to get this over and done with?

Fuck knows. But her tongue comes out to duel with mine, and her arms, strong from her work, squeeze tight and hold her weight so she's easily able to climb me.

It's potent and hot. Her body pressed to mine. Her legs wrapped around my hips. Her tongue in my mouth, and her breath in my lungs. Hell if I haven't thought about this all week.

But it's not real. It's not genuine. They're the actions of a scared woman.

So I slide my hands beneath her ass to help her stay up, but I walk to the stairs.

She makes sounds of pleasure in the back of her throat, like I'm moving the direction she wants. But I climb only half a dozen steps before turning around and sitting so she's in my lap. Then I grab her jaw and disconnect our mouths until we part with a gasp.

Her eyes are wild. Her breath, racing. Her pupils are so dilated, I could almost ignore my instincts and fuck her until she's comatose.

But I can't take what she's not freely, *comfortably* giving.

Damn me and my skewed moral code.

Steal a car, or kill a man? *Go for it, bro.*

But fuck a willing woman when she's so nervous, she's making radical decisions? *Nope. Slow that train and calm her down.*

"What?" She dives in and seduces my neck. Biting. Licking. Tasting, so my toes curl and my cock rages. "What's wrong, Preston? You wanna fuck on the stairs?"

A desperate half-chuckle rolls free of my throat. "Actually, I kinda do. It's worth a try just to see how it feels. But," I catch her hand when she drops it between our bodies and tugs at my belt. "We have to slow down for a second."

"No. I don't wanna go slow." She fights my grip. Battles my will with her own, and yanks her hand free of mine. "Slow is boring. I want to have sex *now*. Then we can have dinner after."

"You wanna have sex now, like it's a fucking chore," I bite out. My cock throbs and my heart yearns to be inside her. But my temper burns, and my instincts say *no deal*. "You wanna get it over and done with."

"So?" She grabs my shirt and yanks it up to reveal my bare chest, but in her haste, snaps my head back when the collar catches my chin.

Nervous, she mumbles her apologies and pulls the fabric away to reveal my face. My eyes. My flattened lips, not impressed with this '*pull the bandaid off*' bullshit.

"I want to have sex now," she whimpers. Leaning closer, she presses her lips to mine and weakens my resolve. Because she tastes like something I shouldn't have, and I'm a man used to sinning.

"I want to come," she whines. "And you're offering. So I don't see the issue."

"You're not trying to enjoy it." I break our kiss, but only to move my lips as far as her neck. To bite. To savor. "You just want the orgasm, and then for me to go away again."

"So? It's sex, Preston! It's casual and string-free. Do you need candles and wine first?"

"No." Angry, I shove up to stand, and elicit a surprised squeal from deep in her throat when I lift her too. Then I turn and continue up the stairs, careful not to stumble and kill us both.

I bury my face against her neck and tug her flesh between my teeth until she cries out. I drag my lips lower, pushing the cotton of her shirt down, then I suckle until I know I'll leave a mark.

Blind, working on instincts, I find the top of the stairs, then I turn right and follow my nose. Because she's a scent all on her own. Sweet and sugary, but floral and delicious too.

I catch fun pinks and purples in my peripherals, brutally reminding me a child lives in this house, but I continue toward the door at the end, and find heaven set in the center of the room: a massive bed made beautiful with fluffy pillows and soft throws.

My cock throbs in my jeans, and when Nicole grinds against me, she brings me closer, closer to a point of no return.

For right now, I can be rational. I can be sensible and sensitive to a woman who desperately needs me to make good choices for us both. But if she continues to rub her fiery pussy over my crotch, I'm gonna find myself unable to say no.

It'll still be consensual, because she's saying yes.

But in her heart and mind, I know she'll regret us.

"Jesus, Preston." She reaches down and pulls up her own shirt. Rushing us along. Demanding we move too quickly. But instead of giving in, I continue into the attached bathroom and set her on the cabinet lining the far wall.

I plop her down with a thud—a reset, the way I might reboot a malfunctioning computer—and as she looks around, dazed at my actions, I turn to the massive shower and flip on the taps.

While she quietly panics, I glance down at the lump in my jeans, then to my belt, half undone. As steam fills the bathroom, and Nicole's face drains dangerously pale, I finish unfastening my belt and unsnapping the button. Then, before she can run out of here screaming, I make my way closer and press an intoxicating kiss to the center of her plump lips.

"If you won't slow the fuck down," I pant, because it's not like I don't want her too, "I'll *make* you."

Grabbing her hand, I wrap my belt around her wrist once and feed the leather through the steel head, then I grab her second wrist and repeat my moves until she's bound and stuck.

She looks at me in horror. In fear. But mixed with that is a frantic dose of *yes fucking please.*

"You won't quit touching me, even when I tell you to stop."

"Preston—"

"And you won't stop undressing me, even when I'm not ready to be naked." I jerk the belt tight and grin when she gasps. "You're not making sound choices for yourself, Feeney. So I'm gonna be in charge of those for now."

A fiery red blush replaces the paleness in her cheeks and, I swear, makes me come a little in my shorts. But I absorb the electricity firing through my veins, and slowly, carefully, lower her bound hands until her knuckles brush over my cock.

Together, we groan.

"Come off there." I speak softly, almost silently, and pull her forward until she touches down on her feet, and her breath comes out on a panting frenzy. Then I lower to one knee and go to work on unfastening her pants.

Button. Zipper. I press a kiss to her belly and feel her nerves return—not nerves for sex. But the kind that announce she's insecure. Shy. In her fucking head, like she so often is.

I bite her stomach and draw a pained squeak from somewhere deep in her chest. But it replaces the waves of worry pulsing through the large bathroom.

"You're gonna stay out of your own way." I shove her pants down, and since I'm feeling a little... eager, I take her panties with them in one swoop. Then I'm left staring at her pussy, the stubble of a week-old shave bringing a smile to my lips. "You're gonna do whatever the fuck you need to do to be here with me, in the now, and not off somewhere else, thinking about the rest of the world."

"I can't help—"

I bite her hip, so she swallows and shuts her damn mouth for a minute.

"You *will* control it. I'll help you." Lifting her leg and pulling her pants and panties away, I set her foot down and go to work on the other.

"Every time you start to obsess about anything that isn't me, you just say '*I think*'," I chuckle, "and I'll fix it."

"But I thi—"

I slide two thick fingers inside her dripping pussy and hold my breath when she screams.

Her hands drop to my hair, pulling so I feel the fire in my scalp. Her knees wobble, weak when I drag my hand down, then thrust back in again and claim her.

"I said, *stop* thinking." I lean in and slide my tongue between her folds, groaning when she comes in my hand. Filling my palm, and whimpering at how easily I make her explode.

"Preston—"

"I can control your body, Feeney. I can make you feel whatever the fuck I want you to. But you need to stop overanalyzing everything." I pull my hand away from her core and look down at my palm, slick with her juices. With nowhere else to put it, I press it against my stomach and wipe her on me.

Because why the fuck wouldn't I want her on me? She's already under my skin. There's no reason to stop that shit now.

Slowly pushing up to stand, I arch my back and press a kiss to her bare ab. Then her ribs. I slowly unfold myself, but stop at her tits, still covered in her everyday, no-frills, cotton bra.

But hell, like that doesn't do it for me.

Straightening out and pressing my chest flat to hers, I reach around her lithe body and work on the clasp at her back. I see myself in the mirror behind the counter. I see my fingers, and the small hooks that keep her bra closed.

I unsnap them, one by one, and study the harsh red line marking her back, from where she leaned against the counter, using it to remain standing while lost in the throes of her orgasm.

"You're so fucking beautiful." Releasing the final hook, I pull back and let the fabric drop away until I get a perfect view of her mouthwatering tits, with perfect, pink nipples that make my tongue come out in want.

Crouching again, I take the first between my lips, and hold her hip when she starts to fall. "You're the sweetest thing I've ever tasted." I switch sides and take the second between my teeth. "And I've eaten a fuck-ton of your cupcakes this past week."

She chokes out a desperate laugh and drops her bound arms over my shoulders to hug me tight. "You're gonna make this weird again. I think—"

"Oop, there you go *thinking* again." Releasing her breast and straightening my back, I slide my hands beneath her ass so my fingers bruise her flesh, then I pick her up and walk her toward the shower. "You gotta stop doing that, babe. It ruins the moment every single time."

"What are you—" She squirms in my arms, and twists like the thought of a shower is terrifying. "Preston, you're still half-dressed!"

"I know." I stop at the entrance to the massive glass cubicle and set her on her feet, then when they try to move forward to help her escape the steam, I press my hand to her throat, startling her.

Sliding the pad of my thumb along the front of her neck, I push her slowly backward. "Under the water, beautiful."

Panic swims in her eyes as she lifts her hands. "Your belt is gonna get w—"

"I seriously don't give a fuck about my belt."

I guide her under the spray until her hair darkens, and water soaks me up to my shoulder and flirts with the hem of my jeans, then I let her go and shove my zipper down so her eyes follow my hands. "Touch yourself."

Stunned, she glances up again. "What?"

"I said," I push my jeans down, then bend to unlace my boots. "Touch yourself."

"Preston..." she breathes. "I can't. I don't think—"

"There's that word again." I kick my boots off and toss my jeans and shorts so they hit the floor with a *splat*. Then I step into the shower and cup her face until she stands on the very tips of her toes. "So now I'm gonna need you on your hands and knees."

Her eyes flash with fear. And desire. And fuck knows, a thousand other emotions. "What?"

"You started thinking again. So..." I push her down. Down. *Downnnn* until she bends her knees, and her eyes drop to my cock.

"You want me to..." Considering, she licks her lips. "You want me to suck?"

She sounds so terrified, but keen at the same time. Her warring emotions wreak havoc with mine, so a desperate chuckle escapes my throat and leaves me breathless. "I would kill a man if it meant you would suck my cock. But that's not what I want right now." I reach down to cup her face, then I push her further down and groan when she presses her hands to the tile floor, and her ass and hips are all I see.

They're a beacon, beckoning me home.

"This is a good shower." I lower to my knees too, and pick her hips up so she's forced to hold all her weight on her bound hands. It's only for a moment, just long enough to place her where I need her, then I set her down again so the head of my cock touches her asshole, and a frantic whimper tumbles free of her throat. "It's roomy in here." Small talk. Helps me not come. "I like it."

"Um..." She chokes out a breathless giggle. "Thanks, I like it too."

"Are we still doing the '*Preston can do whatever he wants, and Nicole will say no if she doesn't like it*' thing? Or do you wanna give me your hard noes right now, before I start?"

"Oh god." She drops her head and rests her elbows on the unforgiving tile floor. "I can't..." She shakes her head. "You just do you," she rasps. "I'll tell you if I don't like it."

"Thank god."

I smack her ass with a *crack* loud enough her neighbors will hear. Then when she cries out, I grab her hips and open her ass as wide as she can handle. Burying my mouth between her cheeks, I eat her up and sprint faster toward my own completion with every lap of my tongue.

"Come again," I command. "But when you're done, I don't want you to say that fucking word."

She cries on the shower floor, shuddering under my touch and angling away from the spray of water. "Preston—"

"Just stop saying it." I smack her ass a second time, and growl when she spasms.

She opens her legs wider, inviting, tempting, and dribbling with pleasure. My cock knows what's so close. It's desperate to enter. Impatient to claim.

I drag my hand from her pussy and around to her ass, and because I can't help myself, I grab my dick with the other and pump.

Once. Twice. Three times, so my balls bunch and ready to spill my seed.

"Fuck me, Preston." She stays down, her weight on her elbows and her ass in the air, but she twists her head so her dazed eyes lock on mine. "Please."

"Not yet. Not even fucking close." I grab her hips and yank her so she slides on the tiles and her asshole crashes against my lips. Then I take. I take. I take so much, I could almost feel sympathy for the way I make her scream.

But those are good sobs. A cathartic and pleasurable weeping that I pride myself in eliciting.

She creams, over and over again, so her desire washes along her thighs, and her legs pulse from the way I make them shake. Then I lift just one and flip her so she lands flat on her back and the air in her lungs races out on a gasp. Tugging her closer until her ass hits my knees and her legs hang over my shoulders, I eat her pussy too, since I want the trifecta.

Her mouth.

Her asshole.

Her sweet, sweet cunt.

"Preston!" She comes, so fucking quickly, so easily into my mouth, and cries out from the sensations bubbling in her blood.

She tightens her legs over my shoulders, like she thinks she can trap me here and control my movements, but I slide two fingers into her pussy and smack her ass with my free hand. Then I catch her legs when they grow weak and threaten to fall.

"I'm not done yet." I keep her legs on my shoulders, but I reach between them and cup the back of her head until she's forced to use her abdominal muscles to sit up. Then I take her mouth with mine so our tongues duel.

She doesn't worry about tasting herself on my lips. She doesn't over-think her position, or the odd angles I force her to contort to. She just feels. She's in the now, exactly like I fucking wanted.

"You wanna suck my cock now, Feeney?" I keep ahold of the back of her head to help her stay up, but I bury my lips against her throbbing neck and leave my mark. Here. There. Everywhere between her throat and her tits. "You wanna taste me yet?"

"Yes." She drops her head back and pants, clamoring for air and fighting to keep her mind away from what we're doing. "Yes, I do. I think—"

"Aw, there you go again." I release her head, but I keep watch to make sure she doesn't rap it against the unforgiving tile. Then when she's laid out, her hands still bound and on her belly, her chest heaving for oxygen, I let her legs fall free of my shoulders, and I push up to stand.

I intend to walk out of the shower. To find a new way to torture her. But for just a moment, I look down at the most beautiful woman I've ever met, wet and wanting and more desperate for my cock than anyone ever in the past. Her lips are swollen, and the bruises my teeth leave behind litter her chest, because I'm a possessive motherfucker who likes to mark what belongs to me.

My breath races too; I'm not immune to this torture. I'm just a willing sacrifice.

"You're perfect," I murmur, softer than I mean. Then when her eyes change from an anxious hunger to something else, something... gentler, I step out of the shower and snatch a towel from the railing.

Wrapping it around my hips and bending to collect my jeans, I snatch my wallet from the back pocket and toss the rest away. Opening the leather and taking out two condoms, I bite the corners between my teeth and leave everything else.

Finally, I come back into the shower and grab Nicole's bound hands. I pull her to her feet, only to grin when her knees turn weak and she needs to lean on me to support her weight.

If she doesn't use me, I suspect she'd simply melt back to the floor.

"I have two of these," I grit around the foil between my lips, then I scoop her up and throw her over my shoulder so she squeals.

I slap her ass and kick the shower tap off—she's a single mom with bills to pay, there's no need to land her with a massive water bill on top—then I carry her into her bedroom and rub my palm over the part of her ass that burns from my slap.

"Only two," I continue. "Which means I get to come twice tonight."

"Okay..." Her voice crackles and breaks on a whimper. "That's—"

I flip her over my shoulder and slam her to her bed so the covers puff up with a noisy *fwump*. Then I spit my rubbers to the side and crawl over her. "You didn't say *think*," I move between her legs and place my knee at the apex of her thighs so she can feel me. So she can grind. "But you were still thinking."

"That's not fair." She scooches just a half an inch down the bed and uses my thigh exactly how I thought she would, rolling her hips and whimpering from the contact. "You're making up your own rules as you go."

"Maybe. But that's what I do, Feeney." I take her hands and shove them above her head with a violence that makes her eyes widen. But she's not scared. She's not even concerned. Mostly, she wants to see where I'll take her.

Lifting my head and glancing around the room for a moment, I spy a dressing robe at the end of the bed. So I twist and grab it in one hand, then steal the sash that goes around her waist.

The whole garment smells of her. It's soft and warm and wafts of flowers and sugar. But it's just the sash I need.

Tying the length around the belt circling her wrists, I climb over her, making myself vulnerable to a bite to my stomach if she wanted to, then I fasten the sash to the headboard and lock her down so she no longer gets to touch.

She craves control, so I take more of it away and force her to trust me.

The alternative, of course, and the risk I take, is that she has a complete fucking meltdown and screams for me to stop.

Please don't scream for me to stop.

Finishing the knot, I look down and study her face. Her curious and hungry eyes, and the way she suckles on her bottom lip.

Yeah, she ain't saying no yet.

Fire burns in my veins, and my orgasm teeters dangerously close to the edge. The moment I plunge deep inside her, it's gonna be all over for us. So I bring my legs to her sides, instead of between her thighs. I crawl along her body so my hardened cock taps her chest. Then I grab it and squeeze tight enough to make us both groan.

"You wanna taste my cock, Feeney? Or are you still busy thinking?"

"I wanna taste." She licks her lips—whether to prove her eagerness, or simply because they're dry and needing the moisture, I don't know. But she squirms under my body and lifts to come closer. "I'm ready."

"Are you thinking? Are you gonna regret this?"

Frantically, she makes a *"nuh-uh"* sound in the back of her throat, then surprises me when she slides her tongue along the tip of my cock.

I throw my head back and cry out, while she bends and stretches and tries to take more of me. Her hands are stuck, and her chest is pinned to the bed by my weight. She can only move as far as her neck allows, and still, she sends me wild with just the tip of her tongue.

"Untie me." She fights her restraints so the bed squeaks from the movement. "Let me do it properly."

"This *is* proper." Lowering my gaze and fisting my cock, I twine my free hand through her hair and hold her up. When I tilt my hips, she takes half of my cock between her lips and draws a desperate cry along my throat.

"Fuck!" I pull her hair too hard. I shove my hips forward too quickly. I treat her like a toy rather than a beautiful, seductive, living and feeling woman. But when she swallows me down, and her eyes watch mine with a dangerous intensity, I know she doesn't mind.

"Fuck, Nicole." I rock forward and fuck her mouth, drawing me close, close, too close to my peak. "Jesus." I fall forward and rest my forearm on top of her headboard.

Which only gives her more of my cock to work with. She lays her head flat and uses her teeth to threaten me.

I can't walk away. I can't do a damn thing but let her suck me off and study her eyes with every thrust.

"Shit," I breathe. I brought her in here to screw with her some more, but then I let her lick my tip. I let her taste. And now I can't stop. "Feeney."

She bites me. It's a fast nip, just enough to warn me, then she licks where she bit and swallows me deeper. "I thought I wouldn't like this," she pulls back to give herself room to speak. To breathe. "When you told me to get on my knees, I thought I would hate every second of this."

"You're still thinking," I pant. My hips keep moving, even without her lips wrapped around. "Quit it."

Snickering, she tilts to one side, bridging until I take a hint that she wants to turn us over. She can't use her hands, and not in a million years could she flip us if I don't want her to. But hell, if that's what she wants...

I tip to the side and flop to my back, then I drag her up and over and place her on my hips.

She freezes for a beat when my bare cock and her fiery pussy touch. I mean, the chances of my little soldiers charging in there and making a home are low. But they're never zero. And the panic in her eyes says she's brutally aware of that.

Sliding down my body and stretching her arms as far as they could possibly go, since they're still attached to the headboard, she takes my cock in her mouth deep enough that my orgasm threatens to explode.

Willpower is the only thing that keeps me from drenching the back of her throat.

"Fuck, Nicole." I buck my hips and grab her dripping hair to control her head. I count it down in my mind. I do exactly what I punish her for —I think and count and obsess over numbers instead of *feeling*—and when I'm on the precipice of detonation, I yank her head back and growl at the wild look in her eyes. "Condom."

I release her head and snatch up a foil packet, then tearing it open and stealing the rubber from inside, I toss the trash away and furiously roll our protection over my dick with a speed that brings me closer to completion.

"Dammit," I grunt out. Then I grab her by the hips and lift her from the bed with a savage strength that comes from desperation.

Sitting her on my hips, I give her only a second to adjust, to think, to voice her objections. Then I lift her again and bring her down over my steely cock until she swallows me up. She rides me with a fluidity that sends me insane. She rests her hands on the headboard and rolls her hips to find a speed that makes us both weak.

But I'm not so weak I can't take her tit between my lips and bite down until she shatters around me.

Like a fucking series of explosions, she bucks and screams, helpless to both her body's release and the ties keeping her hands still. She cries out and comes, squeezing me impossibly tight, and whimpering when it all feels too much. And because she falls freely, out of control, she drags me over the edge so I fill my condom.

Maybe I bite too hard. Maybe my hands bruise. Fuck, maybe my hips mark the underside of her thighs because of the way I push up. But she doesn't complain, and when she's all wrung out and her body is draped across my chest, she doesn't whine when the aftershocks rocking through my veins make my cock twitch. Instead, her pussy flutters tighter, and her walls clamp down to trap me inside. My hands come to her ass, and my fingers squeeze until I leave bruises there too.

But still, she's officially done thinking. She's a bundle of feelings and exhaustion. Of being in the now, and not worrying about everything else.

Jesus.

I did what I came here to do: I fucked her into a comatose state. But now, ironically, I can't turn my brain off.

I've found my drug of choice. The one woman who can send me insane and calm my frenzied brain, all in the same breath.

I found her once. Then I found her again.

And now, I'm not sure I ever want to let her go.

We doze. And touch. And kiss. And at some point, because she did as she was told, I unbind her hands and breathe in the scent of her still-wet hair.

I lie awake in the middle of her bed, and she stays resting on my chest. Less anxious than last time. Freer in the way she strokes the hair shadowing my pecs.

"That felt good." Silence hangs but for the chirp of bugs outside, and the *shhp-shhp-shhp* of a sprinkler in someone's garden. With a breathy sigh, Nicole hitches her leg higher on my thighs and presses a gentle kiss to the side of my chest. "I was ready to come home and rage-clean my kitchen, but—"

"But I provided a better alternative." Pleased with myself, I stroke the ends of her hair and simply... exist. Be. Inhale her deep down into my lungs and know, if I let myself think too much, I might spiral into a dangerous *what the fuck am I supposed to do with this woman who, against her own will, took a slice of me?*

Because she did. She bewitched me. Her innocence. Her drive. Her resilience, and her no-bullshit attitude about life.

Maybe this is another of my toxic traits coming to fruition—to feel for someone who is emotionally unavailable to me. But here we are, and I'm not sure I'll ever get that piece of me back.

"Are you hungry?" She keeps her voice down, her tone soft and somewhat shy. But when the silence hangs a little too long and I don't answer with a vehement *yes*, she pulls back to catch my eyes. "Preston, are you—"

"Are you gonna cook for me?" I arch my neck and take her lips with mine.

Pleasure vibrates in my veins when she doesn't hesitate. Doesn't even pretend to think about my request. I pucker, and she accepts.

Fuck if that doesn't feel good.

"I could cook." Placing a hand on the center of my stomach, she pushes up straight so she's leaning over me, and her long hair dangles to brush my cheek.

She's beautiful in the dusk light. The sun's rays are hidden behind the mountains, so I see her silhouette more than her features. But her lips curl into a breathtaking smile, and then it's she who initiates a kiss.

For the first time ever, she asks for something pure and real and without worrying or expectations.

"I don't have steak, though," she warns.

I choke out a soft laugh and push up to sit, only to wrap my arm around her torso and shove her to the mattress so she lands with a *thwump* and her eyes show a moment of alarm. Fear. Excitement. Her tits bounce, and then her hips lift when I take a peaked nipple between my lips.

"You taste so fucking good." I switch sides and slide my free hand along her torso. Over her belly. Past her hip. Then I slip two fingers inside her pussy, and growl when her eagerness holds them tight and pulls me deeper. "Shitttttt."

"This again." She rolls her hips and fucks herself using my hand, closing her eyes and tilting her head back so I catch a beautiful glimpse of her curved neck. So delicate. So strong.

Then I chuckle. *So marked.*

Smug, I press a kiss to one of my larger bruises and know she'll be pissed when she sees what I've done. But I'll be damned if I can find a scrap of remorse for my actions. "You're gonna have to wear a turtleneck to work."

"Don't care." She whimpers and draws herself closer to a new release. "Shit, Preston."

Some might call me a petty man. Others might consider me cruel. But I tug my fingers from her pussy, stunning a delicious gasp from deep in her throat, then I slip them past her lips and take pleasure in the way she startles at first, then sucks them clean and drops her hand between her legs to finish what I started.

"Get up." I hook my finger in her mouth and drag her closer until our lips touch. "Cook me some dinner."

"What—"

She's still riding her own pleasure. Still working herself into a frenzy.

So I trap her hand to keep it still. Then I kiss her again. "Feeney? Cook me some dinner."

"You're an asshole!" She yanks her hand from my grip and swings out to hit me.

But I'm faster. Agile. And I was expecting retribution. So I bound from the bed with a laugh and snatch my jeans from the bathroom tiles. Stepping into them and turning back to study Nicole starfishing her bed, I shake my head and continue walking. "We'll come back after we eat. Then I'll finish you off."

I tap her foot as I pass, only to walk faster when she growls. "I'm starving. Where's your hospitality?"

"I hate you!" Her voice echoes along the hall. "Did you hear me, Preston Danes? I hate your stupid guts."

"Mm. I heard you, babe."

I pass the pink bedroom, careful not to look inside and invade a little girl's privacy, then I start down the stairs and take myself on a Feeney home tour.

"I like the pictures along here," I call back.

She has family portraits on the wall, going all the way down the staircase in stepped-down increments I'm certain she spent hours measuring and perfecting. Pictures of her and Axel. And others of her and the beautiful little girl I met on Wednesday. The one who looks a hell of a lot like her mother, but with the subtle features her father's genes added. I see pictures of Juniper and some older Feeneys—grandparents, maybe—and then I stop and smile when I find Maya on the wall of love.

Maya, a kindergarten teacher, with her sweet little five-year-old students in a group.

My Maya... who is not *my* Maya, but fuck if she isn't worth more to me than family.

"Kitchen's to the right."

I spin at Nicole's throaty, post-sex, seductive voice, and press a hand to my aching chest when she appears at the top of the stairs in a tiny nightie that'll live in my dreams for the rest of my life. Black silk, thigh-high, with a split to add to my heart palpitations.

I'm not sure if she wore it to make me pant for her, but the result comes all the same—especially when the slip pushes her tits up and makes my mouth water, knowing how good they taste.

Descending the stairs and beaming when she reaches my side, she brushes gentle fingertips along my bare back and saunters on, leading me the way the pied piper led... whoever the hell he led.

There's no chance in hell I won't follow.

Nicole heads into her kitchen and flips the stove on without pause, then she moves to her fridge and peruses the contents for a long beat. While she thinks on that, I pull up a stool at the counter and simply watch her.

The refrigerator light shining through the thin scrap of material covering her body. Her long hair draped over one shoulder, and plump lips, growing thicker because she chews on them.

"How hungry are you?" Glancing over her shoulder, she catches me staring down at her bare legs. Her perfect ass. Her perfect... everything. "Preston?"

I drag my gaze up and stop on her dancing eyes.

"Starving?" she clarifies. "Or peckish?"

"Does my answer change whatever you're cooking?"

"Sure." She grabs out a stick of butter and a carton of milk, then she wanders to the corner cabinet and takes out a frying pan.

Because the sun is getting too low, and the nighttime, too dark, she moves to the lightswitch by the door and flicks it on so we lose the shadows of lust and secrecy, and instead, are bathed in harsh fluorescent light. But it's not so bad, because now I see her peaked nipples through the silk.

A sly grin works across my lips, and when she glances down and figures out why, she huffs and crosses her arms. "Grow up, dummy."

"Never." I rest one elbow on the counter as she wanders back with her pan and sets it on the heat, while with the other hand, I reach into my jeans and adjust my cock so it doesn't press so aggressively against the zipper. "Growing up is a trick. And," I add when she flattens her lips, "why does my answer change your cooking plans?"

"Because if you're starving, I'll cook pasta and fill your stomach. If you're just a little hungry, I'll make something smaller."

"Mm." I roll my bottom lip and think. "And what do *you* wanna eat?"

Considering, she drops a glob of butter in the pan and settles on a shrug. "I kinda really want bacon and eggs." She goes back to the fridge and grabs a packet of bacon, then she juggles a carton of eggs and closes the door with a flick of her hip. "I can still make you pasta if you want."

"Nah, what you've got works fine." And because sitting *all* the way over here while she's *all* the way over there—one counter and five feet away—sucks, I push up to stand and wash my hands at the sink. "I'll help you."

"Oh, no, you don't—"

I turn and snatch up a clean towel folded on the counter, meeting her worried stare with a look of my own. "I wanna help."

I toss the rag back down and move closer until our chests touch and her breath feathers along my lips. Leaning in, I press a kiss to the side of her neck and inhale. Because we're on the clock. Soon, she's gonna flip and kick my ass out. "I *want* to help."

"O-okay." Timidly setting the carton of eggs by my hand, she twists so her back is to me, but she tugs strips of bacon from the pack and drops them into the sizzling butter. "I don't think—"

"Don't think at all." I hug her back with my chest, then I slide my hand over her shoulder and around to stroke her collarbone. "The way you insist on thinking all the fucking time," I murmur by her ear. "Isn't it exhausting?"

"Yeah." She chokes out a laugh that brings a smile to my face. "I'm literally always in a state of exhaustion. It's part of my personality now."

"Which I think is cute... most of the time." Lifting my hand and cupping the bottom of her jaw, I pull her head back until I have access to her mouth. "But when you're hurting yourself to do it," I pull her bottom lip between my teeth until she moans, "it's no longer cute. Tell me something about your life I don't know."

"What?" Confused, her eyes search mine, while bacon pops close enough to burn us both. "You don't know anything about my life," she sniggers nervously. "I could tell you anything."

"So," I drop a second kiss on her lips before releasing her face and resting my hands on her hips. "Tell me something. Anything. First thing that comes to your mind."

"Tit for tat?" she counters instead. "I'll tell you one, you tell me one?"

"Sure." She smells like sex. And shampoo. And me. And a bakery. And every other sinful scent I could imagine. "Tit for tat. You go first."

"Fine." She adds more bacon to the pan and hums in the back of her throat like it helps her think. "I was homecoming queen. I rocked a tiara and had a double page spread in our yearbook."

"Aww, popular girl." I nibble on the shell of her ear. I know my cock presses to her back, but for just a moment, the smell of frying food gives me something else to think about. "I didn't go to homecoming," I admit, fulfilling my side of our deal. "I didn't even graduate high school."

"You didn't?" She reaches out for the carton of eggs, since my offer to help was mostly a lie. I just wanted to be close. To touch her. To taste. "But you work in IT, right? Doesn't that require a degree?"

Fuck. "Well... yeah. I tested for my GED when I was older, then did my diploma through an online program." *Fucking liar.* "Natural ability gets me through doors others can't."

"Lucky you." She cracks an egg into the pan, like my explanation works just fine for her. "Do you have siblings? I can't remember if I already asked you that."

"None that I know of." I allow my hands to explore. Her belly. Her hips. Her ribs, and then down to her ass. "My parents probably made more, but I don't know for sure."

"Makes dating tricky," she teases. "How can you know you're not hitting on your half-sister at a club sometime?"

"Well..." I bury my face between her neck and shoulder and bite the warm skin there. "Do you know both of your parents?"

"Yes."

"Are they still together?"

"Yes."

"Are their names Patricia and Henry?"

She pauses for a beat, then shakes her head. "No."

"Then you're not my sister. Thank god." I bite and make her squirm. "Because your ass tastes good."

"You're so gross!" She tries to step forward, to escape my grasp, but the stove bars her way, and my body blocks every other direction. "Preston!"

Chuckling, I slide my hand up and cup her breast. "Do you have siblings apart from Axel?"

"No." And because she's a prisoner to my touch, she drops her head back to rest against my chest. "Just one sibling, and you've already met him. Do you like your job?"

"Yes. Do you like yours?"

She pants. And sighs. And melts in my arms so I'm forced to hold her up or risk letting her drop to the floor.

"Yes," she whimpers. "I love my job. It's hard work, long hours, a metric ton of stress, and I sit at the top of the chain, so all blame lands in my lap if we mess something up. But yeah." She reaches out to switch the burner off, then turns in my arms and stands on her toes to press a kiss to my lips. "To build a business from the ground up, to see its growth and celebrate its wins," another kiss before stepping away and pulling plates from a high-up cupboard, "I love it a lot. You mention natural ability," she twists back to catch my eyes on her ass. Only to smile when I bring them back up and pretend I'm not objectifying her body. "Would you ever consider branching out on your own and working for yourself?"

"I've been working for myself for the last few years." Since I can't touch her, and our food will burn if I continue to distract her, I find something else to give my attention to. Spying a loaf of bread on the counter, and a foot from it, a four-slice toaster, I get to work adding one to the other and contributing my portion to tonight's meal. "But working for Checkmate comes with stability and the perk of learning from someone much smarter than me."

Circling around to the cutlery drawer, I take out knives and forks for us both, plus an extra butter knife for the toast. "I'll try Checkmate out for a while and see how things go. Then I'll reevaluate." *Once I access Mancino's systems and become the direct reason for their undoing.* "We'll see how I feel, and what Sophia thinks of my job performance. Do you ever want to adopt a dog?"

"What?" Stunned, she turns my way and studies me with eyes that scream *what the fuck?* "Where the hell did that come from?"

I move to the cupboard she took plates from and grab an extra one for our pile of toast. "When we were at the park the other day, your daughter told Axel she wanted to get a dog."

"Ugh." She rolls her eyes and lifts the pan from the stove with one hand. With the other, she holds a spatula and begins filling our plates. "What did he say?"

When the toaster pops, I begin spreading butter on each slice. "That he's not getting a dog, because he works too much, and you're not getting one either, because you're busy and have no time for one."

"She's been asking for years." She puts more than double the amount of food on one plate compared to the other, then snatches up slices of toast as I finish them, and tosses them on top. "I can't afford a dog, Preston. I don't have time to groom or walk or train a dog. I don't want to spend my precious free time picking up steaming piles of crap, and I don't want my house to smell of dog. So," she sets the pan and spatula in the deep-set sink and turns back to brush her hands together. "My daughter's gonna have to get a new dream."

Pushing the fuller plate across the counter so it stops before the stool I was sitting on before, she brings the second closer to her and picks up a triangle of toast to bite into. "Do you want children?"

Her cheeks flame when her question seems to register in her mind.

"That sounded way too serious. I just meant—"

"You meant what you said," I cut in. "But you didn't mean for there to be any strings or insinuations attached." I forgo my silverware and pick up a slice of bacon. "Calm yourself. And..." I shrug. "I don't know. I've never been at a place in my life where I considered it."

"Do you hate kids?"

"No," I scoff. "I think they're the cutest little shits to ever walk the planet. Maya's always being stopped in town by five-year-olds who wanna chat, and the guys down at the gym have another twenty of their own who are always hanging around. Dudes I work for have a bunch. And this new friend of mine," I add slowly, carefully, "Axel Feeney, has this niece I got to hang with at the park one time."

I take another bite and smile as momma-bear's eyes warm. "I like kids. They're innocent and funny and often speak their minds in a way adults just don't do anymore. But will *I* ever make a kid?" I look down at my dick, like seeing where my sperm comes from will somehow help me know. "I dunno. Maybe. Maybe not. I don't have strong feelings either way yet."

I toss a slice of bacon into my mouth and chew. "Your first rodeo sucked and the horse you chose was a prick. Are you gonna have kids or marry ever again?"

She barks out a laugh and shakes her head. "No."

Her certainty makes my brows shoot high in question. "No to both? Never?"

"My first horse was horrible," she reiterates, "and my child is my kryptonite. I won't hand that power over to a man ever again. If I ever *say* I have the itch for more kids, consider that a cry for help and get me out of there."

I glance down at my plate and snicker. "Noted. Marriage?"

"Scam. Never again."

"And yet," I counter through flat lips, "you make money off the wedding industry."

"I lost a fortune getting married. Now it's my turn to take some back. You ever getting married, Preston Danes?"

My stomach dips at her sultry, troublemaking tone. But I pick up my silverware and cut into my eggs with slow, deliberate moves. "If you'd asked me that a year ago, it would've been a flat out *fuck no*." I scoop runny egg into my mouth and groan, because I'm starving, and this tastes delicious. "I didn't think I could ever like a woman enough to latch on for a lifetime."

"But?" Turning on her heels, she goes to the fridge and shows off entirely too much ass cheek as she peruses her options. Beer? Wine? Water? She makes a sound of approval in the back of her throat before selecting a couple of juice boxes.

Bacon. Eggs. And juice in cartons that sport Paw Patrol characters on the side.

"But what?" she asks again when I don't answer. "What happened in the last year that changed your mind?"

"Cole met Maya." I accept my drink and peel the straw off the side. "He met her and fell in love really fucking hard. So..." I shrug and stab the straw through the top. "Made me kinda consider what it could be like. She'd have to be amazing, though. Like Maya."

"Like Maya..." Her brows lift in challenge. "You got a thing for your best friend's wife, Preston?" Picking up a strip of bacon, she bites off the end and stares deep into my soul. "You setting up impossible standards? Or having an emotional affair with someone you shouldn't?"

I take a sip of my apple juice and meet her stare with my own. "They're clearly not *impossible* standards, since Cole found his in a dance club and followed her around until she agreed to marry him. And, emotional affair?" I set my juice back down. "The thing that makes her so amazing is her love for my best friend. If they're no longer in love, that perfection ceases to exist. If that's all shattered, then I go back to being my bitter, un-marriable self, and life goes back to normal."

"It's cute how your beliefs in marriage and commitment hinge on someone else's happiness," she smarts. "Will you ever adopt a dog?"

I snort and cut into my egg. "Maybe. Someday. I like 'em enough, and who doesn't want that unconditional love waiting at the door when we get home from work?"

When I've smashed through two-thirds of my meal, and Nicole is still on her second strip of bacon, I nod toward her plate. "You always eat slow?"

"Mm. Yeah." As though to prove her point, she sets another bite of bacon in her mouth and chews. "You always swallow yours whole?"

"Gotta eat fast when you're poor and competing with others at the trough. Slowest goes hungry. What are your hopes for the future?"

Confused by my turnabout, she asks, "Huh?"

"Five years from now, where do you wanna be? What's life look like?"

"Oh, well..." She rests her elbows on the counter and her face in one hand. "June will be eleven. Pre-teen. Hopefully still as amazing as she is now. With any luck, my store will still be open and my bills with be paid."

"You wanna expand and make it bigger?"

She shakes her head, an instant response that says she's already thought about it. "I don't want to be in charge of a massive corporation where I'm delegated to a desk and managing staff. I want to bake. I like waking in the early hours and working in the dark while everyone else sleeps. I like the creativity in what I do, and the freedom to create what I want. I mean," so gently, so carefully, she reaches for her juice box and brings it to her lips. "I still have to make some of the same things every day, since they're guaranteed sellers, and customers expect them. But my cupcake variations are a fun surprise for us all. I can make whatever I want taste and look however I want, and more often than not, the customers who come in trust me enough to try them."

"I've yet to eat a Juniper's cake I didn't like," I tell her. "You've proven to your client base you make quality. So now they'll follow you anywhere."

"Pretty much," she sighs happily. "And I love that about what I've done. That trust. The guarantee that, even if it looks different or tastes different, chances are, most will probably still like it." A warm blush fills her cheeks. "I love my job. Which is your favorite so far?"

"Cake?" Surprised by her question, I run through the dozen flavors

I've consumed this week alone. "The rainbow one." I meet her beautiful eyes. "It was my first, and fuck if it didn't leave an impression. And," I add with a soft chuckle, "I didn't even know the baker was *you*. I didn't know the chick from the wedding was the one who made the orgasmic desserts."

She clicks her tongue and reaches out for a triangle of toast. "And now you do. Is your work boring?"

"Boring?" I think of Tony Mancino. Of mafia families. Sex trafficking. Drugs. Guns. *Multiple* millions of dollars, and drone-flown explosives like the kind Sophia wants to drop in the guy's yard someday. But then I remember *I work in IT*, and tone down the smug pleasure zinging through my veins. "It's not boring to me."

"Is it repetitive?"

"It can be, but that's the job, right? You measure the same amount of flour each morning, no? Start the same ovens. Turn them to the same temperature. Whip the same recipes for icing. Knead the same doughs for bread." I take a bite of my toast and smile, realizing even this bread was made with *her* hands. "Repetition is everywhere, Feeney, but that doesn't mean we hate it."

"I guess." She drops her gaze to her plate and nods. "Why do you insist on calling me Feeney?"

"For the same reason everyone else calls you Feeney." I watch the way her eyes soften, warm, and sink deeper into mine. "Axel does. And Hannah, too. Because maybe you married a dude with the name Scott, and maybe you're keeping that name for your daughter's sake. But that's just a formality. A literal contract you signed."

I set my fork aside and pick up my juice. "Beneath all that shit is a woman who was born someone else. A little girl who lived most her life with a different name. I figure you don't need to be called Scott any more than you already are. Banks, school, the DMV. More repetition. So..." I bring my juice closer and take a long sip. "I wanna remind you who you are beneath the bad things that happened. I wanna be..." I shrug. "One of the good guys in your life. Whatever happens, and whoever we become in the future, I'd like to be someone you remember with a smile."

Nicole's eyes glitter with emotion. Her shoulders slump, and her mouth opens to speak. But then a phone trills from somewhere else in the house, a chirping sound that echoes off the hardwood floor and steals the softness from her expression.

From relaxed to alert, she shoves up to stand tall, knocking her plate so the ceramic bounces on the stone countertop. Then she dashes out of the room to search for the device.

Maybe she reacts this way to all phone calls. Or maybe that ringtone is set for one person in particular.

Grabbing my plate, then moving around the counter to take hers, I place them both in the sink and try to mind my own business.

I really, truly try. But I hear her voice. The panic in her tone. And her bare feet sticking and releasing from her wooden floor.

"Hello?" Her voice bubbles with uncertainty. "June Bug?"

I turn from the counter in silence and wander toward the doorway separating the kitchen and the front entryway. I keep my movements quiet, my presence unknown.

But then Nicole speaks again, and my heart jumps in my chest.

"Oh, Noah..." She exhales a defeated sigh. "Is June okay?"

"She's fine."

I don't have to be near her to hear. He doesn't even have to be on speaker for his douchey voice to carry through the house.

"We were just settling in for dinner and thinking of you," he continues. "Junie was wishing you could be with us, actually."

That's when I step through the door and make myself known.

To her. Not to him.

"June and I could drive back down tonight," he pushes on, unaware of the current pulsing from her burning eyes to mine. He's oblivious to the sexy gown she wears, and the way her chest heaves for oxygen.

Accepting she has nowhere to go to escape my ears, she simply moves to the stairs and sits on the fourth one up.

So I come into the room and slide my ass down to sit with my back against the door. Silent. Unspeaking. And insanely curious to see her interact with the man who once held the world in his hands.

"It's only an hour drive," he charges on, despite her silence. "And June could sleep in her own bed tonight. *Hocus Pocus* is on TV at eight-thirty, so we could get there just in time and settle in for that."

"Noah..." Lowering her face to her hand, Nicole crushes her eyes shut. "You can bring June home if that's what she wants. But you're not staying here."

"But, Nick, it could be—"

"No." Opening her eyes, she glances across so all I see is despair. And stress. And heartache. All because of a single phone call. "Is June there? Does she wanna speak to me?"

"Hi, Mommy!" I hear her voice. Her sweet squeak of happiness. And then I see how Nicole's posture changes fractionally. "Hey, Mommy! I wanna say hello."

"Noah," Nicole tries again. "I'd like to speak to June, so if you could—"

"No." From sugary and faux-charming, to a cold, rage-filled denial. "This is my time, Nicole. You have no right to infringe—"

"You called me," she snarls. "You started this, Noah. And our court orders clearly state June can communicate with the non-custodial parent at any time, and the custodial parent must facilitate that communication."

She evens her words and speaks robotically. On rote. Like she's memorized and used them a million times in the past. "This, and every phone call I ever have with you, is recorded for everyone's safety, Noah. You and I both heard her ask to speak to me. So if you refuse, I'll have to document your breach." Pausing, then taking a deep breath so her chest grows larger, she looks up and pins me with a desperate stare.

My child is my kryptonite. I won't hand that power over to a man ever again.

"Please put June on the phone."

"I was calling to do *you* a favor," he bites out venomously. "To bring her back so you can spend the night together. And what do I get for my kindness?" The hatred in his voice has me balling my fists and readying to smash a bastard's face in. "I get it thrown in my fucking face!"

"Please stop shouting." Calm. Collected. Practiced. Nicole battles Noah's rage with hypnotic composure. "Please don't cuss in front of our daughter."

"Nicole!"

"Mommy?"

"Please put June on the phone," she asks again, almost too gently, so I worry her kindness is an invitation for him to walk all over her. "Noah?"

"Fine!" He snaps out the word, then tosses the phone to a solid surface—maybe the kitchen counter—so the sound crackles through the speakers and prompts Nicole to pull it from her ear or risk damage to her hearing.

"Mommy?" Small hands fumble the phone, and excited breathing makes my heart sprint faster. Then, "Hey, Mommy! Can you hear me?"

"Hi, baby." Nicole's entire countenance softens so I'm almost tempted to climb up off the floor and head over to sit next to her. To hold her. To squeeze her close.

But I don't dare. Not while she's on the phone with her daughter. And not while Noah is slamming doors and stomping around his place like a dick.

"Do you wanna video call, honey? Would you like to do—"

"Yes!"

In my mind, I see the little girl pull the phone from her ear, just like Nicole does. Then I catch the real-time transformation of Nicole Feeney, from the shrunken woman who has to speak to her abuser, to the mom who cherishes the fucking earth her daughter walks on.

As both women get their tech organized, then the call pops onto speaker, Nicole's happiness notches up a thousand degrees, and with it, the way my stomach tugs in her direction. The way I crave her company. Her body. Her attention.

Fuck, I crave her smile, and yearn for the day she rewards me with that kind of unconditional trust and freedom.

"Hi, baby." Nicole's eyes shimmer with happy emotion. "Oh, wow. You have food all over your face, huh? What did you have for dinner?"

"Lamb curry," the little girl grumbles. Then quieter, "It was disgusting. But Daddy said I had to eat it because I wasn't getting anything else."

I see every tiny notch dug from Nicole's heart. Every nick. Every slice. It gives *death by a thousand cuts* a real-life, practical visual for me to witness.

Leaning closer to the phone, she whispers, "You have snacks in your bag, right?"

"Yeah. I ate enough lamb so Daddy wouldn't get mad at me. But I'll sneak a snack when I go to bed."

"Honey." Nicole's voice breaks. "I'm so sorry you—"

"Daddy said I was coming home to sleep tonight," Juniper's voice cheers instantly, brushing aside the threat of starvation, solitary confinement, and abuse. It's easy for a child who hears it often enough. I know from experience that kids too quickly become desensitized to things that would horrify others. "Am I coming home tonight, Mommy?"

"No." Exhaling, Nicole brings a hand up to swipe her cheek. She's not crying. But she's hurting. She's hurting so fucking bad. "You're not coming home tonight, Bug. Daddy was mistaken."

Daddy was angling for a sleepover with Mommy, and now that he isn't getting it, he'll punish both girls.

"Oh, well..." In response, June's voice falls quieter. "Okay. But I get to come home Monday, right? No matter what?"

"Absolutely." Nicole sits taller and smiles for her baby girl the way my mother never did for me. "I hope you have a fun weekend. Maybe ask Daddy to take you to that trampoline place tomorrow. That way, you can jump your sillies out all day."

With witnesses. And minimal contact with the douchebag meant to supervise you.

"Meanwhile, guess what Mommy has to do?"

"What?" June's disappointment makes way for curiosity and glee. They call that ability to bounce back *resilience*. "What are you gonna do, Mom?"

"I have to call Uncle Axe in the morning and make him fix my car again." Playfully, she wrinkles her nose and makes her daughter giggle. "The silly thing didn't want to work this afternoon, so I guess it's gonna have to go to the car doctor."

"Miss Alesi owns a mechanics, Mom! They're the car doctors, so they can probably fix it for you."

"Fix what?" The sound of Noah's demanding voice and his stomping feet sets my teeth on edge. "What needs to be fixed?"

I hear the shuffle of the phone. The quick movements and panic that makes tension sit thick in the air. Then June's bubbling tone. "Just the car, Daddy. It's being stupid."

"You're having car troubles, Nicki?"

I hate hearing his voice. I hate knowing he treats these girls like shit. I hate his very existence, and I hate the courts for not only allowing his abuse, but practically enforcing it.

"Nicole?" he barks out again when she doesn't speak. "Are you having car trouble?"

"No." She fakes a smile and looks dead into the phone. "Just the radio. Can you put June back on? I'd like to say goodnight."

"If you're having car trouble, and my daughter's primary mode of transport is not reliable or safe—"

"Like I said," she grits out, "the radio. June Bug, honey?" She lifts her voice to bypass her gatekeeper. "Baby? Mommy's gonna hang up, okay? It's dinnertime now, and you'll want to get ready for bed soon. Which means I have to let you go."

"Okay." Juniper's not holding the phone, which means Nicole doesn't get to see her face. But she gets those final words. "I love you, Mommy. I love you zooper duper."

Broken, sad, but held together by willpower and stubbornness, Nicole fakes a chuckle and kisses the pads of her fingers. "I love you too, baby. Zooper duper. I'll see you after school on Monday. Noah," her face hardens, and her smile drops away to reveal something much colder. "Goodnight."

She presses her thumb to the screen and kills her call before setting the device on the stairs. Then she simply lies back.

Resting her head on the stair a few up from where she sits, she lowers her legs so they stretch all the way to the floor, and her tiny slip dress reveals too much thigh. Too much everything.

But I no longer feel that dizzying hunger from earlier.

Pushing to my feet in silence and closing the space between us, I move onto the stairs, but place my feet on each side of her torso so I stand over her.

Her eyes are closed and her arm laid over them both. Her lips are parted, like she needs the extra help to breathe, and her chest heaves as she searches for calm.

For peace.

For a fucking morsel of patience for the man who continues to treat them like shit.

"Hey?" I crouch so I'm almost—but not quite—sitting on her.

When she doesn't respond, I carefully pick up her arm... and find tears streaking along her temples. "Shit, Nicole." My stomach falls at the defeat that burns in her expression. "Babe?"

"Just give me a second." Her voice catches, and her sternum bounces from a sharp inhalation of air. "Just a second, then I can rein it in and be back to how I was before."

"I'm not looking for a fucking front."

I take her hands in mine and move down the stairs until I'm no longer looming over her, then I tug until she starts folding my way. Pulling her up into my arms and pressing her head to rest on my shoulder, I turn us toward the room to the right of the front door, where carpet can be seen through the doorway, and streetlights out front illuminate half the space.

After allowing my eyes to adjust to the new darkness, I find the shadow of a couch pressed against a wall, then I drop down so the cushions eat us up. But I keep Nicole in my lap and wrap my arms around her torso while she holds on.

She doesn't weep. Doesn't sniffle. She's not putting on a show or looking for sympathy.

She's just... living the life she was handed, and taking her minute to collect herself.

"How hard is it to hand her over every weekend?" I murmur.

She swallows down her tears and shakes her head. Fast. Sharp. A statement. "Every *other* weekend. And often, it works out to be once a month, or even once every six weeks, because Noah claims to be busy and forfeits his time."

Pushing up and resting her forearms on my shoulders, she looks anywhere but at me as she swipes a hand beneath her nose. "Last year, he went four and a half consecutive months without seeing her. He didn't call. He didn't tell her why he wasn't around." Bringing her gaze back to mine, she pulls her bottom lip between her teeth and nibbles. "I figure he must've found a new girlfriend to schmooze, and having an ex-wife and a part-time kid wasn't working with the story he was telling her, so he just... didn't come around. It was all so polite and formal when he texted." She laughs, but it's a sound of heartbreak, not humor. "*Kind regards. Dearest Nicole.*" She sniffs. "He just sent it, like it's so easy to not see your kid for that long. Then he was silent, for months. And they were the best months of my entire year."

Finally, she lets a whimper free of the bottle she tries so intently to trap her feelings in.

"Life was so quiet and peaceful. And it's not like June enjoys going there anyway. But she was five, Preston." Her eyes burn. "How do you explain to a five-year-old that her father doesn't give a shit, without saddling her with lifelong trauma she'll carry into adulthood?"

"I don't know." I slide my hand along her arm and up to cup her cheek. Because I was that five-year-old once. And the fact I'm thinking of my parents now probably means I'm still carrying my trauma. "I don't know what you could say that would help her."

"There's just..." she shrugs. "There's nothing *to* say. Because a parent shouldn't do that to their child. No matter what, no matter how much they hate or love or want to control their ex, they should never treat their child with anything but unconditional love."

"I'm sorry he does the things he does to you." I push my fingers through her hair and hold on tight. Because I worry she's readying to run. "I'm sorry he doesn't love June the way she deserves."

"He doesn't love at all," she chokes out. "He's incapable of loving anyone but himself. But the worst part..." She drags her forearm across and wipes her nose. "The worst part is that he doesn't love himself at all. He's miserable and drowning in self-loathing, and because of that, he can never find genuine happiness. So my poor baby has to visit this person whose only emotion is hatred, and we both have to trust he'll bring her home again."

She turns her face and presses her lips to my palm. "It would be easier to hand her over to a stranger. A complete, pulled off the street, no clue who they are, random person. Because most are good, right? *Most* people carry with them the need to protect a child, even if they have no clue who the child is. It's built into our DNA, I'm certain of it."

"Yeah." I stroke her cheek and think of the little girl I met earlier this week. The one I thought was Axel's.

Though Axel was a dude I'd met just a minute before that, already I was prepared to protect her. It didn't matter to me who her parents were or where she belonged. She was there, and I was too, so my existence would center, if only momentarily, around making sure she was safe and happy.

"I think most people are good," I concede. "I think we hear about the worst, and sometimes, that can make us worry about humanity. But I think most folks would protect an innocent kid."

"Right," she breathes out sadly. "Most would die to help a child we don't even know. So how can a man actively not care about his very own? Will there never come a time where he just wants to be healthy for that beautiful baby girl he helped create?"

"Not everyone is good, Nicole." I straighten my back and bring her closer until her face stops just a hair's breadth from mine. Until her eyes lower, and the tears shimmering in them reflect an image of myself back at me. "*Most* are good," I allow. "But not all. And it fucking sucks that June got one of the not good kinds as her dad."

"Because I chose wrong," she whimpers. "Because I got pregnant and trapped in a life I hated."

"And then you found freedom again." I press my lips to hers and taste tears on her tongue. "He *tricked* you, Feeney. Then he controlled you. But you got out anyway. And ya know what?" I pull her face down and wrap my arms tight around her shuddering torso. "You get her twelve days out of fourteen. You get to show her the love she deserves, and the home we should all strive for. She has Axel to teach her what a healthy man looks like, and she gets to see you *thriving* in this world. She'll learn what boundaries are, and there will never be a day when she's afraid to tell you how she feels."

"She has to spend nights in a home she's abused in."

"Ordered by the courts," I argue. "Not by you. And if you don't follow the rules, you risk the orders being flipped and *him* getting her twelve days out of fourteen."

"Oh god." She convulses in my arms and shakes her head. "I won't let that happen."

"Exactly." I press my lips to the center of her forehead and close my eyes. "You got her out, Nicole. You got both of you out. And now you get eighty percent of her childhood to remind her that she's a Feeney too, so she can go to that asshole's home and remember she's strong and brave and wonderful. We both know he'll try to tear her down—it's who he is, because he's miserable and hates his life. But June has you to look up to. She has the strongest, bravest role model on the fucking planet."

I drag her face up until her eyes flicker open and her lips open into a beautiful pout. "What you give her is more than a lot of other kids get."

"You're being obnoxiously sweet."

I choke out a laugh and pull her supple lips between mine for a beat. "I'm telling you a truth I'm not sure you've ever stopped to consider. You didn't *choose* to give her an abusive father, Feeney. *He* chose to abuse. He tricked you, and wouldn't have let his mask fall until after the marriage certificates were signed and you were exactly where he wanted you."

Unconvinced, she brings her hands up to scrub at her eyes. "I should've been smarter."

"Yeah?" I nod toward her front window. "Go tell that to every other woman who married a guy just like him. Go tell them they're stupid and weak and should be ashamed of themselves."

"What?" Dropping her hands, she glances out the window, like there's an actual crowd waiting for her to speak. "No, that's—"

"Mean?" I insert. "Not true?"

"It's cruel! Why the hell would you kick someone when they're already fighting to survive?"

"Exactly." I pinch her chin between my fingers and pull her around until our lips clash and her breath warms my lungs. "If you wouldn't say it to others, then you gotta stop saying that shit to yourself."

"It's not the sa—"

"No, it's worse. You wanna bake a cake?"

"Do I want to..." Her eyes spring impossibly wide. "What?"

"Bake a cake." I stand from the couch, lifting her with me, and laugh when I grunt from the exertion. Then I set her on her feet and throw my arm over her shoulders. "I don't get off on fucking women when they're having an emotional overload about another man. It would be insensitive and unkind. But I don't wanna leave yet. And I don't wanna watch *Hocus Pocus*, since that was Dipshit's suggestion. So..." I lead her into her kitchen and smack her bare ass, sending her stumbling forward. "Let's bake. I like cake as much as the next guy, and I've been a little obsessed with Juniper's Bakery since I got my first taste."

"It's Friday night." She purses her lips and shoots a frown in my direction, but she still goes to a corner cabinet and takes out a mixing bowl. "You want me to work on a Friday night? *That's* insensitive and unkind."

"We can make it fun."

I head to the fridge and peruse my options before settling on a can of whipped cream. Taking it out and flicking the cap off, I shake it and tip my head back to fill my mouth.

"Disgusting," she grumbles with a roll of her eyes. "Do you not care about your calorie intake each day?"

"Fuck no." I stroll across the kitchen and pin her against the cabinet until the door snaps shut and a squeak of surprise rolls along her throat. Then fisting her hair and dragging her head to the left, I squeeze cream along the column of her neck, and lick it off to the humming pleasure that follows from deep in her soul. "And these kinds of calories never count."

"I thought you didn't wanna fuck a sad woman?" Setting her hands on the counter to keep her balance, she drops her head and closes her eyes as I slide my hand beneath the slip of silk. "Something about insensitive."

"I'm not fucking you." Stepping back, I grin when she thinks I'm giving her space. But then I sweep her up in my arms and lay her flat on the island counter so her nightie slides along her trembling thighs, and her breath races to a dangerous staccato. "I'm making a cake."

I drag the tip of my finger along the middle of her torso, up to the valley between her breasts, before tugging the silk down and squeezing cream onto her peaked nipples.

"Oh god." She rubs her thighs together in anticipation. "Preston."

Leaning in, I lap up the creamy dessert I've prepared for myself, and groan at the desperate cry that escapes her throat.

"Fuck, you taste good." I switch breasts, since I'm a man of equality and all that shit. Squeezing cream onto the pink tip, then licking it off until goosebumps sprint along her skin.

"You're supposed to be baking, Feeney." I make my way to the end of the counter, so I get a view straight between her legs, though she tries so hard to press them tight and keep me out.

Instead, I set the can down and grab her ankles. Yanking, I pull her along the counter until her ass rests on the edge and her pussy drips with frantic want. "I intended to eat cake." I set one of her legs on my shoulder and lay a kiss on the side of her knee. Then the second, repeated with another kiss. "But now I have this meal all laid out for me." I cast a look along her body, stopping on her face, and smirking when her eyes latch onto mine. "And you don't look all that sad anymore."

"Fuck." She drops her head back so her skull raps against the stone counter. But she doesn't complain, and I can't seem to fight the hunger burning me from the inside out. "Preston…"

"Relax." I slip a finger between her folds and thank god for the second condom I brought along tonight. I slide my tongue from the side of her knee and follow the line of her thigh closer, closer, closer to her apex. "You don't have to do any of the work, beautiful. I'm gonna take care of us both."

Preston

WITH SPRING ONIONS?

At some point after eating my dessert on the kitchen counter, and carrying a beautiful woman up to bed at eleven, I catch some sleep and *don't* get my ass kicked out of Nicole's home.

She didn't ask me to leave, nor did she seem all that nervous as I held her in my arms and drifted off to sleep.

But I know she's not entirely okay with sharing a bed, and I'm painfully aware she's apt to sneak out when a man isn't paying attention. Which means when I feel the bed move, and my eyes snap open to middle-of-the night darkness, I lie still in bed and watch the shadows as Nicole does what she did before.

She slips a shirt on and fixes the buttons. She snags a hair tie from the bathroom, and whips her hair back into a ponytail.

All in silence.

I watch her wander past the clock on the bedside table—four-twenty-four a.m.—then my stomach hollows as she tiptoes out of the room and dumps me just like last time.

She's not ready to commit even a single night. And fuck, it's not like I can blame her; she clawed her way out of the fire and made a safe haven for her and her daughter. The fact she let me into her home in the first place is a wonder. So her sneaking out again... not surprising.

I lie in bed for a little while longer. To give her the space she desires. To give myself time to come to grips with the emotions hammering my system.

Because I'm deep in *like* with a woman who doesn't really want me back.

I care how she's doing, and I care that she's not sad. Dammit, I care more than I'm comfortable admitting, and the reality is, even if she could like me back, what we have is built on half-truths and dangerous omissions.

"I work in IT" is the most vanilla bullshit description I could ever give for my job. But to tell her otherwise is impossible.

Hi, I'm Preston Danes. I steal, hurt, destroy, and sneak for a living. I've killed a man in cold blood. And hopefully soon, the explosives I deliver to a certain mafia compound will kill a few more. But it's all good. You can trust me to be in your life. What, with an innocent child in the mix, and a vindictive, controlling ex-husband on the side.

Frustrated, I toss the sweet-scented blankets off my body and push up to sit, then I drop my legs off the side of the bed and stand to go find Nicole.

It's practically the middle of the night, and it's insanely shitty of me to let my presence scare her out of her own bed. So if she'd prefer I sleep on the couch, then that's what I'll do. And if she wants me to go home, I'll do that instead.

Maybe in a week, she'll invite me back again. Or in a month, when June's with her dad, and Nicole has a second to breathe and think for herself again.

Soft music comes on downstairs, making me turn toward the bedroom door with a frown, then the clanking of pots and pans sends my mind spinning.

What the fuck?

Bypassing the bathroom—my curiosity is a thousand times more demanding than my bladder—I step into the hall and head down the staircase in silence.

Oh look, here I go sneaking again.

"Hey, Axe." Nicole's cheerful voice makes me pause, and the fun beat of Meghan Trainor brings a momentary smile to my lips. "Why do you have a filthy face?"

"Just got back from a job." He's tired. Grumbling. But as I stop by the doorway and lean against the frame, I get a view of, not just Nicole dancing around the kitchen in a shirt I recognize as the one I wore to Cole's wedding, but Axel too, his face on her phone, propped up on the counter.

His eyes swing my way, but he doesn't announce my presence yet. "Just a small structure fire," he continues for his sister, his face black with soot and dust, and his hair, wild with sweat and water and fuck knows what else. "Put it out, and B-crew are mopping up, since our shift is almost over."

His lips twitch as his sister dances around and starts mixing things in her bowl. "What've you been up to, Feen? Anything you wanna tell me about?"

She sashays by the fridge and takes out milk and eggs. "I had a date last night. And I have four dozen cupcakes to deliver to the shop in a few hours. Oh," she sets her things on the counter and goes back to the fridge for butter, "my car is acting up. Can you take a look today? I know you're tired, but it won't start, and I swear," she tosses the butter down and fists her hair in frustration, "I'm gonna stab someone if something else goes wrong on that piece of shit."

"Maybe you could ask your other friend to help. He's good with cars, isn't he?"

"My other friend?" Genuinely perplexed, Nicole grabs her supplies and gets to work cracking eggs, clueless to the fact I'm so close. "Do you mean Preston?"

"Mm." Axel's eyes snap across to me. "Do you still see him?"

"Yeah." I don't have a view of her face, so I can't know if she's smiling. But she sighs, and that feels good too. "We're still kinda hanging out. He was who I had a date with last night, actually."

She pauses, as though to re-count how many eggs she's used. Then she gets back to work. "I kinda had sex again."

Her brother barks out a laugh and scrubs a hand across his face. "At least you didn't lie. Was it fun?"

"The sex?" She spares a fast glance for her phone and wrinkles her face. "Wildly inappropriate. You're my brother!"

"I meant the date, dummy. Did he treat you well?"

"Mmm." She grabs a glass bowl for the stick of butter, then puts the lot into the microwave and hits the timer. "He treats me... not like glass."

Satisfied with her answer, she goes back to cracking eggs. "He's a little rough around the edges, ya know? There are no flowery words or over-the-top gestures. There's just him, calling me out on my shit, and sometimes pressuring me into uncomfortable conversations."

"Pressuring?" Vicious eyes whip back to me. "Tell me more."

"Not like..." She shakes her head and bops her way back to the microwave when it beeps. "It's not like when Noah would pressure me into things that would hurt me. With Preston, it's more like he's making me uncomfortable for my own gain. So I can be brave, or stand up for myself, or experience something fun and new."

"Like a one-night stand." He drops his gaze. "Tell me less."

She sniggers. "Like that." She pours melted butter into the pot and slowly adds milk. "I'm a grown woman, Axe. And single. There's no reason for me not to have casual sex with someone like him, so he just... I dunno." She shrugs and heads to a large drawer to take out a mixing... spoon. But it looks more like a stick. "He helps me do things that are new and exciting. But not dangerous or anything. I'm not jumping out of a plane."

"No, but you're having sex with a stranger." Axel's voice turns a little harder. "You using protection, Feeney?"

"Yes." She flicks her stick-spoon toward the phone. "Of course I am. And your question is inappropriate."

"I have a vested interest in your well-being. Sex is fun," he assures her, "but herpes isn't, and neither is an unwanted pregnancy."

"It concerns me that you have firsthand experience with herpes," she taunts. "Be sure to warn Hannah before you make a move. And there will be no unwanted pregnancies. I've spoken my boundaries and held to them."

"First of all," he rolls his eyes. "I have no STDs, jerk. Second, I'm not making a move on Hannah. She's a teenager. And third, your boyfriend's behind you."

"What?" She spins with a skid, flinging cake batter against the cabinet as she goes, then she slaps her hands to her mouth and gasps. "Preston!"

"He also heard the thing about herpes," Axel giggles. "But those are the breaks, man. Preston?" He moves his head, like that'll somehow help him see around her. "Why the fuck are you in my sister's kitchen at four in the morning with no clothes on?"

"Wait," another voice demands on his side of the line. Then a second face forces itself into the frame. "What the fuck? Who is that asshole?"

Nicole's eyes glitter with terror. And humiliation. And six thousand other emotions as she looks me up and down.

Thank god I didn't come down naked.

Slowly, when she remains mute and unable to move, I wander closer until I get a clearer view of Axel and his friend. "Who are you?"

"I asked you first," the other guy bites out. "Why are you at her house at this hour?"

"Preston Danes," Axel chuckles. "Meet Lieutenant Nixon Rosa. He has a sister too, and he's not cool with her dating."

"This isn't dating!" Nixon explodes. He, too, has a black face and tired eyes. "This is *sex*. Your sister is having sex, and you're smiling about it. What the fuck is wrong with you?"

"Well, she's not having sex *right now*," Axel laughs. "I sure as shit wouldn't be on the phone to watch it. And you need to mind your business, Lew. Go stress out your own sister."

"I can't! Because she's married and in love and blah, blah, fuckin' blah." Then he looks to Nicole, though her eyes are still on me. "Are you married to this man, Nicole? One-night stands are filthy and not okay."

"Are you married to the Italian goddess who owns the new hotel in town?" Axel counters savagely. "Or is that a one-night stand situation?"

But as Nixon's feral sneer turns on his own team member, Axel hastily adds, "Sir."

"It's a *none of your damn business* situation. And you're on the clock." Nixon looks to us. "Nicole! Put some pants on and send him home. He can come back with a ring or an apology."

"Well, he already brought the herpes," Axel cackles. "So it's a free-for-all at this point."

Stunned, mouth agape, Nicole sputters, "I'm hanging up." Then she turns her back to me and kills her call so Axel's and Nixon's faces give way to a black screen.

Gingerly, she sets the phone down, and the spatula thingy beside it. She doesn't whirl back my way. Doesn't rush out an explanation or babbled words. Instead, she presses her hands to the edge of the counter, much like she did last night. "Uh..."

"Can I come closer?" I want to. I'm hungry for her touch. But I'm aware she's not a 'next day' kind of woman, and we're officially past our *date*. "Nicole? I—"

"I wasn't sneaking out." She spins then, and leans back to rest her hands on the edge of the counter. Swallowing so her throat bobs and her cheeks flush with a pink blush, she drops her gaze and studies her bare legs beneath her shirt... my shirt. "I have to work," she murmurs. "But I would have come up to bed when I was done. And if you were still asleep—"

"Would you have woken me with your mouth wrapped around my cock?"

Her head whips up, and her molten stare locks onto mine.

"Would you have been sad that I was still here?"

She shakes her head before I finish my sentence, then presses a hand to her stomach and chews on her bottom lip. "No. I was kinda hoping you'd hang out for a little longer. I have all day." Then she crooks a thumb over her shoulder to point back at her half-done work. "Well, except for that. But I would've been done in a little over an hour, and I could have come back to bed and—"

"Fucked me awake?"

"Do you always have to be so crude?" She asks a question, but it sounds like a statement. Then she twists on her heels and snatches up her stick thingy. "Sure," she bites out. "Maybe. I liked sucking your cock last night, so who knows, I might've done it again. Or sex. That feels good too. But you make it weird and grate on my stubborn side, so now I can never wake you up like that."

Chuckling, I close the space between us and stop only when my cock nestles against her ass and my arms come around her stomach. Then I bury my lips against the side of her neck and bite where I've already bitten a few times before.

"You have hickies, by the way." I slide my tongue across the marks, and grin when she stiffens with surprise. "You probably haven't seen them yet, since you got dressed in the dark. But it would be shitty of me not to point out that you just talked to your brother, almost naked, with hickies on your neck."

"Pig." She stirs her batter inside a pot larger than any other I've seen in my life, but she doesn't smack me away when I slide my hand under her shirt.

My shirt.

Our shirt.

"I have to bake these," she mumbles, less fiery now that we have skin touching skin. "But I'm glad you're still here."

"I won't slow you down." I nibble the shell of her ear and smirk as she gets back to work. "Wanna get breakfast with me later?"

"Here?" she asks. "Or out in public?"

"Which do you prefer? I'm easy."

"Here." She pours other ingredients into her bowl and stirs so her hips shimmy with the movement. "I'm not ready to go out yet."

"With me?" I tease, knowing her reasons, but still fishing for a full explanation. "Or in general?"

"Both. I'll need to cover my neck with makeup. I'll have to shower again, wash and dry my hair. And then I have to accept that everyone in this town involves themselves with everyone else's private lives, like how my brother knows about his boss' new lady friend. Breakfast in public is more commitment than I can handle right now."

"But you're glad I'm still here." I release her supple body and take a step back, since I'm slowing her down, despite my vow not to, simply by holding on.

I back up further and push up to sit on the island counter, while she rushes to a different cabinet and takes out an electric mixer. "The fact you're glad I'm here means something to me."

"So..." She plugs her machine in and peeks back my way. "Breakfast?"

"Sure. Maybe I can cook, since you did dinner last night."

"Really?" Her cheeks fill with a rosy blush that makes my cock hard and my heart strum a little faster. "You'd cook my breakfast?"

"I had intended to cook your dinner last night, too, but didn't get the chance."

As she gets to work mixing her batter, I lift my chin toward the now black phone. "You want my help with your car today? I do actually have a decent understanding of them, and I've met the local mechanic, so I could hook you up there."

Immediately, she shakes her head *no.* "I can't afford to spend money on a shitty car. And mechanics don't work for free, so..."

"Have you spoken to *that* mechanic? Because I hear he's fuckin' cool, especially when his clientele are chicks who need help and an honest day's work done on their engines. He won't rip you off."

Her tongue comes out, not in a seduction, but in concentration, as her bowl rotates and her stick works batter off the side. "Maybe. I'll consider it. In the meantime, I'll call Hannah and tell her to come pick these up for the shop, then I have a free day." Twisting again, she shows off a sly grin that arrows straight to my groin. "I'm trying really hard not to ask you to leave."

"Oh... Well..." Those arrows fizzle out and dissolve like they never existed. "You shouldn't be *trying* to want me to be here, Feeney." Setting my hands on the counter, I push off and drop to my feet. "If you're not comfortable—"

"It's not that simple," she speaks just loud enough to be heard over the mixer. "I *want* you to be here—more than I expected I would—but I'm chronically accustomed to having space to myself. I'm not used to always being switched on for someone else. However, my desire for your company overpowers my longing to be left alone, so..."

"That was potentially the sweetest thing someone has ever said to me," I drawl. Leaning back against the counter, I shake my head and watch, powerless, as she laughs with abandon and does a mini dance in my shirt.

"You don't have to be switched on for me, by the way," I tell her. "We are who we are. We don't always have to exchange witty conversation and casual flirting. You don't need to host me, and sex is only for when you *want* it. No guilt trips or bullshit in between. It's really that simple."

Her lips remain wide in a stunning smile. "Which is why I want you to stay. I've told you *no* more times than I can count, about more things than I can remember. I say *no* so often, I swear I'm waiting for you to give up and walk away."

"I don—"

"But you never try to guilt me." Leaving her bowl to turn and the mixer to do its thing, she twirls to the island cupboard and taps my thigh to move me out of the way. Then she opens doors and pulls out cupcake trays and sets them by the mixer.

"You never pout," she adds seriously. "You don't whine, or try to negotiate a different outcome once I've spoken my boundaries."

"You told me no to dinner and hanging out." Then I wave my hands along my jeaned legs. "Yet here I am."

"But it wasn't a mindfuck." She greases the trays with practiced moves and flips the mixer off like she's done this a million times before.

Which, I guess, she has.

"You didn't try to make me fold on my boundaries, Preston. You laid out an option for me—we come here, we have sex, we have a good time—and I..." She snatches the massive bowl from the mixer and starts pouring into the trays. "I accepted. But if I said no... like," she glances back, "*actually* said no, and meant it, you weren't going to give me a guilt trip and carry on like a dick. You pick at me, but you never play games. And because of that, my brain is just..." Drawing a deep breath, she exhales again and goes back to work. "At peace when you're around. And that means something to me. But what means the most is that, *if* I decide I don't want you here anymore—"

"I'll just go," I finish for her, acknowledging that I understand her train of thought. "Not because I'm done with you," I clarify, since I want her to understand me too. "But because I won't stay where I'm not wanted."

"Exactly."

She changes the sway of her hips as Katy Perry comes on the radio. "Neither of us will stay in hostile or unwelcome situations. That's a strength for us both, Preston." Setting her bowl aside and moving to the pre-warmed oven, she flips the door open so a heavy waft of heat carries in the air and lifts her shirt to reveal more of her thighs. "I like that we're both here because we choose to be."

She slides one tray into the oven, then turns to grab the second. "We have thirty-five minutes once I close this door." Sliding her tongue along the front of her teeth, she captures my eyes and grins. "Wanna join me in the shower?"

"Fuck yes." I grab the third tray and place it in her hand to save us time. Then I watch, bated and waiting, for her to close the oven door. "Ready, Feeney?"

"I'm ready." She turns away from the oven and wipes her hands on a tea towel "Usually, I would wash the dishes while I wait."

"We'll do them together later." I yank her into my side and pull her into my arms, then together, we dash toward the stairs.

"Thirty-four minutes!" I taunt. Hope and happiness and—hell, I'm still crude Preston, so—*horniness*, all roil in my blood as we sprint up the stairs. "I want at least fifteen of those with my cock nestled in your throat."

"Shit," she pants breathlessly.

But she doesn't slow.

She doesn't stop.

~

Cakes bake. Showers run. Icing is piped in pretty little designs, and makeup is applied to Nicole's delicate neck to cover my neanderthal claims of ownership. Hannah is called, clothes are donned, hair is dried and styled, and awkward throat clearings get us through a visit by the overeager bakery assistant who would rather ask in painful detail the going-ons of last night than help her boss load inventory into the car.

Finally, around eight, when Hannah's car disappears around the corner, Nicole shakes her head at the sudden reappearance of peace and quiet, and turns at the hood of my truck, still parked in the driveway, to stroll back up the porch steps toward me.

"She's so much," she sniggers, taking my hand as she ascends the stairs.

When I stand my ground and pull her against my chest, she accepts my slow kiss pressed to her lips, then rewards me with a hug and a deep exhale that is both calming and content.

On her porch.

Where the whole world can see.

She's choosing to be here in the *now* with me, and not overthink the million things that could bring her grief.

"Breakfast?" she finally murmurs after a minute. Maybe two or three. "What are you gonna cook?"

"My go-to is bacon and eggs." I drag the hair off her shoulder and place a gentle kiss to the exposed skin there. "But since we did that last night, maybe I can think up something else. Do you like omelets?"

She makes a sound of pleasure in the back of her throat. "I love a good omelet. With spring onions?"

"Sure. And mushrooms?"

Her head snaps up like a hound out to hunt, surprising me as she pulls back and scans the street.

"Nicole?" My brows furrow together. "What's—"

"*Shh.*" She takes her hands from my hips and clasps them tight as she nervously looks to the street.

Then a car pulls around the corner at the end of the block, and the woman who was the epitome of relaxation a moment ago now spins out in a frenzy that makes my stomach drop.

She throws herself in my direction, yanks her front door open with one hand, and shoves me toward it with the other. "Get inside!"

"What are you—Nicole!" I stumble over the threshold, but grab the door before she can slam it behind me. "What the f—"

"Go!" she hisses. "It's Noah." She shoves me in again, and swings the door shut with enough force to make the walls rattle.

Then I find myself all alone inside her home, so all I hear is my own breathing, and all I feel is my temper lighting in my blood.

Through the small glass window built alongside her entryway, I'm witness to a sedan pulling into the driveway behind my truck. It's unmarked, the earmark of a detective who no longer has to drive a vehicle with lights on top and garish badges marking the sides.

From my vantage point, I see the back of Nicole's head, and her long, blonde hair bouncing after a fresh shampoo and blow dry. Then I see Noah Scott. The fucking asshole responsible for all the tears Nicole sheds. Dark hair, dark eyes. Jeans and a button-up shirt.

He pushes out of his car, but his eyes burn holes in the side of my truck as he reads the plates and puzzles over the mystery parked in his ex-wife's driveway.

"Mommy!" June climbs from the back seat and dashes from the car with a fluffy backpack bouncing against her backside as she runs. "Hi, Mommy!"

"Hi, June Bug!" Still stunned, but fast on her feet, Nicole lowers into a crouch and catches her baby on the fly. Then she pushes up to stand, tense and staring, as Noah hovers around the bed of my truck.

Like a fuckwit, he actually kicks the tires.

"What are you doing here, Noah?"

My heart thunders, and my hands flex to do something. To go out there and get that asshole the fuck off Nicole's property. He has no right to be here.

But confronting him wouldn't end with him squaring up to *me*. No, that fight would be too fair, when cockheads like him prefer to punish women and children instead.

Impatient when he doesn't answer, Nicole snaps out, "Noah?"

"Whose truck is this?" Suspicious, he brings his gaze up to the porch, only to squint because the sun shines from the east and reflects off the windows. "You didn't come home last night."

"What?" She hitches June up on her hip so both are more comfortable, then she moves and blocks my view.

Or perhaps she blocks Noah's view of me.

"I was here last night," she insists. Giving up on him, she looks to the girl. "Mommy is so happy to see you, Bug, but why are you here before Monday? I'm so confused."

"Daddy said he was worried," she replies on a chirp. "He said you didn't come home *allll* night, so we had to come check you were okay."

"But I talked to you last night," she counters. "I don't..." She desperately searches for understanding. "I talked to you on video call, Bug. I was at home."

"Your car is at the bakery." Noah sets his hands on his hips and tries to make himself larger. More intimidating. But he doesn't wander closer to the porch. Maybe that's a boundary Nicole has already set. A line she refuses him permission to cross. "We drove past it on the way here just now."

"I-I said I was having car trouble," she stammers. "I left it there overnight so it would be closer to the mechanic to check today."

Noah's eyes narrow to dangerous slits. Challenging. Questioning. "You said it was a radio issue."

"It is. But Bug and I deserve a working radio. So the mechanic said he'll fix it today."

Such a poor lie. An embarrassing lie, really.

"And this?" He tilts his head toward my truck again. "A *friend's*?"

"Fuck." When the thought hits me, I drop my hands to my pockets and pat until I find my phone. *Tell him it's the mechanic's truck, baby. It belongs to the mechanic.*

"I-It's the mechanic's," she says, as if my thoughts transmitted straight to her brain.

Inside the house, I hit dial and dash into the kitchen to get space.

"He said I could borrow it," Nicole pushes on, her voice growing quieter as I move.

"Yeah?" Sophia answers my call on the second ring. "What's up, Casanova?"

"I need your help," I rush out. "I'd do it myself, but I don't have my laptop here."

"The *mechanic's*?" Noah pushes. Pushes. Pushes so my jaw grits and my teeth grind together. "You sure about that?"

"Danes?"

"I need you to change the information on my truck. Make it belong to Alesi."

She laughs. "Why? You trying to pin a parking ticket on him?"

"So you won't mind me running the plates?" Noah asks threateningly. Douche-ily. "I could make sure you're telling the truth."

"Excuse me?" Nicole spits out. "You don't get to call *me* a liar." The front door swings open so her voice grows in volume. "Go inside for a second, Bug. Daddy and I have to talk for a minute."

"Danes?"

"Change the fuckin' details!"

When tiny, padding footsteps head my way, I rush through the next doorway and find myself in the laundry room. A washing machine sits on the floor, and a dryer above that. In the sink, a massive wrench lies discarded, but near enough to grab if you know it's there.

"Ace!" I whisper-hiss. "I just need you to do this for me. Please. I'll explain later."

"Fine." I don't think she minds helping out a friend—and I honestly think she gets a sick thrill out of fucking with other people—but she's incapable of doing anything without bitching about it first. "You got baby-daddy problems?"

"Seems that way," I grumble. "Noah's giving Nicole a tough time. He's just turned up at her place uninvited."

"Sounds to me like she needs to invest in an un-papered Glock, and a Griffin home security system. Actually," she *tap-tap-taps* her keyboard, "I'm penciling her in for a system overhaul. Cap can come out and install it for her."

"Hello?"

A sweet little voice brings me around so my feet slide on tile and my vision blurs for a beat of my heart. Then a curious stare looks me up and down, unafraid, despite the feral hiss emanating from my lips because I smash my knee against the corner of the washing machine.

"I met you," June chatters while I drop my hand to furiously rub the ache away.

"Oh dear." Sophia's wicked laugh brings my temper to a fiery peak. "You're in trouble now, Danes."

Trusting her to do the job, I kill our call and slip the phone back into my pocket.

"Um, hi..." I limp-step closer, but stop with six still separating us before I lower into a crouch and replace my scowl with a smile.

As easy as it is to breathe, I fall in love with a beautiful pair of silver eyes rimmed in lashes too long to be natural. And yet, they're perfect and pretty enough to make my heart squeeze.

"Yeah. We met." I soften my voice and swallow the nerves clogging my throat.

I'm your mom's friend.

I'm your mom's one-night stand... twice.

I'm falling deeply in like with your mother.

"I'm friends with your Uncle Axel," I settle on instead. "You remember the other day at the park?"

"Oh yeah!" Her smile lights up her little face and highlights sun-kissed spots on her cheeks. Then she giggles. "Uncle Axe ate your cupcake!"

"He did," I mock admonish. Shaking my head, I purse my lips and keep myself right here with her, when my brain so vehemently focuses on Nicole's enraged voice coming from the front porch.

"You're just leaving her here? You're working? Really? I don't believe you're not checking up on me, Noah."

"Can you believe he ate my cupcake? That was a bit cheeky, huh?"

"Yeah, he eats my cupcakes too," she sniggers. Her lips are a natural rosy-red, and her hair is almost as long as her mom's. "He eats *allllll* the time," she adds. Then she looks around. "Is Uncle Axe here?"

"Uh... no." I push up to stand as she spins on her feet and wanders out of the laundry room. Then I follow her into the kitchen. Slow steps. Plenty of distance so she doesn't get spooked. "But I've talked to him this morning already. He asked me to drop by and pick up something for him."

"Oh?" She swings the fridge door open, casual as can be, and takes out a juice box similar to the ones that accompanied our dinner last night. "That's cool, then."

She slams the door shut and monkey-climbs onto a stool so she can sit at the counter. "I'm glad I'm home." With no clue how bewitching she is, she glances across and meets my eyes. "I hate it at Daddy's."

"You do?"

"*You have a date tonight?*" Noah asks Nicole, setting my blood on fire. And hers too, I'm sure. "*Word travels around small towns, ya know?*"

"*Yeah? Well, not every word should be believed. And even if I did have a date, it would have nothing to do with you.*"

In response, Noah scoffs in the back of his throat. "*It has everything to do with me. If you're dating around, then these people will have access to my daughter.*" He pauses for a long beat before adding, "*June's safety is my primary concern.*"

"*Oh please!*" Then, "*That's why you've brought her home, isn't it? You thought I had a date, so you made damn sure I wouldn't be able to go.*"

"*My parenting choices have nothing to do with your sex life, Nicole. Grow up. I have work, that's all there is to it.*"

"*How do you so easily give up your time with her, Noah? She's the best thing that will ever happen to either of us, but you dismiss her without a thought.*"

"Ya know what?" Pasting on a smile and tuning them out, I come around to the other side of the counter and rest my elbows on top.

It takes June a moment longer to ignore her parents. To bring her attention back to this kitchen. Then her eyes meet mine, and her lips curl into a grin.

"Since Uncle Axe stole my cupcake, I was thinking I should bake more," I tell her conspiratorially. "Ya know, to be fair."

"Sure." Her silver eyes light up with playfulness. "Then you can have *twelve* cupcakes instead of just one. That's fair, because he stole."

"Right!" I turn to the dishes drying on the side of the sink and take out the massive bowl Nicole used earlier. "So that's what I'm gonna do. I'm gonna bake and eat ten." I peek over my shoulder. "You and your mom can probably have one each as well, since I'm using your kitchen."

I head to the fridge and take out butter and milk, then I move to the pantry and grab a massive salt shaker. "I can't wait to eat these." I set the salt down right in June's line of sight. "I'm starving! I haven't even had breakfast yet. So—"

"You can't use salt!" The perfect tinkling of childhood laughter makes my stomach twist and my heart ache. Then I hear the scrape of her stool on the floor as she climbs down and snatches away my faux pas. "You need sugar, silly!"

"What?" I turn at the sink, giving her space, and make a funny face. "What do you mean we don't use salt? It looks exactly right."

"You're supposed to use sugar," she snickers.

Switching out the shaker for a pound bag of sugar instead, she brings it to the counter and plops it on top. Then she goes back and peruses an entire array of boxes with pictures of cupcakes on the side.

"I'll help you make these," she declares, pulling one out and showing off kiddie cupcakes with Barbie graphics on the side. "They're way easier than the ones Mom makes. And they say all the instructions on the side!" She tosses the box beside the sugar and shoots me a disdainful side-eye. "That way, you won't mess it up."

"Oh, well..." I flip the tap on and start washing my hands. "I'm so glad you're here to help."

"Sometimes boys just don't know how to bake properly." She rolls her eyes and climbs the stool again to perch on top. "My dad doesn't cook either. My mom had to do *allll* that stuff when they were married." Then she flashes a giddy smirk for me. "Now she cooks for just us. And some-times Uncle Axe."

"Uncle Axe sure is lucky." I switch the tap off and snag the towel to dry my hands.

"Of course she can stay here. Unlike you, I want to see my child. But you don't get to come onto my property and check on me. My life is none of your business."

"So what's your favorite meal that your mom cooks?" I shake off the adult issues, knowing Nicole is safe. She's unharmed, physically, and right now, I'd do more damage by going out there than if I stayed put. So I brush away my fighting instincts and bake with a child instead. "What's your absolute favorite food to cook in this kitchen?"

"Hmm..." June taps a finger to her plump lower lip and jumps up to perch her backside on the counter. She crosses her legs, so her feet end up on the countertop—something her mom probably wouldn't be pleased about, but I can't find a single fuck to give.

If she wants to sit up there, I'm here for it. And if she looks like she might fall, I'll make damn sure to catch her.

"I really like baked dinner," she answers. "Like, baked lamb." A childish, slow hum of pleasure rolls along her throat. "I *loooove* baked lamb. 'Specially on Sundays. 'Cos Mom doesn't work Sundays, so we have all day to make it and make the house smell nice."

A core memory for the girl. A scent that'll stick with her for life. Because she has a mom who gives a fuck and fights every damn day to keep her daughter safe.

"I love a good Sunday roast, too." I grab a silver straw from the drawer and hold it the way Nicole wields her mixing spoon. "Okay, I'm ready."

"What?" June chokes out a giggle and crawls across the counter to open a different drawer. "Here." She thrusts the tool forward.

When the rubber end loudly slaps my chest, she snaps her head back to meet my eyes with fear in her expression, and a quiver to her jaw. "I-I'm sorry. I didn't mean to hit you."

"Oh, honey." *You're not allowed to hug her, Pres. You can't fucking touch.* "It's okay." I paste on my best smile and wait as the terror slowly recedes from her eyes. "It didn't hurt. And you didn't mean to do it." I wink and watch as she carefully crawls back to her sitting place, then I drop the scraper into the bowl and go to the fridge for a carton of chocolate milk. "This one?"

"The white milk," she snickers. Not as freely this time. But she's trying. She's getting a feel for who I am, and hoping against all hope I'm not like her dad. "You could probably use the chocolate if you want, but you're 'sposed to use white. Besides, chocolate is more expensive, and Mom might get cranky about wasting."

"We definitely don't wanna make Mom sad." I toss the brown milk back and take out what we need instead. "What ne—"

"My dad says mean things about my mom when I'm visiting with him."

My hands keep moving. My smile, plastered on and working overtime to remain. But through tight teeth, I grit out, "Hmm?"

"He says she's the reason we're not one family anymore. And that she doesn't even want me, because I use up too much of her time, and she wishes she could work more."

"Juniper..." I set my things down with a thud and press my elbows to the counter. I stare deep into her eyes and vow to make this all better. To make both of them safe, and him... irrelevant. While simultaneously working to ignore how badly I want to crack her father's skull open with my bare hands. Or tear the tongue from his mouth so he can never talk shit about Nicole again. "First of all, which name do you prefer? June? Junie? Bug? Or something else?"

"Juniper." Her eyes dance with approval. "Because that's my real name, and that's what my mom named the bakery."

"Juniper." I press my lips together "That's a really pretty name."

She preens under my compliment. "Thank you."

"You're welcome. Now listen. Your mom wants you more than anything else in the whole wide world." I hold the little girl's stare so she knows I'm not talking simply for the sake of hearing myself speak. "You have no clue how much she loves you. Or how hard she fights to make sure you're okay."

"I know." She brings her hand up and nibbles on her thumbnail. "Mommy loves me very much."

"Yes. She does. And if anyone," *like your piece of shit dad*, "was to say different, they'd be telling a lie. *You* know she loves you, so you don't have to worry about what other people say. They're telling lies."

"Liars are bad people." She sits taller and reaches across for the Barbie box. Slowly, she begins peeling the cardboard open. "My daddy tells lies a lot."

"He does?" I mean, *I* fucking know that. But what does *she* know? "Did your mom say so?"

She shakes her head with a fast *whip-whip-whip* from side to side. "No, but I hear him tell lies. Like, he's telling her he has to work tonight." She scrunches her nose. "He doesn't. He didn't even get a phone call this morning."

"Oh, well, maybe he—"

"And like, he tells me to tell my teacher that I get smacked at home."

Her simple, seemingly innocent words pull me up short. "What?"

"He said to say it to Miss Blake last year. He said I *have* to, because he's the dad, and I'm the kid, and I have to do what he tells me to. And if I don't, I'll be in trouble with the police."

"D-did you?"

Nicole's existence hangs in limbo every time this prick gets a bug up his ass. False reports. Lies. Made up stories of abuse.

"Did you tell Miss Blake that your mom hits you?"

She opens the box and tears the inner plastic with her teeth. Then she pours the lot into the pot with a contemplative sigh. "I told Miss Blake that Daddy told me to say it. So then he got into big trouble."

I have only a minute to feel relief. To thrill at the little girl's courage.

"But then Miss Blake called my parents for a meeting and told them what I said. So then Daddy started shouting at Miss Blake." She chews on her bottom lip and sets the empty box aside. "I didn't mean to get Miss Blake in trouble."

"You didn't." I pick up the box to read the instructions on the side, then I take two eggs from the carton and crack those into the bowl. "Miss Blake wasn't scared or mad, Juniper. But your dad was being a bully, so she stood up to him to make sure you were safe." I carry my eggshells to the trash and wipe my hands on a paper towel. "Did you know I know Miss Blake? She's my friend in real life."

"Really?" Her eyes light up at that new knowledge. "Like, you know her *outside* of school?"

"Yup! She's my really good friend, which means I eat dinner at her house a lot. And do you wanna know what I know about her?"

Like it'll help her hear better, Juniper presses her hands to the counter and leans closer. "What do you know?"

"That she's brave." Pushing the bowl aside and meeting the girl on her level, I grin when her lips curl up to the side. "She's braver than anyone I know. And her husband fights... like, for his job. So he's really strong too. And her friends can sometimes be kinda scary." *Too much, dickhead.* "So you don't ever have to worry about Miss Blake getting in trouble. You can tell her *anything*, and she'll make it all better."

You tell Miss Blake, I amend in my mind, *Blake will tell me, and I'll fix whatever needs fixing.*

"Anyway." I turn to the oven when I remember we haven't preheated it yet, and stare at the knobs.

I can access Griffin's servers in under three minutes from a remote location. But turn on an oven?

"Here." Snickering like she thinks it's cute I'm stupid, Juniper climbs off the stool and comes around to the stove. Then she leans too far over the top, terrifying me that she might someday burn herself. But she switches the oven on and sets the temperature with practiced moves. "Haven't you ever baked before?" She rolls her eyes and steals a baking tray from the drying rack and hands it to me. "I'm only six and I know how."

"Because your mom made sure to teach you." I give her space to walk by and head back to her side of the counter, then I set the tray down and search for my next step.

In response, Juniper snatches up the cupcake paper cups and tosses them so they smack my arm.

She stares for a minute, no doubt wondering if I'll tear her up for her disrespect. But when I tug the packet open with my teeth and make the action extra silly, she sits tall on her stool and watches me with glee in her eyes. "Do you think my dad will stop fighting with my mom soon?"

Fuck me. And Noah. And the fact this little girl knows way too much. "Hopefully," I concede gently. "But don't worry, I'm listening out. Making sure your mom is safe."

She exhales a soft sigh and nods. "Me too." Dragging her bottom lip between her teeth, she worries the skin and sets a pit of anxiety deep in my belly. "Sometimes Daddy punches things when he gets mad. So I always listen out to make sure Mommy is safe."

I don't mean for my eyes to turn to lava. Or for my body to turn toward the door. I don't mean to crush a paper cup in my hand, and I sure as shit don't mean to grill the girl. But I do anyway.

"Does he hit *you*, Juniper?" Even in my rage, I slowly begin pouring batter into the cups. "Does he ever hit you when he's angry?"

She nods. Short. Simple. She's not even snitching on the asshole. She's just... relaying a fact. "Sometimes. But he doesn't call it hitting. He says it's a swat on my butt, and he wouldn't have to do it if I behaved better."

Releasing her lip, she slides off the stool and leans toward the door, as though to peek out at her mom. "He sometimes hits Mommy too. But mostly, he grabs her arm. Here." She lifts her left arm and points to her elbow. "She *hates* it when people do that now. Even if they're not Daddy."

People like me. At a wedding. Trying to stop a beautiful woman from walking away.

Fuck.

"Just go, Noah!" The front door swings open so Nicole's voice carries louder and brings both me and Juniper to an anxious pause. With a sharp intake of air, the little girl dashes back onto her stool so it rocks on its legs, while I pour cake batter with lumps in it. "Just leave," she adds on a venomous bite. "We'll see you next week."

Does she know how much her daughter hears when they're arguing 'in private'? Does she have any clue at all how wise and protective her six-year-old is?

"June can call you tonight when you're done working."

"He's not working," Juniper mumbles, watching my hands like they're fascinating to her. "He just wanted to check on her, 'cos he thought she was on a date."

"*Shhhh.*" I keep my voice almost silent and my hands busy, while at the front of the house, the door slams shut and a car engine fires up in the driveway.

"We should put those in the oven now," Juniper announces too cheerfully. A little on the childish side. "I'm starrrrving. I can't wait to eat one."

"June?" Nicole's voice comes a little short. Concerned. Then she charges into the kitchen and stops on a skid when she finds us together. Smiling. Baking.

"Oh, you..." Horrified, her eyes whip to mine. "Um, Preston."

"Preston came over to get some stuff for Uncle Axe, Mommy." She slides off her stool and skips toward her mother. Too casual. Too happy. Grabbing her hand, she brings the woman back and pulls a second stool out so it scrapes along the tile. "But Uncle Axe ate Preston's cupcake the other day. So while you and Daddy were talking, I said I would teach him how to make a fresh batch."

"You..." Nicole's mouth hangs agape. "You're baking?"

"He was gonna use salt." Giggling, Juniper climbs up to sit on the stool to Nicole's left. "He was getting the ingredients out of the cupboard, Mommy, but instead of getting sugar, he got salt."

"Oh, well..." She looks around, reeling at the scene she's walked into. *Did she think I'd be hiding in her closet? Or maybe I could've climbed out the window.* "Using salt is a bit silly, huh?"

I click my tongue and set the empty bowl aside. "I'm just not very good at baking," I tell her. Since obviously, Juniper and I are on the same '*let Mommy think everything is under control*' kick.

Opening the oven so hot air gusts out and warms my jeans, I set the cupcake tray inside, then gently close the door once more.

Grabbing the tea towel and wiping my hands, I turn back to both

Feeney females and smile. "Juniper was just saying she's hungry for break-fast. And I could do with a yummy omelet. So I thought, since I'm here, and Uncle Axe is still busy at work, I could cook something."

I study Juniper instead of her mother, since Nicole's on the verge of kicking my ass out. "Do you like omelets?"

"Mmhmm." The little girl bobs her head and beams with happiness. "With spring onions?"

"Of course."

Nicole
TELLING THE TRUTH

Hours after Noah's surprise visit, and after that, our omelet breakfast and cupcake dessert, Preston remains in my home. He hangs out with my daughter. Plays Mario Kart and kicks her ass at least half the time. He plays Go Fish against her, and runs with the story of being her Uncle Axe's friend.

Not mine.

Not a date.

He's not a boyfriend, or any connection June may feel inclined to report back to her father.

He's just... Uncle Axe's buddy, from that time they went to the park.

Lunch passes, and Preston's phone buzzes with a semi-regular consistency. He checks it only when June isn't paying complete attention to him, and he doesn't touch me. Not once. Not even sneakily when she's turned the other way.

His behavior is entirely relaxed and appropriate, but while he appears to be chilled the hell out and having a playdate with a six-year-old, my mind swirls with racing thoughts.

A thousand of them each minute. Going a million miles an hour. A hundred questions a second, and not one of them has an answer, despite my obsession with puzzling them over.

So when June announces she's going upstairs to change her outfit, I corner Preston in the kitchen with ferocity in my voice. "How is it possible your truck tags came up with Angelo Alesi's name when Noah ran it?"

He casts a look to the door, and then up when we both hear footsteps through the ceiling. When he knows the coast is clear, he pushes his fingers through my hair and tugs me forward until I fall against his chest. He slams his lips to mine and drags my tongue in to play with his. Intoxicating. Delicious. Devious.

"I work in IT. I work for Soph." He adds each answer between biting nips. "I heard Dickhead threatening to run the tags, so I made a call and dealt with it."

"That's illegal." But I wrap my arms over his shoulders and twine my fingers behind his neck. I let him take me. I let him claim, and steal, and secret away what we have, because I've never in my life seen a man treat my daughter the way he has today. "How often do you do illegal things?"

"Somewhat regularly." He bites my chin, then buzzes his teeth along my jaw. "We should actually talk about that sometime soon."

"About..." My mind is fuzzy, lust-filled, and yet, acutely focused on June's footsteps in her room upstairs. "Talk about what?"

"Me." He places his hand under my chin and brings me to the very tips of my toes.

He's always so rough. So demanding.

And always so tender and kind.

"I'm pretty fucking sure I feel *love* for you, Nicole. It hurts, and it's terrifying, but I'm the guy who takes whatever is handed to him, and I make it work. And I don't lie to the people I love. Which means at some point, we have to discuss me. All of me."

"You've... lying?"

"It's what I do." He tilts my head to the side to make room for his tongue along the column of my neck. "Juniper's the fuckin' coolest, by the way. You should be proud."

"Preston..." My brain says he doesn't get to talk about her. My heart says why the hell not? He's the best man she knows besides my brother. But my loins win out and demand I pay attention to the way his tongue scrambles my every sensible thought. "I don't... I don't think—"

"You know I hate when you say that. But since you're a mom today, and Juniper is here, I won't do anything about it." He slaps a kiss to the middle of my lips and pushes me away at the first sound of my staircase creaking under the weight of a six-year-old. Then, "Fix this." He touches his own nipples, and sniggers when I glance down to find mine erect. "It's noticeable."

"Asshole." I fold my arms and turn toward the doorway as June wanders through.

"Hey, baby." I study her long-sleeve shirt beneath flower-decorated overalls with the strap tangled over her shoulder. A fresh new look, compared to the leggings and shirt she came back from Noah's in. "I like your outfit. Super cute."

"Thanks!" She skips past me like my posture is completely normal, and past Preston like his smirking presence is absolutely usual to her. Then she goes to the fridge and swings the door wide to peruse her options.

"It's gonna be dinnertime in a little while." She snatches out a carton of milk and sets it on the counter. Then, after slamming the door shut, she carries a stool around and climbs up to take a plastic cup from the too-high cupboard. "I was wondering if you wanna eat with us, Preston?"

"Wait." I spin around to catch his humored gaze. "Baby, hang on."

"What?" She climbs down and sets the cup by the milk. Then she drags the stool back into place and starts pouring. "Preston is nice, plus he's still waiting for Uncle Axe to come visit. And it's nearly dinnertime, and I like him." She spills milk over the side of her cup, then overcorrects her aim and almost loses everything, until Preston steps closer and takes the carton.

"Thanks." She smiles up at him and accepts the hand towel when he passes it with a wink. "I'm getting kinda hungry," she continues. "And it's still a bit early. But dinner could be nice. And you could call Uncle Axe and tell him to come too."

"But, baby..." My heart thunders at the implication of her words. *A dinner. The three of us.* "I'm sure Preston is—"

"Can I teach you something?" Speaking over me, Preston waits for June's nod of approval before he heads to a half-used loaf of bread on the counter. While June tosses the soggy towel away and climbs back onto her stool, Preston wanders back with the loaf.

Taking out a single slice and setting it on the counter beside the little yellow plastic cup, he turns again and heads back to the pantry. "Tear that up into chunks," he tells her. "Like," turning back, he holds his fingers about a half inch apart. "That big."

Grabbing the bag of sugar, he closes the door and sets it on the counter with the rest of his supplies. Finally, he takes half of the slice and begins pulling chunks away and dropping them into her cup of milk.

Much to June's dismay.

"What are you doing?" she scowls.

"This is what I used to eat for breakfast almost every single day." He tears off another chunk and drops it in her milk. "It's not very good for you, and it doesn't come with any nutritional value at all. But this is what poor people eat when they've got nothing else."

While June keeps working on her half of the bread slice, Preston goes to the cutlery drawer and takes out a spoon. Then he opens the sugar and scoops a little out.

And I... stand on the outside, looking in.

"So, you've got milk," he murmurs. Too sweet. Too patient. Too... perfect. "Then you have your bread, which will fill your tummy when you're desperate. Then," he sprinkles sugar over top and hands her the spoon. "This makes it sweet and delicious. Now give it a try."

"But it's just milk and bread." Her cheeks flame pink as she digs her spoon into the concoction and comes out with a pile coated in crystalized sugar. "You're making soggy bread, Preston."

"I'm making a meal you can almost always have, no matter where you are. Most folks have each of these ingredients. Not always," he adds seriously. "But often, even in the least-equipped kitchen, you can find these things."

He watches my baby with adoring eyes as she sniffs at her spoon.

"This was what I ate more often than not when I was a kid," he tells her. "Which is probably why I'm so short."

"Short?" She looks up at him and giggles. "You're huge."

"My friend Cole says I'm short," he laughs in response. "But thank you." He preens under her words and casts a sly side glance my way. "Do you like it?"

"I don't..." June sniffs her spoonful again. "I don't know. I'm scared to taste it."

"Oh please." He grabs a second spoon and digs it into her cup without asking. Then he fills his mouth and smiles so milk rests on his lips. "Yummo."

Convinced, June slides her spoon into her own mouth and closes her lips around her newly discovered meal. She ruminates on it for a moment. Tasting. Chewing. Two little lines form between her brows, and her head tilts to the side like it helps her think. Then she swallows the lot down and flashes a playful grin. "Yum!"

"That's what I'm saying, baby girl." Grinning, he peeks over at me. "Dinner sounds great, by the way. And if you call Uncle Axe, maybe he can have the burned cupcake no one else wanted to eat."

June throws her head back and cackles. Because I guess their private little jokes revolve around picking on Uncle Axe. "We won't tell him it's burned! We'll make him bite it first."

"That sounds fantastic."

When his phone chirps in his back pocket with a ringtone we haven't heard all day, Preston reaches around and takes the device out to stare at the screen. Then he looks to June and winks. "Excuse me for a sec. My boss is calling, and I might get in trouble if I don't answer."

Her dancing eyes pop wide, then she swings my way. "Lucky you don't have a boss, Mom. No one can get you in trouble."

"That's because Mom's a badass." Preston answers his call, but then his words register in his brain, and his expression turns minutely rueful. "I mean, Mom's a bad*butt*. Super smart and awesome for starting her own business." He brings the phone to his ear and escapes my glaring stare. "Ace. What's up? Tomorrow?"

He doesn't leave the room, but he strolls to the doorway so he's not obnoxiously talking in our space.

"Mom?"

My eyes are on Preston's back, but at June's gentle whisper, I head back to the counter and pick up the spoon Preston left behind. "Yeah? Can I try your new recipe?"

"Sure." She pushes her cup an inch in my direction and turns on her stool so her knees brush my hip. "Can we have dinner with Preston tonight? Pretty please?"

"Um..." I glance to his back and frown at his serious stance.

"I can come over around noon and test it. No, I..." He pauses. "I've got nothing else going on."

He's got nothing else going on.

"I think maybe he's busy, baby."

"But he said dinner sounds good," she pleads. "He said that—"

"Sometimes adults say things just to be nice to kids." I hate myself for dulling the sparkle in my daughter's eyes. I hate always being the realist in her life. "I just..." I hate how her expression drops. "He might be busy, honey. That's all I'm saying."

"But if he's not?" she negotiates. "If he wants to stay for dinner, can he?"

"Yeah," Preston wraps up his call. "I'll be there. Okay." He nods once. Short. Sharp. Decided. "See ya."

"Mom?" June hisses. "Please?"

"Sure." I exhale a defeated sigh and make sure not to be looking as he turns. Like his plans are none of my business, and his *I've got nothing else going on* doesn't hurt my feelings. "If he wants to," I tell her quietly, "he can."

"Yes!" She bounces in her chair and meets Preston's curious stare as he comes around.

"Mom said it's okay if you stay for dinner, Preston! What do you wanna eat?" She stands on the stool, though she knows she's not allowed, and half-crawls onto the counter to get closer to him. "What do you like to eat? I like all sorts of things."

"Hmm..." Making a show of thinking about his options, he slides his phone into his back pocket and wanders in our direction. "Do you like steak? Because I've been thinking about grilling since yesterday, and the weather is pretty nice." He peers my way and settles into an amused smirk. "A good, thick steak, for a guy who used to go hungry, is everything I enjoy in life now."

"I *love* steak!" June thrusts up tall and wobbles on her chair. She over-balances and topples backwards, but Preston is too fast. Too protective. He grabs the pocket on the front of her overalls and keeps her steady before I even get the chance to react.

"Careful," he cautions seriously.

"Oops!" She giggles, like falling to a tile floor and breaking her arm won't hurt. "Good catch, Pres. Can I call you Pres?" She wrinkles her nose. "I like that name better."

"Of course. You can call me anything you want so long as your mom is okay with it. So, do you wanna eat steak for dinner? I can run to the store and buy some."

"Sure! And tater tots too?"

Shrugging, he releases her overalls now that she's safe. "If that's what you want."

"I do. But... Mom said sometimes adults say things to be nice to kids, like saying they wanna stay for dinner, but they don't really mean it."

"Well..." He casts a side glance my way, chuckling when I groan and bury my face in my hands. "Sometimes that's true. Lots of adults say things they don't mean sometimes. But not me." He meets my gaze and holds it for a long, heated beat, before looking back to June. "Not to you. Whatever I say, I mean, okay? Because it's important that you know you can trust me to always tell you the truth."

Preston

FLYING EXPLOSIVES. TOTES FINE.

I headed back to my cottage around eight last night. Early enough for the little girl who was happy to stay awake, but not so late that I was tempted to beg to stay over.

Breakfast. Lunch. *And* dinner, all on the same day.

No matter how much I wanted to chain myself to Nicole's oven and stay in her home forever, I knew she was on the edge of a nervous collapse, terrified I might screw up and add trauma to the load her little girl already has to carry. So I cooked steak and kept my distance. Then I settled in on the long couch to watch a movie, and kept my hands really fucking still when June decided to climb onto my lap.

Nicole's face, in response to her daughter's proximity to me, fell so pale, I worried she'd keel over and pass out.

She was long ago scarred by a man who abuses her daughter on a daily basis. So now, she's terrified to let another into Juniper's life. Can't be vulnerable if you don't open yourself up. And a six-year-old can't be disappointed if she's never given the chance to trust someone new.

Fuck, but I kinda want them both to trust me.

Juniper chilled on my lap the whole way through the movie, and since Nicole was to my right, and the television, toward my left, for an hour and a half, the little girl's eyes were pointed and focused away from her mother. Which made it possible for me to touch. A minute here. A minute there. To stroke Nicole's arm. To twine our fingers tight and assure her that I see her.

I'm attached.

And if I can help it, I'm not leaving.

But now it's Sunday. Work calls, Sophia is demanding, and Nicole needs time to breathe. So I pull up outside a bunker-like building I've never visited before, climb out, and grab my laptop before closing the squeaky door and heading toward the entrance.

Gunshots come from inside. Repetitive. Concurrent. Measured. So although it kinda sounds like I'm walking toward a war, I know I'm actually approaching a firing range.

"Danes!" Sophia spins the moment I come through the doorway, then rushes in my direction while a line of men practice their shots thirty feet away. Jay. Kane. Even Griffin. And at the end, Spencer Serrano, who I know owns this place.

Sophia carries a laptop, too—it's what we do—but she sets hers on a counter lining the wall and summons me past a short, red-haired woman whose smile is small and elegant. She's sweet. Innocent, despite being my age. Maybe even a year or two older.

"We're heading out back," Sophia announces in a momentary lull between shots. "Bishop!"

"Yeah?" Kane, Jay, and Griffin all turn at once.

"I meant Jay," Soph laughs. "We'll be outside."

Then she shoves a heavy security door open to reveal a massive yard made up of targets and hills, piles of rubble one might use to take cover, and ditches dug into the ground that others might call a weapons pit.

"Where are you on Mancino's system?" She walks two feet ahead of me, always moving fast, always on the go, and makes a beeline for a small wooden shed.

For a moment, I wonder if she's heading to an old-style outhouse, but my curiosity dissipates when she opens the door and reveals a cache of tools and equipment.

"Are you in?"

Shrugging, I wait a few feet back and watch the ballerina dig her way through the artillery I doubt the cops know about. "I *could* be in," I murmur. "I've mostly been working on my malware, since I'm confident we can slide in unnoticed. Once we have access to their servers, we need to be able to do something with it."

"So…" She tugs out a flying drone that spans about three feet wide, four feet long, and has to weigh an easy sixty pounds. "Have you discovered yet what you can control once you're in?"

"Yeah." I know she knows already. She's a fucking genius, so any question she asks me, she already knows the answer. "Not only can we access his computers, finances, and security, but we can control his power grids, communications, and manpower. Mancino's mansion has its own private electric source, backed up by no-fail generators. Lines are underground, making them secure against attack."

"Which is why we can't shut him down by destroying his source of power."

"Not physically." I accept the drone when she passes it to me, and set it on the grass while she goes back in and reemerges with actual explosives.

I take a long step back, like the extra six feet will save me from losing my fucking face.

"We can't cut the wires," I clarify. "But Mancino's place is controlled via his servers. So we can literally shut his electricity down and stop the generators from kicking in."

"Via malware?"

"Yes."

My heart skips when she turns and places a fucking bomb in my hand. Like, an actual explosive.

"Uh, Soph—"

"Stop being a pussy and set it down by the drone. Tell me more about Mancino's setup."

"It's, uh…" I walk slowly. Carefully. I don't think I breathe, and if a man has the ability to stop his heart for a minute, I'd do that too.

I set down the small, tube-like canister and step away.

"It's all hidden behind a firewall," I tell her. But fuck if I don't have a frog in my throat and nerves tickling my chest. "His security is tight, but once we scale the wall, it basically all blows open, and we can do whatever we want."

"What should he have done differently?"

"Segment. A man needs communications to run an empire. He needs money. He needs weaponry. And he needs a standing firewall shielding each of these things separately. Instead, he's got everything tossed in together. So once I'm in, he loses it all."

I swear, my bowels liquify when she casually tosses another explosive into my hands the way one might toss a hacky sack.

"Dammit, Sophia!" I place the bomb down and give myself space.

If they blow, we're all dead anyway. But hell if I'm not gonna take that extra four feet just in case.

"Once I'm in Mancino's system," I continue, "I'll be able to shut down his gates, his security outposts, all communication, and electricity for the entire property."

"Which means what?" She comes out of the little shed and sets down a final two canisters with the others. "What are you gonna do for us with that information?"

"Close the gates and keep everyone inside the property. And I'll lock the garage, so his soldiers can't access their vehicles. Communications go down, so they can't discuss what the fuck is happening with each other, or with anyone on the outside. Additionally, once I shut them down, they lose their access to anti-air technology."

"Which means..." She comes to a stop beside her drone and grins. "They can't shoot us down except with whatever weapons they have in their hands."

"Right..." I juggle my laptop and frown. "What exactly are you looking to achieve with this mission?"

"Mostly, I wanna scare them." Opening her legs wide and straddling the drone, she turns it on its top and gets to work fastening the canisters to clips soldered on post-manufacturing. "If soldiers die," she clicks an explosive into place and *doesn't* twitch, though I sure as fuck do. "Then that's fine. They're on the wrong side of our war, anyway. They participate in, and encourage, the selling and victimization of innocents. So if their faces melt, and they lose a limb in the fray..." She clicks another on and reaches out for a third. "No biggie. We don't particularly want Mancino himself to die, since our mission goes deeper than that. He runs a trafficking line that, so far, I haven't been able to infiltrate, so if we kill him before we dismantle the line, someone else will just pick up where he leaves off."

"So how does attacking his property open him up to discussing business with you?"

She grabs the next canister and fastens it to its clips. "First of all, I'm

238

hoping he'll have documented his processes, so it'll all be sitting in the servers for you to hand to me. But as a backup, he has a daughter he's obsessively protective of. She rarely leaves the compound, and her only public appearances are alongside other wealthy, dangerous families who have a connection to her father. They consider themselves untouchable while on their property, so the mission is to breach that space and remind them nowhere is safe."

"And then?" I press. "What?"

"Jay!"

As her husband and his brothers cross the lawn, she waves them closer and noisily works to lift the drone on one side.

I'm certain she intends to flip it, but she places far too much fucking pressure on one corner, so all I see in my mind is a skin-melting explosion and my obituary in the paper.

"We breach," she grunts out, "Mancino feels unsafe. And since the only thing he wants to protect more than his business is his daughter, we offer personal security, and plant a man inside the estate."

"Then you figure out the supply lines for his operations," I conclude.

I keep my distance as Jay and Kane oh-so-casually flip the jacked-up drone and place it on its feet.

"So my job is just a smokescreen?" I ask. "A distraction?"

"You're a skilled technician proving himself valuable to my team." Soph steps away, digging her phone from her pocket and tapping at the screen. "But you're still new. So until I know what you're capable of, what the hell else do you want me to do with you?" Peeling her eyes from the phone and glancing my way, she lifts a questioning brow. "If you screw up and alert them to our presence in their systems, then it's all over anyway. So although you may consider a smokescreen kinda lame, what you're doing is actually a big fucking deal. Jay?"

She passes her phone to her husband and sidles up closer as he, with a flick of his thumb, fires up the drone. The little engines purr, and the rotors spin with a sizzling *zzzzzz* of speed.

"Send it up the hill," she murmurs. "Then drop them. I wanna see how accurate we can be."

"Easy peasy." His smile is playful, like this is just a computer game, and not real artillery that could kill a man.

"When can we expect you in, with malware in place, and complete control of the estate?" Sophia asks me. "How long do you need?"

I narrow my eyes until I feel the severe line that forms between my brows. "You could do all this on your own. Why invite me in at all?"

"Because I get off on training folks who wanna be as smart as me. And when that someone has the natural ability you have, and the hunger for knowledge, but a past that has tried to kick your ass..." She lifts her shoulders in a brief shrug. "Makes me more inclined to do so."

"Charity?" I scoff. "You feel bad for me, so you gave me a job."

"Enterprising," she argues right back. "I can't do everything all the time, and Griffin is married to a cop, which means he's not allowed to help me achieve all my illegal, homicidal goals." She grins and turns her head to follow the flight of the drone. "It's a job, Danes. It's a paycheck you're earning. What the fuck is the problem?"

"He's feeling icky about his unlawful actions," Kane grumbles from Jay's other side. "Everyone knows you're dating Nicole Feeney now. And anyone who has spent more than a minute in town knows she used to be married to a cop who wants her back. He's as crooked as they come, he does a drive-through of this town five days out of seven, and he almost caught you at her place yesterday."

"Drop one," Soph instructs.

So Jay does. Like it's not a big fucking deal, he releases a canister and turns his face as it detonates against the ground and makes the earth shake from the explosion.

"Fuck!" I use my laptop as cover and twist away from the gust of wind that barrels past us from the blast. "Dammit, Sophia!"

"Noah Scott is obsessed with his ex-wife," Kane continues, like dropping bombs is a totally normal Sunday activity for the Bishops. "He's not gonna share her willingly. And your rap sheet's gonna be on his fridge the second he catches wind of your name."

"His rap sheet doesn't exist," Sophia inserts arrogantly. "Not even a detective will smell a rat when he tries to run his name. Drop it."

She turns her back when Jay drops another, but her eyes burn deep against the side of my face. "Scott won't be able to pull your name. He won't have any fuel to screw you with. But she has a kid, and that kid needs protection. So if you like her for real, she deserves to know the truth about us. That way, she has all the information when she's making a choice to be with you... or not."

"You're the one who told me to tell outsiders I work in IT," I growl. Lowering my laptop, I turn back to study the fucking divots in the hills that make up Serrano's property. "You gave me those instructions, Ace."

"For randoms," she counters. "Spouses don't count. So if you think she's special enough to become your person, then she deserves to know. And if you don't think she's that special, then you probably shouldn't be at her house when Scott is nosing around and causing trouble."

"That prick needs to be dealt with too." I twitch when Jay drops a third bomb. But I guess I've become less sensitive, because I don't bother bringing my laptop up as a shield this time. "He hurts them, Ace. Both of them."

"So..." Slowly, her lips curl into a sadistic grin. "Do something about it."

She steps toward Jay and takes back her phone, while in my back pocket, mine buzzes with an incoming text.

"This works," she tells the rest of the team. "Small enough not to destroy the house, large enough to tear some assholes up. Stealthy enough," she flies the drone back this way, though I don't miss the fact it's still armed with three bombs, "no one's gonna be able to stop us."

"Cocky," I grumble.

"Confident," she asserts. "I know my team and what we're capable of. And you... well, for now, you're a fun pet."

Shaking my head, I turn toward the bunker and pull out my phone, spying Nicole's name flashing on my screen.

I wish it was a call. I wish I could hear her voice—or better yet, see her face if she wanted to FaceTime me. But I have to acknowledge that it's best we don't do that at this particular moment.

In no universe is it a smart idea for her to listen to these jerkoffs blow shit up.

So unlocking my screen and heading back inside the building, I open her text and read.

'Hey. Just checking in to say hello. I know you're working, so... I won't bother you. Did you hear that sound a minute ago? June reckons lightning crashed down right outside our door. But... it's not storming. I figure maybe a car backfired. But anyway.'

Then a second text buzzes through. *'Axel came by and worked on my car today, since we didn't get to it yesterday. It's all fixed now. He also recommended the mechanic, so if I have trouble again...'*

Then a third. *'Sorry. Nevermind. Ignore me. Small talk feels weird. See you around.'*

She's turned shy. Nervous and fidgety. If I was with her in person, I imagine she'd be wringing her hands and walking away.

And I... would bring her back to me, grab her face, and kiss her till she stops overthinking.

Quickly, I type and send, *'I heard it too. It was loud.'* Not a lie. *'I'm glad your car is fixed. We had so much fun hanging out yesterday, we ran out of time. But if you have trouble in the future, you can call me. I'll help you.'*

Now it sounds like I'm telling her we probably won't see each other any time soon. *Fuck.*

'Thinking of you and Juniper...' I pause and consider deleting the last bit. She's protective of her daughter, and I'm a random guy she had no intention of introducing to her if not for a series of unfortunate events. But then I decide, fuck it. I say what I mean, and I mean what I say.

'I had a lot of fun with you both yesterday, and I appreciate that you let me hang out. I know you're scared to let me close, but I'm glad you did.' Then I stop and snort. *'Even if it was under duress. I was actually thinking... we should get dinner again soon. Like, an actual date. Next time Juniper is with her dad, or when you can wrangle Axe into babysitting.'*

I hit send on my long-ass text, but then doubt rushes in.

Nice one, dickhead. Now she'll think I'm trying to brush her daughter to the side.

So I hit dial and cut straight to the fuckin' point.

"Hello?" Nicole's sweet exhalation of air makes me smile. "I was still reading your text."

"The end says I wanna take you out to dinner." I set my laptop beside Sophia's and head through the front entrance of the building to stop by my truck. "But I mentioned Axe babysitting June. And then I felt like an ass, because it kinda sounded like I didn't want her around. Which is not how I feel."

"You're just..." She hesitates. "You're really intense, Preston. You wanna date?"

I lean against the hood of my truck and nod. "Yes. Like, share a proper dinner. I'll pick you up. You'll wear a cute dress. Maybe I'll fuck you somewhere I shouldn't before we get to the restaurant."

A slow, satisfied smile rolls along my lips when her breath comes faster.

"Then I'll drop you off at your door. And if we do that a hundred times and you're still interested, then maybe we can tell Juniper I'm *your* friend, not Axel's."

"A-a hundred?" she stammers. "You'd wait that long?"

"I'll do whatever I need to do," I assure her. "I'm not here to confuse that little girl, Nicole. But I like her. Like..." I rub a hand across my face and chuckle. "I fucking adore her. So I'll stay Uncle Axe's friend for as long as it takes. Then, someday, maybe after she's comfortable with me, and Detective Noah Scott walks in front of a fucking train—"

"Oh god," she groans. I know she's at home. Cartoons play in the background, and Juniper's playful chatter implies Axel is there too. But Nicole's breathing changes as, in my mind, she pushes up to stand. "Preston, I—"

"Where are you going?" I block one ear, so I can hear her end of the call better. "You're moving."

"Upstairs," she murmurs. "Privacy. This thing with Noah," her voice comes out softer. Secretive, so Juniper doesn't have to hear. "It's a lot, Preston. It's... a *lot*. And eventually, you're gonna get tired of all the drama."

"Like I said," I drawl in response. "Maybe someday, he'll walk in front of a train."

"Yes, well..." I swear, I can hear her roll her eyes. Then the soft snick of a door closing. "I live in perpetual hope. But on the off-chance that never happens... He's a massive part of my life, Preston. I don't want him to be," she laughs. "I honestly wish I never had to speak to him again. And though I'm not supposed to say so, I know June feels the same way. But it's the way it is. He's here, he has a right to see her, even if we both hate it, and for as long as she's a child, he's going to use her to punish me. Which means I can never actually date. I can't let him know that much about my private life, because he'll use it to hurt us more."

"So you're just gonna stay single the next twelve years? Hide your feelings because your *ex* will have a problem with it?"

"It's the way it has to be. Him knowing wouldn't be worth the headache, and anything he finds on you, he'll use. He's a cop."

"And I have no criminal record," I press back. *Another lie. Dammit.* "He won't find anything with my name attached to it, Feeney. And when he figures that out, he'll realize he has nothing to hurt you with."

"He'll make stuff up!" she bursts out. "He'll find an old, forgotten speeding ticket, a parking fine, *something*. He'll say you're an unsafe driver."

I bark out a laugh. *Unsafe driver!* I was a career fucking car thief who only ever scratched *one* ride.

Cole's.

"It seems silly to you," she sighs. "I know it sounds dumb. But it's my reality. So if you want to hang out, you do so as Uncle Axe's friend. If you don't want the drama, then that's fine too."

It's not fine. It's the fucking opposite of fine.

"I won't hold a grudge," she promises. "And I won't get in your way around town. We could just be friends, and I—"

"Holy shit, woman." I look to the gun range's front door and catch sight of Sophia and Jay hovering nearby. They're ready for me to come back to work. "I asked you out on a date just a few minutes ago. Now you're giving me the *'we can still be friends'* talk?"

"I'm not—"

"Friends don't fuck the way we do."

"Preston..."

"Friends don't have what we have. And friends don't feel a burn in their gut when the other friend says *let's just be friends*."

"Preston, you're making this—"

"Dinner. Like a real fucking couple. But for the first hundred, we don't tell Juniper. What Scott doesn't know won't hurt him. After that, maybe you'll be as invested as I am. And maybe by then, you'll be done letting him dictate your life. You're allowed to date, Nicole. You're allowed to live your life. He doesn't actually control shit unless you let him."

"And you?" she challenges. "If he finds out your name and starts giving you a hard time?"

"Ha!" I welcome the opportunity to have my own personal beef with him. I relish the idea of him stepping up and dealing with me instead of punishing them. "He can do whatever the fuck he wants. My records are clean, and whatever ammunition he wants to make up after that, a court-room will insist he prove it. Since he can't, he'll run out of fuel and move on with his life."

"You make it sound so simple." She drops down on her bed. I can't see it, but I hear it in the way her breath rushes out. "You don't know him, Preston, so it all sounds so trivial to you."

"I know guys just like him, babe. They're all the fuckin' same. They bully those they consider weaker than them—which, by the way, is why he comes at Juniper more than he comes at you. You're a grown-ass woman who puts him in his place and asserts her boundaries. Sometimes they waver," I allow, knowing she tries so fucking hard, but has to pick her battles. "Sometimes he gets away with more than he should. But mostly, you've got him pegged. Juniper, though..." I shake my head and turn my back on a watchful Soph. "She's six. She doesn't have the same power you do, and no matter what, she still has to spend time with him. The fuckin' law says so. But I'm telling you, Nicole, they're all the same. They're weak-ass bullies who back down once someone stronger than them steps forward."

"And let me guess," she huffs around impatience. "You're gonna be that guy, right? Big, bad, strong Preston Danes wants to be my hero?"

I scoff. "Big, bad Momma Bear Nicole will be her own hero, and I'll cheer you the fuck on. Because that's who you need in your life: a support system, not a security system."

She draws a deep breath, then lets it out again on an exhausted sigh. "Preston..."

"Dinner." I cut in again before she starts her next sentence with '*I think*'. "Just you and me, so Juniper's not placed in a situation where she has to lie or keep secrets from Dickhead."

"But we don't call him Dickhead..." Soft laughter rolls off her tongue. "Right? It's best not to get into the habit, so you don't accidentally let it slip in front of her."

For a reason I'll never truly be able to explain, an old memory jumps into my brain. A guy Cole and I used to know. An asshole who gave us a hard time, when life was already doing so well kicking our asses.

"So, there was this guy I used to know when I was a teenager." A slow chuckle makes my chest bounce. "He was the building super for the apart-ment where Cole's mom used to live."

"Preston, I..." She pauses for a moment. "Why are you telling me this story?"

"It comes with a point," I laugh. "I promise. So this building super, his name was Frank Belcher. Well, it was probably something more French, like *Boucher*. But we always heard it like Belcher."

"Because teen boys are unkind and immature?"

"Shush! Anyway, this dude was a fuckin' dick to us. Cole's mom was never up to date on rent, and she smoked so much, the walls and curtains and shit were black. She never fed Cole, and she always had guys coming and going. In fact," I add quickly. "I'm pretty fuckin' certain she paid her rent more than once by sucking Belcher's dick. Which only made him meaner on the months she had no money *and* wouldn't suck him off."

"Horrifying story," she drawls. "Not at all child-friendly."

"I won't tell Juniper," I snigger. "Anyway. Cole and I, being energetic, mouthy teens—"

"As in, destructive," she inserts, "with gutter mouths and no filters. Nor did you possess manners when speaking to the poor old man trying to manage a building."

"Shh! You're rooting for the wrong person in the story. Dammit, Feeney."

She chokes out a soft laugh so the sound weaves all the way into my belly and settles somewhere near my heart. "Sorry. Please go on. I'm riveted."

"You're a pain in my ass. But this guy, Frank Belcher, was always on our case. Cussing us out, throwing tools at us if we walked past his door at the wrong time. He was fat and lazy, always had food in his hand. And he knew we were hungry, but he would toss his leftovers in the trash rather than give them to us. He was just a nasty piece of work."

"Are you nearing your point?"

A frustrated growl vibrates along my chest. "You're nearing a spanked ass next time I see you. You've got sass on the phone, Feeney. Jesus christ. Just shut up and let me tell you about Felcher."

"About..." A heavy silence hangs for a beat. "What?"

"So, Cole and I were teens," I continue, like the word I've just spoken isn't truly fucking disgusting. "And teens often hear filthy words. In fact, the dirtier it was, the better. And one of those days, we were on Urban Dictionary and saw that word, felch. Felching." I giggle today as much as I did back then. "To felch means to... Ya know what? Look it up yourself. I can't in good conscience say it."

"Oh wow..." Her words come out on a wondrous murmur. "That bad?"

"It's next-level. But 'Frank Belcher,' when said really fast, kinda comes out like—"

"Felcher," she whispers. "You started calling him that?"

"We absolutely did. And he didn't even know what the word meant. But the name stuck from that day forward, and it was fucking hilarious."

"I don't..." I don't have to see her to know she shakes her head. "I still don't understand your point."

"You don't want me to make a habit of calling Noah *Dickhead*, just in case I slip up and say it in front of Juniper. So..." I flash a wide grin, the way thirteen-year-old me did way back then. "I'm gonna call him Felch. It'll make me ridiculously happy, Juniper won't know what it means, and if it gets back to Noah..." I shrug. "If he knows what it means, then it confirms what we already know about him. And if he doesn't, then no harm, no foul. Life is still good."

"So... your answer, when I asked you not to refer to my daughter's father in a derogatory way, was to revert to your immature, potty-mouthed teen self?"

"Yes. And I'm quite comfortable with my choices. Dinner?"

A heavy breath races along her throat and stops with a quick intake. "Fine," she concedes, exasperated. "I have a big job to complete by next Saturday, and June has school all week, so I can't do the next six nights, but—"

"Next Saturday?" I ask hopefully. "It can be a celebration for a job complete. It'll be the weekend, so you'll be able to spend all of Sunday chilling with Juniper. And I..." A slow smile works across my lips. "I have something to look forward to."

"Next Saturday," she agrees. "But only if Axel can babysit. I won't put her with anyone else just so I can date, Preston."

"I understand. She adores Axel, so it's okay to let them have their time. But random babysitters are a no."

"Her childhood is already sprinting away so quickly," she sighs. "I refuse to give up more than I have to. And I'll never toss her to a stranger for the night just so I can be out having fun without her."

"I'll work around whatever you need me to work around," I rush on. "If Axel can't hang with her on Saturday, you and I can reschedule. But if he can, and she wants that time with him, then I want to help you find out who Nicole Feeney is beneath being a mom and a baker."

"Danes?" Sophia's voice brings me around with a frown.

When our eyes meet, she tilts her chin in that *'come here'* gesture everyone knows.

"Sounds like you've got to run," Nicole mumbles. "I'm sorry for texting you while you were working. I didn't mean to—"

"Be so needy?" I turn back to my truck and smirk, knowing I make the woman on the other end of the call blush. "You didn't mean to show your cards first and admit you missed me?"

"I don't m..." I see in my mind the way she scowls. "It's not like—"

"Well, I missed you." I rest my elbows on the hood and lower my voice. "I really enjoyed being with you Friday night, Nicole. And spending time with you and Juniper yesterday was..." I shake my head. "Good for me. You're scared to rely on anyone, even for company. But I..." I shrug. "I'm not scared to admit I have feelings that involve you and my heart. So... whatever. I'm gonna tell you when I miss you. And I'm gonna come around as much as you'll let me. I'm gonna wanna hang with Juniper too, because she's the sweetest thing since sugar bread dipped in milk. And hell if she doesn't like me too."

"Preston, I don't..."

"You're scared to let me close to her, because you're a mom and your job is to protect her from instability. But, babe, whatever happens between me and you, I'm gonna be whatever she needs. Forever. She needs a guard? I'm gonna protect her. She needs a friend? I can be that too. She sneaks out to a party when she's sixteen and needs a safe ride home?"

"She's gonna be in big trouble," Nicole laughs. "And if you give her that ride without telling me about it, thus becoming her accomplice, then you're both dead."

"I'll be her safe choice whenever she needs it," I press. "But I won't lie to you. I won't let you or Juniper down, so—"

"You keep calling her Juniper." Curiosity pulses between us, while fifteen feet behind me, Sophia shuffles her feet impatiently.

I know I have to hang up. But I'm not ready. I don't want to let go yet.

"Everyone else just calls her June," Nicole continues. "Or Bug."

"I asked her what she'd prefer," I murmur. "Yesterday, when we were baking. She said she likes to be called Juniper, so that's what I'm doing. Listen—"

When Soph's exasperated throat-clearing comes at my back, I exhale a frustrated sigh and bring our conversation to a close.

"I have to go. But I like that you texted me. Keep doing that. Reach out to me, Feeney. I wanna feel wanted too."

"Okay, well..." Nerves swirl between us. "Alright. I will."

"And if you hear more cars backfiring, don't stress," I chuckle. "You're safe. I'll come see you sometime this week, okay? No commitment," I add quickly. "Just a man, buying a cupcake from a beautiful woman. If I hang out for five minutes while I eat, then that's what happens."

"I'll be busy," she insists. But I swear I hear her smile. "I have a five-tier wedding cake to deliver by three o'clock Saturday. And it's gotta go to the city, so—"

"Will you be delivering it yourself?"

"No. The event planner has someone coming to get it. But I'm just say—"

"Busy. I got it. We'll make it work, so I still get to see your face between now and then, Juniper won't know I'm thinking about banging her mom, and you still get to do your work."

"And you're still crude," she responds dryly. "Shall I call you Felch, too?"

I bark out a fast laugh and shake my head. "Definitely not."

"Danes! Let's go already."

"Fuck sake." I turn from my truck and head toward the shooting range doors. "I've gotta go, Feeney. But I'll see you soon, okay?"

"Okay." She hesitates for a beat before finding her bravery and adding, "Thanks for calling. I liked hearing your voice."

"I always like hearing yours. Goodbye, beautiful. Talk to you soon."

She exhales a soft sigh before I hear her push up to sit. "Bye."

Pulling the phone from my ear, I slip the device into my pocket and stop at the door to face Sophia. "What?"

"You gotta tell her." She turns on her heels and heads back into the building that houses entirely too much firepower. "Don't let her find out some other way."

I grab my laptop as we pass it, and follow her through the compound and back outside to find the drone in the sky and its operator grinning like a schoolboy.

"I'm gonna tell her on Saturday." I steer clear of Spencer, and stay entirely too close to my boss. She's the real MVP around here, and the least likely to have a bomb dropped on her head. "We're going out to dinner on Saturday," I continue, "so I'll tell her then. In the meantime, I work in IT, and you'll make sure my record is clear."

"It already is." She turns to face me, and doesn't flinch even a little when the drone spits out its bomb baby and blasts another crater into the hill at the top of the property. "Now, how many power sectors are we talking for Mancino's estate?"

Nicole

SATURDAY IS SO FAR AWAY

Preston texts on and off for the rest of Sunday, and Axel comes and goes like he thinks my home is his. Hannah is in my inbox, vacillating between talking work and making none-too-subtle comments about 'hot brothers'. And Noah tries to call me a thousand times *'just to talk'*, though I ignore every single attempt and give him none of the energy he so desperately seeks.

Now, it's Monday afternoon. My schedule is painfully full, my delivery load is torturous, and my back aches from hunching over my prep desk. And yet, my heart flutters every single time I think of my upcoming date.

Which is far more often than any single-momming, business-owning, busy self should allow.

But I can't help myself. I yearn for Saturday to rush closer. For my next five nights to fly by, and for my life to speed away, all so I can wear a pretty dress and select sexy underwear, *knowing* Preston will only peel them off again.

I thrill at the thought of him picking me up and taking me somewhere private. And maybe, if I'm feeling brave, inviting him over for a Sunday bake, too many cartoons, and hours of hanging out with my daughter.

Because she deserves some of this, too. June deserves to know good, trustworthy men who mean it when they say they have a girl's back.

But, god, am I being naïve? Am I stupid for thinking Preston is being genuine? Are his actions sincere, or is he just saying the things I want to hear?

I want so badly for this to be real. For his promises to be true. For my tiny, glimmering hope to be justified. The hope that we could have something special, that such a thing exists, and I could be the lucky recipient of his affection.

"Nicole?"

Noah burned me so badly, I'm not sure the woman who came out of the fire could ever recognize the foolish one who went in.

"*Nicole?*" Hannah's impatient voice tickles my consciousness.

I hunch over my little steel table in the back of the shop, poring over my planner, fully aware that I have four and a half workdays left before my next wedding cake needs to be delivered and a hefty injection of cash hits my bank account.

It's the last that matters most. That injection is how June and I live another week in paradise.

But in the meantime, I still have a shop to keep supplied and running, which means making stock for the display cabinets and filling bulk orders for school events have me sweating the latter half of this week.

And yet, a small portion of my brain plans what I'll wear Saturday night.

I can't bring Preston to my home afterwards; that would be entirely inappropriate while June is there. But the thought of passing up a night of touching. Tasting. Loving.

It seems like such a waste.

"Nicole!" Hannah snatches my pencil and smacks the top of my head with the end, so I jolt in my chair and topple treacherously to the side.

"What the—"

"I've been calling you." She sets the pencil down and places her hands on her hips. Her lips are wide and smiling, but her eyes... devious. "Are you purposely ignoring me, Feeney, or are you experiencing sudden onset deafness?"

"I was working!" I pick up my pencil and hold it like I might stab a woman. "What the hell do you need?"

"Your attention." She dips her shoulders and shakes her hips suggestively. Then she tilts her head toward the front of the store. "Thought you might like to see."

"See what?" I rub the sore spot on my head with the heel of my palm, then pushing up to stand, I flip my diary closed and wander toward the entryway. "What are you—"

"*Shhh*," she scolds with a finger to her lips, then she tiptoes closer, so together, we poke our heads around the partition.

In the back corner of my store, at a tiny, two-person café table no one ever truly sits at, Preston occupies one seat, while Juniper claims the other.

My heart jumps in my throat, and panic skitters in my blood, but Hannah whips a hand out with surprising speed and grabs my wrist before I can charge into view and save my daughter from her situation.

Except, what exactly am I saving her from?

"He walked in about five minutes ago," Hannah whispers so only I can hear. "June Bug served him and charged his card, and he gave her a two hundred percent tip." Snickering, she releases my hand, knowing I'm not going anywhere. "Then he pulled a little tin of cards out of his pocket and challenged her to a game."

"Boat!" June slaps her hand to a card in the center of the table and scrapes it back in her direction.

"He didn't force her to play," Hannah murmurs. "He didn't even have to convince her. He just ate his cupcake and showed her the tin. And now—"

"She's six years old," I murmur. "He wouldn't have had to try hard." My tone implies I'm mad, but my eyes covet every snapshot I take of this moment.

My baby girl, perched on her knees and swaying with the wobbling table. And Preston, sitting across from her in dark jeans and a black t-shirt, with a black ballcap pulled low over smiling eyes.

His shoulders stretch his shirt in a way that makes my breath come shorter and my stomach twist with nerves. But his infectious laugh when June slaps the pile again and shouts "Cat!" makes my heart jump.

"He's *cuuuuute*," Hannah mumbles. "And June's got him wrapped *all* the way around her finger."

"You're cheating!" June half-dives across the table to take back the cards that Preston may or may not have stolen.

When her flailing arms knock his cap askew, June's entire body freezes, her nerves on edge as she watches for his reaction. But all Preston does is take off his hat, then drop it on her head.

"I didn't cheat." He takes the next card and adds it to his pile. "I'm just better at this game than you are."

"You're a grownup," she giggles. But she pulls back to sit in her seat, and fixes her new hat so it sits comfortably. "You're faster than me."

"Making excuses for being crap at a game is lame."

He slaps the pile and chuckles when her eyes snap wide in shock. "Trees. Pay less attention to me," he coaches her. "And more attention to the game. Then you won't lose as much."

"You said *crap*," June hisses. She casts a side glance this way, but Hannah and I pull back, as though choreographed, so we're not caught. "You're not allowed to say *crap*, Preston. Mom gets cranky."

He chuckles, throaty and delicious. "She's not *my* mom, cutie. I think what you mean is *you're* not allowed to say crap. But I can do whatever I like. If she doesn't like it, she can come talk to me about it."

"He's ballsy," Hannah sniggers under her breath. "He's calling you out."

"Mom will get cranky at you for saying *crap* in front of me."

"Swear to god," I growl. "If she doesn't stop cussing..."

"Oh my gosh, Nicole! Turn around!" Hannah practically shouts, drawing Preston's and June's eyes our way. Then she bats me back from the doorway. "You have work to do, woman! Staring at our customers is not appropriate."

I slap her hands in retaliation and grit my teeth. But heat floods my cheeks. She set me up to be caught. She put me here just so Preston could catch me snooping. "You're a jerk!"

"The after-school rush is done." Spinning on her heels, she starts toward the front of the store. "I had nothing else to do." She passes through the entryway and speaks louder. "Who wants a croissant? Nick baked extras this morning, and they didn't all sell."

"*Car!*" June's hand slapping the table makes me startle as I head back to my seat. "Pay less attention to everyone else," I hear my daughter taunt Preston, "and more attention to the game, and you might not be so crap at it."

"Juniper!" I drop my elbows to the tabletop, and my face in my hands. "No cussing."

"But, Mommy! Preston taught me that word. You should get mad at him, not me."

"Hearts." Uncaring about a little girl's plot to get him in trouble, Preston slams his palm to the stack so the sound reverberates all the way to where I slump on my stool. But beside my planner, my phone chirps with an incoming message that replaces my ire with stomach-dropping dread.

Expecting to find Noah's name on my screen, I peel my hands from my eyes—and frown when I see Preston's instead.

Surprised, I snatch up my phone and unlock the screen. Then I navigate to my text chat and... well, I can't quite explain what happens next. I think I whimper. Perhaps I fall a little more *in like*, but with the addition of my heart being involved.

Juniper said crap. But it's the cutest shit the way she scrunches her nose when she does it. Also, you look pretty today. I miss your face so fucking much.

"Cows!" June's shout makes me jump in my seat.

And your smile. And your lips around my co... nevermind.

"Airplanes, Little Feeney!" Preston slaps the table so hard, I'm not sure it'll still be standing by the time they're done.

But then my phone dings again.

Five sleeps until date night. Did you confirm with Axe?

On Wednesday, I find my life on repeat. June is in my shop, but now she has her own deck of playing cards that somehow magically appeared in our life. I'm out back, working on tomorrow's orders. Hannah's in the front, gabbing on about Axel, since, as far as June's aware, he's Preston's best friend in the world.

And Preston... is bonding with my daughter. Not infringing on my time. Not asking for anything more than a cupcake he refuses to take for free, and a game of cards with a little girl who is more than happy to oblige.

She's been practicing.

And he's... just biding his time and getting through the week. Making my daughter laugh, and sending me filthy texts while I stay put and work through my to-do list.

The bell above the shop door jingles, like it does a hundred times every day, but it's not until I feel the change in the air that I glance up. And frown.

"Oh..." June's laughter cuts off with a gurgle I feel in my gut. "Hey, Daddy."

Panic slices through my blood as I shove up from my chair so the legs scrape along the concrete flooring. Then I sprint the distance between my desk and the entryway.

"I was just playing cards," June continues cautiously. "Preston is Uncle Axe's friend."

I skid to a stop in the doorway just as Noah stands over the tiny, two-person table, his legs set wide, and his hands on his hips.

On his gun.

Hannah's eyes whip my way, while Preston slowly, oh-so-leisurely, rises from his chair and meets my ex-husband's eyes with a barely concealed glare.

"Preston Danes," he introduces himself, extending his hand and placing his body in front of June's. I don't know if he means to, or if he even realizes he's doing it, but he becomes my baby's shield and keeps his hand in place, *waiting, waiting.* "How's it going?"

"Detective Scott." Noah takes Preston's hand so their palms collide with a slap, then he squeezes so his fingers redden in some spots, and turn white in others. I watch Noah's shoulder flex, since his back is mostly to me, and then Preston's eyes, which flicker my way for a fast beat. "Were you just heading out?"

Go away, asshole, I translate. *Leave my possessions alone.*

"No." Flashing an unkind smile as their hands part, Preston wipes his on his jeans, then peers toward the glass front door. "Waiting for my friend to get here."

"You're playing cards." Noah tilts to the side, needlessly proving what the rest of us already know. "With my daughter."

"She's a cool kid. She was raised well."

"Yes, well." Noah takes the compliment like it belongs to him, and turns when I clear my throat. Finding me in the doorway, he amends, "We're doing our best, aren't we, Nicki?" Then he wanders away from Preston.

Away from June, too, which is just another reminder of how much of a dick he is.

I want to see my baby every single day, and on the weekends I can't,

I'm lost and drowning in devastation. But today, Noah walks in and doesn't even get close enough to hug her. Or look into her eyes.

I make my way to the display cabinet and keep it between us, so Noah has less of a chance to pull me into a hug. "What are you doing here? It's Wednesday."

"I miss my family." He says it so easily, so fucking confidently, nausea rolls in my stomach and threatens my throat. "I got off work early today and thought we could get dinner together." Then he glances around. "Where's Axel?"

"Coming," I lie. "He got caught up at the station. Why?"

"Thought maybe he'd like to hang out with Junie tonight." He leans against the glass display case and brushes spider-like fingertips along my forearm.

Twenty feet across the store, Preston's eyes fire up with a manic rage I have no clue how to douse. It's an emotion I haven't explored with him yet. I see the potency. The passion. Though I have no doubt Noah sees neither.

"You want Axel to take care of June?" I take a step back and break the connection Noah is intent on creating. "So you *don't* want to get dinner?"

"No, I do. Me and you," he chuckles. So fucking easily dismissing his own daughter. "We need time just the two of us, Nicole. The adults. So we can discuss adult things. That's the only way we can hope to rekindle what we lost."

"I don't want to rekindle *anything*." The strings of my temper snap, so a haze of red coats my vision. "Dammit, Noah! I don't want to get back together with you."

"Alrighty!" Hannah dashes around the counter, yanks June into her arms, and drops my baby onto her hip. Then she rushes to the front door and swings it wide so the outside breeze gusts inside and blows their hair back. "June and I are gonna go for a walk. Is that okay?" She doesn't wait for my permission. She takes off and releases the door. "Okay! Bye."

"I wanna stay with my mom!" June's shout carries behind them on the wind. "Mom!"

"Noah." My temper simmers and my patience wears dangerously thin as I come closer and set my hands atop the counter. I hold his stare and firm my lips in hopes I can keep my anger in check.

It's so difficult for me not to shout. It's beyond hard for me to speak in a businesslike manner with the man who continues, to this day, to abuse us. But I take a deep breath and stay under control. "I don't want to get back together with you. Ever."

His face burns redder with anger.

"I don't want to go out to dinner with you. Ever. I don't want the three of us to go out, so we can pretend to be a happy family. And I especially don't want to go alone with you, like some kind of ridiculous farce of a date. We're not married anymore, Noah."

I move my hands with a fast swipe when he reaches out to grab. He's predictable, if nothing else, and I learned long ago that his modus operandi is to physically restrain.

"You need help," I plead. "You need to talk to someone about your issues—"

"My *issues*? I don't have any fucking issues, Nicole! I asked you out for the sake of our daughter."

"You need to talk to someone about your inability to move on."

"I don't need to move on!" he roars. "I have moved on. I've been dating. I'm simply trying to co-parent with you effectively and healthily, for the sake of our child. But you're constantly throwing up roadblocks and tossing unfounded accusations at me. It's not wrong for me to want a better situation for my daughter."

"*Our* daughter," I bite out. "She's *our* daughter, Noah. And you're not looking for us to reconcile in a healthy way. You're looking to control and manipulate."

"And there you go again!" He shoves away, but only to pace a few feet to the left. "I said I'd like to co-parent, and you call it manipulation." He stops on a dime and leans closer again. "There's something wrong with *you*, Nicole." Lifting one hand, he taps his temple and sends spittle flying, "Something seriously wrong, up here, that you can hear an innocent request for a parental meeting and call it something else."

"That is your opinion." I give myself space from the counter and fold my arms.

Tears scald the backs of my eyes, not because Noah is shouting at me —I'm used to that—but because Preston gets a front-row seat to the show. When I turn his way, his eyes bore into mine, and his chest inflates with a need to fight. To hurt someone. To take care of me.

You don't need a security guard, you need a support system.

Shaking my head and bringing my gaze back to the man I once promised a lifetime to, I press my lips closed and try, so fucking desperately, to formulate an answer that enforces my boundaries without inflaming Noah's rage.

"I don't agree with what you've said about me." I blow out a heavy breath and stand taller, if only to feel braver. "I don't believe I've twisted your intent, and I don't think you wish to meet me in any way that is healthy or in Juniper's best interest. You are intent on being in our lives, Noah. Except, we're divorced now."

"She will *always* be my daughter." He shoves a hand toward the door, in the direction of the little girl he didn't even greet when he came in here. "And for as long as she's mine, I will be in your lives. And do you wanna know what, Nicole?" He reaches back my way, too quickly, and snatches my hand so an involuntary cry escapes my lips and telegraphs to the world that he scares me. "I have documented every single attempt I've made to reach out, to bring us closer together for Junie."

"Let me go."

"Now, we've come to a point where I have enough evidence to present to a judge. And do you know what I think he'll say?"

I try to shake my hand free. "Noah. I said let me go."

"I think he might consider me the better parent. Our state encourages equal, shared care, Nicole." His eyes scorch with a terrifying fury. "Fifty-fifty sounds good to me."

"Noah—"

"But when I show him your constant refusals to work together for our daughter's sake—"

"Noah!"

"He might just be inclined to flip custody and give her to me. Since I have a proven track record of wanting what's best for her."

"Noah, let me—"

"Alright." Preston's dangerous voice makes my stomach twist. "I heard her ask you nicely." He stalks up behind Noah and grabs his shoulder with a fast yank, spinning him around and slamming his back to the counter so glassware shakes.

Fear ricochets in my blood, because he's almost certainly sleeping in a jail cell tonight. Noah's a cop, and Preston has dared to step forward when most others would not.

But it's the rage in Preston's glare that makes me want to puke.

"She asked you to let her go, asshole. But you didn't listen. So now you gotta deal with me."

"You're gonna want to step away from me." Noah drops his hands to the gun on his hip—not his badge, not even a cell phone. He goes for his *weapon*, because it makes him feel powerful.

But Preston's faster. He wraps his palm around Noah's wrist and twists it back until I swear tendons snap. The pistol falls to the floor, then skitters along the tile when Preston kicks it.

He's so calm. So smooth. So fucking fearless in the face of a gun.

Then he steps closer, so their chests touch and his nose almost touches Noah's. "She asked you to let her go, Scott. Three fucking times."

"You're under arrest," Noah huffs. But fear weaves in with every word he speaks. "For assaulting an officer. And—"

"I've not assaulted you." Preston screws Noah's hand back further, and grins when he elicits a piggish yelp. "I've merely attempted to mediate an issue between an asshole and his former wife. That asshole," he twists again, "turned words into a physical altercation. He grabbed her, unprovoked, and was given three chances to let go. Well, four, actually. Maybe five. But three sounds catchier."

"Preston." My heart thunders so quickly, it stings.

But then the front door swings open with a wild shove, bouncing against the wall so the bells above chime deafeningly loud, and Axel sprints in—only to skid to a stop and try, in the space of a single second, to understand the scene laid out in front of him.

"See?" Unfazed, Preston brings his savage glare back to Noah. "My friend has arrived, just like I said he would. But instead of joining me for a cupcake, he's here to bear witness to your attempted assault of your ex-wife. In fact, it might be in everyone's best interest if he convinces her to get a restraining order on you, considering your complete fucking inability to keep your hands to yourself." His last words come out on a snarl, and with a fast yank, he wrenches Noah's hand back so the bone snaps.

Noah screams out in pain.

"I hope you're not right-hand dominant, Scott," Preston taunts. "It'll suck having to learn to pull your dick with the other hand for the next couple months." Releasing him, he snatches up the discarded gun and pulls it into three pieces with practiced moves.

My mind swirls—*how does he know how to do that?*—but while Noah, sobbing, hunches over so all I see is the arch of his back, Preston walks the dismantled gun to my brother. "I'm surrendering this weapon to a first responder, Officer Asshole."

Preston drops each section into Axel's hand, then meets his stare. "He went to pull this, unprovoked. I might encourage you to add that to the police report."

Then he turns back to Noah. Bending to get on his level, he places his hand beneath Noah's chin the way he's done for me.

When he does it to me, he's forcing me to stand up to my lover. Proud. Able.

When he does it to Noah, straightening his back and demanding his eyes, he's making him look into the face of his better.

"You're gonna leave," he commands on a low rumble. "And you're gonna stay gone, because God help me, I'm struggling not to end your miserable existence right now. If you don't walk your ass out of this store and never come back, the security footage of you pulling a weapon in here will land on the chief's desk within the hour. Unlike you, he's pretty fuckin' good at his job, and I assure you, he has a passion for protecting the residents of his town."

Noah cradles his arm against his chest, sobbing in pain so tears roll along his cheeks and splat to the floor in a way I've never seen from him before. "You're making a mistake, Preston Danes. I'll kill you."

"Eh." With a shrug of nonchalance, he walks to Axel and takes the gun's magazine to pop a nine-millimeter slug free. Then he strides back to Noah, grabs his unbroken wrist, and slaps the bullet into his palm with a wink. "My life has been threatened a thousand times, Scott. And yet, here I am. Still standing. But you..." He glances down at the bullet and smirks. "You'd be doing us all a favor if you put this between your brows and ended this bullshit. Or," he adds happily, bringing his glare back up to look my ex in the eye, "hand it to your captain, and explain where the rest of your weapon has gone."

"I'll end you," Noah whimpers. "I'll fucking destroy you. You'll be in a cell by morning."

Preston only drops his hands to his hips and shrugs. "If that were the case, I'd already be in a cage. If you wanna bring this to a judge, I'm ready to play. I have video, audio, and several credible witnesses, not only to today's bullshit, but to your continued abuse, stalking, and harassment—as well as knowledge of the cute little tracking devices you've slapped on your ex-wife's car over the last several years."

He tips his chin toward the door, and laughs when Noah obediently stumbles forward. "Catch ya later, Felch. It wasn't a pleasure to meet you."

Bested, for today at least, Noah scurries past Preston, then squeals when Axe steps just close enough their shoulders clash with a boom. Finally, he pushes through the door and into the brutal sunlight outside.

I have only a moment to panic because June is somewhere out there too, before Axel follows. He charges in Noah's wake and onto the sidewalk outside. Then the door slowly closes, and the bells above tinkle in faux cheerfulness.

Fresh tears build in my eyes when it's just me and Preston left behind. A sob rolls along my chest, and my breath catches in my throat. "Oh god." I drop my elbows against the counter and my face into my hands, then I cry, when I so rarely allow myself to. "What a mess! He won't let this—"

"Take a breath." I don't know how Preston moves so quickly, but he comes to my side of the counter and tugs me in until his arms hold me up, when I'm not sure I could stand on my own. "It's gonna be okay." He presses a kiss to the top of my hair and croons, "Everything's gonna be okay, I promise."

"I didn't need you to do that!" I shove away from his chest, and hiss when my hip collides with the counter. Then I slap his hand away when, confused, he reaches out for me again. "Preston! You shouldn't have done that!"

"Done what?" His tone turns deadly serious. "What did I do wrong, Feeney?"

"My name is Nicole Scott! And now he knows who you are. He knows you're willing to step in front of me. He knows you care, Preston!"

"I more than *care*," he sneers. "And so fucking what? You asked him four times to let you go. I counted them. Four times! I was waiting for you to take control of the situation, Nicole. I gave you both four fucking chances to make better choices, but he was refusing to listen, and you weren't kicking him in the nuts."

"I can't kick him in the nuts! That's assault."

"So is when he grabs you! I mean, it's also assault when I break his wrist, but hey, it happens."

He crosses the space I placed between us and pushes his hand through my hair so my head drops back and my breath comes to a sharp stop. Then he looks down into my eyes. "I gave him four chances to choose better, babe. But I'm only human, so there's only so long I can stand by and watch another man hurt someone I love."

My heart stutters painfully in my chest. "Lo—"

"If you're gonna throw a fit over my actions, then you do you. Wave your arms and make it a good show. But we have security footage, and we have audio of the entire interaction. We have you asking him to let you go, and we have me, disarming a dangerous man and asking him to leave." He smacks a noisy, violent kiss to the center of my lips before pulling back. "We're not gonna cop flack for this. But maybe now, he'll think twice before grabbing you again."

The bell above my door jingles, then Axel pokes his head into the shop and clears his throat. "Uh..." He remains on the threshold, inside but outside too, and when I turn my head, I find him standing with his legs wideset, and half his turnout gear on. His hands are lifted in surrender, and his hair is in a wild disarray that says he's been working out today and running drills in full uniform.

His brows sit high on his forehead as he looks from Preston to me. "Who wants to fill me the hell in on what just happened? Because all I know is Sophia fucking Solomon called me at work and told me to haul ass over here. Then I find..." he waves his hands around. "*This*. Why did Sophia call me?"

"Because I didn't have your number handy," Preston murmurs. "And I was dealing with a situation here. So I told her to get you." He brings his gaze back around and rests his forehead against mine so I taste his breath on my tongue. "I gave him four chances, Feeney. That's three more than I would give anyone else."

"You escalated the situation." I stick with my argument, though I've lost most of the wind in my sails. "He won't let this go."

"He was pulling his gun," he grits out. "I *deescalated* the situation. Then I gave him an opportunity to step back and think about his actions." With a playful grin, he leans in and presses a kiss to the tip of my nose. "He doesn't run this show anymore, babe. And if he doesn't give you space, he'll know he has to answer to me. Juniper won't have to visit with him for another ten days, and if we're lucky, maybe he'll just fuck right off before then and never come back." Gently, he lays a sweet kiss on the center of my lips that steals the breath from my lungs.

With that one, he tugs my heart over a line of no-return.

Damn, damn, damn him.

"Things are gonna be okay, I promise. Also," he pulls back and flashes a boyish smile. "Three more sleeps till our date."

"Oh god." A drawn-out groan rolls along my throat. "I can't even... I don't..." I push away from him and press my hands to the counter, to hold myself up when all I can do is dangle my head and shake it side to side. "I can't even think about that right now."

Unbothered, Preston starts around the counter toward Axel. "We're best friends now, by the way." He claps my brother on the shoulder and continues to the little table and spilled cards. "As far as Felch knows. So whenever the douche canoe is around, you gotta play the part."

Then he wanders to the shop window and glances out. "Someone go get our girl. She was winning our game of cards, so I want her to finish it out."

Noah

PRESTON DANES

N o middle name.

February twenty-ninth birthday. He's twenty-nine years old, if we ignore the leap-year thing.

He has a master's degree in computer technology from an Ivy League school, and according to the information I can pull, he's a volunteer firefighter, chess master, Eagle Scout volunteer, Guinness World Record holder for the most consecutive hours of Gameboy played—*What the fuck? Loser*—and a teacher of advanced self-defense classes for women on the fourth weekend of every month.

Fucking pussy.

Until recently, he lived on the twenty-ninth floor of one of the more expensive buildings in my city, but a new job meant a new town. A new home. It means he now lives just a couple miles from my wife and daughter. And in the afternoons, it appears he plays cards with June and eats Nicole's cakes.

He stole the life I'm supposed to be living.

His new job title mentions security analysis and information technology specialist. And his bank account—though, if my captain knew I'd dug so deep, he'd have me on administrative leave faster than I could scratch my ass—says he has a modest income and a decent savings account.

He has six figures saved, but it came through consistent injections each month, allocated from his income. Squeaky clean.

"Come on, asswipe." I scroll past his '*I'm a yuppie dork*' bullshit and look for criminal history instead. *There's gotta be something.*

There's *always* something.

"What are you doing?" Detective Drake Banks flops down in the chair across from mine, sporting two black eyes and a filthy smirk that says he's content with how he got them. Then he nods toward my casted wrist, held close to my chest. "What happened?"

"Hurt it at the gym." I look toward my computer screen. "And I'm running a suspected perp. But don't worry about it." I navigate away from the page when Drake pushes up to get a peek. "Nothing's popping yet."

Because Drake Banks is a fucking narc who would send me to the captain before I could turn around.

It's a dark time when a man can't even trust his own partner.

"Who is it?" Suspicious anyway, Drake's eyes narrow. "What case?"

"Something one of my informants fed me. Preston Danes." I switch off my computer and grab my coat from the back of my chair. "His name keeps popping up in my investigation," I murmur, "but his jacket is all but nonexistent. So I'm wondering what he's hiding, ya know?" I swing my coat on, and grit my teeth when my wrist throbs with a deep ache. "Have you heard of him?"

He thinks for a moment as we step away from our desks. "Nah, I don't think I know that name. What case are you looking at him for, again?"

None of your fucking business, asshole.

"Don't worry about it," I answer instead. "Danes can sit on ice for now. How are we doing on the Shapera case?"

"Danes?" Officer Devon, a beat cop I've brushed up against a couple of times in the last couple of years, comes to a sharp stop in the hall and spins back as we pass. "*Preston* Danes?" he repeats. Then he drops his head back and laughs. "What'd he do this time?"

"*This time?*" I swing around and, like a panther stalking his prey, start toward the uniformed officer. "What do you know about him?"

Nicole

PLEASE DON'T MAKE ME CRY TODAY

"Be careful!" I stand in panicked stillness and watch Raul and Jenson load my cake into the back of a delivery van.

They're careful, but it's five freaking tiers of faultlessness they'll have to assemble when it reaches the city.

"Jesus. Oh my god." I mutilate my thumbnail and wince when Jenson's footsteps waver. "You're stressing me the hell out."

"It's fine." He sets the largest, heaviest base slab in the van and turns back to me with a satisfied grin. Brushing his hands together, he winks and moves aside to let Raul set the next layer in. "Client's pretty chill," he adds. "Seems the type that, if we mess up one side of the cake, she'll just turn it around to show her guests the good side."

"The *whole* cake is perfect," I snarl.

My phone chirps in my pocket, so I snatch it out and groan at Noah's name flashing on the screen. Then I kill the call and shove a clipboard in front of Raul.

"Sign here. Acknowledge you've collected the cake, and that it was in perfect condition when you did so."

"Hmm…" He studies the form and wrinkles his nose. Then he turns when Jenson slams the doors shut. "Nah. I don't think I will. Let's get this beauty to the venue before it melts."

"Raul!" My heart thunders as I chase him the length of the van. But

267

then he turns, so our chests crash, and my breath comes out on a fast exhale.

He chuckles, playful, and snatches my clipboard. "You're seriously wound up, Ms. Scott. You need a Xanax?"

"I need you to stop testing my patience." I kill Noah's next call at the very first vibration. "This cake is my mortgage *and* grocery *and* electric money for the entire month. I know you would feel bad if you let me and my daughter starve. So sign the damn invoice and get that payment released to my bank."

With a shake of his head, he sends the pen flourishing across the paper, and hands both back with a twinkle in his eyes. "You need to loosen up, Nic. It's Saturday! Go out. Dress up. Let your hair down."

"I *am* going out," I huff in response. But my cheeks burn with a blush. "I have a date. Soon. And now I have this." I lift the clipboard with one hand, and kill Noah's next call with the other. "Drive safe," I tell them. "If you trash my work, I'm gonna trash your faces." Then I turn away and wave goodbye.

"Wow." Jenson opens his door so the hinges squeak. "That was violent and unnecessary."

"Happy Saturday!" I skip inside my bakery and close the door at the back so the locks snick into place. Then I take my signed release form straight to my archaic computer and scan it in for safekeeping.

Still, my phone buzzes and drags my smile away.

Now that the cake is gone and my workday is officially complete, I snatch the stupid device from my pocket and answer. It's his fifth or sixth attempt, and though I know June is with Axel and can't hear this conversation, I still give Noah the courtesy of manners he would never think to reciprocate.

That's my toxic trait, I think. My inability to treat him the way he treats me.

"What, Noah?"

"You're okay?" His words come out on a concerned exhale that, from anyone else, would make me feel bad for worrying them. But it's Noah, and I know better. "I've been trying to reach you for the last hour, Nicole. Is everything alright?"

"Yes." Dry. Factual. To the point. I can't be my own hero if I allow my emotions to get the better of me. "I'm working." I sit at my desk and open my email so I can let my client know her cake is on the way. "It's Saturday, and I always work Saturdays. You know this. Why are you calling?"

"I need a reason?" His tone turns wounded, but it doesn't elicit the reaction in me he probably hopes.

Back when we were married, I'd have worried I hurt his feelings. I'd have tried to validate him, even at the expense of my own mental health. Now, I see it for the manipulative ploy it actually is.

"You're my family, Nicole. You're the mother of my child. It's reasonable that I care about you."

"No." I shake my head and type my client's email address one-handed. "It's no longer reasonable." Calm. Measured. "The last time you were in my presence, you physically assaulted me, Noah. And you verbally threatened to remove our daughter from my care. Her life is *here*," I remain firm, unshaking, "her stability is with me. So no," I repeat, and tap enter to send my email. Then sitting tall in my chair, I rest my elbow on the desk and focus entirely on my ex-husband. "Nothing you say or do is reasonable. Your threats are malicious, you've never had June's best interests at heart, and your inability to control your temper is both dangerous and documented. So I think we're done with this phone call."

"Wait!" he calls out, just as I remove the phone from my ear. "Nicole! Just wait a second."

I close my eyes and draw a deep breath. Find my patience. *Stay calm. Stay in control.*

Gritting my teeth, I bring the device back to my ear. "What?"

"I just want to know you're being safe," he whispers. If I didn't know him the way I do, I could almost pretend he actually cares. "You had that guy hanging out with Junie. Did you know he's a car thief? A fucking criminal. He's spent time in a cell, Nick. He's dangerous. And I don't like that you—"

You slimy little rat bastard. "You looked him u—"

"And you're always foisting her off on Axel," he pushes on. "I don't know the men you're dating. And I just..." He sighs. "It scares me to think you have this constant stream of guys coming in and out of her life."

If I was less confident in myself as a mother, I might take offense to his words. But the fact is, I long ago learned that accusations from him are typically confessions.

He has a constant stream of women coming through his door.

He is unsafe for June.

He is the unstable element in her life.

He is a bad father.

"Whether I date or not is no longer your business." Standing and hitting the button to switch off my computer screen, I grab my purse and drop my planner inside. "I will always take care of June to the best of my abilities. *Always*. And what I do outside of that has nothing to do with you. I never *foist* her off on my brother. She loves him more than you could ever understand."

Because you don't understand love.

But that's an emotion. Not a fact. And this discussion is for facts only.

"That man she was playing cards with on Wednesday is a special friend of ours. He's been nothing but a positive addition to our lives. And before you ask, *he's* none of your business, either." A smile grows across my lips, smug, because I'm done being controlled by this jerk. I'm done being manipulated.

Most of all, I'm done being afraid.

"You no longer have a reason to contact me, Noah. I've said it before, but you fail to listen. June will be available for your court-ordered visitations. If something comes up, I'll email you. You can call her any day you like, but I want you to do so between six and seven at night, so she has time to eat and get ready for bed at a reasonable time. Phone calls outside those hours will no longer be answered."

"Nicole—"

"It's really this easy," I press on. "I no longer want you." I swing my purse onto my arm and head toward the front of my shop. "I stopped wanting you a very long time ago. And despite your threats, you don't want June. So there's no way in hell you'll fight me for primary custody, because you're too selfish to care for anyone but yourself."

"Nic—"

"You don't even want her for your current visitation schedule. You only want to annoy me. If you truly want what is best for her, then you need to come to a place of acceptance that we're over, you need to stop being so horrible to her when you *do* have her, and you need to find help for whatever you have going on in your head. Because you're not healthy, Noah. Your behavior is not okay. Until then—"

"*Nicole!*" he booms, just like he always does. The faux-caring act is exactly that: an act. "Don't you fucking hang up on me, bitch."

"Goodbye." I bring the phone from my ear and kill the call with a fast swipe of my finger. Then I go one step further and block his number.

I'll reverse it in a couple of days, when he's had time to cool off, so his temper won't spill over onto June. But until then, my court orders are void of a clause that says I *have* to be available to him.

"I'm done." I stop at the entryway to find Hannah mopping behind the counter. "I'm going home," I tell her. "Having a shower and blowing out my hair. Then I'm going on a date with a man who makes my toes curl."

She changes her grip on the mop and uses it to sway and dance. "I wish I was going out on a date with someone who makes my toes curl."

"Someday."

I go to the display cabinet and box up four different cupcakes. One for June. One for Axel. One for Preston. And one for me—a rare decision.

Closing the glass door and grabbing a paper bag to hold the parcel, I turn on my heels and move toward the front door. "I'm going home. I'll see you on Monday."

"Call me later tonight!" she shouts over the sound of the bells jingling. "I wanna know about your date."

"If it goes well," I stop in the doorway and turn back with a smirk, "I'll be too busy to text you. But maybe tomorrow."

"Girrrrrl!" She hugs her mop and laughs. "Get some. I'll talk to you when I talk to you."

"Mmhm." I let the door swing closed and start toward my car parked out front.

I refuse to let anything upset me today. So I ignore the fresh new scratch on my bumper—*the curb came out of nowhere*—and slip the key into the ignition just as soon as I'm in. I don't even care that the engine *rrrr-rrr-rrrr*s in complaint. I simply set my bag and cupcakes on the passenger seat, and try the ignition again. Then, when the car fires up, I close my door and back out of my parking space with a smile.

If I contract a wedding cake for every weekend for the next couple of months, I might buy a new car.

Or if Noah miraculously decides to pay child support.

"Nope." I make a concerted effort not to let myself be cranky, not to let thoughts of my ex tarnish date-day, and turn up my radio as I head toward home.

I find Axel's truck parked out front, like I knew I would. So stopping in the driveway and killing the engine with a flourish, I grab my cakes and handbag, and skip along the path that cuts down the middle of my yard.

I shove through my front door, and can't help the smile that stretches across my face when I hear a loud *thud* then a shouted, "*Cats!*"

"Hey!" Axel's laughter comes from the kitchen. "You cheated!"

"I didn't cheat," June counters savagely. "You need to pay more attention to the game, and less attention to everything else. Then you won't be crap."

"Juniper!" I enter the room to find the Feeney couple at my counter: June perched on her stool, and Axel leaning on his elbows on the opposite side. "No swearing."

"Preston taught me that word," she giggles.

While Axel's eyes are on me, she slaps her hand over the next set of cards. "*Cars!*"

"Stop shouting." Axel growls in response. Then he pushes up to stand and snatches the tray of cakes from my hand before I have time to set them down.

"She's cheeky and mean," he grumbles. But his sour expression turns to a grin when he finds a cake he likes and tugs it from the packaging. "She's getting a little sassy, Feeney. Is she old enough yet to be tied to a streetlamp and flogged with a stick?"

"What?" Cackling, June balances precariously on her stool. "You can't hit me with a stick! That's not nice."

"It's how your mom and I were raised," he argues with icing on his lips. "We turned out okay."

"Hi, baby." I come up behind her and press a kiss to the top of her hair. "No one's hitting anyone with a stick. Now sit on your bottom before you fall."

She drops with a huff, but half-climbs onto the counter to drag the cupcakes her way. "Can I eat one now, Mommy? Even though it's almost dinnertime?"

"Sure." I set my bag on the floor and toss my keys on top. Then I spin in a nervous circle and feel my stomach whoosh. "What time is it?"

Too-knowing, Axel teases and waves toward the hall. "Time to shower and get changed. June and Uncle Axe have a date tonight. I thought maybe I'd teach her how to smoke and light fires. Ya know," he skitters aside when I lift a hand to smack him. "Life lessons. Don't hit! It's not nice."

"Don't teach my daughter those words." *They could be repeated and used against me in court.* "You're supposed to be a good influence, Axel. Not a pain in my backside."

"But..." His eyes dance with deviousness. "I'm only fifty percent of her male interaction now, right?"

"Axe—"

"My bad influence can be canceled out by what he brings to the table, no?"

"I know you're not talking about Felcher," I mumble and head out of the room. Stopping at the base of the stairs, I set my hand on the rail and call back, "Don't talk about any of that, Axel Feeney, or I'm putting you in timeout. Then you'll have to play cards on your own. I'm not messing around."

"Yeah right," he grumbles around a mouth filled with cake. Then, "Hearts!" *Slam.*

Shaking my head, I climb the stairs and grab stray articles of clothing June has left behind. A sweater, despite the warmer weather. A single shoe I know she'll come looking for the match to before next weekend is over. I snag her schoolbag as I pass it, and sigh when I find her lunchbox spilled open inside.

A problem I'll hate myself for tomorrow, when I finally get around to cleaning it.

I'm not fixing it tonight. Nope. Because I have a date.

In my back pocket, my phone vibrates. But dread doesn't come to me like it usually does. Noah's been blocked, and no one else on this planet, besides a judge, makes my stomach turn. So I drop June's bag at the top of the stairs, and her clothes in the bathroom, then I snatch my phone and answer with a grin. "Are you calling to cancel?"

"Fuck no." Preston's playful rumble. His voice, his intensity... *Damn him for making my heart skip a beat every time he flitters through my mind.* "Calling to see if you have finished work and are ready for me. I'm dressed, I brushed my hair and spritzed on a little cologne. Now I'm waiting for you."

"Well…" I move into my room and close the door at my back, then I continue into my bathroom and close that door too. Finally, I flip my shower on, and set the call on speaker before placing my phone on the counter to free my hands. "I'm finished at work," I tell him. "And now I'm undressing."

"Mmm…" That sound alone, that one friggin' syllable, is enough to make my thighs tremble. "So we're close, then. Keep talking to me while you shower?"

"Pervert." But my heart flutters as I push my pants down and kick my shoes aside. "How was your day?"

"Decent." I don't know where he is. I don't know if he's sitting or standing. If he's in his living room, or in his car. But in my mind, as I push my panties down and goosebumps race along my skin, I imagine him lounging in a comfy recliner. "I have this project coming up," he says. "Kinda big." He clears his throat. "Something I wanna tell you about tonight, actually."

"Yeah?" I turn the volume of my call as loud as it'll go, then I step into my shower and tip my head back so water cascades through my hair and makes it heavy. "Something exciting?"

He makes a noncommittal sound in the back of his throat. "Depending on a person's perspective, I suppose. How was your day?"

"Good." I pump shampoo into my palm, then massage it through my hair. As I close my eyes, I can almost imagine he's right here with me. In my bathroom. Chattering with me after a long day of work. "I sent my wedding cake off with the couriers. It's been signed for, which means it's no longer my responsibility. I got a release on the funds, which is always something to celebrate. I have nothing on my schedule from now until Monday, so I'm kind of excited to have tonight with you, and tomorrow with June. And…" opening my eyes, I smile. "I stood up for myself against Noah today."

"What?" Preston's relaxed demeanor zooms away on a single breath. But I don't fear his temper. Or his disapproval. I don't fear anything, because he's never tried to manipulate me through his feelings. "You talked to him?"

"He called five times in a row." Moving on to the conditioner, I work the gel through my hair and take care to massage it into the ends. "I took the final call, to tell him not to call."

"You told him that?"

"Mmhm." *And my stomach still rolls from nerves at the memory.* "I confronted him about his threats to take June from me—he never will. I demanded he seek help for himself—he won't. And I told him to stop calling me."

"He won't listen." Preston's words are the verbal equivalent to an eyeroll. "You've asked for that space before."

"Right. But then I hung up and promptly blocked his number. I'll leave it that way for a few days so he can cool down. Then I'll unblock it and allow him to have access to June again. But I'm done letting him push me around."

Victory warms my blood. Bravery makes me smile.

Maybe I didn't break his wrist or snarl in his face, but I spoke my boundaries. I didn't lose my temper. And I forever intend to hold him accountable for his behavior.

"Best of all," I continue giddily. "I'm gonna start dating."

"Uh..." Preston chokes out a cough. "Excuse me? You're dating *me*. And I'm not done with you yet."

I close my eyes and rinse the conditioner from my hair. "I meant I'm not hiding this. I'm not hiding *us*. Tonight is just for me and you, but tomorrow, I thought maybe you could come over to the house and hang out."

"To your house?"

"Yeah. Hang out with me and June. Stay for dinner. I'm not ready for you to sleep over and stuff yet, but I thought, maybe we could tell her you're *my* friend. Not Axe's. We could tell her we're, like... dating. Ya know?"

"Really?" His breathing grows a little faster. "You wanna tell her?"

"I think so." After squeezing the excess water from my hair, I grab my razor and make quick work of my legs. The faster I get out of here, the faster I get to see him. "It's kind of scary," I murmur. "And god knows, I might be moving too fast. But... she deserves to be a part of this. She deserves to know you as someone more special in her life than Uncle Axe's friend. So..." I shrug. "I wanna tell her."

"Fuck, Feeney." I hear his footsteps—*he's at home*. Then the sound of a fridge opening and closing. "I won't let you down." With a reverence in his tone that surprises me, he adds, "I promise. I wanna talk to you about everything tonight, okay? *Everything.* Then after that, I'm yours."

"Well..." My heart flips, and the sensation is both pleasant and painful. "I can't wait to get started."

"Me too. How long till you're ready for me to pick you up?"

"Uh..." I peer around my bathroom, though I know there's no clock in here. Then I look down my body. Plan my hair, my outfit. "Thirty minutes."

"I'll be there in twenty-eight," he declares. "I can't fucking wait to see you."

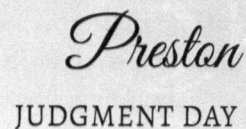

Preston

JUDGMENT DAY

I park on the street outside Nicole's home and walk along the pathway that cuts through her yard. I pass her junkbucket of a car, and vow to tear the engine out just as soon as I can replace it with something better. Then I pass Axel's truck. His presence here, a favor I won't ever forget.

Of course, he loves his niece and wouldn't consider this a favor at all.

But I won't ever ignore the part he played in my relationship with Nicole. I won't toss aside the fact he came to me at my work, and demanded I seek her out and show her who she can be outside of an over-thinking mom, or battered divorcee.

I won't forget that his love and desire for her happiness supersedes his brotherly instinct of smashing my face in for daring to touch his sister.

It's a balancing act he seems to have perfected. And that, I appreciate too.

I move up the porch steps and stop by the front door, then bringing a hand up, I knock, only for an unbridled grin to cross my lips when a shouted "*Dog!*" echoes from deep inside the house.

I've infiltrated their lives against their will. But there isn't a part of me that feels guilty for it.

Really, introducing her family to an addictive card game barely registers on the list of crimes I've committed in my life. And Nicole may hate my guts once I tell her who I really am tonight. Still, I can't let this go on any longer without bringing her in and giving her all the information.

Anything less, and I'm no better than Noah 'Felcher' Scott.

Footsteps echo through Nicole's home, then I glimpse navy on navy just half a beat before the door swings open and I'm presented with Axel in dark blue cargo pants, and a skintight fire department shirt that I *know* he thinks makes him look good.

"Danes." He flattens his lips and struggles with that *loves me/hates me* balance of brotherhood. Lifting his chin in hello, he steps to the side and allows me to come in. "Didn't think to bring her flowers?"

Chuckling, I head toward the kitchen. "And tell June what?" I glance back and meet his eyes. "They're for you?"

He tosses the door closed so it slams with a rattle, then with a shrug, he follows me to the kitchen. "I like flowers. A dude's allowed to be romanced, too."

"Uh-huh."

I step into the room and stop at the sight of a beaming Juniper standing on the counter. She wears my hat atop her head, and below it, her eyes dance with... *could it be love?*

Of course not, stupid.

But affection, yes. And trust.

She's in the middle of the island and mostly safe, but my stomach still twists with worry. "Juniper Scott." I continue in her direction and shake my head. "You know that's not safe."

"But I heard your voice." Just as soon as I'm close enough, she surprises Axel and I both when she throws herself off the counter and jumps into my arms.

Her legs circle my torso, and her arms threaten to choke me out. But she smells of fireball—or, well, cinnamon—and makes a noise in the back of her throat when she squeezes. "I didn't see you all day Thursday *or* Friday," she admonishes. "I missed you."

Well, fuck. Dammit. Fuck.

Pulling back, I hold her with one arm, and reach up with the other to fix the hat she bumped askew. "I missed you too, cutie. I'm sorry I didn't see you yesterday. I got busy at work, and I thought maybe my card games were getting boring to you anyway."

"Nuh-uh!" She pulls back and points to the cards on the counter. "I was just whipping Uncle Axe's butt. He's not as good at this game as you are."

"Har har," *Uncle Axe* rumbles. Then, as though he can't help himself, he crosses to where we stand and takes June from me.

Just like Nicole, he's not quite ready to share.

But Juniper is. She wants me around. And fuck if that isn't a shot of adrenaline to my gut.

"I can't be good at a game I'd never played before." Axel takes his niece and sets her on her butt on the edge of the counter, then he pushes a paper bag in my direction. "Nicole brought you a cake. So eat it and stop infringing on what's mine." He grabs the brim of June's hat and pushes it up to meet her eyes. "Stranger danger, kid."

"Preston's not a stranger," she giggles. "He's your friend, silly."

"Mmhm. But maybe Uncle Axe doesn't wanna be his friend anymore. Ever think of that?"

Amused, I pull up a seat at the counter and tear open the paper bag to reveal a rainbow iced cake. It's like the first one I had from her shop. My introduction to blind love.

"You'll always be my friend, Axe." Taking a bite, I turn to him and grin around icing. "You might even consider me your brother eventually."

"Not ready," he grits out. "Asshole."

"Uncle Axel!" Juniper smacks his shoulder. "Name-calling is mean."

"Yeah, Uncle Axel." I break off a piece of cake and offer it to the beautiful little girl. Payment for having my back.

Just like her mom, a pink blush fills her cheeks and makes my heart grow larger.

"Where's your sister, Uncle Axe?" I glance at the clock on the wall and note she's a whole minute late. "She's not usually one for tardiness."

"I'm here." She rushes into the room with one heel on, and a stunning dress of midnight black, with tiny spaghetti straps that show off her shoulders. She carries her second shoe in the crook of her arm and reaches up to fix an earring. "Sorry I'm late. I've been looking for my earring, but can't seem to find it." Stopping, she drops her heel and steps into it to even up her stance.

Nevermind the fact I'm still stuck on stupid, and my heart, surer than ever that I'm well and truly fucked.

"I don't know where it could've gone," she rushes out. "I never lose—"

"Oh, the silver one?" I ask. "With the little pink stone?"

"Yes!" Narrowing her eyes, she looks to me with suspicion in her stare. "How could you possibly know that?"

I drop my hand into my pocket and finger the bauble I've held onto since the morning I found it.

Part of me mourns giving it back. But the rest of me knows it rightfully belongs to her.

Bringing my hand out again, I turn it palm-side-up and reveal the matching second. "I found this after Miss Blake's wedding." I smile for Juniper, since she and Maya are friendly. *I slept with your mom that night!* Then I preen under Nicole's stare as she gingerly takes the jewelry in her fingers. "I've been meaning to give it back to you."

"You've held onto it this whole time?" With shaking hands, she brings it higher to slide the hook through her earlobe. "And somehow knew I'd be looking for it tonight?"

"I've had it in my pocket every single day since the wedding." But because I can't say a hell of a lot more without Juniper knowing too much, or Axel losing his battle against brotherly protection, I turn back to my cupcake and eat. "I'm starving."

"You look so beautiful, Mommy." Juniper's voice turns softer, the way it always does when Nicole is in the room.

If she thinks I don't notice the act she puts on for her mother, the too-sweet parody she uses to keep Nicole in the dark about how truly clever she is, then she's sorely mistaken.

That doesn't mean I'll call her out and ruin what she's no doubt worked hard to achieve. But I'm aware of it. Which means I'll keep an eye on it as she grows. I'll know she's wiser than she lets on, and wittier than she shows.

She'll be a handful when she's older, and that'll come as a surprise for the woman who thinks her sweet Juniper is naïve to the world around her.

"Are you going somewhere special, Mommy?"

"Uh." Considering, she glances my way for a beat.

This is your show, Momma bear. Tell her what you want, when you want.

"Mommy's actually going out w-with Preston tonight," she stammers. "To get something to eat."

Of course Juniper's eyes light up. "Like a date?"

"Um... well..." Nicole's head bobs before her words are quite ready to admit her truths. "Yeah, kinda like a date. But I won't be out too late, okay? Then Preston might come over tomorrow to hang out and have baked dinner."

The little girl looks from her mother to me. Curious. Probing. "Will you be home before I go to bed?"

Nicole wants to say yes. She's dying to allay her daughter's potential fears. But after only a moment of hesitation, she stands taller and pushes her shoulders back. "Probably not, babe. But I'll be home way before you wake up. Then we can make a yummy breakfast together."

Juniper peers down at the cake I continue to demolish. "Will Preston make breakfast with us, too?"

I stop my movements. Still my chewing. And don't say shit, because this isn't my call.

Do I want to be here for breakfast?

Abso-fucking-lutely.

But am I willing to go at Nicole's pace and be thankful for every morsel of Juniper-time she'll give me?

Also yes.

"Um..." Nicole hedges. "I don't think he'll be here for breakfast, babe. But we'll invite him over for lunch, and then he can stay all afternoon if you want. Would you... um..." she chews on her lipsticked bottom lip. "Would you like that?"

"Yes!" She fixes her hat and tugs it down so all I see are her plump lips curled high. "Yes, I want him to come over all day." She peeks my way. Devilishly knowing. "I'm gonna whoop your butt at cards."

"Oooookay! That's enough." Nicole pulls Juniper off the counter and sets her on her feet. Then she drops into an elegant crouch and cups her daughter's cheek. "Mommy's going out now, but I'll be home later, okay? You can hang out with Uncle Axe for a couple of hours, then go to bed. I'll see you when you wake up in the morning."

"I love you, Mommy." Juniper reaches across and fingers the loose locks of her mother's hair. "I'll see you in the morning."

"Yes, you will." She tugs her baby in and presses a kiss to her cheek that leaves red lips behind. Then pulling back, she doesn't mention the mark.

Axel doesn't mention it either; no one does. Because that's Nicole's gift to her, I suppose. Leaving something of her behind while she heads out on an adventure that is entirely for her.

God forbid she lives for herself for a few hours.

"Come on." Pushing up to stand, Nicole's cheeks warm as she peeks across to me. Then she grabs her phone, and crosses to the handbag she left on her floor to take out her house keys. "You can call me anytime," she tells Axel. "You know the drill."

"Of course." He pushes up to sit on the counter. Then he catches my eyes and purses his lips. "I'll be awake when she gets home. I'll be sure to catch all the gossip while it's still fresh."

"Hush." Nicole fists her belongings in her hands and stops in the doorway to wait for me. "We're going. Don't open the door to anyone while I'm gone. Don't call Felch, and don't let him call you."

She says that word so easily, I doubt she ever took the time to actually Google the meaning. But shit, I won't spoil things for her. Instead, I cross the room and fight every instinct in my body to keep my hands to myself.

"I'll see you later," Nicole says to her brother. "I love you, June Bug."

"I love you too, Mommy! Goodbye, Pres. I'll see you tomorrow."

"Goodbye, cutie." I pause in the doorway and peer back to find the Feeney duo sitting side by side. Crossed ankles. Hands by their thighs, so their shoulders appear larger than they really are. I meet Juniper's eyes. "I'll see you tomorrow. I promise."

Assuming your mother doesn't kick me in the nuts and toss me to the side once I tell her who I really am.

Fuck, but I just made a promise I can't entirely control.

Oblivious to the torment playing through my mind, Nicole lets herself out the front door and onto the porch so her heels *click-click-click* on solid timber. Then she pauses at the top of the steps as I pull the door closed, and waits for the snick of the locks.

"It's still so early." She's stunning in her dress and makeup. Her freshly blown-out hair. Dark lashes, and sex-red lips. But it's still only four in the afternoon, which means the sun glares and forces her to squint. "It feels weird wearing this dress and these heels with the sun still up."

"Mom life," I snicker and join her on the stairs. Then we head down and cut across the lawn.

I open my truck and help her into her seat, then I jog around to my side. But I don't touch as much as I want to. I don't kiss. I don't sneak a feel, or whisper filthy wishes in her ear.

It takes only a minute for her to notice.

"What's wrong?" Frowning, she fixes her seatbelt and glances across until I feel her stare on the side of my face. "Preston, something's going on, and I'm at a point where I don't want to tiptoe around a man's mood. So..."

"I thought we could have dinner at my place tonight." I start the engine and roll away from the curb. *I'm a coward. A pussy.* "It's private."

"Preston!" Despite the fact my truck is moving, Nicole leans across and grabs my chin until her nails dig into my skin and her breath feathers my jaw. "Spill it, or take me home."

"I don't work in IT." I shake her hand off, not because I don't want her touch, but because that particular touch hurts, and I don't want to associate pain with this woman I ran face-first into falling in love with.

When she remains silent, I arrange my thoughts, pull out of her street, and start toward my cabin. "I mean... I do work in IT, in that I work with computers, and I could troubleshoot just about any issue you could ever think of. But..."

I work desperately to think of a way to deliver my news without scaring her away. And while I think, I cross the train tracks heading out of town.

"I don't troubleshoot regular office worker shit. I work in the, uh, morally gray area of things."

In my peripherals, Nicole's eyes narrow to slits. "Morally gray how?"

"Like... you know my relationship with Cole, right? You know we used to—"

"Steal cars together?" She brings her thumb between her teeth and nibbles on the nail. "Yes. *Everyone* in this town knows that. It's a terribly kept secret."

"Well... being morally gray means accessing things I probably shouldn't." A few minutes after leaving Nicole's, I pull into my driveway and bring the truck most of the way around, since I've moved the fallen tree out of the way.

I've taken care of one task at a time around my new home, albeit only when I've forgotten to charge my laptops and have no choice but to abandon my work.

"It means I can edit files, or delete them completely," I explain. "I don't have a rap sheet, Nicole, though we both know I should."

"That's a crime." She's fast. Smart. So as I cut the engine and tug the keys from my ignition, she slides out on her side and burns me with a glare from across the hood. "Accessing police records is illegal."

"Yes." I drop my hands in my pockets and miss the comfort of the earring I've been able to touch for weeks. "Yes, it's a crime."

"Punishable by law," she adds. "Severely."

"A lot of years in prison if I get caught," I agree.

She crosses her arms and goes back to nibbling on her thumbnail. "Do you *continue* to break the law? Or is this past tense?"

Well, shit, babe. I'm preparing to drop explosives on the heads of a mafia cartel soon.

"Come inside." Taking out my keys and selecting the right one, I head onto my rickety porch and unlock my door so it creaks open.

I don't go back to grab her. I don't even hold out my hand and ask for her to make that contact. Because she's entitled to time and space. She's allowed to make her own decisions without my influence.

"I thought I could cook tonight," I tell her gently. Non-confrontational. "And tell you anything you wanna know."

She sidles past me, contorting her body as though to make sure we don't brush against each other as she crosses the threshold, then sets her phone and keys on the table. "Absolutely everything?"

"Yes."

I close the door and flip the locks to keep intruders away. Then I follow her into my kitchen, and after that, my living room.

She's exploring, and I have no issue letting her. Even with my laptop open on the table, and schematics laid out beside it, in full view. I don't fuss about the emails on my screen, or the handheld radio beside it.

Because this is me.

All of me.

And if I want to keep her, then she deserves to know the truth.

"And also... yes," I exhale on my new confession. "I continue to break the law."

She pauses by my couch, and glances down at the new leather three-seater that I replaced my old, lumpy flea-factory with just a few days ago. Considering, she continues to catalog my space. "You work for Checkmate."

I stop in the doorway and lean against the frame. "I do."

"Everyone knows Sophia's company isn't... ya know," she clears her throat. "Completely legit. There are whispers around town that imply she does more than personal security."

"Well..." I shrug. "Some of those whispers may be accurate."

"Do you do security?"

Chuckling, I glance down. "Like, personal security? With my body?" Bringing my gaze back up, I shake my head. "No, I'm not what she calls 'muscle'."

Like my word choice intrigues her, she turns from my updated television set, which still sits upon a humble stack of bread crates, and looks me up and down. "You're muscular." She tilts her head in thought. "Strong."

"I do okay for myself," I concede with a smug grin. Smug, because I'm strong enough for *her*. Because my body is muscular enough to make her happy. "But I'm not like Cole. And I'm definitely not like Serrano or Rosa. They're a whole different level of security guard she keeps on staff. My job is more like... internet security. With a twist."

Pursing her lips, she nods, like I've somehow confirmed something in her mind.

Have I told her too much? Not enough? Have I messed up?

"Tell me about the twist. Without sugarcoating it."

Demand. Cold, hard demand.

"Okay." Pulling a breath deep into my lungs, I drop my hands into my pockets and exhale with a nod of my own. "My current project is to infiltrate a mafia family's servers. Their online security, basically. And then set Checkmate up so we can control it from here."

Her eyes narrow—she's probably thinking *That's not IT, asshole!*—but she meanders the length of my couch and runs her fingertips along the back. "For what purpose?"

Surprised, all I manage is, "Hmm?"

"I already mentioned the whispers about Sophia's company," she explains. Wandering back toward the kitchen, she passes me, so her perfume sits trapped in my lungs. On the other side of the table, she scans my laptop screen with mild curiosity. "It doesn't take a genius to know she's not the local tech support chick for small businesses. Plus, my brother works for Nixon Rosa, and I know Nixon is brother to Troy." She lifts her head and peers up from beneath long lashes. "Troy is the muscle you mentioned just a moment ago, and word travels fast around small towns."

"Everyone knows what's going on over there?"

She shakes her head, so her earrings swing and brush the side of her neck. "Not everyone. But I know Axe, and Axe knows Nix. Nix knows Troy, and those whispers get a little louder when you're friendly with someone. So..." She purses her beautiful, glossed lips and studies my eyes. "For what purpose do you intend to take control of someone else's security system?"

"So we can shut them down." I stand in place an easy fifteen feet from her. Casual, but ready to chase if she spooks. "Strategically," I add as an aside, "we want to take away their eyes, ears, and arsenal at a particular point in time."

"Why?"

"So they can't call for help or organize their men."

"But *why*?" she presses. She's not letting me off without telling her every single thing. "Why would they want to call for help? And why don't you want them to be able to?"

"Because..." *Just say it, dickhead.* "Because we intend to attack them. And it would be beneficial to us if they're fenced in."

Guilty. Proven. Prison. Off you go, asswipe.

Thoughtful, she tilts her head the other way. "Why are you attacking them? What did they do to you?"

My heart thunders, and nerves backstroke in my veins, but I push away from the wall and head to my fridge. Because I'd like a little booze, and better yet, I'd like for her to have a glass of something to take the edge off whatever reaction she might throw at me in retaliation.

Yanking the fridge open and taking out a bottle of white wine, I snatch one of those limited-edition McDonald's cups they give away during Big Mac promotions, and set it on the counter. Then I grab a second for me.

Because I'm not above dulling her instincts and clouding her thoughts, I guess.

Cracking the lid open and pouring, I glance over my shoulder and meet her eyes. "They're a bad family," I explain gently. "They make their fortune in the sex trade. Plus, drugs and guns. So we want to shut them down. But until we can get inside and understand their processes, wiping them out would be like knocking the head off a splinter in your foot. Maybe you took away the bit on top, the bit you can see, but the splinter is still inside, festering and causing infection."

"So... infiltration?" she ponders as I finish pouring the second glass.

Setting the bottle down and picking hers up, I come around the table and stop just a foot away so I get a fresh new hit of her sweet scent. Sex and flowers and sugar. All of my favorite things.

With a considerate smile, she accepts the glass and brings it to her lips to taste. "So Checkmate wants to infiltrate their system to understand what's happening under the surface..." she lowers her wine and still, remains close enough for me to touch. "By attacking and fencing them in?"

"The attack is a ruse, mostly. A show." Trying my luck, I duck a little lower and press a kiss to the corner of her lips. Because I haven't tasted her yet today. I haven't felt her. I haven't touched. "Some men might be hurt, but our intention is to scare them."

"Which brings me back to... for what purpose?"

She's smart. And focused.

"The dude, the head of the family, has a daughter. About our age. She's his most prized possession, so if we scare him enough, he might be inclined to hire personal security for her."

"Muscle? You want to get Checkmate muscle inside his home?"

"Essentially."

And because she's still not running away, I walk to my table and snap the laptop lid closed. Then I assemble a stack of schematics into a pile and add them on top. Finally, I pick it all up in my left hand, and grab her hand with my right, then I lead her to my couch.

Because fuck, I'd like to sit with her. I want to be close. I want to feel her under my skin.

"We've tried looking around at what this guy shows on the outside. But to understand his system," I set my laptop and papers on the crate-coffee table, then I pull her down so we hit the sofa at the same time. She turns toward me, hitching her leg up so her dress slides down to reveal her thigh. "To understand what's actually happening under the surface, we need intel from the inside."

"So scare the guy into hiring one of her staff?" As though she's impressed, she sniggers behind the lip of her glass. "It's a little crass, if you ask me. But you didn't, so..." She takes a delicate sip. "Your job in all this?"

"Sliding into his servers and shutting him down long enough to attack his property." I speak factually. Calmly.

And her eyes narrow. "Will you be onsite for this attack?"

"No. I probably won't even leave my living room."

"Will they know it was you?" she asks next. "Will you be in danger?"

I shake my head and accept her glass when she offers it, since I left mine in the kitchen. I take a small amount on my tongue and savor the burst of fruity flavor on my tastebuds. "No one will connect me to the attack. And *if* there was a trail left behind—there won't be," I assure her, "but *if*, by some crazy chance, that were the case—then it'll lead to Checkmate. Not to me specifically."

"So you're safe?" She accepts her Hamburglar glass and holds it like it's the finest of all crystal on the planet. "And no one will come looking to hurt you because of your job?"

"No. My job is to not be noticed at all." Setting my hand on the leather couch and leaning forward until I taste her fruity breath on my tongue, I press a kiss to the opposite side.

I'd hate for any part of her to feel neglected.

"I'm really good at my job, Nicole. And I'm never in the fire where shit is going down. In fact, I specialize in remote access." Pulling back, I study the slice of fear in her eyes she works to hide. "Sophia's the best at what she does... the best in the fucking world. So we're protected, and anyone I'm attached to..." *Like you. Like Juniper.* "Will never be in danger."

"How can you know?" Her voice comes out on an almost-whisper. "How can you be so sure they won't come for you?"

How can I be sure they won't come for *her*?

"There are a dozen layers of protection between me and the things I do. There are traps laid for anyone who wants to come looking, so at the very first attempt, we'll be alerted, and they'll be shut out. I never work with my name, and neither does Sophia, nor anyone else on the team.

We're ghosts," I press, when her eyes shimmer with anxiety. "No one even knows where to look, because we're just shadows on the dark web. There's not even a morsel of doubt in my mind about it. We're protected."

"I don't..." She shakes her head and drags her bottom lip between her teeth. "I don't understand it all. But they have ways of tracking this stuff, right? Like, IP addresses?"

"Those are for regular people."

When she brings her glass up again to sip, my conscience gets the better of me. So I take her wine away and set it on the table.

I don't want to dull any-fucking-thing when she's being handed the largest pile of dangerous truth she'll ever get in her life. I want her to be sharp. I want her to make her choices with a clear mind.

"IP addresses track your standard John and Suzanne Smith. Those aren't for us."

"And just so we're on the same page..." She peers deep into my eyes. "What you do is not legal?"

I bark out a cathartic laugh and shake my head. "No. But I'm trusting you not to toss me to the cops."

"I was married to a cop." Crashing back to seriousness, she swallows. "And he's not inclined to let me move on."

I cup her jaw and nod. "I know."

"What if he finds out you do this stuff? He knows about the cars, Preston. He knows about the stealing. But what if he finds out about the records and—"

"He won't," I cut in gently. "Unless you tell him. And even if you did, he'd have to prove it. This *can't* be proven, because, like I said, I'm a shadow when I'm working."

"So if I wanted to take this to the local police?" Her silver-gray stare flickers between mine. "If I wanted to turn you over?"

I roll my bottom lip and consider her non-threat. "You could try it, but again, you've gotta prove it. Besides, the chief is basically brother-in-law to a Bishop. I'd say he already knows what happens inside the Check-mate office."

Frustrated, her eyes flare hot. "So they're crooked? You're saying they're aware of illegal activity, but they just let it happen anyway?"

I hate that I've soured her vision of our local police. That I've taken away a sense of security she may have clung to after her experience with Felcher.

"Sex trade. Drugs," I emphasize. "We like to think we're serving society by shutting these things down, Nicole. It just so happens we bend the law a little to achieve our results."

"Which is a hell of a *morally gray* area to work within." Exasperated, she pushes up to stand so her perfume wafts in the space she was occupying just half a beat ago.

Her absence is a shock to my system, but her anger... entirely expected.

"I was already married to a guy who considered himself above the law, Preston." Spinning, so her dress swirls and the ends flutter against her thighs, she stops when our eyes meet. "I can't handle another egotistical narcissist who does whatever the hell he wants, no matter who it affects."

Her fears are entirely fair. So I remain seated, instead of standing up to tower over her.

"Egotistical..." I nod. "Yeah, I've got a bit of that. But I'm not selfish, Feeney. Not in the way you're thinking. I don't get off on a power trip, and I never hurt somebody who didn't deserve it."

"But you consider yourself the decision-maker? *You* decide who is to be punished?"

"No. Checkmate decides." I push up to sit on the edge of the couch. To be closer to her. To pull her back if she tries to sprint away. "Sophia and Kane and Jay and Griffin and the rest of them... *they* decide. And no one, not even Sophia, has final decision-making power. They figure that shit out as a family. They present their proof to the group, and then they determine: one, if their target is exploiting innocents, and two, if they'll step in and stop it."

"So you hide behind a shadow when you're working. And you hide behind a Checkmate democracy when you try to justify your actions?"

"I'm explaining to you what I do! I'm trying to answer your questions factually. You asked if I choose these outcomes, Nicole. The answer is no."

"And I'm trying to determine if the thing you do makes it impossible for me to stay," she grits out. "I'm trying to trust my instincts after so many years of squashing them down for someone else's benefit. I don't know if this thing I feel in my stomach," she slaps a hand to her belly, "is intuition, or if I'm overreacting. Or *under*reacting. Jesus, Preston! I just don't know."

"I don't think you're overreacting." I calm my voice and slow my breathing. "And I don't think you're underreacting. I think you're desperate to know which way to turn... but fuck, I'm desperate to help you understand I'm here for you. I won't put you or June in danger. *Ever.*"

"But those are just words!" Tears, heartbreaking and soul-shaking, squeeze through her lashes and settle on her cheek. "I've been told words all my life, Preston. And a million more during my marriage. But they were never true."

"But I promise, when *I* speak, I mean what I say." I shove up to stand, unable to stay down any longer. But I don't charge forward. I don't grab her, though my hands itch to touch. "I love you, Nicole. I love you so fucking much, it scares the shit out of me. And *worse*," my voice rises. "I love Juniper. I love how smart she is. And how brave. I love how protective she is of you, and how you don't even know the half of it. I love how protective you are of her, and how you would lay down your life just to keep her from hurting."

I step forward, so I feel her panting breath on my lips, her expanding chest in the space between us. "I love being witness to the purest fucking love I've ever seen in my life. And I love that you're tempted to share it with me. You're not yet convinced," I choke out a pathetic laugh. "You're so terrified, it makes you want to puke. But you *want* to share. You want to raise that little girl with a good man."

"You're right," she spits out. "And from what I've learned tonight, it appears the *good man* I chose is a criminal. So what the hell does that say about me?"

Anger burns in my blood. Not because she's mad at me, but because she's mad at herself.

"That family we're looking to shut down," I snarl. "They sell little girls, Feeney. They kidnap them, transport them, and then they sell them to the highest fucking bidder. Girls not a hell of a lot older than Juniper. So if you wanna know what kind of guy you fell in love with, know I'm the one who'll work his hands *raw* to get those babies out of a horrible situation. I work every fucking second I'm not with you, and I do it in silence, because if I screw up and spook Mancino, he's gonna burrow underground, and we'll never get there in time to save them."

I wrap my hand around the back of her head and tug her closer.

Because she makes me weak. Because she terrifies me. So I yank her forward and bring her to the tips of her toes so her exhale fills my lungs. "I'm gonna be good to you, Nicole. For the rest of my life. I just need you to give me a chance to prove it."

"Preston..." Her breath catches on a sob, but she reaches up and wraps her arms around my neck to keep me close.

It hurts to know she's so at war within herself. She doubts herself and destroys the instincts she should embrace. She loves me too—*fucking A, she loves me too!*—but she's been burned before.

"I don't..." She inhales deeply, until her chest expands. "Dammit, Preston."

"One day at a time." I drop my hands to her ass and pull her close. And when she doesn't object, I lift until her legs cinch around my hips. Then I damn near lose my balance when she slams her lips to mine and swallows me down, soul and all.

"I love you." She drags my lip between her teeth, then soothes the ache with a swipe of her tongue. "I'm scared. But my heart wants you more than it's ever wanted anyone."

"So we'll work with that." I back up until my calves touch the front of my sofa, then I sit and bring her onto my lap until she's straddling my cock.

I can't help that she makes me rock-hard. I can't help that my body craves her just as fiercely as my heart craves her approval. But I revel in the way she drops her head back and grinds along the hardened length inside my jeans.

I fall in love with the delicate blue veins in her neck, and the way her throat bobs when she swallows. I luxuriate in her delicious body wrapped around mine, and the trust she hands me, purely by being here.

"Be with me today." I fist her hair in my hand and guide her down to face me, so her swimming eyes flow with lust and a little less fear. "Then maybe you'll be with me tomorrow, too. And the day after that. And the day after that. Until eventually, we have *all* the days." I pull her forward until our lips clash and her tears drop to the tops of my cheeks. "Eventually, we might look back and twenty years have passed. Twenty really happy years."

"Oh god." She crushes her chest to mine and takes, takes, takes everything I happily offer. "Could it be that easy?"

I choke out a laugh and twist our bodies until she lands on the sofa with a thud. Then I crawl on my knees and press my lips to her racing heart. "I doubt it'll be easy. I'm an asshole, and you're stubborn. June's in the middle, and Noah keeps trying to put himself there. But..." I slide my palm along her thigh until I cup her ass. "I'm not gonna give up on the hard days. I swear that to you."

Her spine arches deliciously high, and her core burns furiously hot. "Preston." She pants my name and squirms closer. "Jesus, Preston, I can't—"

"Just give me a day at a time," I plead. "One sunrise. One sunset. So every night when you go to bed, I'll make damn sure I was worth it."

"I want to—"

But whatever she wants is interrupted, when her phone trills and stuns her out of the frenzied lust hammering through her system.

Her breath catches in her chest, and her eyes snap wide as she looks to her right in search.

"Goddammit." Chuckling, since the only other option I have is to cry out at the intrusion, I fix her dress and drag my hand from her fiery flesh. Then I push up to stand and shake my head when my legs tremble. "Where the fuck is your phone, Feeney? I'm gonna kill whoever jumped into bed with us just now."

"It's work." She drapes her succulent body over my couch and throws her arm across her eyes. "It's not Axel or June, and it's not Noah either."

"Because that cocksucker is blocked."

I move into my kitchen and spy the phone on the table, then snatching up the loathed device, I walk it back to the living room and set it on her belly. "Answer," I reach into my jeans and adjust my throbbing cock. "Then suck my dick until I feel better."

She snorts at my command and grabs her phone before the call ends. Bringing it to her ear, she leaves her other arm still covering her eyes. "This is Nicole."

But fuck, of course she shoves up in alarm.

"You'd better be joking, Raul. I'll break your hands if you've..." She snarls in the back of her throat. "Raul!"

"Ugh." I turn from the couch and move to the kitchen to get my keys. Because we're going out, it would seem.

"Well, where are you?" she bites back. "And why the hell weren't you careful?"

I slip my phone into my back pocket, and reach into my jeans to fix my cock, since it won't get any attention for the next little while. Then I grab her keys and head back into the living room to pull her off the couch. I drag her to her feet and tuck sex-messed hair behind her ear. Then I lead her toward my cottage's front door.

"I'll be there in about an hour," she growls to Raul. "And you're lucky! Because I almost chugged a glass of wine ten minutes ago. You're lucky, Raul!"

"Raul's a piece of shit." Leading her out of my cottage and onto the porch, I lock up behind us and mourn the fantastic sex I was about to drown myself in. Instead, I get no nookie, no dinner, and no date. "I hate Raul's stupid fucking existence."

"Yeah," she barks out. "See you soon."

Dragging the phone from her ear and ending her call, she looks around, somewhat dazed, as I open the passenger side of my truck and help her in. "They ruined my cake."

"Raul did?" I slam her door shut and move to my side. "To annoy you?"

"Well... no," she scowls. "But he and Jenson ruined my hard work. And now I have to fix it before our bride turns into a monster."

Twisting in her seat as I start the engine and roll out of my driveway, she brings her thumb up and her nail between her teeth. "I'll be two hours," she mumbles. "Then we can come back here and keep arguing."

I cough out a laugh and bring my old truck onto the main road that leads into town. "Tantalizing offer, Feeney. Where's the cake?"

"At the venue," she sighs. "So I'll have to drive the hour there, fix what they broke, then drive back again. But," she glances desperately to the clock in my dash, "it's still early, right? This can be salvaged."

"No guilt trips." I reach across and wrap my arm over her shoulders, then I pull her in till she's wedged beneath my arm. "No manipulations. No bullshit. You've gotta work, so dinner can wait. I'll hang around until you're ready. And if, by the time you're done, you don't wanna do this tonight, we can try anoth—"

"Wait for me." She cuddles into my side and wraps her arm over my torso as we cross the railroad tracks and breach the edge of town. "Please wait for me," she murmurs. "I'm not done with us for today."

"Alright." I keep one eye on the road, but turn my face to press a kiss to her temple. "Say that thing about love again."

She sniggers and squeezes tighter into my side. "I love you?"

"Yeah. But say it like a statement. Not a question."

"You're so needy." But she turns her face and kisses the ball of my shoulder. "Stupidly, and against my better judgment, it would seem I've fallen in love with you, Preston Danes. We're gonna keep arguing about all the extra stuff, about your work and whatnot. But I love you. So..." She sighs. "We won't quit on the hard days."

"Great." I pull onto her street and note, in my peripherals, a mushroom cloud of smoke billowing from somewhere far away. "Now say it without the *stupidly* part."

She snorts before following my gaze to the fire a few miles away. "Guess a house is lit up on the other side of town," she murmurs instead. It doesn't bring her alarm the way I guess I expected. "I'm glad Axel's finished his shift."

"Want me to pull up the radio so you can listen?"

Stunned, she sits back and studies the side of my face as I come to a stop outside her home. "You can do that?"

"Sure." I cut the engine and take my keys from the ignition. "I could do that when I was five years old. Jesus, you think I'm an amateur?"

"But that's illegal." She stares for a long beat like she thinks she can intimidate me into becoming a law-abiding citizen, but as my smile grows and my remorse remains nonexistent, she huffs and turns to slide out on her side. "I need a minute to adapt to this version of you. Axel!" She charges along the path cutting down the center of her yard, but only makes it as far as the steps before the door opens and he comes out.

He's wary as hell, and quick to scan his sister for injuries. "What's wrong?"

"Raul trashed my cake, so I've gotta head into the city to fix it. Is it okay if—"

"June stays with me?" he cuts in easily. "I'm already babysitting, doofus. You didn't have to ask again."

"Alright, well..." She glances past her brother in search. "Where is she?"

"Shower. She wanted to change into her jammies and settle in for a movie night. I already ordered pizza. Go." He nods toward her car and ignores my existence completely. "I'll see you when you get back."

"Take my truck." I stop her with a hand on her hip, and press my keys into her palm with a quick swipe to trade. "Your car's still acting up. I can't feel good about letting you drive into the city in your bucket of shit."

"It's not a bucket of shit!" She lifts to her toes and presses a kiss to my jaw that has Axel's brows shooting high on his forehead. "But thank you."

"I'll see you when you get back." I watch her walk away, and hate how my stomach tugs at her absence.

The tang of smoke sits in the air, and though I hardly know Axel, I see the way he's attuned to it. Like a hound scenting out his next hunt.

But I'm attuned to something else.

Dropping my hands in my pockets, I keep my gaze on Nicole while she slides into my truck and winds the window down. "Hey, Feeney!"

As our eyes meet and her lips quiver with the ghost of a smile, I lift my chin. "I love you."

"Shiiiiitttttt," Axel rumbles. "Seriously?"

"Love you too." With a roll of her eyes, she starts my truck and checks the mirrors for traffic. But I see her smile. Her satisfied smirk. "I'll see you both soon."

"Hey. Loverboy." Axel walks to the edge of the porch and sits so his feet rest on the step. As Nicole disappears around the corner, with my heart riding shotgun, I turn to see her brother pat the floor beside his legs. "Come sit with me."

I chuckle at the stern tone he tries to scare me with. But I wander his way and drop my ass on the porch beside him. "Yeah." I set my elbows on my knees and dangle my hands between my legs. "I fell in love. So go ahead. Punch me in the face so you can feel like a man."

"I know enough about you to know she's either in the dark about who you are, or she's having a fucking heart attack trying to love you back."

"It's the second." I study the wafting smoke in the distance, but in my mind, I find comfort in the fact she knows now. And maybe she's not running into my arms, but she's not running away in fear either. *We're gonna keep arguing about it.* "I told her everything tonight."

"And she's okay with it? She's still hanging around?"

"She is. '*Against her better judgment*,' she says." Dropping my head, I shake it side to side. "She's trying really hard to process and be okay with things." Then I look toward the street, though my truck is no longer there. "Why'd you come outside thinking the worst?"

Frowning, he follows my line of sight. "What?"

"When we got here, she called out to you, and you came charging out thinking she was hurt."

"She's my sister. It's my job to worry."

I don't believe him. But I can't place my finger on exactly why not.

"Nah... Something's got you spooked. You came out here white in the face. So since we both love the same woman, it might be helpful if you share with me what's got you scared, so we can both make sure she's okay."

"I'm not scared." He narrows his eyes and goes back to watching the horizon. The smoke that drifts black. "I heard you talking the other day about Scott having a tracker on her car. And in the hour since you left, I *swear* it feels like we've had eyes on us."

"Noah?" I glance across the street and search the trees. "He's skulking around?"

"No, he's..." He shakes his head. "I haven't seen him. But you broke his fucking arm, Danes. You disrespected him, in front of her, you're dating the woman he considers his property, and you called him out on stalking and harassment." He nibbles on his thumbnail and fills out the trio of Feeneys who exhibit that nervous tic. "I haven't seen him, but there are whispers he's been asking around about you."

"He doesn't know she and I are dating."

"*Everyone* knows you're dating. But even if he was that fucking clueless, he at least knows you'll step up for her." Shrugging, he drops his hand again and laces his fingers together. "He's a possessive asshole, and no one besides me has ever stood up to him."

"So... what, I should be afraid?"

He coughs out a laugh and glances back to the house. Juniper's in there somewhere, and if he's not careful, maybe she'll hear things she really shouldn't. "I think he's gonna struggle being told no. But he's a coward beneath the bullshit, which means he won't come for you."

"But you think he'll come for her," I conclude. "So when you heard her calling out, you worried something had already happened."

He firms his lips and bounces his knee. Anxious. Anxious. Anxious. "I had a minute where I panicked, sure. And now she's driven off alone."

"In *my* truck," I assure him. "No one but me tracks it. The engine's like new, and the safety features are extensive, considering how old the outside is. Nicole's not gonna have trouble. And if she stops anywhere she shouldn't for more than a minute, my phone will let me know. I'll know where she is, and I'll run my ass there to make sure she's okay."

"So she traded one asshole tracking her for another?"

"Jesus," I scoff. "I'm not tracking her! That's *my* truck, which she just so happened to borrow. Her engine really does suck, and having her stranded on the highway in a vehicle that her ex has a habit of stalking is not something either of us considers a good idea."

Before he can respond, his phone trills in his pocket.

His shoulders broaden, and he straightens one leg so he can dig his hand into the denim, then he tugs the device out and answers it before a single second has passed. "Axel."

Dispatch, I hear his caller say. *Structure fire. You're requested back on duty.*

When his eyes swing to mine, I clap his shoulder and push up to stand. "Go." I glance toward the house, to make sure the front door is open so I can get inside. "If you trust me, then I've got her. I won't screw up, I promise."

He stares deep into my eyes, pained and conflicted, as he tries to decide if his sister's new boyfriend gets to hang with his niece all alone.

I say nothing more, because I don't want to have to convince him. Instead, I remain still, so he knows the choice is truly his.

Possible victims inside the home, his caller reports. *Search and rescue.*

"Fuck. Yeah," he bites into his phone. "I'm on my way."

Before he even hangs up, I drag Nicole's car keys from my pocket and start down the steps so I can move her bucket of rusted steel out of his way.

The engine *rrr-rrr-rrr*s in tired response, but I get it started and roll the piece of shit into the street. Then I climb out again—but not before Axel's already in his truck and backing it out of the driveway.

"I'll eat your pizza," I tell him. "What movie did she wanna watch?"

"*Casper*," he calls out the window. "The '95 version, with that dude. She thinks he's cute."

My lips peel back into a sneer. "She's six years old! She doesn't get to have crushes yet."

"Tell her that!" He idles at the curb and casts a longing look back toward the house. But the smoke in the distance grows thicker. "Shit. Okay." He drops the gear into first and revs his truck. "Don't fuck up, Danes. Or I'm coming for you."

"I've got it."

I start toward the house and hold the front door open as he speeds toward the end of the block, then when he's gone, I turn inside and close up, pushing both locks into place with a snick.

"Oh!" Juniper skids to a stop on the stairs in bunny pyjamas and slippers with massive moose heads on the end. Her hair is wet, and her cheeks are rosy. "Hi, Preston." She looks around me, suspicious. "Is Mommy home?"

"Actually, no." I remain in place and give the girl space to move wherever she'd like. "Mommy had to run out for a cake emergency." I scrunch my nose and grin, so she doesn't think the emergency is something to fear. "And Uncle Axe had to go to work too. So..." I lift my hands and shrug. "I was wondering if you wanted to hang out with me?"

"Okay!" She skips down the rest of the steps and turns toward the kitchen. "But we wanna watch *Casper*." She goes to the fridge and tugs the door open to reveal more juice boxes than any six-year-old could ever want. "Is that okay?"

"*Casper*?" I lean against the doorframe and cross my arms. "How about *Wall-E*?" *No cute boys in that one, you little turd.* "Do you wanna—"

"No thanks."

She grabs two juices and slams the door shut, then she sets them on the counter and pulls a stool toward the open pantry. Climbing—though I'm damn sure she knows she shouldn't—she reaches into the depths of the topmost shelf, past boxes of dry pasta and one-pound bags of flour, then with an exhale of triumph, she reemerges with a block of chocolate bigger than her head.

"Mommy hides the best stuff up high, 'cos she thinks I don't know."

"Oh, well…" Chuckling, I wander around the counter and stop two feet away, only to extend my hands, and grunt when she jumps into them.

She fucking free-falls, and somehow knows I won't drop her.

With a shake of my head, I set her on her feet and snatch the chocolate block back before she can eat her weight in sugar and cocoa. Tearing the packet open, I snap off just one row. "This much." I offer it to her, raising a brow when her lips curl into a pout. "Pizza's coming, cutie. And more chocolate than that will give you a stomachache."

I move the stool out of the way and push the pantry door closed, then I accept the second juice box when she offers it.

But her offer is a slam to my stomach that immediately sends a rosy red blush to her cheeks. "Sorry, Pres."

"I'm not mad, baby. Let's go." I take the juice and head toward the living room. "So, *Casper*? Really?"

"It's totally the best!" She charges on moose-head feet and dives onto the couch so the cushions puff when she lands, then she grabs the remote and pulls up the screen that either she or Uncle Axe already set up. "How long until pizza gets here?"

"I… have no clue." I plop down on her right and set my foot on the edge of the coffee table. Because I'm still a dirty kid from the streets who lacks manners. "How long ago did Uncle Axe order it?"

Instantly, she shrugs. "I don't tell the time very good."

"Well… was it a long time ago? Or a short time ago?"

And fuck, but how does that answer anything when I don't know what long and short means to her?

"Eat your chocolate," I tell her instead. "If you're still hungry after, and the pizza's taking too long, you can grab another snack from the kitchen. Cool?"

She considers my words for a beat, then accepts them with a nod. "Cool. Is my mom with my dad right now?"

"Hm?" My heart skips in my chest and sends a lance of pain biting through my heart. But I calm myself down. Take a breath. Chill the fuck out. Because it's just an innocent, logical question a six-year-old might ask.

"No, Bug. Mom's at work for a couple of hours because she has to fix a wedding cake. And your dad's probably working too. I dunno where he is."

I don't give a fuck, so long as he's nowhere near either of you.

300

But I can't say that out loud.

"Okay." Satisfied with my answer, she tears the straw from the side of her juice box and stabs it in the top. She wiggles in her seat, too hyped already—and that's before she even eats her chocolate. But she casts her eyes to the TV and hits play on the remote to get the opening credits rolling. "This is my favorite movie ever, Preston. You should see Casper as a boy. He's so nice."

Noah

HOW FUCKING DARE SHE?

He's a criminal. A thief. He's everything I take pleasure in arresting, and he's dating my wife?

My wife?

"No."

I sit on the outskirts of town as Axel Feeney, *friend* to the lowlife Preston Danes, races toward a fire.

I didn't set it. I didn't start it. Bums do that sort of thing—and criminals are just as useless as a bum.

I didn't light it, but I don't dislike its timing.

And it puts on a good show. The flames are so pretty, and the smoke is so... dark. So even though it's still daylight out, the sun races toward the horizon, and the moon struggles to win over dusk.

It's my favorite time. When daylight makes way for night.

And *everyone* knows, night is when the best things happen.

Music plays on my radio, and my fingers tap, tap, *tap-tap-tap* in time with the beat. My phone bleats on the passenger seat—short, sharp, chilling trills that serve only as a reminder she cut me off.

Blocked me! That fucking cunt.

"But it's okay."

I pick up my phone and check the screen. *Drake Banks.*

"It's okay," I repeat under my breath. "We'll talk soon, and when she gives me a chance to explain, she'll understand my reasons. She'll unblock me."

Swiping my screen unlocked and bringing my phone to my ear, I narrow my eyes and wait for Drake to speak first.

"Scott?" He's suspicious. *That country-drawl-fuckwit is always suspicious.* But never of the criminals. Only of the hardworking. "You there?"

"Yeah." I reach across to my glove box with my sore arm and drop the flap open. My spare pistol flops free and bounces to the floor with a thud, but I ignore it and fetch my cigarettes instead. I'm not a smoker. Only bums smoke. But one's okay sometimes. *One isn't a habit. It's a stress reliever for the hardworking.* "What's up? We're off shift."

"Just checkin' in," he rumbles. "I dropped by your place to see if you wanted to get a meal over at that bar near the station."

"I'm not home." I press the cigarette between my lips and lean across again in search of a lighter. "I can't hang out tonight."

"Right..." Always suspicious. Never trusting. *A dangerous combination for a cop.* "So where are you?"

"Out." My injured hand shakes, but I find a lighter and bring it closer. My thumb aches, and my wrist is fucking destroyed, but I flick the top —*flick, flick, flick*—until a flame emerges. *So pretty. So destructive.* "I've got something on my mind." Bringing the flame closer, I watch in awe as the end of my cigarette glows red. "I'll see you when we're back on shift tomorrow."

"Maybe I could come to where you are instead."

He pushes. Pushes. Pushes. Like that kid at school who had no friends, but instead of taking a hint, he just nagged and nagged and fucking *nagged* the cool kids to give him a minute of their time.

"I could help with whatever you're doing," he continues. "Then we could hit that bar and grab a burger."

"No thanks." I suck a long line of smoke deep into my lungs—*casual smokers don't die of cancer. That's only for the idiots who do this all the time.* "Not me," I mumble. "Can't be me. 'Cos I only do it once or twice."

"What are you..." Always suspicious. *The worst fucking partner on the planet.* "What do you do only once or twice, Scott?"

"Huh?" Pulling the cigarette from my lips and dropping the lighter into the center console, I frown and exhale white rings into the air. "What's once or twice?"

"You just..." He stops. Then he huffs, like *I'm* the one interrupting his day with an annoying phone call. "Nevermind. Are you... are you okay, Noah? You've seemed a little, ya know, distracted the last few days."

"I'm fine." I set my call on speaker and jam the keys in the ignition to start my engine. But I don't roll forward yet. I can't move until I know which direction I'm heading. "Nicole and I had a fight. But we're gonna sort it out."

"You and Nicole?" He's so fucking nosy. *So rude.* "Dude, you and Nicole are—"

"Gonna work it out." My lips curl into a smile that brings levity to my heart. "We're still young, Drake. You've never been in a relationship that lasts longer than it takes to fuck, so you wouldn't understand. But me and Nicole... we love each other very much."

"Scott..." Suspicious! Never trusts. "I'm concerned about—"

"I gotta go. I'm off shift, and we have no actives. Don't call me."

"Scott!"

"See ya."

I kill our call and jump screens until I find the one I want. Until I find *her*.

Alone. Exactly where I want her to be.

She doesn't hate me like she says she does. She's just tired of broken promises. She's tired of inconsistency.

And of course it seems like I'm inconsistent. *She* moved out, and now she hardly ever lets me come around.

I know the truth. I know my intentions. But in her mind, it sure appears like I'm the inconsistent one.

It's time I prove to her that I'm the man she needs.

That I'm all the man she'll *ever* need.

Hitting my indicator, I pull onto the highway and follow her until we can finally have a little privacy.

"She won't be mad once I explain."

Nicole

SHOULD'VE KEPT MY EYES OPEN

I pull into the parking lot outside Verve, an upscale hotel not so far from the one Cole and Maya had their wedding reception in. Crunching the gears when I push the truck into neutral, I feel mild guilt at the fact I'm trashing Preston's vehicle now too.

It's not enough that I destroy mine. I take down *all* cars, the way the machines tried to kill Will Smith in *iRobot*.

Taking the keys from the ignition and shoving the door open so it squeaks on its hinges, I snatch my phone and drop onto the blacktop in heels that are nothing but a cold reminder I was on a date not all that long ago.

Laid out on a couch, with Preston's body plastered to mine, and his lips peppering a fever all over my skin. His hands on my thighs, and his words racing through my mind.

He's a freakin' criminal.

A... hacker? Is that the right word?

He works for Sophia Solomon, who *everyone* knows is crookeder than Cupid's bow. But... her crooked-ness is for the betterment of society.

Right?

I can't ignore the whispers I've heard floating around town over the last several years. The advice to steer clear of Checkmate unless you want them to know who you are.

But no one has ever said what they do is *wrong*. Only... shady.

"Ugh." I slam the door shut and glance around the mostly deserted parking lot. Deserted, because I chose to use the vendor entrance instead of the main one for guests.

Okay, right now, I need to stop obsessing over Preston's career, and instead focus on my reason for being here.

Cake. Destruction.

Stupid delivery drivers, incapable of steering straight and following instructions.

Fisting my keys in one hand and my phone in the other, I start toward the lit entrance at the back of the hotel. My heels click against concrete, and a soft breeze whips my hair back, so the ends tickle my shoulder blades.

Before I come within thirty feet of the hotel doors, my phone vibrates in my hand. When I bring it up to check the screen, it's Preston's name I find flashing back at me.

Unlocking the device and navigating to our text chat, I walk blind and grin at his words.

Did you arrive safe, Feeney? Treat my truck well?

It's like he felt the crunch of the gears in his heart.

So I tap my screen and quickly reply, '*I'm here. Heading in now. Didn't scratch your beloved truck, but I might've shaved a cog or two off your gearbox. However, that sounds like a you problem. I'll let you know when I'm back on the road.*'

After I hit send and lock my screen, nerves and eagerness and excitement batter in my veins until I unlock it again and type, '*I love you.*'

That doesn't mean I'm okay with his career. It doesn't mean I'm okay with putting my daughter in the middle. It doesn't mean I'm willing to have Noah become our third wheel.

But it does mean... I love him.

"Crap."

"Nicole?"

I skid to a stop twenty feet from the hotel doorway and spin at a man's deep voice.

The parking lot isn't lit all that well, and the sun has lost its battle with the skyline. So I narrow my eyes as the man approaches, and try to make out his features

His swagger is familiar, and his height is... a little over six feet. His shoulders are broad, and his hands hang low, by his hips.

My eyes follow those long lines down, and my heart stutters when I find a gun nestled on his right hip. And beside it, a badge I could recognize anywhere.

"What are you—"

"I need you to come with me." He's fast, determined, and when he charges forward and wraps his hand around my arm, I find he's strong. "Right now."

Preston

ONE. TWO. THREE.

Nicole's doorbell chimes about twenty-five minutes into *Casper*'s attempted charming of a six-year-old child. Twenty-five minutes is all it takes for June to close the space between us on the couch, and lean against my side so her hair tickles my shoulder and her bouncing moose-head slippers play havoc with my peripheral vision.

I see her... her sticky fingers, and her tapping feet.

I see the shadows on the wall, because most of our lights are out, but *Casper* illuminates the living room.

I see the streetlight beyond the bay window, seemingly swaying with the gentle breeze outside.

And then I catch movement on the front porch just a beat after the doorbell rings.

"That'll be the pizza, cutie." Gently, I push her forward and slide out from behind her measly fifty pounds, then I keep hold of her arm, because if I don't, she'll flop back and smack the cushions.

She's lazy like a pig in mud, and comfortable despite the sugar coursing through her veins.

Setting her down and chuckling when she hugs her mooses... *Meese? Moosay? Fuck. I don't know the right word*. I shake my head and make my way across the living room.

I drag my phone from my pocket and unlock the screen with a quick swipe of my thumb. "Hey, Siri? What's the plural for moose?"

'The only correct plural of moose is moose.'

Yanking the front door open, I surprise the delivery boy so he startles. He can't be more than fifteen years old, but he wears a cap low over oily hair and carries a pizza box so large, I wonder where the fuck Axel intended to put all these carbs.

But it smells good, so I find myself not giving a shit about potential leftovers.

"The answer is moose," he says.

When I stop smelling the pizza and instead meet his eyes, he grins.

"You just asked Siri," he tilts his chin toward my phone. "The answer is moose."

"That doesn't even make sense." I open the pizza box and glance inside to find enough melted cheese to drown a herd of moosay. "The plural of mouse isn't mouse. It's mice."

"But a moose isn't a mouse," he smirks. "They're not even related." Then he opens his hand and holds it between us, palm-side up. "That's twenty-three bucks."

"What?" My eyes widen. "That asshole ordered pizza, but he didn't pay for it?"

The kid—whose name sewn into his shirt reads *Josh*—only shrugs. Then he wriggles his fingers, like my moosey-brain needs reminding. "I just deliver the pie and collect the cash. Twenty-three dollars, please."

"Shit, kid." Taking the pizza and stepping back inside the house so his eyes flare wide with panic—*This motherfucker is stealing!*—I set the box on the small entryway table, then come back and snatch my wallet from my pocket.

My phone chirps in my hand, but I'm focused on the contents of my wallet... which are somewhat pathetic. I search each slot, and find condoms, but no cash.

I grit my teeth, then I meet Josh's expectant gaze and laugh. "I don't have any cash. But," I unlock my screen, ignoring the app I designed when it throws up an alert, and instead, navigate to my banking app. Meeting his eyes, I say, "I'm gonna need to transfer it directly over. I'll send forty," I assure him when a cold sweat breaks out on his brow. "I promise. You'll get your tip."

"I-I don't know Pip's banking details," he stammers. "I don't—"

"It's all good."

I skip a lot of the steps most others need to traverse, then I drop fifty in Pip's Pizzeria's bank account and hit send.

"You get a twenty-seven-dollar tip," I tell him. "Make sure you claim it when you get back to the store. And next time Axel Feeney calls in an order, make sure that asshole pays before you cook. He's apt to dine and dash otherwise."

"O-okay." Josh reaches up and fixes his hat. "I'll tell the boss."

"Good kid."

I frown and glance down when my phone chirps again, but before I check it, I look back up and meet Josh's eyes. "Moose? Not mooset?"

He shakes his head. Then nods. Then shakes again. "Mooset is not a word."

"It should be. In fact," I take a step back and tip my chin in goodbye. "If I set up a wiki-page for it tonight, it drops onto Urban Dictionary by tomorrow. By next year, it's in the Oxford Dictionary."

I slam the door and grin when, through the glass, Josh startles a second time. Then, since June isn't crying to be fed, and *Casper* is keeping her momentarily occupied, I check my app and find my heat signature inside the house. Twenty-five feet from my dot, I see another.

June.

Then fifty feet away, out front, I catch another.

That would be Josh.

Locking my screen and reaching back to slide it into my pocket, I scowl when it rings.

It's Saturday night. The weekend. *It's my night off!* But the damn thing won't stop vibrating.

"Fuck."

Bringing it around again and spying Soph's name on the screen, I swipe to answer and lift the device to my ear. "I'm off the clock, Ace."

"You're back on the clock," she cuts in on a dangerous tone. "Axel Feeney was just pulled from a structure fire. He dropped through the floor and fell ten feet."

"What?" My heart thuds painfully in my chest.

I turn toward the living room. Then to the front door. But where the hell can I go?

Nowhere, for as long as I have Juniper.

"What the fuck happened, Ace?"

"Nix is with him," she answers instead. "He's alive, but he's busted up. You're at Nicole's place?"

"Yeah, I'm..." I bring a hand up to scrub over my face. "Shit. Yes, I'm here with Juniper. Does Nicole know yet?"

"No. She's not answering her phone. And Noah Scott crossed into town limits a bit ago, so I need you to stay alert. I've got eyes and ears all over her house, okay? It's not legal, but her ex gives me the creeps. So if he steps on her property, alarms go up and cameras start filming. She can't enter external footage into police evidence—"

"Technically," I scowl. "Neither can you."

"No, but if he comes inside, we're free and clear. If he turns up there and harasses her, he loses his job."

"Unless he turns up tonight," I snarl, unable to stop the grin that crosses my lips. "In which case, he cops a bullet between his brows, and all our troubles go the fuck away."

Silence hangs for a long, heavy beat. Charged. Intense. Finally, Sophia mumbles, "Self-defense makes it okay. And camera footage that shows he attacked you first means you stay outta trouble."

Fuckin' psycho. I bark out a laugh and pick up the pizza box. "It's hardly self-defense if we have time to set up surveillance, discuss the pros and cons of our actions, and contemplate the best way to anonymously drop doctored video to the cops. But I appreciate your enthusiasm, Ace."

Stopping in the doorway and finding Juniper splayed out on the couch, oblivious to the waves that constantly threaten to send her and her mom underwater, I ask Soph, "Is he gonna be okay?"

"Axel? I think so. I've got Troy on his way, and Nix is already there. They'll raise alarms if it's bad."

"And you'll let me know, right?" I glance to the bay window over-looking Nicole's yard and frown at the streetlight dancing in the wind. "As soon as you know?"

"As soon as I know," she confirms. "Keep your eyes open, Danes. It's a full moon tonight."

"Ugh." I continue into the living room and set the pizza down on the coffee table. Then I sit on the edge of the couch, careful not to get in Juniper's way. "I hate the full moon," I murmur. "People are always doing stupid shit this time of the month."

"But not us," she declares. "We think. Then we act. I'm hanging up now. I'll try to contact Nicole again, but I won't tell her about Axel till she's in town limits. Don't want her panicking on the fucking freeway."

"She texted me not long ago, so she's around."

My phone pings against my ear.

"I'll try to call her too," I murmur. "I'll get her back home."

"Alright. See ya. I'll be in contact."

"Wait, Soph?" I call her name, disturbing Juniper's Casper crush-time. "You still there?"

"Yeah." She's busy. Typing. Working. Moving chess pieces across town so everyone is placed where she wants them. "What's up?"

"Can you get me access to this house's surveillance? I wanna see what you see."

"What's wrong, Danes?" I see her smug grin in my mind. Her proud knowledge she'll always be the best. "Can't slide past my firewalls?"

"Not willing to keep using my phone and worrying about a thousand things while watching *Casper* and letting my fifty-dollar melted cheese turn cold. Give me access and save me time."

"Pussy." With a laugh, she kills our call and leaves me hanging.

But just a minute later, my phone dings with a notification.

She's not just sending me access. She's taking control of my fucking phone and mirroring screens. She can read my texts, scour my photo gallery. She can use my account to prank call the CIA, and there's not a damn thing I can do to stop her.

And yet, I trust the psycho with my life.

A good thing, I suppose, as I study my screen, and footage of the street outside is presented to me in high definition.

"Motherffff..." I bite off the remainder of my word so Juniper doesn't tell her mom I can't control my potty mouth even with a child in the room. Then I push up to stand and grab the television remote off the table. "Juniper. Get up, baby."

"What?" Dazed. Confused. Distracted.

I jab the power button so she loses the view of her ghostly boyfriend.

"Preston!" She twists her torso and looks at me upside down. "What did you do that for?"

Nicole

WHERE DID HE COME FROM?

"But how could you possibly know?" My hands tremble. My stomach sinks. My brain screams a thousand things at once, but my body... folds itself into his car when he sets his hand on the top of my head and guides me in. "What do you mean Axel's been hurt?"

"He was called out to a structure fire." He leans over me to fasten my seatbelt, so his aftershave fills my lungs, and his badge glistens in the light from the hotel. "Floor fell through." *Click!* "Busted his leg, we think. But I'll take you to him."

"But I don't..." Tears fill my eyes as he straightens out again and closes my door. My lips quiver with fear, and my stomach whooshes with an oil slick that makes me nauseous.

The second he opens his door and slides in, I turn his way.

"Why *you*? Why didn't Nixon call me?" *Or Preston. Or literally anyone else.* "And where's June?"

"Junie's with Danes. Nixon's busy. Axel doesn't have his phone. But I heard about the incident over the radios, and I knew you were in the city, so I came by to get you."

Starting the car and twisting in his seat to face me, he sets his broad hand on my bicep and smiles. "It's going to be okay, Nicole. I'm gonna take care of you."

"I don't..." I cast my eyes toward the hotel. The doors I'm supposed to walk through. The cake I'm supposed to fix. But my brain can't hold on to those threads. "A-Axel's hurt?"

"It's gonna be okay." Taking his hand from my arm, he pushes the car into drive and brings us out of the shadowed parking lot. "I made a promise a long time ago to have your back, Nicole. I won't let you down tonight."

Preston

SAFEKEEPING

"It's so cool your mom has a television in her bedroom, huh?" I set the pizza box on the end of the bed and wait as Juniper cautiously sets her butt on the corner.

She's attuned to moods. She reads between the lines as easily as any kid who's forced to walk on eggshells and live in an abusive home.

But she trusts me. And for that, I'm deeply grateful.

Moving to the dresser drawers and snatching up the remote, I switch the TV on and search for *Casper*, thankful for the streaming services and syncing between devices. When I've got it queued up, I press play and set the remote back down.

"Come up here." I flip Nicole's covers back and pull them down just far enough to squeeze a six-year-old's butt, then I grab Juniper under the arms and pull her along the bed.

She flicks her moosets off and tucks her feet under the covers, but though her body moves where I ask, her eyes are trained on my face. On my eyes, and the lines fanning from them that signify stress. The firm line of my lips. And the tight set of my jaw.

"Does your mom usually let you hang out in her bed to watch a movie?"

She shakes her head, quick left-right-left-right. "She lets me watch a movie sometimes. But she neverrrrr lets me eat pizza in here."

"Well... that makes tonight your lucky night."

319

A heavy *thud* outside makes my stomach jump, but then a swaying branch tapping the window settles my nerves.

Sort of.

"Not only do you get pizza and a movie tonight, but you get to do it in here. Which is the best place in the whole world, huh? It smells like a bakery in this room, dontcha think?"

A warm blush fills her cheeks as she bobs her head. "I love how my house smells. And my mom's smell is the best of all."

"I absolutely agree."

I drag the pizza box along the bed and open the lid to reveal greasy perfection. I take out a giant slice and offer it, but then I pause with a frown. "Can you eat all alone? Or will you choke?"

"I won't choke." She rolls her eyes and takes her slice. "I'm not a baby."

"Well... no. But I'd feel pretty bad if I went downstairs for a sec, and you stopped breathing while I was gone."

"I won't," she huffs. Taking a messy bite, she grins around bread and shows off an oil-slicked smile. "Where are you going, anyways?"

"Just downstairs to make sure everything's locked up. But—" I set my hand on her shoulder when she predictably pushes up tall. Gently, I force her back so she's half-reclined. "I want you to stay here."

"I could come with you. I could—"

"But I want you to stay *here*. I want you to stay in this bed and not get out, no matter what. Do you promise?"

Too attuned. Too smart.

"Preston, I don't—"

"Do you know what I say to my very, very, *very* best friends in the whole wide world?" Leaning in, I press a kiss to her brow and breathe her in. She smells like her mom. She loves the scent of sugar and flowers and all things sweet, but doesn't even realize she carries it as well. "I tell them I love them all the way to the zombie apocalypse." Pulling back, I reach across and brush tendrils of her hair behind her ear. "I love *you*, Juniper, even more than that. I love you so much, I won't let the zombie apocalypse come anywhere near you."

Pushing up straight, I turn to the television and chuckle at Casper's uncles getting drunk with the human. "I'll be back in a few minutes, okay?" Peering over my shoulder, I hold June's stare. "Promise you'll stay right here?"

Her jaw quivers with the emotion she tries so hard to lock down. But she nods. Short. Sharp. Fast. "I promise."

Then, using my own words, she slices me at the knees—but fuck, I can't find it in my heart to mind.

"I say what I mean," she whimpers.

"And you mean what you say."

Stopping at the bedroom door, I hold the handle in my palm and study the brave little girl dwarfed in her mother's bed. "You're the best person I know, Juniper. And I know a lot of really amazing people." Twisting the handle, I open the door just far enough to fit my body, then I wink because the girl's eyes refuse to leave mine. "Love you, cutie. See you in a bit."

"I won't choke." And yet, she chokes on a silent sob deep in her throat. "I'll see you in a minute."

Nodding, I close the door in silence and make sure the damn thing snicks before I release the handle, then I take out my phone and open it up to study Sophia's security surveillance.

I have to concentrate, because the house is dark, and the screens are tiny. But I find what I'm looking for and start down the stairs.

I have space. I have time.

So I open my text app and find Cole's name. My second-best friend in the whole wide world.

'SOS, bitch. The apocalypse is here. Come to Nicole's.'

Then I move to Nicole's text thread and type, *'Where are you? My truck hasn't moved, beautiful. Has Sophia contacted you yet? She has news from Nixon, but I need you not to freak out, okay? Take a breath, then come home. We'll see you soon.'*

Hitting send, I lock my phone and slip the device into my pocket, then I descend the staircase and hug the wall as I move into the kitchen. The house is dark, so the only light comes from the full moon outside. But I've always had a decent sense for sneaking around.

It's what I do, really. I can skulk through someone else's home undetected far easier than I can accept moose is plural for mooses.

Fucking moosets deserved better.

The back door creaks open, the groaning of the hinges like a cannon shot in the dark home.

The house is hardly silent: Stretch, Stinkie, and Fatso are busy screwing with the ghost whisperer, and the wind outside masks most other noises so a man can creep without worrying about a creaking floorboard.

But the back door opening, and a moment later, closing, is not *nothing*. It's a home intruder. It's malicious. It's an attack on Nicole's safe space.

And it's unacceptable.

"Nicole?" Noah Scott's voice is somewhat... *giddy*. Happy. "Nicole?" he whisper-talks. "Are you here, babe?"

While he wanders one way, I circle back and make my way toward the laundry room.

"Baby?" He tiptoes into the front foyer while I wait at the end of the room in the shadows.

If he starts up the stairs, my plans change. If he heads into the living room, I have time.

"Nicole?" He continues straight, instead of onto the staircase. "Happy anniversary, sweetheart. I've been waiting all afternoon to see you."

He's fucking delusional.

He's officially stepped over from controlling ex to certifiably insane. But at the sound of his cocking gun, I'm reminded he's armed and dangerous.

Crazy, maybe. But a good shot, no doubt.

"Nicole!" From sweet and cajoling, to mean and commanding. "Where are you?"

"In here." I dash into the laundry and snatch up the pipe wrench I saw the first time I ever visited this home. The day Juniper caught me sneaking. The day Noah almost got my name from the plates of my truck.

It feels like a lifetime ago.

Fisting the five-pound wrench in both hands and standing in the shadows just by the door, I wait. And listen. And slow my breathing so I don't drown out the sound of his shuffling footsteps.

Stretchy—or Fatso, or whoever—'wheees!' on Juniper's movie, while wind whips outside, and a tree branch thuds against the side of the house.

"Nicole?" Noah's voice is more curious than suspicious. Clueless.

He's suffering a legitimate mental breakdown, but knowing the man has lost his senses does nothing to douse my need to bring him pain. To remove the gun he would use on Nicole, spin it around, and press the muzzle against his temple instead.

To pull the trigger. To end his life. To remove this problem from the Feeneys' lives.

"Are you in here, baby?" He shuffles on flat feet, so his shadow enters the laundry first. Then his gun. Then his casted wrist. "Nicki?"

When he's far enough in that he can't spin and bolt, I swing out with the wrench and shatter his cast so plaster sprays through the room, pinging onto the tile floor and ricocheting off the walls.

Moving quickly before his cry of anguish alerts Juniper, I wind my arm back a second time and slam the steel down on the side of his neck.

I hear the crack of bone. Thrill in the way his body drops.

Then my head whips up at the wail of sirens outside. They scream in the distance and battle with the breeze, because Cole has no chill.

I declare the zombies have arrived, and his newfound 'strait-laced' life means he calls the cops.

Pussy.

Shaking my head, I kneel by Noah's unconscious form and wrinkle my nose at the tang of urine in the air. He's pissed himself. But I breathe a little easier when I press my fingers to his neck and find his pulse.

"Preston!" The front door slams open, and Cole's voice echoes through the house. "Danes! Where are y—"

"Laundry room," I call out. Then I push up to stand and set the pipe wrench back exactly where I got it. "And stop shouting. Juniper's upstairs."

Cole sprints through the house he's never been inside before. But he knows how to sneak, too. He learned long ago how to explore a dark home and waste no time backtracking. So he charges into the kitchen, then skids by the laundry door and grabs onto the frame when his body keeps going.

Wild-eyed and panicking, he looks me up and down while red and blue lights flash through the windows. "What the fuck happened?"

"Home intruder." I set my hands on my hips and try, sort of, to straighten my smile. "Snuck in the back door. His prints will be on the knob. They'll also be on," I nod across the floor, to the gun, "that. I haven't touched it. I caught him on Nicole's internal security feed, but before I could confront him, he walked in here and slipped on the wet floor."

Suspicious, he scans the floor. Then his eyes narrow. "It's not wet in here."

"Oh, right." I head to the sink nestled against the far wall and turn on the tap. Cupping my hands, I let them fill till they overflow, then I toss the liquid to the floor and smirk. "Dude just slipped, bro. He probably needs an ambulance. I heard his neck break."

"His neck?" Stunned, he looks down again. "Is he alive?"

"Yep."

I stay put as cops rush into the house. Cops I know. Cops who just so happen to basically—though not officially—be on Ace's payroll. "Armed home intruder, Chief. Seriously bad luck he slipped."

Patting Cole on the shoulder, then passing the first cop at the laundry entrance, I make my way to the front door and stop in front of the chief's second-in-command. "Deputy Oz. Any word on Axel Feeney? His niece is upstairs eating her body weight in pizza. I haven't told her about Axe yet. I wanted to know how bad it was first."

"Broken leg." Warily, he scans the room. He was coming here with his lights blazing, and now he gets... a friendly chat? "Smoke inhalation. Sore back. But he's gonna be fine."

Relieved, I reach into my back pocket as my phone trills with a call. Tugging the device out and finding Nicole's name on the screen, I tilt my chin in farewell to the cop, then I start up the stairs. "Feeney?"

"Axel's been hurt!" she bursts out. Tears make her voice thick, and fear makes it shaky. But she's okay. He's okay. "Detective Drake Banks picked me up. He's driving me back now so I can get to the hospital."

"Banks?" I stop at the stair landing and glance down again as an ambulance skids to a stop outside. "Who's that?"

"Drake is Noah's partner," she whimpers. "He said he's been worried about me. Noah's been acting weird and erratic lately, and asking about you at the station, and now Drake can't reach him on the phone. I just..." She makes a frustrated sound in the back of her throat. "Jesus, Preston. I can't focus. Axel's hurt. Noah's unreachable. Drake is here and he's friends with Checkmate—Sophia called and said it's okay that I'm with him. So I don't... I don't..."

"It's fine. Feeney, babe? It's okay." I start toward the bedroom again and leave the town's EMTs to deal with Noah Scott. "If Soph says it's okay, then it's okay. Juniper's eating pizza, by the way. I heard about Axel, too, so I was gonna call and ask if you want her to know tonight, or if I should wait till the morning."

"Tonight." Bursting with fear and unable to hold everything in, she cries, "Bring her to me, please? I can't... please bring her to me."

"Of course." I stop before the closed bedroom door. Before I go in and shatter a little girl's evening. "You should know... Noah dropped by the house."

Predictably, she inhales a sharp breath. "What?"

"Drake was right. Noah's being erratic and dangerous. He let himself in your back door."

"What? Juniper—"

"Is completely fine. She's still eating pizza," I assure her. "But Scott slipped in the laundry room and had a spill. Ambulance is here to treat him."

"A-ambulance?" she stutters. "He's hurt?"

"Quite seriously," I tell her truthfully. "I think he'll be down for a while. And the fact he came in here with a gun means he's going away."

"What the hell is..." She searches for truth. For sense. "Preston, what?"

"He slipped," I reiterate. "But I promise, he's never gonna be a problem for you again."

"He..." She swallows down her breath. Her sob. Her fear. "You?"

"Yeah, babe. Me. Because I gave him four chances to back away from you, but he wouldn't listen." Grinning, knowing my truth may scare her but we'll work through it anyway, I open the door and head in to find Juniper exactly where I left her.

Her eyes swim with anxiety, and her knuckles are deathly white as she grips her pizza. But she remains put, because she promised.

She meant what she said.

"I took care of what needed taking care of," I tell Nicole. "But I did it clean, quick, and with love."

I smile for Juniper, which, to her, is a sign to explode free of her blankets and sprint across the bed. Her mooses bounce on the mattress, then the girl flings herself off the edge and trusts me to catch her.

Our chests slam together with an '*oomph*', but as she wraps her arms around my neck, I set my call on speaker and sit down on the end of the bed. "You're on speaker, Feeney. Someone's been eager to talk to you."

"Mommy?" Juniper squeezes me tight and smooshes our cheeks together. She wraps her legs around my torso and fills my lungs with flowers and sugar. "Mommy? When are you coming home?"

"Preston's gonna bring you to me, okay, baby? Uncle Axel hurt his leg at work, so we're gonna go visit him at the hospital. But he's okay." She pauses for a long beat. "Okay?"

Juniper nods with fast and jerky dips of her head, but she doesn't speak. She can't get the words out.

"She heard you," I tell Nicole. "She's just a little overwhelmed right now. We're gonna put our moose head slippers on now, okay? We'll meet you at the hospital in a few minutes."

"Okay." Nicole's breath comes out on a squeak of upset. Of tears. And anxiety. But she sniffles and pulls it under control. "I'll see you soon. I love you." She pauses, then, "Both of you."

Epilogue

Sometime later

J ay Bishop works a joystick like it's a game controller. He plays while wearing a grin, like this is truly fun to him, but as he weaves a fully loaded drone through the trees surrounding mafia bigwig Tony Mancino's property, he glances my way and waits for my *go*.

"You're up, Danes." Sophia chews on a Twizzler stick and paces the Checkmate office. Back and forth. Back and forth. Because that's how she expels her excess energy. "In three. Two."

I shake my head and do the job I was contracted to do. I walk through the virtual door I created months ago, and seize control of Mancino's system. But I do it in a way he can't know he's being fucked with.

"Sector one is down." I cut the power feeding the security outpost on the northern-most corner of the property, while radio chatter—from *their* radios—crackles to life with panicked questions.

'What's happening?'

'We lost power.'

'Easmon! We need assistance!'

"That damned Easmon," Soph sniggers. Then she lifts her chin in my direction. "Shut down comms. We can't have them calling their mommies for help."

"Shutting down comms." I place a blanket over the entire property, so phones are dead, internet doesn't exist, and stringed-cups become the next best option. "Silence in one."

Chatter dies eerily fast, so it almost feels like I dropped a fucking nuke on their heads and killed them all.

But that's not what I did. Because I don't kill folks these days.

I prefer to break their necks and allow them the chance to live a long, miserable life of perpetual soft-cockedness.

"Sectors two and three," I add, even before Ace asks for it. "Shutting them down." Then I glance to Jay. "You can enter now."

"Fuckin' A." He wields his joystick like he's playing Pac Man. And so with a fast *tap-tap-tap* at my laptop, I fill our office with the audio from the drone.

It buzzes, loud and incessant, but beyond that is shouted commands from Mancino's soldiers. Fleeing men. Automatic weapons.

"They're shooting at me, Sophiiiiaaaa," Jay chuckles.

He might be a bigger psycho than his wife. As he sways in his chair like he's flying inside the actual drone, he watches his computer screen with eagle eyes, then with a giddy smile, he drops the first load—and cackles when an explosion erupts in our office.

"Knocked that motherfucker off his feet," he giggles. "Lemme swing on over to the right."

"They still have weapons in their hands," Sophia grumbles. "Don't let them tag you." Then she glances to me. "Mancino?"

I switch screens and scan the dozen surveillance angles I took control of the moment I slipped into his system. It takes only a second to find him and half a dozen guards charging up the stairs.

"Heading to the north wing," I tell her. "Michelle Mancino sleeps up there."

"Yes, she does." Sophia stops in front of Jay's desk and gives her next command. "Drop the second. Bring it closer to the house, so Mancino knows we're in control. Then I want you to switch out and bring the others in. Surround the property; we have twenty-four packages to drop before they shoot us out of the sky."

"Your dirty talk turns me the fuck on."

He drops the next explosive, and bounces in his seat when it digs craters in Mancino's front yard.

Sophia turns to me. "Report."

But then a droning *brrrrrt* fires across the yard so bullets zing through Mancino's window, and the woman drops to her hands and knees.

"What the fuck?"

"Oop, that was me." Jay giggles. "This is the best RC toy I've ever played with. Can we get one for—"

"No." Sophia wanders my way and bites the top off a Twizzler stick. "Where are they?"

"They're pulling Michelle Mancino out of her room. Heading..." I stop and watch as she dashes to her drawers and snatches something from the top. She shoves whatever it is in the pockets of a slouchy sweater, then she meets her father at the door and is swallowed up by guards. "Heading down now."

"Push them toward the bunker. Jay, you keep hitting them. Empty out before you pull back." Then she charges to her desk and fires up her own laptop. "Now it's time for me to sell my services online."

"No thongs," her husband snaps. "No glitter."

Filling her mouth with candy, Sophia sniggers. "No fun. Romeo," she glances up at her seven-foot-tall soldier. "I'm gonna need you in a minute."

"Fuck you will," Jay growls. Then *boom!* Another explosion rocks the Mancino estate. "I'm all the man you need, Solomon. Don't start playing games."

Things are good these days. Work is... fulfilling, if not a little maniacal. I'm *this* close to convincing Soph to drop a USB in our next target's yard. Juniper's thriving at school, and her cupcake-making skills are still, sadly, better than mine.

Noah Scott spends most of his time in a hospital for the slightly-too-ill-for-society. But it wouldn't matter if his mind healed, anyway, since he can't use his arms or legs to drag his sorry ass over to his *ex*-wife's home.

Which just so happens to be my home, too.

Because we're the *cohabitating* type now.

Yes, it took a minute to convince Nicole to share her closet. No, she won't sleep now unless I'm in bed with her. Yes, I'm fucking thrilled about it. No, I haven't asked her to marry me.

Yet.

Yes, Juniper's adapting to this new life and my role in it—though, *flourishing* may be a better word to describe her infectious smile.

No, Axel isn't coping with his sister's sex life, now that it's recurring and he no longer has to worry about her being alone. But yes, that motherfucker survived a burning building and a ten-foot drop.

Nine lives; that's how I describe him every time he comes over for Sunday baked dinner. He had nine of 'em to work with. Now he only has eight, but hell, eight is seven more than most get... and those extra seven are enough to ensure Nicole sleeps at night.

I pull into a parking spot outside Juniper's Bakery, beside a shiny new Toyota Corolla, and chuckle at the utter *momness* of her ride.

I take pleasure in knowing Nicole's vehicle is now safe. Reliable.

Better yet, it's funded by Noah Scott's pension, now that he lives a life of minimalism consisting of bed pans, pyjamas, and blended meals.

He can't use his hands to swipe his debit card anyway.

Amused, I hook my keys around my finger and slide out of my truck. As soon as my boots hit the asphalt, I close the door and head toward the bakery.

Cinnamon, flowers, sugar, and *Feeney* weave through my senses until I'm gulping down every morsel of deliciousness, and my eyes search the large floor-to-ceiling shopfront window.

I push through the door and lift my brows when I find Hannah swaying with a mop, and Juniper hip-swinging on the little table tucked into the corner of the shop.

She wears shin pads and long socks all the way up to her knees. A maroon and yellow soccer uniform, and pigtails on each side of her head. Best of all, she wears the black hat I long ago decided belongs to her.

"What the heck is going on in here?" I turn toward my baby and try for my sternest expression, but fuck, I can't seem to muster anything more than '*sucked on a lemon*'. "You're not allowed up there, Bug."

"I was dancing!" She drops her head back and cackles, her glee-filled self enough to make my heart run faster. But I learned a long time ago, she trusts me. She trusts without restraint. So I open my arms just in time, and dart forward as she throws herself into the air.

We collide with a *thud*, and her sweet breath fills my lungs to bursting. But I wrap her up close and hold on tight.

"Are you finished work?" she giggles. And squeezes. And presses a noisy kiss to my cheek that slays me easier than any foe I've ever come up against. "It's time for my soccer game, but I've been waiting for you."

"I *am* finished work. And I would *never* miss your game."

I glance across the store when I feel the other Feeney in the air. When I feel her presence. Her happiness. Her love.

Twisting with Juniper pressed to my chest, I find Nicole standing in the doorway, her arms folded, and a smug grin plastered across her lips.

"I'm ready to get this show on the road." With a wink, I bring my gaze back to Juniper. "You gonna kick ass today?"

"Preston!"

"Yes!" June practically vibrates in my arms. "The zombies are coming."

"Well, shit, baby. It's time to whoop their asses."

Continue the Lost Boys Series in Crash & Burn.

Also by Emilia Finn

(in reading order)

The Rollin On Series

Finding Home

Finding Victory

Finding Forever

Finding Peace

Finding Redemption

Finding Hope

The Survivor Series

Because of You

Surviving You

Without You

Rewriting You

Always You

Take A Chance On Me

The Checkmate Series

Pawns In The Bishop's Game

Till The Sun Dies

Castling The Rook

Playing For Keeps

Rise Of The King

Sacrifice The Knight

Winner Takes All

Checkmate

Stacked Deck - Rollin On Next Gen

Wildcard

Reshuffle

Game of Hearts

Full House

No Limits

Bluff

Seven Card Stud

Crazy Eights

Eleusis

Dynamite

Busted

Gilded Knights (Rosa Brothers)

Redeeming The Rose

Chasing Fire

Animal Instincts

Pure Chemistry

Battle Scars

Safe Haven

Inamorata

The Fiera Princess

The Fiera Ruins

The Fiera Reign

Mayet Justice

Sinful Justice

Sinful Deed

Sinful Truth

Sinful Desire

Sinful Deceit

Sinful Chaos

Sinful Promise

Lost Boys

MISTAKE

REGRET

Crash & Burn

Rollin On Novellas

(Do not read before finishing the Rollin On Series)

Begin Again – A Short Story

Written in the Stars – A Short Story

Full Circle – A Short Story

Worth Fighting For – A Bobby & Kit Novella